ABOUT THE AUTHOR

Markus Heitz was born in 1971; he studied history and German language and literature. His debut novel, *Schatten über Ulldart* (the first in a series of epic fantasy novels), won the Deutscher Phantastik Preis (German Fantasy Award) in 2003. His bestselling *Dwarves* trilogy has earned him a place among Germany's most successful fantasy authors. He currently lives in Zweibrücken, Germany.

Also by Markus Heitz

Righteous Fury

THE LEGENDS OF THE ÄLFAR
BOOK II

DEVASTATING
HATE

MARKUS HEITZ

Translated by Sheelagh Alabaster

Jo Fletcher
New York • London

Jo Fletcher Books
An imprint of Quercus
New York • London

ISBN 978-1-62365-704-8

Distributed in the United States and Canada by
Hachette Book Group
1290 Avenue of the Americas
New York, NY 10104

Manufactured in the United States

10 9 8 7 6 5 4 3 2 1

www.quercus.com

To the world's composers,
living or dead,
classical or modern,
my inspiration
as I write

DSÔN FAÏMON

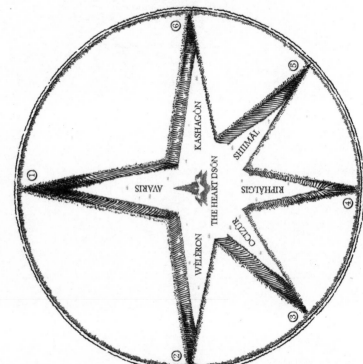

① Status & Wealth
In Avaris there settled those älfar of high status blessed with wealth. Any wishing to reside in this radial arm had to have the support of all the other residents or else had to go.

② Sword & Faith
Wêlêron fell to the warrior class and the priests and all who were involved with magic. But there were few powerful magicians among the älfar people. The magic in their blood did not permit for this.

③ Crafts & Knowledge
In Ocizûr the craftspeople sought their home and exchanged their skills amongst themselves. Different branches of knowledge fused to a unity and they founded schools and places of learning in order to perfect their skills.

④ Art & Death
In Riphâlgis there gathered the artists and they too collected together the various forms of artistry, creating a new art. Fascinated by the subject of death, they liked to utilise the materials that came with the ending of life.

⑤ Growth & Welfare
Shiimäl attracted those älfar who were skilled at farming. Huge farms were established where cattle and crops were raised in this one radial arm for supplying the whole realm.

⑥ Science & Death
Kashagôn is the home of the true warriors! Älfar, male and female, totally committed to the art of warfare came here and founded academies to train the hardest, best and most lethal of warriors.

Dramatis Personae

THE ÄLFAR

Nagsar und Nagsor Inàste, the Inextinguishables

Sinthoras, älf-warrior (Comet faction) and a nostàroi (supreme commander)

Demenion, politician (Comet)

Khlotòn, politician (Comet)

Khlotònior, his nephew

Rashànras, politician (Comet)

Yantarai, artist

Imàndaris, Yantarai's daughter, and a nostàroi

Timanris, artist

Robonor, Timanris's former companion, a warrior (deceased)

Timansor, Timanris's father, an artist

Durùston, sculptor and artist

Arviû, warrior

Horgàta, warrior

Virssagòn, warrior

Morana, bodyguard

Carmondai, artist in language, script and image

Polòtain, politician (Comet)

Godànor, Polòtain's grandson

Eranior, politician (Comet)

Samrai und Chislar, Eranior's personal entourage

Halofór, politician (Constellations faction)

Landaròn, Halofór's brother

Falòran, guard in Dsôn

Ratáris, politician (Constellation)

Armatòn, benàmoi (military leader) in the Gray Mountains

Arganaï, warrior cadet

Tiláris, warrior cadet

Zirlarnor, warrior cadet

Phinoïn, benàmoi of warrior cadets

Itáni, Dsôn artist

Caphalor, älf-warrior (Constellation) and a nostàroi (supreme commander)

Enoïla, Caphalor's life-partner (deceased)

Aïsolon, a friend of Caphalor's (Constellations)

Kilanor, trader, from Dsôn

Veranor, messenger sent by the Inextinguishables

Téndalor, benàmoi of island fort number one-eight-seven

Daraïs, Téndalor's deputy

Ilinia, coachwoman

Yintaï, älf in Avaris

Heïfaton, älf in Avaris

Umaïnor, Sinthoras's administrator in Dsôn

Bolcatòn, academic and chair of the Wèlèron Research Council

Païcalor, blind bodyguard to the Inextinguishables

Ergàta, warrior

Sajùtor, warrior

Ofardanór, benàmoi at the Stone Gateway

THE HUMANS

Raleeha, slave girl to the älfar (deceased)

Wirian, slave to Sinthoras

Farron Lotor, barbarian prince of the Ishmanti

Törden and Famenia, famuli (apprentices) to the magus Jujulo

Olfson and Drumann, Famenia's uncles

Parilis, Famenia's aunt

Khalomein, rebel

Pirtrosal, rebel

Iula, famula (female apprentice) to the maga Hianna

Quartan, cooper, from Duckingham

Geralda, serving woman from Halmengard

Doghosh, commander of soldiers from Sonnenhag

Endrawolt, Doghosh's deputy

Pantako, trader from the barony of Gourarga

Ossandra Ilmanson, daughter of the burgomaster of Milltown

Mollo, Gatiela, Sarmatt, Ossandra's playmates

Welkar Ilmanson, Ossandra's father and burgomaster of Milltown

Jiggon, young slave in Avaris

Hirrtan, Jiggon's father

Elina, Jiggon's sister

Rodolf, Jiggon's grandfather

Irhart, villager

Salisala, villager

Güldtraut, villager

Errec, human slave

Amso, human slave

Omenia, landlord's daughter in Quarrystone

Odeborn, king of Ido

Starowig, ruler of Ido by proxy

THE MAGI

Jujulo the Jolly

Simin the Underrated

Grok-Tmai the Worrier

Hianna the Flawless

Fensa the Inventive

Ortina the Omnipresent

MISCELLANEOUS

Narósil, leader of the elf-riders

Fatunasíl, elf from the Golden Plain

Veïnsa, princess of the Golden Plain

Ataronz, óarco from the vassal nation
Toboribar, óarco prince and leader of the Kraggash óarcos
Shoggrok, a Kraggash óarco
Sardaî, thoroughbred night-mare
Rîm, an Ubari female
Worbîn, a fire-bull

ÄLFAR DIVISIONS OF TIME

A division of unendingness, ten years
One year would be a tenth of a division of unendingness
A moment of unendingness, one day
A splinter of unendingness, one hour

ÄLFAR MEASUREMENT

One pace, one yard

They are said as a people to show more cruelty than any other.

They are said to hate elves, humans, dwarves and every other creature so much that the blood runs black in their veins and darkens their eyes in the light of the sun.

They are said to dedicate their lives exclusively to death and to art.

They are said to use black magic.

They are said to be immortal . . .

Much has been said about the Älfar.

Read now these tales that follow and decide for yourselves what is true and what is not. These are stories of unspeakable horror, unimaginable battles, gross treachery, glorious triumphs and crushing defeats.

But they are also tales of courage, integrity and valor.

Of friendship.

And of love.

These are the Legends of the Älfar.

Preface from the forbidden books which transfigure the truth,
The Legends of the Älfar,
unknown author,
undated

PROLOGUE

What a magnificent assembly that evening! What a magnificent hall!

Never again will such a gathering of heroes be seen in a single place—heroes of such stature, of such power, of such unique nature!

The aura that surrounded each one was clearly visible and almost tangible. And on hearing the heroes speak, ordinary älfar were filled with dread and awe.

I, too, was fascinated.

By each one of them.

By Virssagòn: virtuoso in the arts of war and the skills of the forge, deviser of sophisticated and deadly weaponry and instructor of others in their use;

by Arviù: bringer of death and destruction to the elf realms and whose misfortunes made him the greatest of enemies to the elf peoples. Such was his fame that even today many a fortress bearing his name still stands in the conquered regions once held by the elves;

by Morana: supple and elegant warrior and worker of magic who, while steadfastly resolute toward her deadly foes, harbored an unforgiveable and incomprehensible weakness;

by Horgàta: restless and incomparable beauty, graceful huntress, who never once spared an adversary;

and, of course, I was fascinated equally by the nostàroi, Sinthoras and Caphalor, leaders and initiators of the campaign against Tark Draan, at last granting our people their sweet and cruel revenge. To describe these two leaders would be blasphemy.

For, in truth, no words of mine could match their deeds!

At least, not at that point in time.

No one could have guessed what changes lay in store for them.

Excerpt from the epic poem *The Heroes of Tark Draan* composed by Carmondai, master of word and image

Tark Draan (Girdlegard), Gray Mountains, Stone Gateway, 4371ˢᵗ division of unendingness (5199ᵗʰ solar cycle), summer.

The air was filled with the sound of hundreds of banners flapping in the breeze; occasionally the cry of a raptor was heard as it flew across the darkening sky.

Awe and reverence determined the mood of the silent multitude of älfar warriors assembled on the high plain.

Surrounding the throng, shattered enemy weapons that had been melted down and twisted creatively into bizarre interlocking structures towered into the air—victory columns to symbolize the downfall of the dwarves. But no regard was currently being paid to these abstract works of art: all eyes were trained on the garlanded platform before them.

A low roll of thunder gave the first indication of an approaching storm. Over in the south, black clouds covered the sky as if ready to halt the advance of an enemy; a warm breeze played around the tips of the älfar army's lances and spears and the rivets on their armor.

Carmondai tied back his long brown hair so that the strengthening wind would not whip it into his face and over his paper, and observed the patiently waiting crowd. *It is as if they had turned into statues.* The silver-clad stick of compressed charcoal in his right hand raced across the open page as he drew without looking down at the notebook. He never needed to correct these preparatory studies; he was accustomed to making accurate lightning sketches for the large paintings he would complete later.

The blood-red sun sank behind the Gray Mountains, illuminating the finest of the óarco, barbarian, troll, demi-giant and älfar fighting force. They had gathered to acclaim the Heroes who had made their victory at the Stone Gateway possible.

The groundlings—the defenders of Tark Draan—had been eliminated, their bones serving as raw material for sculptures, musical instruments and decorative souvenirs, wagonloads of which would be finding their way back to the homeland as evidence of the win.

This is only the beginning of an endless river. Our swords will take Tark Draan's last drops of lifeblood. In the margin, Carmondai made a note of the color combinations and appropriate blood types he had in mind for his mural. Groundling life-juice was darker and more mystical than others, he had found, and not easy to work with, but it did give the work a level of integrity not usually achieved through the use of other creatures' blood: minute traces of minerals in the dwarves' blood emphasized the picture's essence through scent, and would intensify the effect of the battle for the discerning spectator.

Carmondai sketched without stopping. He knew the swift lines he was drawing impressed the barbarians who could see his sketches, but this did not satisfy him—any älfar child could do this sort of thing.

He caught sight of the cloud formations as they moved threateningly toward the conquerors. *You shall not stop us.* He took in the gray, white and black as the clouds raced across the sky and then his gaze dropped back to the decorated ceremonial stage and he began to make his way slowly through the ranks of the warriors to study it more closely.

Skillful craftsmen had created the brilliant white base of the podium from split and dried groundling bones; strands from the hair and beards of the defeated soldiers had been used to fasten the bones together. At the rear of the stage, bronze-coated skulls hung from long poles by ropes of braided silver, jangling like bells. Carmondai could hear the sound now that he was closer; the combination of bone and metal produced a strange tone. Their enemies' grimacing features had been transformed into shimmering masks: images of death that would last forever.

In the distance, Carmondai could see standard-bearers beginning to march toward the stage, and suddenly the noble runes of the nostàroi could be seen; blood-red fabric wafting lazily in the breeze. There followed the nostàroi bodyguard in sinister leather armor glittering with engraved tionium plates. The motifs on their helmets signified that each warrior had killed more than one thousand of the enemy.

Carmondai moved away from the stage to get a better view. *Ye gods of infamy, how proud our people are!* His fingers flew, making notes on the figures around him. His skin prickled and the sense of awe sent waves of excitement up his spine.

Suddenly an impatient night-mare's imperious snort broke the quiet and Sinthoras and Caphalor were sighted on their magnificent armored mounts. Caphalor's black stallion Sardaî was taller in stature and more impressive in nature than any other night-mare.

Carmondai registered that he was writing more slowly now. He was deeply affected by the imposing appearance of the nostàroi; their presence swept over the plateau like a spell. The two nostàroi were producing powerful emotions from the assembled troops: respect, worship and fascination.

Carmondai had to shake himself free from their hypnotic effect. He looked quickly around at the crowd, noticing that all were staring at their leaders' noble features, eager for some slight word that might impart to them a shred of this triumphant brilliance.

The effect could hardly be stronger if it were the Inextinguishables themselves who had arrived. Carmondai was convinced that every warrior and any creature present would have followed Sinthoras and Caphalor to the ends of the known world. *What power they have!*

The leaders, their way lined by standard-bearers and bodyguards, halted at the platform.

Sinthoras and Caphalor dismounted and climbed up to the dais. They wore gold-wrought black ceremonial armor studded with jewels. They removed their helmets, displaying fine facial features and allowing their long hair to move in the wind: blond in the one case, black in the other.

Carmondai had heard tell how different these two nostàroi were, in personality as well as coloring; he had heard that Caphalor tended toward the views of the Constellations and that Sinthoras supported the Comets. But now, seeing them together, it looked as if they could be brothers.

Sinthoras raised his right hand and addressed the silent throng. "We are standing on the land of Tark Draan! Do you know what this means?"

A single cry thundered from thousands of älfar throats.

"No army could have achieved more!" he proclaimed. "It is *we* who have defeated and annihilated the groundlings, and it is *we* who will bring down and destroy the elves. We will not only eradicate them, but eliminate all they stand for and all they have created. Nothing of theirs shall be allowed to continue. We shall be their *death*." He lifted his head slightly, the fire of hatred glowing in his eyes. "For the Inextinguishables!"

Again the response came back a thousandfold.

Carmondai's heart beat quickly in his chest, while his pen scurried across the paper. *Every fragment of this event must be recorded for posterity—every fragment! I am witness to our people's greatest victory. I must miss nothing.*

"We shall bring death into every last corner of Tark Draan. Kingdoms will fall under our yoke, fortresses will burn to the ground and we shall create such art as has never been seen before. We are the new rulers here!"

Not even the loudest clap of thunder could compete with the älfar warriors' voices and the roars from the other creatures. To Carmondai's mind, the sound had penetrated deep into Tark Draan. He imagined the inhabitants quaking with fear and turning their ugly heads toward the Gray Mountains, aware that their end was nigh. *I must start my new poem this very day.*

The nostàroi, like two gods come down in grace to their worshippers, received the adoration and acclaim of the crowds.

Finally Sinthoras raised his arm and the assembled throng fell silent. "The first victory is with us. In the coming moments of unendingness we shall flush out the groundling tunnels to ensure nothing and nobody can attack us from behind. Find their treasure hoards, take what you can from their storehouses and send it all as tribute to Dsôn Faïmon. Caphalor and I will now decide our strategy for delivering the final blow—the exterminating blow—to Tark Draan."

Caphalor now spoke. "But this evening you shall celebrate what we have achieved so far. Take your ease, drink with your comrades and companions, and then"—he drew his sword and pointed toward the south where the dark clouds glowered—"let us stamp out this elf brood!"

The nostàroi withdrew, mounted up and disappeared over the edge of the plateau, while the älfar and their allies tirelessly called out their leaders' names to ear-splitting applause.

Carmondai had never in all his long life experienced such deep admiration for anyone. It struck him that with commanders such as these the army would be victorious in any campaign, however taxing the fight.

In response to whistles, fanfares and shouted orders, the assembled troops dispersed: älfar in a disciplined fashion, barbarians in a less orderly manner, orcs and miscellaneous creatures in shambling disarray.

Carmondai stayed where he was, taking in the scene. *Tark Draan has nothing to compete with our army. In less than a third of a division of unendingness we shall have achieved our goal.*

He sauntered off, watching the river of soldiery streaming into the groundlings' former stronghold. Having left his luggage with one of the gate guards so that he could arrive in good time, he was dressed in light traveling attire and as a result, felt vulnerable and out of place: he looked far too peaceable.

Carmondai reached the top of the plateau and looked out over the camp. Tents were set up across the mountainside, strictly segregating the various warring races, from one another. Many unresolved enmities left the allied factions prone to disagreements, and the nostàroi were keen to keep this to a minimum. Each individual commander was responsible for internal discipline within his camp. Much of this enmity was down to the intensely motivating effect of greed, which Carmondai was fascinated by. *That's where the differences lie: the lower orders will die for the sake of gems and riches, while the higher beings kill for their ideals.*

He stood watching the óarco horde as they shoved and pushed and punched each other. No surprise that these green-and-black-skinned beasts with their decorated tusks and their stinking fat-coated armor tended to try to bump each other off at the slightest annoyance.

"Ye gods of infamy, would you look at that scum," he murmured. "They are a disgrace."

"But we'll be leaving them here, of course," said an älf-woman at his side. She had come up close on her night-mare, unheard over the whistling wind. "That way we will be permanently free of them in Ishím Voróo." She smiled at him. "You must be Carmondai?"

He took half a step back to see her better. Her armor told him she belonged to the nostàrois' personal guard. The symbols on the tionium-reinforced leather cuirass showed her to have killed over one thousand enemies, and proclaimed her as the unpartnered daughter of two great warriors.

She looks so young. Carmondai was usually quite good at guessing the age of other älfar, but her face was hidden by a half visor. *Fifty? Sixty? But how could she have killed so many in that short time?* "Yes, that's me." He looked at her inquisitively and received a slight nod in return.

"Then I have an invitation for you. The nostàroi have heard that you are with the troops here and they want you to be present at supper. You are to record the event in word and picture so that the Inextinguish-ables may receive a report drawn up by an inestimable talent."

Carmondai felt hot and cold shivers run up his spine. At first he was flattered, but then his old resentment reared up: he hated taking orders. It was not only that he considered himself an artist of high repute. If it had been his own idea to take notes and to sketch the occasion he would have considered it an honor to be allowed to do so. But like this . . .

"What's wrong?" The älf-woman was astonished at his hesitation. "Tell me what you have planned that's more important and I'll kill who-ever it is you are meeting, then you'll have no difficulty deciding."

Her remarks amused him. "Why don't they find an ordinary scribe?"

She leaned forward, crossing her wrists on the pommel of her saddle. "Let me put it this way, O Master of Word and Image: an invitation from the nostàroi is not something you can decline." Her words were spoken carefully, but were as cold as the breath of night. "If you fail to accompany me willingly I shall find other ways to take you to the nos-tàroi, and believe me"—she said, sitting upright again but keeping her voice low—"I am perfectly capable of that."

"Oh, you are?" replied Carmondai with a dangerous smile that did not quite match his harmless appearance. There was an icy silence, but after a short while his curiosity got the better of him and he sighed, relenting. After all, the woman was attractive. Warrior-women were not normally his type but this one had a certain something. "Do I get to know your name?"

"Morana, my mother called me." She held out her hand. "Will you ride with me or do you want to walk? My night-mare is good natured. He doesn't usually bite."

His arm stretched out toward her as if of its own accord, then his hand clasped hers and he swung himself up behind her. She wore an unfamiliar perfume that came through over the metallic leather smell of her battledress and he could see strands of black hair escaping from under her helmet. "Take me to the nostàroi. I shall thank them in my own words for their *invitation*."

With a laugh, Morana urged her mount in a ruthless line through the horde of óarcos, who protested vociferously, dodging the night-mare's snapping teeth. Lightning flashes played around the stallion's fetlocks, sparks scorching the ground and an occasional óarco leg.

Morana headed for a smaller gateway guarded by two impressively armed warriors that was free of gathering crowds. *It must only be available for älfar use.*

These gatekeepers saluted briefly and let them pass.

Morana slowed her night-mare as they moved through the passage; the walls threw the sound of its hooves back to them.

Carmondai looked around and smiled at the groundlings' crude art. Their wall sculptures demonstrated an intention to create something beautiful, but their clumsy dwarf hands were never suited to delicate work.

"When did you arrive?" Morana asked.

"Today: I couldn't get away from Riphâlgis any earlier. I admit that I'm furious to have missed the storming of the stronghold, but I did get to hear the speeches. And now I'm to be the *guest* of the nostàroi."

"You would have loved it. It was the best battle even I have ever seen!" Morana guided her night-mare through the right-hand opening. Their heads nearly touched the vaulted ceiling.

Carmondai noted the chiseled runes but could not read them. *As primitive as all the rest of it.* "I know," he sighed. "I had no end of trouble with my night-mare and then of course it decided to depart into ending-ness just as I was on my way here."

Her stallion snorted and they came to a cross-tunnel where they had to wait; a group of älfar in leather aprons were carting dwarf cadavers away. When they saw the riders they moved back to let them pass.

I want to see what they're doing. "Wait for me." He slid down and moved over to the workers.

With a mixture of disgust and fascination, he looked at the gross, pale bodies of their enemies closely. He saw that each had been stabbed neatly through the heart. They had not fallen in battle. *They've not got the slightest bit of refinement about them. It's as if their god was just experi-menting: getting his hand in before creating something to be proud of.* A second cart carried barrels of sloshing liquid; a smell of stone and metal indicated it was dwarf blood.

He greeted the älfar and took out his notebook. "What are you doing with this?"

"We are preparing them according to instructions." One of the älfar answered, looking puzzled. "Have you been sent by the nostàroi to supervise?"

"This is Carmondai, master of word and image," Morana said. "He is sending a report to Dsôn Faïmon about what's happening here in the Gray Mountains."

"Carmondai?" A gray-haired älf bowed his head. "I am an admirer of your art. I never thought I would have the honor of meeting you. My name is Durùston."

Durùston! Carmondai knew the name. He was a sculptor from Dsôn and well known for his stela carved from metal-clad bone and preserved intestines. Anyone who was anyone would have one of these commemo-rative slabs displayed in his home. "Greetings. You are indeed known to me." He indicated the piles of corpses. "Will you be using these in your next works?"

Durùston smiled. "Parts of them. I asked the nostàroi for permis-sion to use any groundling remains that weren't needed for another purpose." He pointed down the corridor. "I've set up a workshop in an old forge. My slaves and my apprentices are processing the cadavers: bones and tendons for sculptures, blood and skin for inks and pigments, hair and beards for paintbrushes. But really their beard hair is too coarse for delicate work—we have to boil it in vinegar to soften it—and then there's the transport through Ishím Voróo. I'm not sure it's really worth it . . . it might even be better to sell it for scrubbing-brushes."

"A tradesman now?" Carmondai asked, with a laugh.

Durùston looked embarrassed. "I sometimes do think of the times to come when my name might no longer be so well known." He turned to go. "You are most welcome to come to my workshop if you'd like to do some sketches. The dwarf anatomy is quite instructive; it might be useful knowledge for future battles."

"Future battles?" Carmondai exchanged glances with Morana. "I thought we'd defeated them all."

"No. Not yet," Durùston answered. "A few stubborn bastions remain, deep in the Gray Mountains. The main victory is ours, of course, but groundlings are tough. We'll have dwarves to deal with for quite some time, mark my words." He gave the signal to move on. "You are welcome any time," he said again, as he followed behind the cart.

"Thank you," Carmondai called after him, then he stowed his notebook once more and went back to the night-mare, allowing Morana to help him up. "What did he mean, do you think?" he asked.

They moved off. "Just what he said: there are still some isolated pockets of groundling families—they are quite stubborn, but they won't hold out for long." Her words sounded confident, arrogant, almost—as if the matter were of no consequence. Of course, it wasn't for *their* armies.

They rode in silence through the underground realm that had so recently fallen into älfar hands. Spattered bloodstains lined the walls: dark-red reminders of the original occupants of these mountain tunnels. *Durùston must have removed all the bodies.*

After some time they arrived in an area where the dwarf runes carved on the walls had been smashed with hammers, and älfar banners and flags, prominently displaying the insignia of the nostàroi, hung from the high vaulted ceilings: to be forgotten was the fate of those defeated in war.

Carmondai looked at the ceiling. Even if he was not necessarily anxious at the thought of a mountain's worth of solid stone above his head, he was not exactly at ease. Back in Riphâlgis, his own house gave unrestricted views over a wide valley and he loved the open vistas. Here he felt constrained, as if buried alive. *The sooner I get out of here, the better.*

"That's where we are heading," said Morana, pointing to a massive gate made of gold—its carved decorations had also been destroyed: hammered flat or levered off, and now four älfar guards flanked the gateway. "It used to be one of their throne rooms, I think, but the nostàroi live there now." A young älf hurried up and led their stallion off. The guards at the entrance stood aside to let them through.

Carmondai's heart started to race. He was not properly dressed to meet the nostàroi and there was no time to go and change. But on the other hand, he did not want to give them the impression that he cared about his apparel—an artist did not have to feel in any way inferior to a warrior. *And I want them to know I have come because I wish to be here, and not because they have summoned me.*

When he walked into the vast hall, he could see tall five-sided columns rising up into the darkness and five älfar in the middle of the room, sitting at a stone table laid for a banquet.

It was clear that Sinthoras and Caphalor, side by side at the head of the table, held equal status as joint commanders. Carmondai did not recognize the other three, but that was no surprise: he had long given up a warrior's life for the sake of art, so he had no idea who was currently in favor. *They look impressive, nearly as fine as the nostàroi themselves.*

As an artist he had learned to focus on tiny distinctive details when observing people or objects closely. He grasped immediately that this was an unusual gathering.

The armor worn by the brown-haired älf on his right, for example, was of incomparable quality. It was thicker than was usual, but did not look like it would restrict the wearer's movements, though the decorative sharpened rivets on the breastplate and over the shoulder and back area would probably mean he wouldn't be able to lean back very comfortably. Two long swords rested on his thighs.

Opposite him sat a pale-faced warrior who had eschewed armor altogether. His wide silk robes were multi-layered and flattering in shades of red, green and black and he wore delicate gloves that had false silver nails at the fingertips. His dark hair was held in check by a broad black band embroidered with white symbols. Another älf stood behind him bearing a thin, steel bow three paces in length, and carrying a quiver of arrows at his belt.

"Noble lords Nostàroi!" Morana bowed toward them and Carmondai felt he should follow suit. He dropped his gaze, although this meant losing sight of the assembled company. "I bring you Carmondai, the master of word and image," Morana announced.

"My dear Carmondai, we have been so looking forward to having you here," said Sinthoras, his welcome delivered in a slightly patronizing tone. "You are just in time."

Carmondai raised his head and regarded the blond nostàroi who, like Caphalor, was dressed in ceremonial armor. "Forgive me if my delight is not entirely boundless. I was given the impression that I was to serve as some sort of scribbling secretary, not as a master of the written word," he countered. "You could have got any schoolboy to do the task." He pulled himself up to his full height, heart thumping wildly at his own audacity.

Caphalor looked mildly amused. He folded his arms. "There you are. I warned you he would take umbrage." The other älfar at the table laughed, but not in a condescending manner. "I should have put money on his reaction."

Sinthoras did not seem to take offense at Caphalor's critical words. He gestured toward one of the free set places. "Please take a seat and forgive me if our *request* for your presence has upset you in any way. We are, of course, well acquainted with your artistic reputation. We felt you were the only älf up to the task."

Carmondai moved over to a high-backed dining chair. As soon as he was seated, he was served dark red wine in a crystal cup. He was still not able to quell his nervous apprehension. *What task will they ask me to perform?*

"May I introduce the others?" Sinthoras asked.

Carmondai inclined his head slightly as platters and cutlery were brought in and set before the guests. To his surprise, Caphalor gestured to Morana to join them at table. She had already removed her helmet and cloak and handed them to a slave. If he was interpreting her expression correctly, she had not been expecting this either.

"I will tell you now: you are in the very best company." Indicating the älf in the flowing robes, Sinthoras continued, "May I present Arviû, our army's finest bowman? He commands the long-range archers. Opposite him is Virssagòn, warrior and master at inventing weaponry and devising new ways for the army to use them."

The name Virssagòn was familiar, but he had never come across the name of Arviû before. He bowed to both. "An honor to meet you."

"At your side we have Horgàta, the deadliest female warrior ever to confront the enemy here in Tark Draan," said Sinthoras.

Carmondai turned to look at her more closely. Her features were perfect, symmetrical and stunningly attractive. Her armor was similar to that worn by Morana but with more in the way of decoration. Surprisingly she bore no weapons and her long blond hair was intricately braided with jewels and carved bone ornaments.

"And Morana here is the second-in-command of our personal guard detachment," Caphalor rounded off the introductions. "Like yourself, she does not know why she has been asked to join us tonight." Everyone, apart from Morana and Carmondai, laughed in response.

Carmondai laid his folder on the table, his posture clearly indicating that he would not be writing or drawing anything until he had heard an adequate explanation as to why he had been summoned. "Most noble Nostàroi, I had been intending to express my displeasure at the manner of my *invitation* here in no uncertain terms, but I admit you have roused my curiosity. And if the food is any good I may find myself forgiving you both." *Ha! That surprised them.* His heart rate, however, had doubled, and his mouth had gone dry.

Sinthoras's countenance darkened and a single jagged anger line shot from the bridge of his nose down to his chin, as if to slice his face in two.

The room fell deathly silent and even the servants froze. For three, four, five blinks of an eye nobody moved, nobody spoke.

Then Caphalor let out a short peal of laughter. "So, our Carmondai is a master not only of word and image but also of sarcastic comment!" He unfolded his arms. "It is good that you make no bones about who you are and that you demonstrate your pride rather than choking on it."

"What did you expect, knowing his previous history?" asked Horgàta.

"Don't try that one too often, Carmondai," Sinthoras said in a low voice. "There are those I know whose pride cost them their life." The jagged black line faded and disappeared. He reached for his cup and raised it, addressing the company with a toast. "Here's health to the Inextinguishables, success to our Tark Draan campaign and an end to the elves!"

I will have to be careful. There's something momentous in the planning here and I'd like to be part of it. Carmondai drained his cup to quench his thirst and started to relax.

The nostàroi seemed to enjoy making their guests wait while the mouth-watering spicy aroma from the first dish infiltrated the cavern, but soon enough slices of tender, rosy, grilled meat were served on polished bone plates for their satisfaction.

While eating with gusto, the artist looked around at the assembled company, fixing the appearance of these important älfar in his mind. He would need to remember them clearly for the pictures he would make later. He noticed a few swift glances exchanged between Caphalor and Morana. *But I don't think they are a couple.*

No one spoke. People were cutting their food, chewing, swallowing, cutting, chewing . . . the horn cutlery made a slightly abrasive sound on the bone plates.

After the first course was cleared away, the servants brought in a map that nearly covered the whole table. It was a map of Tark Draan, with all the topography and features so far known—and it was mostly blank.

Sinthoras stood up, a full wine cup in his left hand. "As you can see"—he gestured to the map—"we need much more information. We have already sent spies disguised as elves out into Tark Draan: they will report to us on troop strengths and deployments, exactly where the borders run, any alliances or animosities between the various kingdoms, and, most importantly, the specific location of the elf realms." He spoke dispassionately, yet he had fire in his eyes. "We *have* heard that some barbarians are versed in magic here. They could prove a difficulty and must be eradicated as a matter of priority. We deal with them before tackling individual rulers."

Caphalor took over, brushing back the strands of black hair that had fallen into his face. "Assuming that word about the fall of the Stone Gateway will soon be widespread, we have to get our information very quickly." He turned to Carmondai. "Would you be willing to record this for us *now*?"

Carmondai hesitated, but then stretched out his hand to take up the pen. "I may regret it later when I'm laughed at for being a mere secretary to the nostàroi."

"Not a soul will ever dare to laugh at you. Your name will be cited on a level with our own and with those of these älfar here at our table," Caphalor announced. "Well, perhaps just *under* our names."

"Shouldn't we subject him to some sort of a test first?" objected Arviû. The archer's tone implied that he did not think much of Carmondai, or at least did not agree with his presence. His resistance also indicated that he was unwilling to share any glory. "Does he deserve the honor of carrying out our task?"

Envy. Carmondai studied the bowman. "How do you envisage this test? Would you like a specimen of my handwriting, or shall I do you a quick sketch perhaps?" he asked amiably.

"Don't they say that the sword is mightier than the pen?" Virssagòn broke in with a smile to indicate that the suggestion he was about to make was not to be taken too seriously. "How about if I challenge him to a fight and we give him a pen to defend himself with? If he wins, we'll accept him."

Seeing that the nostàroi were not interfering, Carmondai assumed that this banter was the actual test he was to undergo. *They want to observe my reactions.* "Arviû and I shall fight, each with a pen. I'll hold mine in my hand; he can put his on the end of an arrow," he retorted.

"So, if you insist on a test, Arviû . . ." Carmondai made as if to get up out of his chair.

"That won't be necessary. No test is required," Sinthoras said swiftly, as if afraid he had let things get out of hand and that this reflected badly on his own and Caphalor's positions of authority. "We have chosen you both—Morana and yourself, Carmondai—to carry out one of the most vital tasks in our campaign."

Carmondai was relieved to hear it and immediately picked up his pen. He suppressed the question about what they intended to do with the army in Tark Draan. He glanced at Morana, who looked just as taken aback as he was. It was clear none of the others had reckoned with this turn of events, either.

His hand sped over the page, sketching and noting details: faces, armor, gestures, who was sitting where—he would need all this for the monumental work of art he had in mind.

He imagined the canvas at least ten paces long and six paces in height. This would enable him to show the hall properly. *I'll include the shattered crown of the groundling king,* he mused, working on the composition: a long table, the light falling just so, columns here and here, the nostàroi in all their glory. Their glory would have to be just that little bit more glorious than that of the other notable älfar in the picture. Deep in thought about what colors to choose for his palette and what materials he would need, he let the nostàroi's words fade to a pleasant background murmur.

"Carmondai, what are you writing?" he heard Caphalor say. "Nobody has been saying that much, but you are making pages of notes."

Lost in his plans for the mural, it took him a moment to notice that anyone had spoken to him. His creative spirit protested at the interruption. "What was that?" He cleared his throat and reached for the wine while he tried to collect himself.

Arviû leaned forward to see what was written in the notebook. "He hasn't written anything. It's just drawings." He gave a scornful laugh. They were obviously not destined to become true friends. "How will that help to preserve events for posterity? Aren't you supposed to write down our commanders' words? Were you going to make it all up later?"

The hostility in Arviû's voice made Carmondai uncomfortable. *What have I ever done to him?*

"Carmondai, I know how easy it is for an artist to get distracted," said Sinthoras mildly. "But you must concentrate and keep your visions under control. Write down what we are saying. Afterward there will be time for drawing and painting."

Carmondai nodded and tried to ignore the patronizing tone. *I fear I shall have to practice this skill.* He took a sip of wine. "It won't happen again—but you must admit that the visual effect here is fascinating, overwhelming!" He was looking directly at the graceful Horgàta as he said these words, prompting a smile from Virssagòn.

"Why don't I start again?" said Sinthoras. "And this time, master of the word, please write down for the generations to come what specific tasks the nostàroi in this exact splinter of unendingness are delegating to our very best älfar."

Chapter I

Distrust, it is said, is the best protection against surprise and death.

But in the long course of their existence the älfar had forgotten how to be suspicious.

> *Because they had courageous and skillful warriors in their armies.*

> *Because they had vassal peoples under their control.*

> *Because they had built fortresses, defense moats and protective walls able to withstand any onslaught.*

> *And because from birth onward their particular qualities enabled them to defy death.*

But there came the day when the älfar would have needed all their old suspicious qualities.

> *Because fate sent them a forgotten enemy to test their mettle.*

Epocrypha of the Creating Spirit
Book of the Coming Death
11–19

Ishím Voróo (Outer Lands), former kingdom of the fflecx,
4371ˢᵗ division of unendingness (5199ᵗʰ solar cycle),
summer.

"I saw the remains of the border palisades over to the left." Arganaï rode his fire-bull along the broad path that had once led to the gateway into the kingdom of the fflecx.

There was nothing left now. A fire had entirely destroyed the defenses: The brightly colored paint used to daub the wooden posts had been highly flammable—a crucial mistake on the part of the builders—and the gnome-like former inhabitants, the alchemancers, had been wiped out.

Arganaï and his six-strong troop of young älfar cadets had been given the mission of inspecting the region in order to make a detailed map. They were also under orders to report any changes.

Arganaï could not be sure what the benàmoi had meant by "any changes" and so it was his plan to pay close attention to every minute detail of the landscape.

Jumping the blackened stumps of the palisade, they entered the barren region. However ridiculous the fflecx had looked, they had been greatly feared because of the poisons they knew how to concoct. For a long time they had been thought to be inviolable, but that had ended when most of them were killed by the mist-demon—the remainder had been finished off by Caphalor. Arganaï looked over at their placid fire-bulls. They had not been entrusted with night-mares; they would have to earn the right to ride one of those valuable beasts, but Arganaï did not mind: Worbîn, his own mount, had served him well. Even if fire-bulls were not as swift or as elegant as night-mares, they were more or less unstoppable: the long horns and their metal coverings set with blades could remove or destroy any obstacle, and their black coats, which ran to a rust color over their breasts and flanks, gave the beasts the appearance of flames and made it look as though they were born to fight.

Arganaï looked around him. There was nothing moving save a few white seeds floating about and the air shimmered with heat. He was bored, his clothes were sweat-soaked and the armor made him hotter still. If it had been up to him he would have taken off the protective leathers, but if the benàmoi came across any of them without armor they would all be in trouble. *Why does it have to be so hot? It's like an oven.* He had his lance in his right hand; the end supported by a thong attached to his stirrup. "Spot anything unusual?"

The responses sounded decidedly unenthusiastic. Nobody was putting any effort into the search at all. Except for Tiláris. She was looking around eagerly, sniffing the air as she turned around in the saddle.

"What is it?" Arganaï took hold of his water pouch and moistened his brow. The liquid was as warm as he was, but at least it would wipe away the sweat. He was looking forward to having a bath.

"Haven't you noticed? There are no insects."

"It'll be too hot for them," grumbled Zirlarnor, as he sought shade by a tree, but dry leaves covered the ground around it: it was dead, there would be no shade there. "I know just how those insects feel."

Arganaï looked around more carefully. There wasn't a fly to be seen. No beetles. Nothing. *By all the unholy gods!* "Zirlarnor, write that down. She's right. It's very unusual." He told the others to spread out over the area. "See what insects or animals you can find."

Now for some real research.

Every movement made the älfar sweat more and the fire-bulls struggled in the increasing heat, so they took things as easy as possible.

Even so, Arganaï soon emptied his water bottle and began to look for a stream. *I can't believe the fflecx would have stored all their drinking water in flasks.*

His fire-bull snorted and twisted its head around so fast that the iron-clad horns made a ringing sound.

"Have you found something?" Arganaï muttered to his fire-bull. He gave the beast its rein and it led him through leafless shrubbery to the edge of a pond. The water was black as pitch and stank.

The young älf leader wrinkled his nose in disgust. "No good for us," he murmured, and was about to turn his mount away when he caught sight of a creature that looked like a wolf lying on the desiccated grass. It got up and growled at him, crept over to the water, drank, choked and trembled all over, but kept on drinking more and more of the dark liquid.

"A sotgrîn." Its behavior was worrying. *It must be sick.*

The predator's cunning black gaze fixed itself abruptly on him, then on his fire-bull. Black water dripped out of its muzzle onto the grass like ink and the creature gathered itself to attack, uttering a low, threatening growl.

"Aha, someone wants a taste of our flesh." Arganaï tapped his mount's neck. "Watch out, Worbîn. Looks like we're not going to be bored for much longer."

The sotgrîn launched itself at them with a roar. The fire-bull responded to its rider's gentle pressure on its flanks and lowered its horns, catching the beast with a glancing blow before tossing it violently to the ground. The sotgrîn staggered up and tried a second assault. This time Arganaï directed the bull to skewer the animal's throat with a sideways thrust: the sotgrîn was suspended in midair, yelping, gurgling and flailing wildly as dark red blood drenched its coat.

"Well done, Worbîn." The young älf had not had to do anything, really, except to sit at his ease in the saddle and direct the fire-bull from there. He watched the death throes of the sotgrîn with curiosity as the beast finally weakened and gave up its last breath, its life juices running down the bull's horn.

The blood made Arganaï think of the brackish water in the pond. He bent forward and sniffed.

"Right," he murmured. The creature's coat gave no indication of its having rolled in the black water, so the smell did not come from there. *We must record this at once.* He called out to Zirlarnor, "Over here! I've found something. Bring your notebook and—"

The sotgrîn opened its eyes and growled viciously, even though it was still transfixed by the horn of the fire-bull. It struggled hard to free itself, but in vain.

"By all the ungodly ones!" exclaimed Arganaï. "It was just playing dead!" He took his spear and rammed it straight into the creature's body. But the sotgrîn only fought more tenaciously than ever, burying its teeth in the wooden shaft.

"What's happening . . . ?"

With an audible *rip*, the flesh of the sotgrîn's throat tore through and the animal landed on the ground on all four paws, blood still pouring from the gaping hole in its side. Without hesitation, it launched itself for another attack.

How on earth? Arganaï aimed his spear again and stabbed at the creature, which seemed totally unaware of its injuries. On the contrary, it snapped at the legs of the fire-bull more ferociously than ever.

The steed made a mighty leap aside to avoid the deadly teeth, but the rider himself was now in direct danger. Would nothing stop the sotgrîn? Finally Arganaï got the tip of his spear through the creature's ear and thrust hard. It emerged on the other side of the sotgrîn's head.

The sotgrîn collapsed immediately and remained motionless.

Arganaï pinned the animal to the ground with his spear before jumping down from the saddle. He drew his sword and approached cautiously, mindful a further attack might be in the offing. *I won't give you a chance to try that one again.* The fire-bull lowered its metal-clad horns in readiness.

"Hey!" Arganaï shouted. There was no response from the sotgrîn. *Better be on the safe side.* He sliced the creature's head from its body and a last surge of blood followed. "What's your secret . . . ?" he muttered to himself. Then he saw the pond. *You drank that water! Is that what let you withstand all those injuries?*

"Zirlarnor!" He called. "Where are you? I've found something really exciting. The Inextinguishables will be all over us in gratitude. We'll go direct to them and not tell the benàmoi. We don't want him taking all the credit."

Arganaï went back to the stagnant pond. The smell was worse than ever, yet there were still no flies, nor were there any other insects. There was nothing living in the water, either.

He knelt down, leaning on his sword. *What is this stuff? Is it some of the alchemancers' leftover poison?*

His own reflection looked eerie: the black eyes were taking over the whole face, swallowing up the other features and leaving only a dark hole. Arganaï shuddered. Despite the intolerable summer heat, an icy chill ran up and down his spine. He found it almost impossible to drag himself away from the image of his dark, cruel brother under the surface of the pond.

He was so distracted that he did not notice the sword he was leaning on begin to fall. His sword blade slipped down into the soft ground and he fell headfirst into the black water, clamping his lips shut at the last minute.

He sank into the oily depths, his sword lost on the bank. Flailing wildly, he tried to swim back up to the surface, but soon realized that he was actually heading farther into the pond.

It can't be that deep! He suddenly had the impression that someone's fingers were grasping him. *No! What is happening . . . ?*

He was running out of air. Getting desperate, he kicked out and thrashed with his arms, finally struggling up to the surface again.

The sunlight dazzled him, but he had never been happier to see it. He hurled himself up onto the bank of dry, rustling grasses and only then gasped in the air. Brown and black weeds clung to him in a slimy mass.

"Ye unholy gods," he panted, rolling onto his back. Fear was making him tremble all over. *That's not just something the fflecx left behind by mistake. What terrible power is hidden in that pond?* He pulled his feet out of the black morass, afraid those claws might try to grab him again.

Raising his head he could see the pond was no more than two paces across. *I must have been imagining it! How could I have nearly drowned in something that small?*

"Zirlarnor, where the blazes are you?" he yelled. "I nearly . . ." Arganaï froze. He had picked up the scent of raw meat and fresh blood. He turned, pulling his long dagger out of its sheath on his leg.

The sotgrîn lay where Arganaï had beheaded it, but his fire-bull was gone—all Arganaï could see was a pile of guts on the trampled, bloodied grass and a broken-off horn stuck in the ground. *What does all this mean?* Worbîn was an experienced battle-steed and always came off best in any fight. Nothing could have beaten him in such a short time, let alone have butchered him and carried off the carcass. *What awful curse has touched this land?*

The young älf warrior got to his feet, dagger held pointing down. He staggered past the pile of intestines and followed the bloody track leading through the thicket. Red blood dripped on him from the dry foliage.

He moved silently, alert for danger. The idea of meeting a predator able to dispatch and drag off an adult fire-bull as if it were a sack of feathers did not fill him with delight. And now he did not even have his sword for protection.

The track brought him back to the place he had left his troops.

His black eyes widened as he stepped out of the bushes: the grass had been trampled down and there was so much älfar blood on the ground and splashed on the leafless trees it was as if it had been poured out from buckets.

There wasn't a sound, or a trace of his companions—apart from the blood.

His heart thumped painfully in his chest. He would not have wanted to admit it, but for the first time in his life he was experiencing true terror. It was urging him to save himself and flee, abandoning his men. *Flee . . . from what?*

I can't do that! What will I tell the benàmoi when he asks what happened here? Arganaï's thoughts were jumbled. It was something to do with the pond, surely? Was there a creature living in the water? Had it come out and killed them all?

He noticed a second track and made his way forward. There were marks everywhere he could not identify: hoof-prints and deep furrows filled with blood. And then he found pieces of älfar armor, shards of metal, and severed locks of brown hair. Despite the destruction, the air was perfectly still.

Arganaï was overcome with fear once more.

He halted, planting the toe of his raised boot behind him, instead of in front. He started to withdraw as slowly and quietly as possible so as not to attract any attention from the creature that could kill and dismember älfar and fire-bulls as if they were toys.

There's nothing I can do on my own. He turned and ran as fast as his legs would carry him. *I have to find the benàmoi and make my report. I don't care if they think I'm a coward.*

He never stopped to rest, only once to take a drink and to throw off some of his heavy leather gear. *It doesn't matter what I look like. I've just got to get back in one piece.*

Sometimes he sensed he was being followed, but whenever he turned to look, there was nothing and nobody to be seen. He put it down to the stress he was under.

Without his fire-bull, and even though he kept up a steady pace, it took him until sundown to reach the place where he had agreed to meet the benàmoi. His legs were killing him and he fought for breath as he struggled up to the vantage point. He saw Phinoïn, his commanding officer, leaning against a rock.

Arganaï staggered up to him with an overwhelming sense of relief. "Phinoïn!" he gasped. "I—in the northwest . . . at the border with the fflecx . . ."

He fell silent with shock at the sight of his benàmoi.

Someone had thrust iron bolts through the armor at shoulders, breast and neck, anchoring him to the rock so that he appeared to be patiently waiting for his scouts to return. A pool of his own blood spread out at his feet.

Suddenly, the commander he had assumed dead saw him and gave a groan. "Run. You must warn Dsôn! If you don't—"

Violet-colored light fell on Phinoïn's face, coming from behind the scout. The benàmoi's eyes widened and he opened his mouth to utter a blood-curdling scream.

What . . . ? Arganaï was about to vault to one side but mid-turn he was dealt a blow on the back that had him hurled to the ground. The impact knocked him unconscious.

Tark Draan (Girdlegard), Gray Mountains, Stone Gateway,
4371ˢᵗ division of unendingness (5199ᵗʰ solar cycle),
summer.

That's a lot of material. Carmondai was sitting in the accommodation the nostàroi had given him surrounded by loose pages that had been drawn or written on.

Notes, lightning sketches, detailed drawings, resonant turns of phrase . . . it had all resulted from that evening session with the nostàroi, and it was all waiting for him to put it into some sort of order.

He leaned back against the wall, closing his eyes. He wanted to recall every visual detail of that important meeting.

Each of them had been sent away with specific tasks that they could perform better than any other älf, and Carmondai should have been starting on the preparations for his journey: there were lists to make, things to pack . . . But his muse demanded that he be creative: he was obsessed by the image of Horgàta raising the cup to her lips.

She is incomparable. He opened his eyes and grabbed a pen and some paper. He would not be able to rest until he had completed the drawing in his mind.

As he worked he became more and more absorbed. Soon he moved away from the table and went over to perch on the uncomfortable bed. He adjusted the lines, rubbing out and drawing anew until he had perfected the image of her face. She was smiling gently as she sipped from her cup of wine.

That will sell well. Carmondai propped the picture up and stood well back to observe his work. *Yes, not bad at all. Likenesses of our heroines will be much in demand, and that will help me fill my empty coffers.*

He went over to the table and drank some water, letting his gaze roam.

The chamber ceiling was only just high enough for him, but all the furniture was undersized; if he lay full length on the bed he knew his legs would hang over the end. In fact, he would probably do better to sleep on the floor.

I miss home. I hope there'll be some houses somewhere in Tark Draan with a bit more room. Carmondai put the mug of water down and

suddenly remembered that he had a meeting he should be at. *Curses.*
Casting a final glance at his drawing of Horgàta, he picked up his notebooks and hurried out of the room. *But she was worth it.*

Carmondai looked carefully at the corridor he was in; without a guide
like Morana, he'd managed to get hopelessly lost.
I'm sure I've been here before. He knew he had an excellent sense of
direction above ground, but these corridors all looked exactly the same.
Even the carvings on the walls were incredibly similar.

Fortunately, his wanderings had given him the opportunity to be
a secret observer to an óarco celebration. From some kind of naturally
occurring rock balcony, he watched as his allies enjoyed the groundlings'
extra-strength beer. Their celebration was worlds away from the sophisticated revelries of the älfar: drunken óarcos lay under the tables, others
were scuffling and fighting, some of the females were spreading their legs
for whoever came out the winner, while some were stealing jewelry from
the ones that were asleep; trombones and horns screeched, drums and
cymbals crashed—you could not call it music—and the *stink* had been
something else!

As he'd watched, Carmondai's contempt for the green-skinned monsters had reached record levels. When he was back home he would show
his fellow älfar sketches of the beasts to make them appreciate what a
good idea it had been to entice these creatures away from Ishím Voróo.
*Curse those wretched groundlings! They must have deliberately con-
structed these tunnels in order to confuse.* Carmondai came to a crossroads
he recognized. He contemplated a moment before taking a different
option to the one he had before, but his choice was more out of desperation than conviction.

He was really looking for Arviû in order to pick his brains about
archery, but if he did not find the way soon he would miss him: the master bowman would not be in the Gray Mountains for much longer. *Who
knows when I'll have another chance?*

Carmondai started to jog.

Though he had told Morana that his night-mare had departed into
endingness, he had made the story up so as not to look a fool in the eyes

of the important älfar: he had actually never possessed such a creature. He had been out of funds for too long to have ever bought anything so expensive. Only the wealthy could afford night-mares, and only those in the army were given them. He was neither.

His paintings were popular, but they did not fetch a high price. That is why this campaign to Tark Draan was so important to him: it was just the thing for his art. He could pick up the odd trophy and find plenty of inspiration that could translate into money later.

The tunnel was slowly opening out. It led into a hall where there were boxes, barrels, chests and sacks piled high against the walls. Some had been opened, and in the faint light of some shimmering blue moss he saw vegetable roots, spices and salt scattered on the ground.

I wonder where the wretched mountain maggots kept their gold?

Something whizzed past his nose and collided with a metal object that clanged and smashed before he even knew what had happened.

Turning his head, he saw a long black arrow embedded in the padlock of one of the chests. The lock had burst open under the impact.

"You're late, Carmondai. We were meeting at the seventh splinter of unendingness," someone called, the voice echoing. "I have all but completed my practice."

Carmondai turned around and saw Arviû's silk-clad figure at the other end of the hall, he raised his arm in greeting and strode over to the archer.

He's more than 400 paces away. Even with my own excellent eyesight it would have been difficult to make out such a small padlock from that far back. Four servants were standing by Arviû holding quivers stacked in readiness. Arrayed around them were stands containing various different types of bow; some three paces long, others as short as half a pace. Arviû himself held a tall, steel bow that glinted in the torchlight.

This is going to be fun. Carmondai approached the archer and bowed. "My greetings, master of the—"

Arviû dismissed his words with a hand gesture. "Masters of any art do not use titles when they address each other. We know who we are. Forgive me if I was abrupt with you at our first meeting, I think I was just surprised. It won't happen again." He paused. "You wanted to learn about archery?" Arviû's blue eyes were smiling at him now. "But doesn't every älf know how to use a bow?"

"Well, I know how to shoot," said Carmondai, staring at the range of weapons with curiosity. "I could hit a target, but I'd never have been able to destroy that padlock."

Arviû smiled. "How do you know that was what I was aiming at? My target might have been the leather strap you carry your folder with."

Carmondai glanced at his right shoulder. The end of the strap had been cut clean off.

Arviû handed his steel bow to a young älf, who put it away. "I was aiming for the strap and for the padlock, Carmondai. And if you ask me why, it's because I can." He pointed to a black, varnished bow as tall as an älf and a servant brought it over to him.

So he's not conceited at all. Carmondai could not help grinning.

"I know what you're thinking; you think I'm bragging, I can read that smile of yours." Arviû was enjoying himself. "Some who have shown me a lack of respect have paid for it with their lives."

Carmondai stopped being so cheery. He opened his folder and took out the pressed charcoal-dust writing implement he was so proud of having invented. "That was a very impressive shot. Could you tell me why you use a steel bow? What is the string made of?"

"I usually use the steel bow if I don't know what the climate will be like in a certain area, as it's not badly affected by weather variations like a bone or wooden bow would be.

"The string is silver wire and just as resistant to changes in the weather as the main structure, but I use natural strings more often." Arviû caressed the black bow. "This one is made of many parts glued together. It has a much greater range than the steel bow."

"How far will it shoot?"

"With a bit of practice, about a thousand paces in the normal shooting posture, but there's another method. If you lie down on your back and use your feet to support the bow while you pull back the bowstring with both hands it shoots much farther. Unfortunately it's not very accurate, but in battle there's a lot to be said for sending a dense shower of arrows down on the enemy before they begin to fight." His face took on a contemptuous expression. "I don't use that method as it's inelegant and clumsy. I teach it to others, though; one never knows when it might come in useful, but there'd have to be a real emergency for me to employ it myself."

Carmondai had never heard of this type of archery. "And how far could that method get you?"

"As long as the bowstring doesn't snap, between 1,500 and 1,800 paces. It's a good ploy for a surprise attack on an army. The best of the barbarians' bows can't get farther than 500 paces." Arviû was enjoying Carmondai's astonishment. "I know you have never been a passionate archer."

"I was certainly never very good at it." Carmondai's gaze took in the various bows, some of which were asymmetrical. *No untrained* älf *would be able to use those ones.* "The nostàroi said you were in charge of the long-distance warriors."

"I trained the benàmoi and advised them on the kinds of bows and arrows to bring on campaign." Arviû went over to the quivers and selected a few samples. "Some of these are traditional älfar arrows, but I've improved the design. Just because something has been around for hundreds of divisions of unendingness doesn't mean it has to be good." He showed Carmondai the shafts. "Look at the fletching here. We used to use eagle feathers because of the birds' noble natures, but I use black goose feathers and cut them into shape. They are stronger, so the arrow's flight remains true. I don't care if my arrows are noble; I want them to be lethal."

Carmondai sketched as he listened.

Arviû showed him various arrowheads. "I had the best smiths in Ocizûr work on these for a division of unendingness until I was satisfied. Nobody else can supply that standard. If you save money on the arrowheads, you reduce the effectiveness of your army, then you expend more effort and risk losing more of your own ranks."

Carmondai made a note of what he was told.

"Look here; these are the main shapes we employ. First you have the narrow shaft with a four-sided arrow tip. I designed them on the principle of the cutleaf tree foliage—they are excellent for cutting through light armor." He turned it in his hand, then picked up the next example.

"Then we have the barbed arrowhead, which is nice and slim, and then the forked version: useful for causing heavy bleeding in an enemy when you're dealing with opponents not wearing armor. Or you can bring down their mounts with these, of course. Then we have the smooth, simple variety with a long, straight tip, but they have more weight in them to take care of those in heavy armor. All the others are variations on these basic shapes."

Arviû was getting carried away with his own skills and artistry and Carmondai did not want to spend the rest of the present moment of unendingness listening to the archer's monologue. "Right. I've got all that. Could you tell me about the fighting procedure?"

"Have you forgotten everything?"

"No." Carmondai cleared his throat to cover his discomfort at this question. "But I want to hear it from you."

"I understand. In combat, it's all a question of what situation you are in. I've trained the long-distance warriors to be adaptable: each one has a horse, two longbows and one short one, eight dozen arrows with inter-changeable arrowheads and light body armor for optimum mobility—armor like my own. They carry a container with utron viper poison, in case an opponent proves too tough." Arviû raised his arm to show Carmondai the forearm guard and a ring he wore on his thumb. "I don't just use my fingers to pull back the bowstring: sometimes I use my thumb, too, and the ring helps to protect the skin. My pupils have all learned this method; they know it helps them if they're keeping up a prolonged bout of shooting. It's another tactical advantage we have over others." He replaced the bow in the stand. "Any further questions? However infinite, my time is precious." He turned around and instructed his servants to pack away the equipment. "I'll be leaving soon, to carry out the will of our nostàroi."

Carmondai realized the archer was offended. *Perhaps I upset him when I interrupted him just now?* "One more thing: this armor, it's made from some sort of textile; is it really sturdy enough?"

Arviû gave him the sort of look you would give a child who had asked a stupid question. "That's another thing you ought to know your-self, Carmondai."

"But it will be better in your own words."

Arviû's face showed scorn as he continued his discourse. "What you see here is the top covering, worn over a long surcoat composed of many layers that are glued together. These provide flexibility and provide plenty of protection against sword thrusts and small missiles." His smile was cold. "An archer will always be more concerned about his own ease of movement. That's what will enable him to knock an enemy out before he has a chance to strike." He ran his hand over the fabric. "Soft silk can withstand steel if you know how to conduct yourself. End of story." With a wordless gesture the älf strode off, followed by his retinue.

Carmondai watched the älf leave the hall in silence, then finished off his drawings and put his notebooks and writing implement away.

He paused for a moment and thought carefully—recently he had been confronted with many things that reminded him of his past, and he did not want to let the past affect his behavior in the present—but his spirit was undisturbed. *I don't know if that's a good thing.* Carmondai sighed. *The old life, I'd like to forget all about it.* He let his gaze wander across the hall one last time. He went back to the storage chests wondering what else Arviû had been aiming at.

The archer's arrows had destroyed every lock. He had not missed a single target.

Carmondai wrenched the shaft out of one of the chests. The arrow tip was designed to penetrate metal. With one arrowhead like that an archer could pierce and kill three or even four barbarians all at the same time. *I've heard that's how Arviû tests out his modifications: aiming at prisoners in body armor.*

He dropped the arrow and walked rather aimlessly along the corridor. He didn't have a lot to do until the evening, when he had a meeting with Virssagòn, to learn about his recent innovations in weaponry.

An army could not afford to take an entire new range of weapons and armaments with them: forging huge numbers of newfangled swords, lances and axes would be ridiculously impractical. But Virssagòn had other talents the nostàroi might want to employ: where others bore details on their armor denoting the number of enemies dispatched, he bore a single rune that indicated he had simply stopped counting, so great was the number. Carmondai knew of no other warrior who had distinguished himself in that way. Not even Sinthoras or Caphalor.

And myself? How will I fare in the coming divisions of unendingness? He had mixed feelings about his appointed task.

On the one hand he felt flattered, but on the other the risks were enormous. It was quite possible none of his reports and poems would ever reach their intended audience in Dsôn Faïmon, because he might be killed during his Tark Draan mission: stabbed or strung up, crushed by a falling rock, tortured by barbarians, or come to some other unglamorous end.

Carmondai was so deep in thought he was not paying attention to where he was going—until he noticed the corridors were getting narrower and the ceiling lower. He assumed he had been moving away from the stronghold and was inadvertently on the point of exploring the realm of the groundlings. All by himself.

Not the brightest of ideas. He glanced down at his short sword: not enough in the way of defense. He turned back.

He eventually reached a hall where a group of óarcos were tucking noisily into stewed meat and gnawing on the bones; Carmondai had no wish to know what kind of meat it was.

This is no place for me.

One of the monsters raised its head and grunted. The whole group stopped guzzling and stared at Carmondai. A furious roar swelled up. There was no mistaking the invitation to depart.

What an ugly bunch. Looks like they wanted to keep their party strictly to themselves. He was not keen to enter into negotiations with these allies, so he skirted the gathering, keeping to the cave walls. "Revolting, stinking scum. Even a tenth of a division of unendingness ago we'd have chopped your heads off and ground your guts for paint," he said to them in the dark language, with a steady smile on his face. "I hope many of you die horrible deaths in the Tark Draan campaign. If necessary, our own warriors will see to that as soon as we have no further use for you."

"What was that?" one of them growled in a barbarian dialect. "Wot you mumbling bout?"

"I said I did not wish to disturb you at your fine meal." This time Carmondai was using the same primitive language. "I do not want to share.

It is all yours, but would you please be so kind as to tell me how to get to where my own folk are camping out?" They still did not understand what he was saying, so he repeated his request slowly.

Instead of giving him a sensible answer, they chucked away the bones they were chomping on and came over to him, drawing their swords. One of them gave an ugly laugh. "Snooooty clever dick," one of them roared. "Think you can make stoopid jokes with stoopid talk like stoopid flowers?"

As the beasts approached, a wall of óarco beer-breath rolled toward him. He recognized the smell from the other hall. Carmondai looked to his left and saw an empty barrel, once full of dwarf ale.

Oh. Thanks a lot, gods of infamy! Just my luck to run into a horde of drunken óarcos raring for a fight. He took a step backward and moved his drawing folder safely onto his back.

"Let me ask you nicely one more time," he said, but the way they laughed made it clear they were not going to oblige him with the information he wanted.

Chapter II

You know Death comes in many forms.

Most pose no threat to the älfar.
Age is of no significance.
But Death does not give up easily. He is greedy and desires to fetch as many beings as he can into the endingness where he dwells.
This is why he has devised sicknesses, war and other miseries for barbarians, óarcos and other miscellaneous scum.

And sometimes, the gods of infamy decreed, Death will appear in person to those who continue to flout his power, so that he may fell them with his own hand.

Epocrypha of the Creating Spirit
Book of the Coming Death
19–30

Ishím Voróo (Outer Lands), Dsôn Faïmon, Dsôn,
4371ˢᵗ division of unendingness (5199ᵗʰ solar cycle),
summer.

Polòtain cast his eyes critically over the onyx marble statue of an älfar warrior in full armor. Contrary to traditionally favored poses, this life-sized representation did not show the subject in fighting stance. The soldier bore his weapons on his back, with his three-cornered shield in his right hand; his left arm was raised, the index finger pointing accusingly. In denunciation.

Sunlight from the high studio windows illuminated the work, making it glow as if lit internally. Long dark bands within the stone showed like veins, and there was a burst black lump in the center.

"I particularly like the way you have rendered the broken heart, Itáni," Polòtain murmured as he placed his hand caressingly on the statue's cold neck and pressed his forehead against the stone brow. "My dearest Robonor," he whispered. "How I miss you."

"My heartfelt thanks for your appreciation and praise." Itáni moved away from the wall where she had been leaning. She was wearing a gray and white robe covered, as were her face and hands, with light-colored dust. "It has been an honor to carry out this commission for you." She went around to the rear of the statue and squatted down to point out where she had emphasized the wound in the älf's leg, inserting red gold and allowing it to run down to denote trickling blood. "The alloy I have used absorbs heat by day and allows the wound to appear to shimmer by night. No one passing, even at a distance, could fail to notice."

Polòtain took a deep breath. "A masterly work of art, Itáni! I shall pay twice what we agreed. No one else in Dsôn could possibly have done better." He ran his fingers over the black embroidered runes on his grayish yellow robe. Two badges of honor shone at his breast. These were decorations granted him for his past achievements. They were as nothing to him now.

"I am humbled by your generosity." The artist stood up and bowed to him. "I know it is what you asked for, but would it not have been appropriate to portray him in a heroic pose?"

"A hero's life was not granted to him. He was not granted the chance to join the campaign against Tark Draan and to fall honorably in battle when his time came," Polòtain replied in a somber tone. "He was betrayed and killed in the most cowardly manner. I want everyone to know! The statue of my great nephew will be a permanent reminder to the guilty until his death is avenged."

Itáni summoned a slave by giving a short blast on a whistle she wore around her neck. Refreshments were brought; she partook of fruit wine while Polòtain selected the stronger brandy liqueur. "You realize what this may mean for you?" she asked carefully.

"It is good of you to want to warn me, Itáni," he replied with a sad smile.

"I'm just afraid of losing my best patron and ending my days penniless," she joked. Then, becoming serious, "Even you cannot risk challenging a nostàroi in this way. He has become very powerful. After the victory in the Gray Mountains he will be able to ask the Inextinguishables for anything he wants. He will go crazy when he hears about Robonor's statue because he'll know exactly what it means."

Polòtain's melancholy smile had not faded. "Have I told you where I want it to stand?"

She narrowed her eyes. "I thought it would be in front of your family house in Avaris."

He shook his head, the long blond hair with its gray strands brushing his dark summer coat.

"That would not have the desired effect." Polòtain swirled the drink in his cup. "I have purchased a trader's stand on the marketplace. For one division of unendingness the pitch belongs to me."

"But that's immediately opposite the nostàrois' plaque of honor," Itáni exclaimed. She was also aware that one of the main roads crossed that square. Whenever the nostàroi entered Dsôn, he would perforce pass the statue. He would have to walk past this life-sized accusation. "By all that's infamous! Sinthoras will hate you for that."

Polòtain lowered his head, lines of fury crisscrossing his face. "And what do you think I feel for my great nephew's murderer? Admiration? I am the only älf in Dsôn Faïmon to detest the nostàroi, the greatest general in the history of our peoples, from the bottom of my soul. I detest him to such a degree that I do not even wish him to enter endingness. I want him crushed and humiliated before me in the gutter! Then I shall press his arrogant face into the filth with my foot, so his lungs fill with excrement and he suffocates!" The cup shattered into glass slivers in his hands. "You see how this unimportant, trivial matter upsets me," he whispered. "Here I am destroying your valuable tableware."

Itáni sent for water and a cloth so that he might wash his hands. "I am glad you have not injured yourself." Slaves appeared and swept up the broken pieces. "I understand how you must feel, my friend."

"The worst thing is that nobody else seems to object to how Timanris openly betrayed him," he said as if he were on his own, while he wiped his hands. "She has taken up with the murderer of the älf who worshipped her and with whom she should have produced at least one child." He sighed deeply, as if unable to bear the sorrow any longer. Polòtain focused his black eyes on Itáni. "Can you arrange to have the statue erected on the marketplace? Your people will know how to handle a work of art better than my slaves will."

She bowed. "Of course. I'll see to it at once." She drained her cup. "Onyx marble withstands all weathers and won't be affected by frost. But it will be vulnerable to cuts or blows. You should set a guard if you want it to last. I fear there will be more than one attack made on it. Either Sinthoras will pay someone to do it, or it might be defaced by frenetic admirers of the nostàroi, who will be calling you a liar."

"I've thought about that. I'll come up with something." Polòtain shook hands with her. "My thanks again for this incomparable likeness of my beloved great nephew. Until we meet again." He departed, escorted to the door by a slave.

Polòtain left the house of the sculptress and suddenly felt a pain in his heart. He put his hand to his breast and took deep breaths. His grief at Robonor's passing caused him more anguish than any physical injury he had ever sustained in all his time as a warrior. And yet his distress would serve as a motivating force. He would not give up until revenge was his. He dismissed his litter-bearers. He wanted to walk and follow his own thoughts.

Polòtain found it unbearable that Robonor's own father had done nothing but was prepared, on the contrary, to believe the line that his son had died in an accident and that it had been so decreed by fate.

But Polòtain was all too familiar with this kind of fate: älfar hands had given fate plenty of help here. He was well versed in such intrigues; were it otherwise he would not himself have achieved such a high position among the Comets.

The Comets were convinced that the future of the älfar depended on expansionism, increasing the territory under their control. The Constellations, on the other hand, insisted the best strategy was to build more and better border defenses. Each faction had been trying to persuade the Inextinguishables that their own view was the correct one.

The sibling rulers would, of course, be deciding for themselves what should happen in Dsôn Faïmon, but the views of their people and, in particular, of the elite were important.

Polòtain had retired from his function as a Comet leader nearly ten divisions of unendingness previously to live on his estate in Avaris, leaving Robonor in charge of his city property in Dsôn. But when Sinthoras—a member of the same political faction as himself—acted with such despicable trickery, it was more than his soul could bear to sit and do nothing. He still had his network of connections in all six of the radial arms. He had already received a promise that should soon be bearing fruit.

"I'll have you on your knees, Sinthoras," he murmured. "Don't you dare get killed in Tark Draan. I want you to have victory after glorious victory. The greater your fame, the more devastating your subsequent fall. How I shall enjoy it!"

Polòtain had no eye for the magnificent architecture around him; this was a part of the city where many artists dwelled. He ignored the convoluted buildings constructed in gray and colored wood or in compressed stone incorporating thin metal layers, with their decorations in white and black bone tiles, their carved window frames and many other features. He did not look at the cleverly sculpted evergreen bushes with their ornamental artworks tinkling in the gentle breeze.

He had lost all interest in art because beauty no longer had any relevance for him. Such was his hatred of Sinthoras and Timanris that he had thrown out a number of outstanding pieces of work her famous artist father had created. He had gotten the lowliest of his household slaves to carry them out onto the street and destroy them in public view.

He took no notice when passers-by greeted him. He slouched along until his legs started to hurt and he was forced to use the litter his servants were carrying. After all, he was getting old.

When he thought back to his dreams of the future! Everything he had hoped and planned for his beloved great nephew! "My young hero—cut off in his prime," he sobbed, burying his face in his hands, and wiping his tears on his sleeve.

Polòtain had thrown off his deepest despair before returning to his city residence; grief paralyzed one and prevented any clear thought. This was the most grueling battle he had ever waged and it was against an enemy in his own ranks and for whom he felt the most devastating hatred.

His servants halted and Polòtain got out of the litter.

Before he was halfway into the forecourt, his great-grandson Godànor rushed over, dressed in a black robe with wide white leather straps adorned with gold and silver at hip and across the chest. "There you are at last! You have a visitor."

Polòtain suspected he knew who the visitor could be; would this be the promised assistance? "Why are you making it so mysterious?"

"I'm not. Ask me whatever you want." Godànor took his arm and hurried him across the courtyard toward the slaves' quarters.

"Slow down! I've been walking all day." Polòtain decided not to ask who was waiting for him.

Passing the slave building they reached a small smithy and Godànor opened the door.

There were two armed älfar waiting inside, their light armor marked with the insignia of Eranior. They had tied two humans, chained together, to the anvil. The barbarians were in dirty, torn clothing and cowered in fear as Polòtain and his grandson entered. An acrid smell from one of them suggested he might be suffering from some unpleasant chronic disease.

"Samrai and Chislar," Godànor introduced the älfar at arms, then pulled out a letter to give his great-grandfather. "They brought you these two barbarians and this letter."

Polòtain broke the seal and read the few short lines which wished him every success with his interrogation. These men were apparently two of the three slaves found brawling in the street on that fateful night. Robonor had been on the point of arresting them when he had been killed. The note went on to say that something extra would be arriving shortly.

Polòtain was elated. These barbarians were vital pieces in the mosaic of his case against Sinthoras!

He handed Godànor the letter and gestured to the ragged prisoners to stand up. They struggled to their feet at the anvil, their chains tightening. "Whose slaves are you?" He resented having to use their language. He took a fire iron and shoved it into the glowing furnace, telling Godànor to work the bellows.

"Do you mean who we belong to or do you mean who we serve?" came the reply from the barbarian who stank slightly less than the other one.

"What is your name?"

The slaves exchanged glances as if they were trying to ensure they did not say the wrong thing.

Polòtain used the fire iron to sweep red-hot coals in their direction. There was a smell of burning: clothes, hair and skin. The men screamed and batted the coals away as best they could. "Look at me, not each other!" he ordered, a terrifying coldness in his voice. "Did you serve Sinthoras?"

They shook their heads.

"Well?"

"I am Errec, and this is Amso. We . . . serve Halofór," stammered the less unsavory one. "We always have done."

"Landaròn's brother?" Polòtain broke into a malicious grin. Landaròn was Sinthoras's cousin and it was pretty clear that he would have done him the odd favor or two. "Did your master tell you to stage a brawl in front of the slaves' tavern?" He pulled the iron out of the fire and held the white-hot tip against the chains at the man's wrist. Smoke rose and heat transferred from one metal to the other. "What happened the night of the street fight?" He glared at the men in turn. "There were three of you, I understand. Where's the other one?"

"Dead. Under a carriage," Errec rushed to answer, already in great discomfort. "Lordship, please! The fight was because he insulted us back at the inn. We dragged him outside to give him a beating but then the guards showed up and we made a run for it." He shrieked and the smoke was different now. The stink of charred flesh spread throughout the forge.

Amso rolled up his eyes and collapsed, forcing Errec nearly to the floor with him. He started to choke, bringing up black blood, and his whole body was trembling.

With his free hand Polòtain raised the heavy forge hammer, letting it fall on the man's head, cracking it open. "He was useless. Let's concentrate on you." The älf laid the cooling fire iron back into the furnace. "Who did the third man work for?"

"Our master, too," Errec screamed in terror. "I swear I'm not lying, noble lordship! We weren't told to fight!"

Polòtain recognized the desperate light of truth in the barbarian's eyes and felt bitter disappointment fill his heart. His neat theory about the brawl having been orchestrated as a distraction was proving baseless. "I think I should make sure you are not lying," he said, pulling the glowing iron out of the coals.

"I'm not! I'm not! I'm not lying!" he shrieked.

Polòtain turned his face away in disgust. "Silence! You offend my ears!" And with that he rammed the fire-iron into the man's open throat.

White steam hissed from the man's throat and a stifled gurgling sound was heard. The fire iron still deep inside his convulsing body, Errec fell half onto the floor, half onto his friend's shattered head.

"Get rid of them both!" Polòtain ordered, turning on his heel. "Feed them to night-mares or do whatever you want with them! I don't want the bodies found." He left the forge with Godànor following.

As they crossed the courtyard they saw a guard being escorted in through the gate.

The armed älf marched up to them. "Greetings, Polòtain," he said respectfully, handing over a leather parchment roll. "I have been instructed to bring you this message and to wait for your reply."

Godànor frowned and was about to say something, but Polòtain smiled and held out his hand for the parchment. He had an inkling what it might contain. "Thank you. Go with Godànor and wait. You will be given refreshments. It's been a hot day."

As the others went into the house, Polòtain opened the thin leather roll and extracted a sheet of paper bearing words in Eranior's handwriting.

My esteemed Polòtain,

The guard bringing you my letter is the one who inflicted the leg wound on your beloved nephew Robonor that night.

Do with him as you will to get the truth from him.

Find out whether it was an accident or whether he was paid by some third party.

You have a free hand because officially I sent him to the Tark Draan campaign with the troops to take a message to my niece. If he never arrives they will assume something untoward happened on the journey.

Don't let the fact that he is a relation of mine hold you back. It is a branch of the family I do not care for. Do whatever is necessary to bring Sinthoras down. You have my support.

My sincerest good wishes for the continued strength of the Comets,

Eranior

Polòtain's mood improved.

The barbarians had not delivered the information he craved. It would go better this time.

He was sure he would be able to get what he needed for his revenge scheme. It *had* to succeed! It occurred to Polòtain he could attach bits of the guard to the statue of Robonor. That would show whoever was behind the attack.

He hurried into the house and went to the reception room where visitors would normally leave their cloaks and their slaves.

Godànor was sitting next to the guard on a narrow bench and they were chatting together. A carafe of water stood on a small table at their side, along with two silver beakers inlaid with bone decorations.

"You have brought me a very pleasing message," said Polòtain warmly, with no need to dissimulate. "I'll prepare my response right away." He made as if to pass by the two of them but stopped short. "Tell me, don't you want to go to Tark Draan to do battle with the elves and their allies? You look as if you were born to greater things than just being a personal guard. What is your name?"

The younger älf looked up in surprise. "My name is Falòran. Yes, that's what I was intending to do. Why do you ask?"

Polòtain indicated the sword at the guard's side. "Because of your weapon. I'd say it was a superior piece of work, not the sort of thing an ordinary guard would use."

"I haven't had it very long. I had it made in the forge Xermacûr runs. It is indeed not something I would normally have been able to afford."

"So you've come into some money?" Polòtain's question seemed harmless. "A guard won't earn much."

"Yes . . ." Falòran was regretting what he had said and he shifted uneasily on the bench. "An . . . inheritance."

"Ah, so death has its uses? That's encouraging to know." Polòtain gave the guard a reassuring smile. "I agree: that blade should only taste very special blood."

With lightning speed he drew the sword and rammed it deep into Falòran's shoulder through the body armor.

"Like your own," he hissed. "A traitor's blood!"

The guard let out a yell of pain and raised his fist to strike at Polòtain but Godànor sprang to his side and restrained him.

Polòtain's laugh was icier than the blades of the western wind. "I have some questions for you. And you shall give me the answers I want. All of them. This I swear by all the infamous gods." He twisted Falòran's arm, making the älf collapse. "Let's take him to the forge." Polòtain left the sword in the body of the unconscious guard. "This is the traitor that prevented Robonor from stepping out of danger when the stone block came down."

"I thought he must have something to do with it from the way you were speaking to him." Godànor grabbed Falòran roughly and hauled him out of the room, across the courtyard and into the small smithy they had so recently left. The two dead slaves had been removed, but the bloodstains remained and the stench of burned flesh hung in the air.

Polòtain followed on his great-grandson's heels, annoyed with himself for losing his temper. He had Godànor tie the prisoner up so that the tip of the sword—still embedded in Falòran's body—came to rest inside the furnace.

They chucked a bucket of water over Falòran to bring him around. He opened his eyes and understood the situation immediately. "I . . . should . . . have known," he hissed through lips taut with pain. "It seemed like . . . a rum mission . . . from the very start."

"If you had relied on your instincts you wouldn't be sitting here in chains, but you were not bright enough to do so," Polòtain responded, applying the bellows. Flames shot up and sparks flew as the heat increased. "Now the furnace will heat your precious sword; your flesh will start to cook and you will die in intolerable pain. *Or*, you can tell me who paid you to injure Robonor and you can go free."

"Did someone tell you it was me that caused his leg injury?"

"Was that not the case?"

Falòran nodded and screwed his face up in pain. "Yes, it was me. But it was an accident! I swear by the Inextinguishables."

"Tell me what happened in the alley. Perhaps I will believe you." Polòtain stopped the bellows. The sword had a rosy glow to its tip and the heat would be creeping nicely along the blade toward the älf's body.

"We were on patrol through the alleyways. Robonor was uneasy and kept glancing up at the roofs, as if he was looking for someone up there. He must have shaken whatever was bothering him off because he gave the order to return to base. Then we heard a shout from the alley we had just left."

"Robonor was already concerned about safety?" Polòtain urged.

The guard nodded, his jaw clamped tightly shut against the pain; sweat shone on his top lip. "We ran back into the alley, two on each side of him, me behind, our shields half-raised. Then we saw the slaves brawling at the other end and Robonor thought we should take a look. We intended to let them finish their scuffle, then given them a whipping and taken them back to their masters." A cry of pain forced its way out of Falòran's mouth. The blade was too hot now to be borne.

"Speak quicker, so that your discomfort doesn't last too long," said Polòtain.

"We stopped a few paces short of the ruffians who were fighting." Falòran groaned. "We noticed at once that they were unmarked, so we couldn't see whose slaves they were. One fell to the ground and it looked as if the fun were over. Robonor was about to issue an order when there was a scraping sound from up above us. He jumped back, into me . . ." He uttered a prolonged cry, then fought for breath.

Godànor inspected the place where the blade emerged. "His shoulder is well done now," he informed Polòtain. "He'll soon be cooked through and we can feed him to our slaves." He grabbed hold of the älf's hair. "Do you want to end your days in a barbarian's stomach? Is this the entry into endingness you have always longed for?"

"It was an accident!" Falòran yelled, the veins in his neck standing out with the effort. "Robonor crashed into the edge of my shield, cutting his leg. He stumbled and was hit by the falling masonry. I was thrown backward by the impact and escaped the same fate. Robonor saved my life!" Tears were streaming down his face. "Please, Polòtain! I swear I am telling the truth."

Polòtain's emotions were in uproar. He did not want to believe—no—he could not *allow* himself to believe that Sinthoras had nothing to do with his beloved great-nephew's death. It could not have been a chain of unlucky coincidences. There must have been some intrigue behind it. *Someone must take the blame.*

In spite of what the guard had told him, Polòtain remained convinced that Sinthoras was behind it: the masonry block had been pushed off the roof by an unknown hand. He would prove it in court—until then he must gather the necessary testimony. The nostàroi was not going to escape punishment—Polòtain would see to that.

Shaking, he dropped the chain that activated the bellows and put his hand on the hilt of the sword. "You owe your life to him?"

"Yes," gasped Falòran, exhausted. Sweat ran down his face in rivulets.

"Then you would do *anything*, I'm sure, to prove that he is a hero—and a victim of someone else's machinations."

"I—"

Godànor took over the operation of the bellows.

"Yes, yes!" Falòran shouted in fear. "I'll do anything for Robonor!"

Polòtain grasped the sword hard and pulled it out of the guard's shoulder; there was a hissing sound as the red-hot tip came through his flesh. "Don't worry about the wound. The heat will have cauterized the blood vessels." He put the sword back into its sheath. "You shall be my guest and be given everything you need. Soon, Godànor will bring you a witness statement to sign. My family and I will provide you with all the protection necessary for your safety."

Falòran was not listening. He had passed out.

Godànor watched as Falòran's face relaxed into unconsciousness. "He can't have sustained many injuries in his life if he couldn't take more than that," he said.

"We were lucky he gave in so soon, otherwise we'd have ended up killing him and would have gotten nothing out of him." Polòtain was slowly calming down after the exertion and excitement. The relief was enormous. He still did not have any genuine evidence, but a falsified statement would work just as well when it came to damaging the reputations of both Sinthoras and the treacherous Timanris. He would set down the words of the statement as soon as he could, then Falòran would put his signature to it, thus transforming it into truth.

He looked at his great-grandson. "I have a task for you, Godànor."

"Whatever you like."

"I want you to get up onto the roof of the building the masonry fell from. Examine everything minutely. Look for any scrap of material, any mark, the smallest of scratches—make a drawing of anything you find. Then you're to interview all the residents of the building. Ask them what they heard that night. Tell everyone you meet that you are looking for further evidence of

Sinthoras's involvement in Robonor's death. Remember: *further* evidence! And mention in passing that you already have a witness."

"I understand: they will pass the rumor on and it'll do the rounds all over Dsôn. It'll be talked about in every single radial arm of the state!" Godànor untied Falòran so that the guard's body tipped forward and came to rest on the floor. "I am fortunate that you have taught me so much, Great-grandfather." He indicated the unconscious älf. "Where shall I take him?"

"To the guest quarters. Treat him well and see that he is watched. As soon as he has signed the statement he's to be allowed to leave."

"But . . . when Sinthoras finds out that he is our witness—"

"He will have him killed." Polòtain smiled. "That's exactly what I hope will happen. We will still be able to bring his statement as evidence, but if a guardsman who tried to speak out against the nostàroi ended up dead . . . ?" He strode off toward the door of the forge. "Of course, we let Falòran believe that people will be protecting him at all times."

Godànor nodded.

Polòtain left the workshop, humming a tune.

It might have looked like a lost war first thing that morning, but it had turned out to be merely a lost battle, followed by a victorious one. Somebody would be losing the war soon, but it was not going to be Polòtain.

Tark Draan (Girdlegard), Gray Mountains, Stone Gateway, 4371ˢᵗ division of unendingness (5199ᵗʰ solar cycle), summer.

Carmondai was actually too early when he arrived for the troop commanders' conference, although he had been afraid he was running late. This was why he had not changed. He hastily tried to remove the greenish black marks from his cloak and surcoat. The substance did not only smell unpleasant, but stuck like glue. *Can't be helped now . . .*

The nostàroi were already in the hall, both in ceremonial attire. Sinthoras was seated, listening intently to a standing Caphalor. Suddenly his features lightened and he jumped up and took his dark-haired friend by the shoulders, embracing him joyfully.

Carmondai realized he was witnessing a very personal moment and felt awkward. Clearing his throat, he addressed the nostàroi. "Forgive me for barging in," he said, stepping back out of the room. "I had no intention of disturbing the noble lords."

They turned toward him.

"Not at all!" Sinthoras gestured to him to approach. "Come in! I would like you to write something special for the generations to come, and for the whole of Dsôn, my dear Carmondai! Though my words to you are meant as a request, not an order, of course!" The exuberant way in which Sinthoras was speaking marked a significant change from his usual sarcastic demeanor.

Whatever it is Caphalor said, he is mighty pleased about it. Carmondai came over and unpacked his writing folder in readiness. The ugly greenish black blotches on the cover were all too obvious.

"Óarco blood," said Caphalor. "Let me guess: you were running out of ink and just in the nick of time an óarco was foolish enough to cross your path, so you bled it."

Sinthoras laughed. "What's your story, Carmondai?"

"It's a little embarrassing: I got lost and when I asked a group of óarcos for directions, the conversation was not as courteous as I imagined, so I was forced to defend myself. I really could not help it"—he tapped his writing folder—"this folder and its immeasurably valuable contents had to be protected at all costs."

"Of course," agreed Sinthoras, but he did not seem interested in the details. "Your documents will be even more irreplaceable when you have recorded that my beloved Timanris is still among the living." His smile grew even wider.

Being part of the cultural elite of Dsôn, Carmondai was aware that Timanris was the daughter of Timansor, one of the most celebrated artists of the realm, but it had escaped his notice that the nostàroi and she had developed a close relationship. "Has she been unwell?" he inquired carefully.

"We could put it that way," Caphalor said. "We had been tricked by the false report of her demise and the news had affected my friend here greatly. I am all the more delighted to be able to put his mind at rest."

Carmondai made a note of this happy turn of events and recalled how Caphalor had lost his own life-partner—rumor had it she had been slain by a lovesick obboona. He had been sorely grieved by her loss; misery was still apparent in his eyes. "This is a happy day, indeed," said Carmondai.

"Do you have a partner at home, waiting for you? Or perhaps she has accompanied you?" Sinthoras looked at him expectantly.

"Or he, of course?" added Caphalor. "If that is the case, perhaps you would both want to join the Goldsteel Unit of Friends?" He smiled. "No—not your kind of thing, I think. I understand your fighting days are over." He looked pointedly at the óarco bloodstains as if to say, *I don't believe a word of your story.*

"Neither a male nor a female partner," Carmondai answered. "I broke off all my commitments before leaving for Tark Draan. I would not have expected anyone to wait for my return. In my experience, even two moments of unendingness can be an extremely long time." He paused a moment. "Forgive me, Nostàroi, but the Unit of Friends is with our army?"

Caphalor nodded. "The Inextinguishables sent them to join us. We have placed them under Virssagòn's command because he is in charge of the barbarian troops. The Goldsteel Unit will be a whip he can employ if there is any insurrection."

Carmondai was impressed to hear this; he wrote it all down.

As far as he knew, the Goldsteel Unit of Friends was composed of 150 pairs of same-sex lovers—mostly males, but also some female älfar couples, who made up the core of the Inextinguishables' personal guard. The advantage of lovers was that they would look out for each other's safety in battle, supporting and protecting even more than conventional warriors would normally do. They had the reputation of being the hardest, most merciless fighters at the front where resistance was greatest.

I must be sure to take a look at them. They are said to be a veritable adornment for the army—from their stature right down to the body armor.

Every day that passed showed Carmondai that he had been right to join the Tark Draan campaign. Some of his friends had pronounced his plan to be madness because of the dangers involved, but they had had no idea of how much artistic material there was. None of the naysayers had ever, for example, seen the Goldsteels in action. Some thought they were only a myth. He could take home evidence of their existence.

"I want to ride home to see Timanris." Sinthoras drew a deep breath. He was consumed with desire and it was torturing him. "I need her!" He sent Caphalor an imploring glance. "I have to see her! Do you think you can hold the fort here till I get back? Nobody has to hear about my leaving the troops for a few moments of unendingness. I'll travel in secret. Please! It'll be some time, anyway, before the scouts return with their reports about Tark Draan. We'd have to wait . . ."

"Off you go!" Caphalor interrupted. "Go now and see Timanris. Embrace her and see that she is well protected so you never go through what I did." He placed his hand on his friend's arm. "You have been given a taste of what it means to lose a loved one. May it never become a reality for you."

Carmondai observed the nostàroi closely. *They care about each other—true friends, although they are so different.*

"I thank you. I am in your debt. I'll stay until after the briefing session, then I'll head off. I'll go in disguise and keep it quiet." Sinthoras hurried out.

Caphalor read Carmondai's thoughts. "Please do not record that Sinthoras is leaving; not now at any rate. Perhaps in the future, when we have conquered Tark Draan, it will be appropriate to tell of this venture. It would not go down well with the army to know that their general is leaving the field for personal reasons."

"Wasn't he correct about the scouts still having to—?"

Caphalor broke in and this time it was not a request, but an order. "Why don't you go and watch the Goldsteel Unit in training? Write what you like about that, but don't mention Sinthoras's visit to Dsôn. I want you to regard this as a secret we three share."

You are telling me what to do. Again. As if I were just a secretary. Carmondai inclined his head. *What would you do if I gave your secret away,*

I wonder? "As you command, Nostàroi." He slapped his folder shut and put away his writing implement. *One day you will come to see that your authority is merely lent to you and can be removed on a whim. You are an instrument of your rulers' power, just as I was once.* "As there is still time before the meeting I'll go and change." He turned, on the point of leaving the hall.

"If you have some free time in the next few evenings, I'd like to talk to you about Enoïla," came the milder voice of Caphalor from behind him. "It is right that her memory be preserved for posterity. I would never have been made Nostàroi if it had not been for her. The whole nation should know this. She deserves it."

"Gladly." Carmondai left the hall swiftly and went to his quarters to change his stinking clothing.

One thing was certain: this campaign was providing everything a successful epic needed.

CHAPTER III

The Goldsteel Unit of Friends—I had thought they were the stuff of legend.

But I saw them myself. These warriors were proud and beautiful and splendid. I shall never forget how they looked in their armor, with the light of never-ending love in their eyes.

One hundred and fifty couples; male and male, female and female. Wonderful and deadly.

Blessed by the Inextinguishables and bound to each other by the greatest affection and the noblest of feelings, they defied endingness in the belief they would spend eternity in each other's company.

And their fighting prowess is without compare.

Where a sword is wielded by mere strength and pure reason, love is a thousand times more powerful.

For love will kill to protect love.

There can be no more formidable incentive.

Excerpt from the epic poem *The Heroes of Tark Draan*
composed by Carmondai, master of word and image

Tark Draan (Girdlegard), to the southeast of the Gray Mountains,
4371ˢᵗ division of unendingness (5199ᵗʰ solar cycle),
late summer.

Morana looked toward the northeast where a vast plain stretched out
to the horizon, warm yellow in the evening sunlight, as if gold were the
crop to be harvested. There was a large barbarian settlement on the edge
of the plain. *My quarters for the night. My hunting ground, too.*

She felt uneasy; she was not in her normal protective armor, she hated
the elf costume she was forced to wear and she had had to leave her
night-mare behind in order to pass as a friend to the barbarians. She
looked up at the sky. The daystar would soon set, then she could risk
entering and exploring the nearest barbarian town. By night her disguise
was more convincing because her eyes did not go black after dark, and
that was the only physical distinction between the älfar and the elves.

Language was no problem, because the dialect was similar to that of
the Herumite tribe in Ishím Voróo. If her pronunciation was not quite
correct she could get away with it by saying she was an elf and not accustomed to talking to barbarians.

She had noted how highly the elves were held in local esteem. *Every-*
body trusts the elves—this should make things easy for us.

She galloped in the direction of the town, but it still took three times
as long to cover the distance on a horse than on the slowest night-mare.
When she got there, she found the gate was unguarded, but a couple of
bored soldiers were chatting idly nearby. One of them was munching an
apple. They did not notice her.

Morana was able to ride into the town unchallenged. *I'll wager you*
would not even notice an army marching in.

Her disguise was working brilliantly; the barbarians were staring
at her as if she were some divine being. *I should be more friendly*, she
thought. She waved at people and they responded with cries of delight.
To her relief she noted they were not attempting to follow her. That
would have been too much.

She halted at an inn with a red goblet on its sign. It was a single-
story building, but it had a tall tower built onto its side. *Excellent!* She

dismounted and led the horse to the stables next door where a youth in simple clothing was shoveling manure on to a cart. "Room for one more?" she asked.

He looked up at her and then bowed so low that the tip of his nose nearly touched the toe of her boot. "For such as you, lady, we would always have room," he said. He dropped his fork and took hold of her reins. "Father! Father!" he called across the yard. "Come quick! There's an elf! A real elf!"

Morana did not want to attract further attention. "Don't bother, boy..."

Five heartbeats later and a barbarian with a beer-stained apron stormed out. "Are you out of your mind? What are you...?" then he saw Morana and stopped blustering to run over and bow. "O Being of Light, Goodness and Joy, Knowledge and Delight," he addressed her, his words stumbling out so fast that she found it hard to follow what he was saying next. She picked up the phrases "best room," "every wish" and "no better inn in all Quarrystone."

When he finally stopped talking she assumed that it was her turn to say something. "You have my thanks. I wish to have the room at the top of your tower," she requested civilly but clearly. *How could he possibly turn me down?*

"Of course, of course. I'll get it prepared at once." The barbarian moved aside. "Please take a seat in the taproom in the meantime, Being of Light—"

"I would prefer simply to be addressed as *elf*," she said, cutting short the flow of praise. Her unease was growing. "And please do not go to any trouble with the meal; bread and butter will be all I require." She lifted down the saddlebags and walked over to the inn, the landlord buzzing around her like a bumblebee around a flower, bowing and scraping and opening the door for her.

The taproom was full of barbarian men and women. All of them stopped talking and stared at her. A few continued to drink or to put food in their mouths. She heard a couple of belches. Morana had to control her features so as not to show her disgust. Her inclination would have been to draw her sword and forcibly prevent them from eating and drinking in her presence. But, on the other hand, these simple creatures did hold a certain fascination for her. *How ever can they live like this?*

The innkeeper scurried to her side. "Would you speak to them, noble elf?"

"My . . . may my gods be with you," she managed to say. "Long life to you all." *I wish you a long life so that I may be the one to bring about your deaths.*

Applause broke out and the people shouted their gratitude: thanks she did not want. The smell of their bodies, their clothes and their breath was almost unendurable. "Show me the room and bring me the refreshments I asked for," she muttered to the innkeeper. "I . . . am very tired."

"Of course!" He called to someone behind the bar and hurried off ahead of her, leading the way.

The way to the room was up an old spiral staircase. As they climbed, the noise of the taproom faded and Morana felt the tension ebbing from her. Muffled conversations and even snoring could be heard behind some of the doors they passed.

"You are not one of the elves from the Golden Plain, are you?" asked the landlord, stopping for breath on the stairs.

"No," she admitted at once. "I am from the south. From far away in the south."

"Oh? There are elves in the south? I didn't know that."

"We are a young nation. We avoided contact for a long time but we are changing our policy now. Before I meet my relations I wish to rest and then I'll travel on first thing in the morning." She found the lie came out pat. She had given versions of this story several times recently. "Why does your inn have a tower?"

"It used to be a border lookout post," he explained. "It's from the times when humans did not trust the elves and all sorts of creatures used to wander the flat lands." He paused, leaning back against the wall, out of breath. "One moment," he panted.

"You don't come up here very often," she commented.

"Never, noble elf. I would normally leave that to my wife and my daughter." He wiped his brow. "But you will love the view. The tower is higher than the new fortress. Seventy-eight paces high; you'll be able to look down and watch your relations getting their supper ready."

Light footsteps approached up the stairwell and soon a young girl of perhaps one and a half divisions of unendingness had overtaken them, bringing a basket of bread, some butter and a jug of water. The goblet on the tray showed smear marks at the rim.

"Omenia, my youngest." The landlord took the tray from her.

I won't be letting my lips touch that cup, for sure. "Thank you, my child." Morana said. "My, you are very tall." *She's the first one I've seen whose bones would be any use at all. The others would only serve to be ground down as chippings for our roads.*

"Would you be so gracious as to give her your blessing, elf?" the landlord asked hopefully. The little girl lowered her eyes.

I am sure you would not wish an älfar blessing for your daughter. Morana was about to improvise a gesture, but then had second thoughts. "It would be something no mortal has ever received from me before," she told the father, placing her forefinger under the girl's chin and tilting her face upward. She smiled into the child's unwavering eyes. It was as if the young girl were challenging her. *Had she seen through the disguise?* "This could hurt a bit."

"She is very brave," the innkeeper said, delighted at the honor.

"In that case . . ." Morana put down the saddlebags she was carrying, took out her dagger and made some marks with the blade tip on the girl's brow, while she used her free hand to hold her fast by the chin.

Omenia whimpered but Morana did not loosen her grip until she had completed the rune. Then she planted a kiss on the child's skin, tasting blood.

"That will keep you safe from the death which is shortly to sweep this land," she whispered into the small ear. "You shall be the only one in Quarrystone to survive." The girl began to tremble. "And if anyone should ask you what happened, tell them: the elves brought death to the town. If you speak to anyone about this now the power in the rune on your forehead will disappear." She planted a second kiss, turned her around and urged the child down the stairs. "Get them to put an herbal bandage on that," she called after her.

The landlord looked concerned. "What . . . what have you—?"

"An ancient ritual to keep away evil. A little pain and some bleeding are an essential part." Morana wiped the child's life-juice from her lips and then bent to pick up her bags again. "Shall we go up?"

The rest of the way neither of them spoke. All Morana could hear was the innkeeper's labored breathing. He pushed open the door at the top of the stairs, put down the tray and turned around, giving Morana a searching look. Then his head dipped. "Thank you for blessing her," he mumbled, a little late in the day.

Morana merely lifted her hand in acknowledgment.

She waited for the door to close behind him and the sound of his footsteps to die away before she opened the windows that went all the way around the chamber. A summer breeze wafted in.

She could smell grass drying, could hear the buzz of insects and the hum of people chatting and laughing in the streets below.

Morana laid her saddlebags on the old table and moved over to the window that faced east. *The home of the elves of the Golden Plain.*

The land rolled away toward the darkening sky, broken only by a few gently rising hillocks. A small number of trees, mighty specimens, grew straight and true and rose taller than her spy tower—as if determined to touch the heavens. Morana had never seen the like, either in Ishím Voróo or in Dsôn. A few miles away a river meandered through the landscape, lights appearing on its banks as the night deepened.

Elves. There are still some of you around. For now.

Morana was gripped by excitement now that she was so close to the enemy—she was probably closer than any of the other scouts.

When Caphalor had chosen her for the mission, she had been surprised, but honored to think how great his confidence in her must be. The nostàroi would be planning their attack strategy based on the reports she made.

This would be easy territory for the archery divisions. And for the cavalry, of course. She took out parchment, a quill and ink, and began to note down her observations. *Do I dare explore the Golden Plain, I wonder?*

She was eager to find out whether the elves had strongholds and how many elves would be garrisoned there. She leaned out of the window and looked up. Outside, there was a perilous staircase that led to the very top of the tower. *I'll tackle it at daybreak tomorrow; I'll be able to see more then.*

She reached for the food on the tray and tried the bread, which tasted better than it looked. She did not touch the goblet, but drank the warm water from her own leather bottle. Then she skimmed through her notes as she ate the rest.

The closest target for the nostàroi was in the north, not far from the Gray Mountains. The barbarians called it Lesinteïl and it was apparently hilly, unlike the Golden Plain. Morana had also heard of a place called Âlandur, said to be a heavily forested and difficult terrain, but she did not yet know its location.

That was why Morana had decided to go east to explore the Golden Plain. She thought that, if it were indeed a plain, it would be particularly easy to conquer. A traveler had also told her about a place called Gwandalur. It was said that there the elves worshipped a dragon that periodically laid waste to the surrounding land, devouring the barbarians' crops.

Morana underlined the relevant passage twice. *That's all good. If the elves are not in favor with the locals in Gwandalur, we can march in as liberators. That should make things even easier.*

She smiled, not quite believing that Caphalor valued her opinion on all of this. She remembered how he had looked at her. *I must not take this too seriously. I am merely one of his personal guards and one that he values highly enough to send on an important mission. But . . . I certainly find him attractive.*

Morana watched the evening unfold in Quarrystone. Those still abroad in the streets and alleyways carried torches or lanterns to light their way. Candlelight shone softly through the thick, opaque panes of their cottage windows.

Look at them trying so hard to drive away the dark. And yet they fail. She took off her elf disguise and drew on the black clothing she had brought in her saddlebag. *They don't realize that darkness is aggravated by light and will increase in intensity to stifle it.* Morana climbed up onto the window seat and crouched there for a few heartbeats. *If you accept the dark it will work for you.*

With a powerful leap she catapulted herself through the air to land far below on a sloping roof, sliding down the wooden tiles nearly to the gutter. She caught hold of a chimneystack to steady herself. This marked both the beginning of her exploration of Quarrystone and the imminent demise of the town.

I have something to celebrate, she remembered. *This is the thirtieth settlement I will have explored.* She moved in a crouching run along the rooftops, heading for the castle in the middle of the town. If the guards there took their duties as lightly by night as they had done by day, it would be simple for an älf to penetrate the fortress. She smiled. *This land is just begging to be invaded. We should go ahead and do it before someone else gets the idea.*

Tark Draan (Girdlegard), far to the south of the Gray Mountains, 4371ˢᵗ division of unendingness (5199ᵗʰ solar cycle), late summer.

Patience was not Horgàta's strong point, although one might have expected otherwise, given her immortal status.

But it was patience that was demanded of her now as she made her way through the wilderness of Tark Draan. She rode without using roads and paths, aware that her night-mare would attract attention, particularly in the dark when sparks played around its fetlocks. If she were spotted, she would have to kill those that had seen her—a trail of dead bodies would be difficult to explain and her mission *had* to remain a secret.

At least I'm making good progress; there's less dense woodland here than I thought there might be. The mission she had been given by the nostàroi would take her deep into enemy territory, to a point around 600 miles south of the Gray Mountains. This would be the assembly point for the hidden army: a secret reserve and surprise element that could be called upon to join the battle if they were needed. And Horgàta was now their commander.

The cavalry of this force alone numbered a good 5,000 warriors already. Any hiding place for so many fighters and their mounts would have to be carefully selected, so Horgàta had left first in order to check out the site. If she found it unsuitable—strategically unsound or too easy to discover—she would have to decide where to send all the other troops and leave signs and messages for the ones yet to arrive.

She had not bothered to disguise herself as an elf because it was essential not to be seen at all. In any case, the dark provided enough cover. Occasionally she would stop and consult the map, navigating by the stars and moon to assess how far she had already traveled. At least the stars were the same here as they were in Ishím Voróo.

Less than a mile to go and I'll have covered all 600. Horgàta reined her night-mare in on a slight rise and let her gaze take in the horizon, then leaned forward and patted the neck of her steed. The animal snorted quietly, white foam flying from its lips. She looked down the steep side of the hill.

Below lay a small town with a low defense wall that would not serve for much more than encouraging the cattle not to stray. *The meeting point must be down there somewhere.* She tried to guess the number of inhabitants from the houses.

"A few thousand," she whispered.

An idea occurred to her.

She noted a wide path on the slope beneath her that led straight up to the settlement. Every so often a lane would branch off toward buildings on the banks of the little river. She could see millwheels turning and lamps burning inside the mills. The barbarians were obviously still at work although it was night.

Horgàta dismounted. "Wait," she commanded her night-mare and she started to climb down the steep cliff face, recent chisel marks telling her that she was in a quarry.

She jumped down from rock to rock, balancing carefully, and had soon covered several hundred paces of vertical distance. Toward the bottom of the quarry there was some scaffolding that enabled her to move more quickly.

With one final leap she reached the ground. The path she had seen led to piles of stones ready for transport. It looked as if quite hefty boulders were being extracted. *Building materials, I expect. They must ship it along the river.*

Then Horgàta noticed an entrance leading into the mountain. She hurried through, making no sound.

Like everywhere else she had been in Tark Draan, nobody was on guard duty. The barbarians relied on the groundlings keeping watch at the mountain passes, so they would probably only have to fear the occasional band of robbers. Monsters like the óarcos and trolls must have been eradicated—or were in hiding.

This made it easy for Horgàta to examine the tunnel. She took a torch from the wall and lit it with a flint.

A tunnel three paces high and ten paces wide had been fashioned through the rock and there were deep ruts cut into the floor. *Carts?* She made her way farther along.

The tunnel sloped upward and opened out into a cavern that had formed naturally, but the barbarians had adapted it; there was a dark lake in the middle and next to it, a human-built scaffold tower that led up to enormous stalactites. Some had been partially removed, but others were still intact. On the right-hand side of the cave there were some rafts tied together, forming a makeshift bridge across to a snowy white wall. *I wonder if the stone being quarried is particularly valuable?*

The banks of the little lake were piled high with crates that were filled with pieces of stone. A system of ropes and pulleys connected the floor to the roof of the cave.

Horgàta turned around and looked down the tunnel, then back to the lake, crossed the bridge and pulled out one of the long poles that supported the scaffold to test how deep the water was. *Less than seven paces and the edges are quite flat.*

Horgàta dismissed her original idea, because now she had a new plan. But she would not be able to implement it until sufficient numbers of älfar had arrived.

The Inextinguishables have sent their blessings. She left the cavern and returned to her waiting night-mare. *The nostàroi could hardly have chosen a better place for their secret army to assemble.*

Tark Draan (Girdlegard), Gray Mountains, Stone Gateway,
4371ˢᵗ division of unendingness (5199ᵗʰ solar cycle)
late summer.

Something's up. Carmondai strolled through the tunnels, no longer
finding them as difficult to navigate as he had done previously. After
the incident with the óarcos, he had made sure he knew all of the most
important of the passages so that he would not get lost again. Now he
was on his way to find Caphalor for one of their regular meetings. It was
hardly a true friendship they shared but their relationship was amicable
in a way that would not have worked between himself and Sinthoras.

He thought hard as he walked: the mood in the Gray Mountains was
changing. The nostàroi had not made use of the initial euphoria to whip
the troops into a conquering frenzy and sweep through Tark Draan, and
nobody but himself and Caphalor knew the real reason: that Sinthoras
was not in the mountain. If his absence was noticed and the cause discovered there might be a mutiny.

But if we wait much longer the campaign will have to start in winter.
Carmondai did not have any illusions of grandeur about his own strategic planning skills, but he knew you did not attack when the ground was
covered in ice and snow. And nobody knew what the climate was like
in the winter months in Tark Draan. Carmondai smoothed down his
midnight blue robe as he entered the hall once again. The dark-haired
nostàroi was waiting for him by the map-strewn table.

"Carmondai, good to see you," came the welcome. Caphalor was not
wearing ceremonial attire, but a flowing silk robe in dark gray and red.
"I'm sure they tell you more than they tell me: what is new? Is my army
buzzing with rumors and unrest?"

Carmondai conjured up a half-hearted smile as he pushed back the
hood from his brown hair. "The älfar are well disciplined and that will
always be the case, even in a hundred divisions of unendingness. But
the óarcos are roaring through the tunnels like fire-bulls looking for
mates; they start fights for the stupidest of reasons and they brawl with
anyone they come across." He came over and placed his writing folder
on the table, opening it to show some of his latest notes. "The trolls have

split up and are all over the Gray Mountains, while the demi-giants have decided to head south into Tark Draan. They are determined to get out—"

"I know," interrupted Caphalor, irritably. "I've sent twenty pairs of the Goldsteel Unit after them to talk them around. Or to kill them. What about the barbarians?"

"You're close with Farron Lotor, aren't you? Wasn't there that slave girl . . . ?" Carmondai leafed through his records then noticed the nostàroi's displeasure. "Am I wrong about that?"

"No. But I would prefer you not to mention Raleeha. She is . . . *was* a slave and does not deserve to be named." Caphalor took a sip of steaming tea. "I have not seen her brother Farron for a long time. He told me she was found dead on the battlefield."

Carmondai took a breath and continued away from that topic. "In any case, the barbarian troops are still behaving, but they are ill at ease. Most of them thought they would have invaded Tark Draan by now and be preparing to dig in for the winter in newly conquered land. Instead, they are cooped up here with the worst kind of beasts for companions." Carmondai leafed through his notes for a moment then found another item that he wanted to bring to Caphalor's attention. "I also hear there is still trouble with the groundlings."

"You mean the dispersed groundlings?"

Carmondai nodded. "It's said they have laid traps and killed a lot of our allies. Apparently the insurgents are always killed, but . . ." He trailed off and indicated the walls. "The first barbarians are already showing signs of mania due to being cooped up in here, and are beginning to think the mountains can give birth to more groundlings whenever and wherever they like."

Caphalor leaned on the table. "I wish Sinthoras would get himself back here," he complained. "Then we could set off."

"You gave him permission to go," Carmondai said.

"I know. It was a bad idea. I allowed myself to become sentimental." He pulled a map of Tark Draan over; troop movements were displayed with colored threads. "Until he comes back, why don't you look at my plans?" He handed Carmondai a page of notes explaining which color stood for which army unit.

"I'm no tactician."

Caphalor gave a low laugh. "No, indeed, you are not. But I've listened to suggestions from my best soldiers and now I'm keen to hear the views of a poet." He handed him a cup and poured him some tea.

Carmondai studied the map. The colored threads formed an intricate web suspended over the north of the land. "So, I'm one of your advisers, now? How have I earned this honor?"

"I'm not one to bear a grudge. Sinthoras may be different, but I'm not going to exclude good advice—wherever it comes from." Caphalor laughed. "Perhaps this is a kind of test. Maybe I have invented this set of troop movements purely to check whether or not you would betray my plans?"

Carmondai could not help laughing. Feeling a little lighter, he studied the notes with care. The trolls had been placed in the west, the óarcos would work in a broad sweep to the south, flanked by the ogres and the demi-giants. All the monster divisions were to be accompanied by älfar units, and the barbarians from Ishím Voróo would be bringing up the rear. Elsewhere, a regiment of their own warriors was detailed to deal with the elf realms. *Revenge on the elves is reserved for our kind.*

"This is only a provisional plan because I need to wait for the scouts to report back," he heard Caphalor say. "This strategy is based on their initial messages."

Carmondai tapped his chin with the forefinger of one hand. It all seemed to make sense. *But . . .* "What about the barbarians in Tark Draan who can do magic? Have you considered how to handle them? Or have you discounted them as presenting only an insignificant risk?"

"An excellent point! It seems our poet has a good head on his shoulders. My advisers did not come up with that objection."

Carmondai drank some of the fragrant tea. *An infusion of thujona berries: a precious commodity!* The dried fruits that made up this tea were only available to the wealthy. It was an infusion that refreshed and cleared the mind like the music of a soul-toucher. This was only the second time Carmondai had ever had a chance to taste it. Carmondai smiled.

"I thought you would appreciate the drink," Caphalor grinned. "To return to your objection: my spies report that there are six so-called magi: three men and three women. They live with their pupils and have very odd names, like—" He fished out a piece of parchment from among the maps. "Here we go: Jujulo the Jolly, Simin the Underrated, Grok-Tmai the Worrier and Hianna the Flawless, Fensa the Inventive, and Ortina the Omnipresent." He let out a peal of malicious laughter. "Amusing, aren't they?"

Carmondai made a note of these names. "Might it not be dangerous to underestimate these wizards? We don't know what they might be capable of."

"I have fought against the botoicans," Caphalor cut in harshly, as if insulted by the remark. "I learned one thing for certain: there is no need to fear a magician if you shoot straight and your arrow reaches his mouth before he has spoken his spell."

"Of course," said Carmondai with false cheerfulness, striking himself on the forehead. "I was forgetting. You called me in to congratulate you on every aspect of your plan and to write it all down in my book: Caphalor planned the Tark Draan campaign strategy all by himself while Sinthoras was swanning around in Dsôn being romantic!" His jolly tone faded abruptly. "Nostàroi, you asked me for my opinion and I gave it to you. If you don't want to hear what I have to say, don't ask me to come here." He was surprised at his own audacity. *Is this the effect of the berries, making me so outspoken?* Strangely, he felt no fear. His words and thoughts had never seemed clearer.

Caphalor took a deep breath, but no fury lines appeared on his face. "None of my benàmoi would have dared to say that. They certainly would not have phrased their objections so strongly."

"Maybe we can blame the tea."

"That's why I gave it to you," the nostàroi said, smugly. He raised his glass. "My scouts had been told to explore the enchanted lands and find out where the magi live. You may have forgotten what we said a few moments of unendingness ago. At the briefing session."

Carmondai did remember. "You are of the opinion the magi don't present a danger?"

Caphalor nodded. "If what we have been told is true, they can only do magic on their own territory because they need to use the energy sources there. When away from home ground they are presumably easier to defeat than an unarmed barbarian."

"Presumably," stressed Carmondai. "And how do you propose to find out whether your spies' reports are actually true?"

"We shall see." Caphalor sat down. "I must thank you for the descriptions you have sent back to Dsôn. People there are very enthusiastic. They are behind us totally, and those who think differently have been more or less silenced."

Carmondai attempted to suppress the effect of the thujona berries, but his soul felt light and his lips were eager to form words that he saw as glowing symbols in the air. *They look so beautiful! I must say these things!* "The Constellations will be doing what they always do; they stand on the firmament and look down to watch what comes to pass," he blathered, annoyed with himself for not finding a more elegant expression; he was supposed to be the master of words, after all. "But I hear they have never forgiven you for being a Comets supporter." *I never meant to say that!*

Caphalor's lips narrowed. "So? I have never been one for politics. I want nothing to do with it."

"But the Comets regard you as one of them. And you left Dsôn Faïmon to make yourself their willing tool."

All at once the fury lines broke out across Caphalor's face and he jumped to his feet. "Don't you dare impugn my reasons for joining the campaign," he shouted. "It's not for the Inextinguishables, nor for the vanity and greed of the Comets that I'm laying waste to Tark Draan. And I don't care about the Constellations either."

Carmondai was fascinated: he could see the words Caphalor had uttered shimmering bright red in the air, quivering with hatred and fury.

Caphalor strode toward him and Carmondai was suddenly afraid for his life. The nostàroi grabbed him by the collar and swept him up into the air. "It is for *my own* motives that I shall be burning Tark Draan to the ground. My own! This land bears the blame for my—" He stopped speaking abruptly, his whole body shaking, and he thrust Carmondai aside. The writer managed to keep his balance but collided with a chair. He sat down and stared at Caphalor.

The nostàroi's hands were clenched fists. He was breathing quickly. A single tear made its way down his cheek and splashed to the floor.

Carmondai heard the tear fall as loud as if it had been thunder. Suddenly he understood. *In his eyes Tark Draan is responsible for the death of his life-partner!* "I understand—"

A whispering, falsely friendly voice was heard in their heads: <Oh, is this a difficult moment?>

Carmondai looked around in surprise. No one had knocked. He saw a flurry at the doorway and cried out in horror. *The mist-demon!*

The thujona berries gave Carmondai the ability to see him not as the silver shimmering ghostly apparition others had described, but as a terrifyingly ugly visage that kept changing shape and spoke with many mouths. The words it spoke hung in the air like toxic, acid syllables. Carmondai slid back to avoid them and fell from his chair.

Caphalor turned to the mist-demon and attempted to control his own distress. "This is indeed not a good time, but we will make ourselves available for you nevertheless."

The terrible cloud drifted closer.

Carmondai managed to get back on his feet and put the table between him and the demon. *This is the most dreadful of our allies!* His gut reaction was to flee, but he grabbed hold of his last vestiges of courage, honor and pride; if Caphalor was staying, he would stay, too.

<Too good of you, Caphalor. But I'm looking for Sinthoras.>

"He is with the troops," the nostàroi replied.

<I've been looking for Sinthoras for a very long time and I'm surprised to note that I have had no success. Is there a possibility that he may have gone away?> The cloud went dark, with a few greenish yellow stars appearing in the middle. <Don't you dare to lie to me, älf!>

"He will be back soon," Carmondai said without thinking, in the hope the demon would go away once it had heard what it needed to know.

<Soon? How soon?>

"He was needed in Dsôn for some very urgent matters. As soon as these have been dealt with, he will be returning," said Caphalor, without looking at Carmondai. "It is better if the troops don't know."

<You include me with your troops? Are you out of your mind?> The cloud turned into a dark green mass with bright blue tentacles. <It's me you have to thank for the fact that you are even in Tark Draan! Without me you would never have gotten here!>

"And nor would you," countered Caphalor. "We need each other."

Carmondai had to admire the nostàroi's composure in the face of this evil presence. *But then, he didn't have any of the thujona tea, did he?*

<We have an agreement: I open the gates to Tark Draan and you conquer it for me. That's what Sinthoras swore, in the name of your rulers. I won't give you a second reminder about our pact.> The cloud swirled around the älfar. <I am fed up with waiting, älf. If the campaign does not get underway before the winter, I shall turn my force against the óarcos and the other creatures. I want my fun, one way or the other.>

By all the gods of infamy! Carmondai was trembling uncontrollably. He was so close that if he stretched out his hand his fingers would be right inside that cloud. His hypersensitive imagination showed him how his flesh would drop away from his bones and his soul would be sucked up by the demon. The tentacles grabbed for him . . . "No!" he shrieked, hiding behind Caphalor and shutting his eyes.

"I cannot promise we shall have started the campaign before winter, but our preparations are coming on apace. Our spies are out exploring Tark Draan so that when we invade we will—"

<I already know how big the enemy's army is,> whispered the cloud smugly. <There is no need to send out spies! You could roll through the land like a storm, a tempest; a wave of steel! Who would show resistance? The peoples of Tark Draan have no idea of what awaits them— and they'll bow down to me!>

Carmondai could no longer bear the words. He cowered and stuck his fingers in his ears to keep it out, but he could still hear the demon's words. *I must get out of here!*

<This winter, älf! Or I'll demonstrate what was intended for your enemies on your armies!>

Carmondai waited several eye-blinks, but the demon said nothing. He opened his eyes carefully—and saw the nostàroi. Caphalor's expression was somber, but the fury lines had disappeared. "I was . . . it was s-s-so . . ." Carmondai stammered, trying to cobble together an explanation for his cowardly conduct. "The tea . . . by all the gods of infamy, you should have seen what I saw! That demon is worse than—" He raised his arms and uttered an involuntary sound.

"If a poet is lost for words it's obviously not a good sign. I should not have served you that tea without asking first." Caphalor laid a hand on his shoulder in forgiveness. "Go and rest. I must send out messengers to bring Sinthoras back here." He left the room.

What have we got ourselves into with that demon? Would our own forces not have been sufficient to take the Stone Gateway without his help? Carmondai sank down on the nearest chair, burying his head in his hands.

He sat there for a long time, trying to sort out his thoughts and waiting for the after effects of the tea to recede.

When he felt steadier, he reached for his writing folder and put down what he had experienced in words.

Every now and again he took some of the herbal drink Caphalor had been drinking. His throat felt dry and sore. Then he noticed that the goblet contained diluted thujona juice.

Surely he must have seen the same things I did if he was drinking that stuff, too? How could he bear it? Carmondai could only think that the depths of despair Caphalor had been forced to explore in his grief must have been worse than anything the demon could offer.

CHAPTER IV

Have you heard of the Wandering Towers?
They withstand storms with their special powers
and can snap thick iron bars in two.
Three of them to kill a thousand of you!
To deal them death only poison will cope.
Miss your chance and there's no more hope!

Nursery rhyme *The Towers that Walk*
1st verse

Ishím Voróo (Outer Lands), former kingdom of the fflecx,
4371ˢᵗ division of unendingness (5199ᵗʰ solar cycle)
late summer.

Arganaï did not know where he was or who had taken him prisoner.

He had been given brackish water to drink that had probably come from a puddle. Some kind of food the texture of bread had been thrust into his mouth, but it was not bread: it stung his torn lips and seemed to wriggle in his mouth when it was moistened with saliva. But it stopped the hunger.

He lay on a dry earth floor, tied up and blindfolded. To judge from the animal smell—and the sound—he had been put in a hole in the ground, perhaps some predator's burrow? Arganaï guessed it might once have been a sotgrîn's home.

He had been forced to relieve himself in his clothes and every couple of moments of unendingness he was hosed down with hot water. This humiliating treatment made him hate his torturers still more.

He racked his brains to try and work out who might be holding him captive.

It could not be the fflecx; this was not the way they fought and treated enemies. And anyway, the fflecx had all been wiped out. Barbarians or óarcos were just as unlikely: none of their warriors would have been able to kill and dismember a grown fire-bull. It could be some of the huge monsters like trolls, demi-giants, ogres . . .

But the noises I heard—it doesn't make sense. Arganaï could not stop himself thinking about the attackers. *That unearthly roar! And what about the violet-colored lights?*

The earth shook around him and bits of soil rained down. At regular intervals there were vibrations that felt like the impact of a battering ram.

They are driving posts into the ground. Arganaï sat up and slid back up against the side of the hole. The älf had spent some time exploring his dungeon carefully, even though he had had to crawl, worm-like, to do so, and he had discovered that his prison cell was around two paces by four, and from the way sounds echoed, was probably about two and a half- to three paces high. The exit was blocked by what felt like a huge stone. He had come to no useful conclusion and his torturers had given him no opportunity to escape.

So he would have to sit and wait.

He listened out once more.

The impacts were not so strong and not so frequent now; but there was a steady drip of water that had not been there before. Some of the drops landed directly on him.

Does that mean it's raining? Arganaï imagined the water seeping down through the earth into his prison. *I hope it won't be just a short shower! Maybe the earth walls might soften . . .* Hope welled up: he might yet be able to get away.

The slow dripping sound changed to distinct trickles—the weather was on his side!

His breeches and back became wetter as his dungeon was thoroughly soaked. The earth slowly grew softer. Arganaï kicked against the wall and his foot went straight through. He redoubled his efforts until he judged he had made an opening he would be able to squeeze through.

He had no idea where the hole led to, of course. He rolled around and stuck his head through, listening hard.

He could hear the noise of rushing water coming from below and it was cooler than in his cell. Had he discovered some underground stream? It might enable him to escape. Or it might drown him.

And how far down is it, I wonder? He used his shoulder to nudge a lump of clay into the hole, but the noise of rushing water was too loud for him to hear it fall.

Gods of infamy, I place my life in your hands. Arganaï turned around again and worked his way, feet first, into the hole, sliding over the muddy soil until he fell through the air and landed in icy water.

The current dragged him along.

Arganaï did not know which way was up. He held his breath for as long as he could as he scraped against rock walls and barged against stones. Finally something snagged and pulled away his blindfold.

He still could not see; it was pitch black in the water. The bands holding his wrists had caught on something and did not give way, making him a prisoner in the river.

Not like this! Not here! Arganaï lashed out, his feet meeting resistance. He pushed as hard as he could.

The icy water had numbed his muscles and was forcing its way into his mouth, trying to get him to take it into his lungs. The need for air was unbearable and he saw colored rings in front of his eyes . . .

There was a crack and Arganaï screamed with pain as his left hand fractured and slid out of the bindings. As he screamed the river forced itself into his open mouth.

The älf coughed and spluttered, swallowing yet more water while the river dragged him on. Then he was falling through air again. He landed on a hard surface and vomited the water out, fighting for breath. He had landed beside a small waterfall that emerged from the rocky slope before heading vertically downward; if he had fallen a few paces farther, Arganaï would have ended up at the bottom of the cliff. After a while he noticed that he had exited the tunnel into daylight.

I . . . am . . . alive! He looked at his injured hand. The restraints had broken the joint of his thumb and the bone fragment was visible, sticking up through the skin. If that bone had not given way he would have drowned in the stream.

He slid over to the rock wall on his knees, where a thicket of night fern with its large black fronds would hide him.

The pain was bearable if he gritted his teeth hard. He remembered similar discomfort the first time a fire-bull had thrown him, breaking his right arm. *It will heal.*

He raised his head to risk a look over the top of the fern.

He found himself on a sort of shelf, less than two paces wide, underneath an outcrop. He looked along it: there was a path there, and the foliage would give him sufficient cover as he moved along should his enemy turn up unexpectedly. He paused a moment to remove the bindings around his ankles, then moved off.

The rock shelf led him to a flat piece of ground the fflecx had once inhabited. There were strange, brightly colored houses with gnome heads painted on them and tubes and pipes made from copper; wood and glass had been used in constructions that joined the buildings together chaotically. There was no sign of any inhabitants.

I would have been surprised to see any. There were no signs of violent destruction, or fire here, but the gnome-like creatures had all been killed—there was no reason to suppose there were any left.

He did not bother to search the buildings and workshops of the poison-blenders. It was much more important to find out about the mysterious creatures he had heard while imprisoned in his dungeon.

He moved as fast as he dared through the deserted village, his injured hand throbbing painfully. Immediately behind the dwellings a small forest began. He slipped into the trees and made his way through the undergrowth parallel to the path.

There was another rumbling sound and the earth beneath him shook; he heard timber crashing to the ground.

They are felling trees! Arganaï hurried to see what was happening. With the noise that the creatures were making there was no need for him to keep silent as he moved. The effort made his hand hurt badly; next time there was a crash of falling trees he permitted himself a groan.

Rounding a corner, Arganaï reached a vantage point and heard a dull roar. *That's exactly what I heard before something felled me!* He made his way to the edge of the clearing cautiously.

Suddenly, all was silent. It was as if the creatures had noticed he was nearby. All work stopped, birdsong was audible and a light breeze rustled the leaves on the trees.

Arganaï saw great tree trunks that had been felled, their branches removed. Wood fragments showed they had been hacked down with axes—and not with the small axes barbarians or älfar would wield, either.

Arganaï crept slowly out from concealment and raced over the clearing, going from one tree stump to the next until he found one he thought he could climb to get a better view.

From his new vantage point he could see how big the clearing was: a broad path of felled trees had been hewn through the forest.

So where are they? They must be hiding somewhere. Arganaï jumped down off the tree stump and continued on his way. The cleared path led southeast toward Dsôn Faïmon. *By all that's unholy, what are they up to?*

Less than twenty paces in front of him one of the trees shuddered as if it were being cut down. The branches shook and the foliage trembled, and some leaves drifted to the ground. There was a renewed thud, accompanied by a dull roar and then the tree's natural anchor gave way and the trunk snapped with a loud crash.

Arganaï sprang to one side just as the broad canopy of the tree smashed down exactly where he had been standing. He quickly hid in the branches, spying out from between the leaves. *Where are you?*

But again, he could see nothing.

It seemed that his injury was eager to cause maximum pain and he was unable to stop a loud intake of breath.

Rapid footsteps thundered in his direction.

Did they hear me? Arganaï ducked down and saw a huge shadow wielding a mighty ax the length of a grown älf.

No! He lay flat and rolled over to the right.

The ax blade whistled through the foliage, splitting branch from trunk, then buried itself in the earth by his foot and was yanked back up. There was a loud roar and a violet-colored light that illuminated the leaves he hid under. Then the ax blows continued to rain down. Arganaï slithered toward the end of the tree like a snake, desperate to avoid the blade that was being wielded untiringly, slicing through even the thickest of the branches and splitting the trunk itself.

Arganaï dived out from under the tree and ran faster than he had ever run in his life.

He raced along the cleared path, realizing that his speed and flexibility would give him the best chance if he took this direct route. He never once looked back. Fear that he might stumble if he did so and thus end up back in the power of the unknown monsters kept him going. The knowledge that they had felled these enormous trees by hand only served to increase his terror. *The Inextinguishables must be told! They—*

A dull whizzing sound warned him and he dodged to the right,

It was not a moment too soon: an ax only just missed him before it buried itself into the nearest tree. The pace-long blade was thicker than his hand was wide.

Arganaï left the cleared path and ran into open country. He could see a few wooden palisades erected by the fflecx had remained untouched by the fire that had destroyed the rest. But that was not what astonished him now.

For the first time he saw the alien creatures that chased him. They were tall and broad, and some of them wore armor that made them appear broader still, while others wore nothing but a short leather apron. Their skin, Arganaï saw, was pale gray and their bodies were extremely muscular. Their faces terrified him. Strong-jawed mouths held protruding needle-sharp canine teeth, their heads were bald, bony and hard, their yellow-veined eyes violet and they took in air through three holes in the middle of their ugly faces. At about four paces in height, none of them was shorter than a demi-giant. Two of them had two humps on their backs, as if they were starting to grow wings.

They were all working at splitting the tree trunks and binding them together into rafts or mobile defenses. Their movements were swift and adroit, a quality that differentiated them from all the other outsize creatures that Arganaï knew of. Over to the west, a former fflecx dwelling had greenish-orange smoke rising up as if the alchemancers were still at their wicked poison-brewing.

It did not take Arganaï long to come to the only reasonable conclusion: *they are planning to cross the defense moat and attack us!*

In calmer times the mere thought of an enemy crossing the huge defense canal would make anyone laugh out loud. Sometimes, of a winter evening, älfar would gather and tell tales of roving barbarians or hordes of half-crazed óarcos attempting to cross the cleared strip of land that bordered the water. No boat intended for the crossing had ever made it to the banks of the river. Catapults manned by älfar soldiers were an excellent defense. No single outside force in the whole of Ishím Voróo had ever reached Dsôn Faïmon.

These creatures reminded Arganaï of a legend. It told of a people that the Inextinguishables had to defeat with trickery because they would have outclassed the älfar in conventional warfare.

Defeat . . . But he had always understood they had been so defeated there was not one left alive. *By all the powers of infamy! Could these be—*

He heard a loud roar behind him and the creatures raised their heads. Purple eyes stared directly at him.

Arganaï stopped running and took a step back. These creatures would certainly run as fast as he could; he would only stand a chance of avoiding recapture if he could be more nimble and quick on his feet.

The first of them grabbed their tools and raced over; heavily armored creatures swarmed toward him from all sides, attempting a pincer movement.

I've got to get out of here! Arganaï raced off, going south, where there seemed to be fewer of the enemy.

But his body was letting him down: his legs were giving way and he was fighting for breath. He had to find somewhere to hide to get his strength back before he could continue his flight.

O gods of infamy, can't you stop up their ears and shut their eyes for them? Make them run straight past me! Arganaï hurled himself into the undergrowth and buried himself in the pile of dead leaves between two fallen trees. He shut his eyes and breathed quietly.

And waited.

And waited . . .

In the middle of the night Arganaï shot up in pain.

I fell asleep!

The moon was shining down on him through the foliage and his right hand was burning like fire. The filthy water and the earth he had rolled in had caused the wound to fester.

But pain means you are still alive.

They didn't find me! Arganaï pushed his way out, listened hard and made his way cautiously forward, always stopping to listen out . . . *Ye gods of infamy! You have indeed protected me. I shall make offerings to you.*

He stood and began to run south again, bathed in the friendly silver light of the stars.

He stopped to eat some berries and roots he found along his way, then took a drink from a small stream. He kept looking behind him, fearing that the huge monsters were on his tracks.

By the evening he had reached the edge of Dsôn.

Not long! Letting out a sigh of relief he continued his journey, sure that the watch would have seen him coming by now. He imagined the orders being given to get the catapults ready.

Exhausted, Arganaï managed to raise his uninjured hand in a wave . . . then he heard a dull roar behind him.

He dropped to the ground and rolled quickly to the side.

A viciously barbed spear, twice as long as he was tall, flew over his head and embedded itself in the sandy soil. It had a ring at one end with a rope attached for instant retrieval of the weapon.

"Fire!" Arganaï shouted to the fortress garrison on the island, as if his voice had the slightest chance of being heard over the water. He rolled to the right, jumped up and raced across the flat open ground with the very last of his strength. There was no cover. It felt as if he had never run so slowly in his life. "Loose the catapults, for pity's sake!" he cried.

One half of the bridge to Ishím Voróo was let down and a cavalry unit rode out toward him. Hefty thuds told Arganaï that the catapults had fired a first salvo to deter the enemies' attack. His eyesight was now restricted to tunnel vision. He ran toward the warriors riding toward him.

They'll save me! A cloud of arrows whirred over his head, targeted at the edge of the forest.

Not until Arganaï was safely up behind the rider on one of the stallions did he really believe he had escaped with his life. "I must . . . get to . . . the . . ." His voice failed completely.

"We'll see you are all right. You'll feel better soon," said the älf who had pulled him to safety. "Who were the Ishím Voróo scum who dared lay hands on you?"

"I saw them!" he groaned. "They have come back!"

"Who has?" asked the solider.

"Dorón . . . ashont . . ." Arganaï whispered, afraid he would not live long enough to deliver the vital message. His people must be warned. The horror redoubled in his mind as he breathed the name. "It's them— the dorón ashont!"

Tark Draan (Girdlegard), to the southwest of the Gray Mountains, 4371ˢᵗ division of unendingness (5199ᵗʰ solar cycle), late summer.

As dawn broke, Morana made her way to the top of the tower, spying out the land to the east and observing how, as the daystar rose, the plain changed color from dark yellow to gold.

She put her hand slowly into the pocket of her robe and took out a small round flute the size of a child's fist. She had fashioned it out of the skull of a young óarco; it was one of the first things she had ever made and it served as a charm, bringing her the luck of the north wind.

She placed her lips on the double opening and blew softly into it. *Just so you know that we are here* . . .

The wind of the dead was brought to life. It was like the shrill noise of a storm raging over sharp cliffs. There followed a deep resonance just beyond the range of the audible. The reverberations of the double flute were guaranteed to drive away any semblance of clear thought and to put you into a trance—it was a sound to chill the soul.

Morana varied the tones by covering one or other of the skull's holes with her fingers and feeling how the vibrations affected her. Her vision became blurred. Certain warriors found the music heightened their mood to one of tense and furious aggression.

She ended her concert.

Listen to my message, townspeople and elves alike: I send you the wind of the dead. Nothing will save you. As she put down her flute her eyesight gradually cleared.

She could see the river with the elf settlement on its bank; behind the river, gigantic trees stretched up toward the sky.

They have not bothered with fortifications, only a couple of isolated watchtowers. Morana could hardly believe her good fortune. *We'll be able to take the whole plain in a matter of a few moments of unendingness.* The nostàroi would be delighted to lead the initial attack on their sworn enemies.

Morana would leave Quarrystone that night and head into the Golden Plain. Perhaps she would even be able to deceive the elves, but she did not really intend to meet any of them. She wanted to take a look around; set foot on enemy territory and sink her fingers into the soil—a symbolic claim for her own folk.

She let her eyes drift over the landscape once more—*wait, what is that?*

On the horizon she saw the edges of an immense opening in the earth. She could not be sure of the dimensions, because there was a small forest blocking her view, but she felt sure that it was no ordinary mine. She would have to inspect this from closer up.

She swung herself away from the roof and down the side of the tower to reach the window of her room. She would not leave her room again until the evening, otherwise the color of her eyes might attract suspicion. And she had plenty to do: she had to finish writing up her night's findings.

Quarrystone held no further secrets for her; she had noted every weakness in the town's defenses. In her opinion, a unit of twenty älfar warriors could take the place with ease. The barbarians would wake up the following morning astonished to see älfar banners flying from their castle battlements. *A nice little extra when we conquer the Golden Plain. We can extend the castle and make a proper fortress out of it. It can serve as a bastion against the human armies.*

Morana jumped back into her room.

She landed next to the table—and found herself confronting an elderly elf leafing through her notes.

He wore a brown leather upper garment and green breeches tucked into high boots. His gray hair was gathered into a knot at the back of his head. Looking up, he addressed a few words to her, which she could not understand. He seemed friendly at first, but became unsure when he noticed the black in her eyes.

Morana saw that he carried a knife at his side and that a longbow and quiver had been placed against the wall. *He must be out hunting.* "Greetings," she said, speaking the language of the barbarians and attempting to remain calm so as not to unsettle him—in case he had not already started to suspect.

"May Sitalia be with you," he responded hesitantly. "Forgive me for entering the room like this. The landlord was proud to relate that an elf was a guest at the Red Goblet, but I was wondering why you had not come a little farther to stay with your own kind." He gestured to the east. "It would not have taken long and the accommodation would have been so much better." He put his head on one side, his hand still on her pages of notes. "He thought you were from the south."

Morana could tell that he was on his guard now. She had no idea what the elves knew about the älfar, but she assumed there must at least be legends about them. *He is old, so he will know the stories. Is he playing with me?*

"Yes. I'm here as a messenger from our Queen Emifinia, to visit you here in the north," she lied. "My name is Morana."

The elf bowed. "My name is Fatunasíl. That's our town down there by the river. I would be happy to escort you. I expect you would like to meet our princess."

"It would be an honor. My queen wants to put an end to the estrangement between our peoples. We are in some trouble." Morana appealed to his sympathy, which would, with any luck, serve to allay possible doubts.

"What has happened?" Fatunasíl had not moved and his hands were still resting on her notes, as if trying to read her words through the fingertips.

"Our harvest failed and we can't feed ourselves on barbarian corn." She tried a smile. "We had hoped you might have something easier to digest."

"Of course." Fatunasíl tapped the sheets of paper. "This script is new to me. It's unlike any handwriting used by local elves. And your eyes are dark. Why?"

"It's a special characteristic. It's to do with the water." Morana was sure the elf did not believe her and was trying to trap her with his questions.

"That tune I heard just now . . . Was that you playing?"

"Yes. It was to welcome the daystar; it's a traditional tune."

"I see." Fatunasíl grew more earnest. "You gave the innkeeper's daughter a strange blessing. He had asked for Sitalia's help, but the symbol on the girl's brow is not that of our goddess." He frowned. "How do you explain that?"

Morana crossed the room silently and pushed the door shut. "Time is up for the town," she said. "The residents will give their bones for our works of art and their blood will be used for noble paintings; their tendons will serve as strings for our instruments and their skin as canvasses or parchment. The little girl will survive because *I* have granted her life." She gave a grim smile. "Sitalia's blessing would not have helped her."

Fatunasíl said something in his own language, drawing his knife and hurling it in her direction.

Prepared for this attack, Morana was able to step aside and grab a fistful of arrows from the quiver by the wall; she threw them at the elf.

He raised his arm to protect his face. The force behind the thrown arrows could not at this distance pierce his flesh with deadly effect, but was sufficient to graze his face, neck and forearm.

Morana used the confusion to draw her short sword for close combat.

Fatunasíl ducked under her attacking thrust, collecting a kick in the belly and a cut across his back. The light leather shirt offered little protection and the wound gaped wide, revealing the white vertebrae before his red blood gushed over it. He screamed.

Having silenced his voice with a blow to the nape of the neck, Morana then turned over his body as he slumped to the floor at her feet. She placed the tip of her sword at his throat and was pleased to see the blood pour out right and left. She must have found an artery. "How many are there of you?"

Fatunasíl gulped and cursed her in the elf language. "I know what you are," he stuttered through his pain. "Sitalia sent you to us to bring us back to the path of righteousness. We had not been walking the right path for our people."

"No. It was the Inextinguishables that sent us to eradicate you," she replied. "Tell me what that hole is I saw from the tower, over to the east of your land."

He averted his gaze and turned his face away.

She knew Fatunasíl would not tell her anything about the elves of the Golden Plain. "Congratulations," she said darkly. "You are probably the first elf in Tark Draan to die by our hands. I shall ensure your name goes down in history. Your death is named Morana." She shoved the blade deep into his throat and then abruptly upward inside his head. Fatunasíl gave not a single death shudder.

How does one of your kind die? She stared at him in curiosity, noting how his pupils contracted smaller than frogspawn before turning opaque and glassy. Then they widened, replacing the blue as if to make space to allow the soul to escape.

I want to witness that many more times! She stood up and studied the corpse carefully. *What shall I take as a souvenir?*

She could have cut off the head and preserved it in honey, but she did not know what adventures awaited her in Tark Draan. It might be risky to have an elf head found in her saddlebags. *But hair would be all right.*

She cut off his hair with her sword and soaked it in the pool of blood.

"That's a fine reminder," she said quietly, lifting the red-stained strands to dry in the sunshine.

As if nothing untoward had occurred, Morana sat down at the table to bring her notes up to date, paying no further attention to the corpse.

She spent the rest of the day in her chamber, writing and drawing. She sent the innkeeper away several times when he came up to ask if there was anything she wanted, perhaps concerned about the sudden disappearance of his second elf guest.

Morana could not resist making a sketch of the dead Fatunasíl's face. She recorded his death mask on a separate piece of paper and drew his profile and several close studies of his eyes, concentrating on producing an exact representation.

When the sun had gone down and her own eyes were no longer black, she got her things ready and then poured lamp oil out onto the floor and the dead body, ignited it with a spark and watched the flames begin to dance.

I have killed the first of the elves! Morana felt elated as she left the room for the tower stairs. She headed out of Quarrystone at a gallop, having paid neither the innkeeper nor the stable boy. She did not want the townspeople to remember their elf visitor fondly.

She looked back over her shoulder.

The top half of the tower was burning, sending flames and smoke out through the dusk. The first fragments of the building were starting to fall away, starting fires on the roofs of nearby buildings. She knew that the barbarians would not be able to fight the blaze in the tower because it would be impossible to reach. They would have to wait until it burned itself out or until it had reached the lower floors where they could try to douse it with buckets of water thrown from neighboring roofs. She turned again and headed east toward the border with the Golden Plain. It struck her with immense pleasure that the town was the first to be set on fire by an älf. Her deeds here had set a development in motion that no one in Tark Draan could stop.

Ishím Voróo (Outer Lands), Dsôn Faïmon, Dsôn,
4371ˢᵗ division of unendingness (5199ᵗʰ solar cycle),
late summer.

Dsôn is as glorious as ever! Even in the pouring rain! After his endless ride
and the protracted sojourn in the groundling caves, the dark heart of
his homeland appeared more stately and impressive than ever. This was
where he truly belonged; there was no denying it.

In spite of his promise to Caphalor, it went against the grain not to
announce himself as the nostàroi and receive the appropriate praise and
acclaim—especially as he would not have to share the triumph with
Caphalor. *But it can wait for now.* Sinthoras had to smile when he pictured
the faces of the guards who had let him pass. They had been nearly pros-
trate with respect and admiration. He had found this very gratifying. They
swore they would keep his presence in Dsôn Faïmon secret. He didn't
doubt they would; they had been proud to be taken into his confidence. It
was enough, for now. *I'll send them over a few bottles of good wine.*

Sinthoras rode along the main street that led from the north to the
Inextinguishables' tower. *Shouldn't I at least go and pay them a visit?*

After a moment's thought he decided to go straight to Timanris to
surprise her. He was so keen to see her and take her in his arms once more.
By all the gods of infamy! How distraught I was at the news of her death!

The power of love had revealed itself to Sinthoras after the many
divisions of unendingness he had mocked and denied it. Before falling
for Timanris, he had only entered into socially advantageous relation-
ships. He had been astounded to find his soul could blaze with fire for
an älf-woman with no social status, but she had won his heart without
any discernible effort on her part.

He passed huge buildings with pillars of black and gray basalt, and
approached the marketplace, where only a few stalls had been set up:
the bad weather was keeping most of the inhabitants indoors, so it was
difficult for the traders and merchants to do much business.

I need a present for her. He had some gems in his pocket taken from
the groundling treasure chests, but he was not sure this kind of jewelry
would appeal to her artistic nature. The gold the mountain maggots

produced had a certain value, but that stemmed from the substance itself, not the handiwork. Sinthoras was eager not to offend his beloved.

As he looked around, his attention was caught by a new statue. Sinthoras wondered why there were two armed guards by the plinth. Their shields bore the insignia of the Polòtain family.

Has somebody died? Sinthoras rode over to the statue and realized who it portrayed. *Robonor?*

The face carved in onyx marble bore unmistakable signs of pain and accusation. The outstretched arm pointed to Sinthoras's house, and the wound on the leg, glowing red, was visible from far off.

But that's . . .

"Hey, you two!" The hood Sinthoras wore concealed his face and the guards looked up at him with bad-tempered expressions. "Who put this statue up?"

"Take a look at my shield, if you want to know that," came the gruff answer. The bad weather must have gotten to the soldier.

"So it was Polòtain himself?"

The watchman nodded.

"And no one stopped him?" Sinthoras could feel his fury growing: a burning wave sweeping through his body and jagged lines forming on his face. *How dare he place a damnable lie like that in the middle of the marketplace?* He rounded the artistically perfect statue. Its significance was appalling. "How long has that been here?"

"Since the end of early summer." The guard looked at him more closely. "Don't try to touch it. Do you hear? We're here to make sure you don't."

He assumes I'm going to do something about this hideous defamation! Sinthoras felt the urge to overturn the statue and have his night-mare crush it with its hooves. *What other lies has he spread while I was away on campaign?* A block of ice formed in his stomach, caused by anger and fear.

"I certainly won't be touching it." Sinthoras turned his night-mare and ordered it to shit on the statue. The shouts of the guards had no effect and Sinthoras rode off.

The wind brushed his hood from his head, the cold rain cooling his face. *Think hard! What can you do about it?*

Sinthoras felt destiny had brought him back to Dsôn. It was fitting that no one knew he was there. He had an advantage over Polòtain's family in that respect.

Why did he . . . ah! He is Robonor's great-uncle. Directly after the guardsman's death there had been rumors that Sinthoras had arranged the accident in order to get Timanris's betrothed out of the picture. Caphalor had warned him of them at the time: everyone knew what he and Timanris had been up to before Robonor had been killed. High society in Dsôn had been enjoying the gossip, but had fallen silent after his promotion to nostàroi.

I got back here in the nick of time to force their lies back down their throats! He pulled his hood back up, determined now not be recognized.

As he made his way to Timanris, the humiliation and shame got to him and he racked his brain as to what he should do next. *If anyone knows the scandal surrounding my name, it'll be Timanris.* He trusted her not to tell anyone else that he was here in the capital.

He reached her house. The door was opened by a slave.

Sinthoras pretended he had been sent to deliver a personal message to Timanris. He was told to wait in the corridor near the pantry until she appeared.

Although his face was in shadow, his intended life-partner recognized him at once. "You?" She stopped short two paces away. This was not the cry of joy he had expected.

What effect have these poisonous rumors had on her? Sinthoras felt sick as a storm raged in his insides, leaving him cold as ice. "I . . . had to see you. I was given false news of your death . . ." The words tumbled out and he stepped up to her, sweeping his wet mantle from his shoulders to fall to the ground, revealing his light armor and weapons belt. "I have not been home yet. Nobody must know that I am here: I should not have left the troops—but I needed to see you and to take you in my arms." He reached out for her.

Timanris stiffened, her beautiful face a closed mask. "Did you come because of me or because of what they are saying about you here in Dsôn?" she asked with a quavering voice.

"I have no idea what people are saying!" he insisted. "I've just seen the statue Polòtain has put up. Is that what you mean?"

The älf-woman lowered her head, a strand of hair falling across her features. "You have no idea what it has been like for me while you've been away," she muttered resentfully. "Everybody's talking about us, even if they won't say anything to my face. They say you had Robonor murdered." She stared at him intently, her eyes narrowing. "Do you remember my asking you whether you had anything to do with the accident?"

Sinthoras nodded quickly. "Yes, and I told you that I had nothing—"

"I know. You vowed you were innocent. But how can Polòtain be telling anyone with an ear to listen that he has a witness statement incriminating you?" She brushed his hands away. "I'm giving you the opportunity here and now to renew the oath you swore or to confess to having lied, Sinthoras."

He felt weak and hurt. The quiet realization crept into the rational side of his brain that it was love that had dragged him into this mess. "I swear by my life, by the Inextinguishables, by my ancestors and by anything else you like: I had nothing to do with Robonor's death!"

"And that you never ordered anyone to injure him, or ever expressed it as a request?"

"I swear it, Timanris."

At that she stepped into his arms and embraced him wordlessly.

However, his reaction was different from usual: it was not the warm response he usually felt when she touched him.

Sinthoras stroked her slender neck. "What else is wrong? I can see there is something else . . ."

Timanris took him by the hand and led him to her chambers. Two slave girls were sent to bring tea. Sinthoras and Timanris sat down at the window, looking at the splendor of Dsôn.

He would have liked to kiss her, but did not have the courage to do so. As long as there was a shadow over their meeting he did not feel secure enough in their relationship. He took her hand and waited to hear what she had to say.

Timanris looked at him questioningly. Hidden behind the consternation and doubt in her eyes, he recognized the tenderness she still obviously felt for him, but he realized he was on the point of losing her completely.

"I fell down the stairs, I am told," she began. "I must have grabbed hold of a spear from the wall . . . I ended up very badly injured. The healers were hard-pressed to keep me in the sphere of unendingness." She waited until the slaves had served the tea. "I had memory problems. I could remember nothing about the accident, or about the period immediately preceding it."

Sinthoras was on glowing coals. *What is she trying to tell me?* "I am so grateful to the gods of infamy that—"

Timanris raised her left hand slightly. "I have not finished. Everyone thought it was an accident, and so did I—until Raleeha ran away. She had left a letter for me, saying she had acted on your instructions!"

His heart stood still. "No!" he gasped. "You . . . how can you believe . . . ?" He did not know what to say. "You are everything to me! I never—"

"She wrote that you had promised to apprentice her to the best artists in the land if she did it," she said, her voice shaking with emotion. "She said you had told her you no longer loved me and wanted to enter into another arrangement. A relationship that could further your career and help you in politics." Timanris shut her eyes and reached for her marble bowl of tea. "I would not believe the words of a slave girl, Sinthoras . . ." Her voice broke. "But together with the rumors here in Dsôn, and then with Polòtain's accusation, well, it nearly . . ." She fell silent, but opened her eyes and regarded him.

Sinthoras felt his mouth go dry. There was a metallic taste on his tongue as if he had swallowed blood. He had to take a mouthful of tea before answering. "I took Raleeha's eyesight because she was careless. She must have wanted revenge for that," he said slowly, emphasizing each word, hoping that Timanris would comprehend. "It was her that brought me the false news of your death! She had forged your handwriting—"

"Raleeha was blind! How could she forge my writing?"

"By the gods of infamy, I have no idea! Maybe she had help. Maybe from my enemies, from Polòtain and his friends, to weaken my position."

Sinthoras cupped her face in his hands. "Can't you understand? She wanted me to stay in Tark Draan! My grief at your death would have kept me away from Dsôn forever. She wanted to destroy me, far from home, so that she could go about ruining my reputation at home." Sinthoras thought this was an appropriate explanation. *That's it! That makes sense!* "They gave you Raleeha's letter so you would lose faith in me and never try to find me." He stroked her fragrant hair. "They want to tear us apart. They want to rob me of the love and support of the one I carry deep in my soul."

"Their plan so nearly worked," whispered Timanris, tears flowing down her cheeks. "Forgive me for doubting you. I should have listened to my heart, because it always took your side." She pulled him to her. "I swear I shall never doubt you again."

Relief flooded through him and his fears were suddenly as nothing. Warmth spread, invading every last corner of his body. Overjoyed, he pressed her to him. "We shall win. We shall defeat Polòtain with his own weapons!"

"Yes, we will," She gave him a long and passionate kiss on the lips. "We'll start tomorrow morning. But this night belongs to you and me."

Sinthoras surrendered to her caresses.

But as he did so, a voice inside whispered that he was a deceitful fraud.

Chapter V

The first elf blood, spilled by Morana.
Without doubt, an exceptional achievement.

But more great achievements were yet to come, even if the Heroes did not know it, as they covered mile after mile in the far lands of Tark Draan.
Back in their homeland, thought so very secure, these warriors would soon be sorely missed.
And there was no way to order their swift return to Dsôn to give succor to the älfar folk by their presence.

I cannot say whether a warrior such as Virssagòn, unbeaten in battle, or such as the nimble Horgàta, would have stood a chance against the horror that strode through Dsôn's alleyways, streets and elegant squares.
One thing was certain: the Heroes were missing.

Excerpt from the epic poem *The Heroes of Tark Draan*
composed by Carmondai, master of word and image

Tark Draan (Girdlegard), far to the southwest of the Gray Mountains, 4371st division of unendingness (5199th solar cycle) early autumn.

A rain-laden wind was whistling through the gaps around the shutters, making the nervous apprentices doubly anxious. But nobody did anything; the student magi remained at their desks, scribbling away by candlelight, their young faces tense.

Jujulo the Jolly sighed, wondering if he was the only one who could hear the wind howling outside. He got up from his comfortable armchair on the dais.

Twenty of his best students were puzzling over the tasks he had set them. Any who failed the test would be making their way home tomorrow and would revert to being the offspring of some noble lord, or a merchant's son, or a farm boy, or a young laborer—with one thing in common: they would have missed the unique chance of one day taking up a position as magus.

Jujulo the Jolly was well named—he was never moody or bad-tempered, and did not like it when others brought their foul moods into his school and home: an old, stately building on a hilltop surrounded by a town called Duckingham. His multi-colored kaftan and curly-toed shoes also complemented his personality and completed the eccentric picture he projected; anyone would be forgiven for thinking him a fairground attendant or a court jester. He was already over eighty sun-cycles old, but looked much younger, so that anyone meeting him for the first time might have said he was fifty.

Jujulo walked over to the windows and fastened them shut. *A magus must never get distracted, otherwise he can't concentrate, and if he can't concentrate, his spells won't work.*

He stood with his back to the exam room listening to the quill pens scratching away, satisfied that they were all concentrating hard. *Yes, they are writing as quickly as they can. They are good boys.*

Jujulo returned to his chair and made himself comfortable, sipping his tea and nibbling the odd biscuit the cook had baked for him: nice and spicy, just the way he liked them. *I wonder if they will do better than the girls?*

The magus taught the girls and boys separately. He always found that a male apprentice would learn better with other boys, and a female apprentice did better if instructed in a group of girls—there were fewer distractions.

He could still hear the wind howling. *A north wind, of course.*

His thoughts strayed to the Gray Mountains: those majestic peaks that were home to the fifthlings. The dwarves knew their way about the mountains like nobody else. He had twice taken up their invitation to visit and had admired the stone friezes in the halls, their forges and workshops, ingenious irrigation systems, and of course, the fortifications at the Stone Gateway.

However polite the dwarves had been, he could not avoid the feeling that they did not have a very high opinion of humans, or magi for that matter—dwarves did not hold with magic. However, if that was the case, they thought even less of elves. But for some reason the dwarf king liked him and a real friendship was developing through their correspondence.

Jujulo used to think that the dwarves were a little slow, but he had soon realized that this was due to their native stubbornness: they were quite prepared to listen to others' views, but they would always stick to their own opinion, and this somewhat hampered discussion. Now, something else was worrying him: he had been waiting for a response from the dwarf king since the summer, when Jujolo had invited him to visit the magic realm of Jujulonia, together with his retinue; he had expected to hear back immediately.

But there had been no answer.

And the messenger he had sent was missing: his famula Famenia. She was the best student in her cohort and it was not just the invitation she had been entrusted with. Jujulo had instructed her to entertain the dwarves with some indoor magic to whet their appetites.

The magus sipped his tea noisily. *I wonder what's afoot in the dwarf realm?* Had the fifthlings perhaps forced their king to abdicate? Was there a dispute between the various clans? Or were the odd creatures fed up with his magicking? Or perhaps an accident had occurred—a flood maybe, or some gas seeping into their mines and tunnels?

He spotted one of the young students trying to copy from his neighbor. "Watch it, Törden! This is your last warning, boys. If anyone else tries to cheat, you are out on your ear!"

Törden went red and doodled on his paper.

Jujulo had to stop himself from breaking into a grin. *As if I would not have tried the same trick.* He thought back to when he had studied under the magus Erinitor the Unrestrained. His master had thrown an inkpot straight at his head upon seeing him attempt to cheat. He still had the dark blue mark where the bottle had broken the skin. *The fact I tried to cheat didn't stop me being chosen as Erinitor's successor though, did it?*

He had finished his mug of tea and the pot was empty. He took another biscuit and made a swift gesture with his right hand.

A shimmering teacup appeared and shot off through the closed door: a simple message spell to get the cook to bring what he wanted. Easy as pie.

The famuli, he noted, were not letting themselves be distracted. He supposed his little tricks were perfectly normal to them now; they had all been at the school for so long.

Voices were heard out in the corridor and the door burst open. Jujulo recognized the soaking wet figure on the threshold as Quartan, the cooper. He was bleeding badly from a cut on the top of his arm. "Master Jujulo!" he called with horror in his voice. "Come quickly! You must— It's the elves! They are attacking us!"

The apprentices all looked up and started whispering to each other, regardless of Jujulo's reproving glance.

The elves? The magus got up out of his chair. "That can't be true! We're so far away from the nearest elf realm . . . why would they attack us?" He looked at Quartan. "Are you sure?"

"I saw it with my own eyes!" The cooper gripped his injured shoulder. "One came out of the shadows as if he had been spat out of the dark. He stormed into the middle of our guilds meeting in the council chamber. I'm the only one to escape, because I—" He sobbed. "Master, please! Do something!"

"Indeed I shall!" Jujulo rushed past the wounded man and stormed out of the hall.

"Magus, what about the examination?" Törden called after him.

"You have all passed. Stay where you are, all of you," he instructed as he hurried out, grabbing his raincoat from its hook.

Quartan soon caught up with him. "I can't let you face them alone, master."

"It won't be elves, my friend. That's for certain."

"But the ears are all pointed and they—"

"I'm sure that's what you saw. It'll be a gang of robbers disguised as elves," Jujulo said as he ran. "They want to frighten you so that nobody puts up any defense." *There can't be any other explanation. There's nothing here in Duckingham the people of light could possibly want.*

The dwarf king's warning came to mind; he had always insisted the elves were treacherous. "Beware of the elves! Trust them and you'll live to regret it." Jujulo could almost hear his friend's growly voice. "They only act in their own interest—they think they are so much better than everyone else. It's us dwarves that protect Girdlegard. Yes, we even offer the pointy-ears our protection, although they deceive us. The long'uns forget so quickly who they owe their prosperity to, calling us mountain maggots, nothing but treasure-hoarders, bad-tempered little black-smiths only good to trade with. But if we didn't keep the Stone Gateway safe, the whole of Girdlegard would be awash with evil."

The words resounded in Jujulo's head as they came to the first houses, but the town looked peaceful enough. There was no sign of any invasion.

It's so quiet. Jujulo slowed down and gathered his thoughts in order to be ready with a spell if it should prove necessary. The ground at his feet was charged with a magic force, so he was not worried about confronting an enemy. There wasn't much that could go wrong.

"What is wrong? Where are the guards?"

He heard footsteps receding.

Jujulo turned to Quartan and saw that the man was making himself scarce. "What is happening?"

"Forgive me, master. He made me do it! Otherwise . . . Forgive me!" the cooper stammered, before he turned and ran.

"Who? Otherwise what?" Jujulo shouted after him while preparing a defense spell. He had been lured into a trap—the elves had not attacked at all. *But who could be after me?*

He heard a dark laugh from the shadows.

The hairs on the back of his neck stood up and he was filled with fear that grabbed at his heart with a cold hand; it started to beat frenetically and his chest was suffused with pain. *What is happening to our town?*

"You have all that power and yet you dress like a fool," an eerie voice mocked in a half whisper. "You could rule over the whole of Tark Draan! Take a look at yourself. Aren't you ashamed to be seen like that?"

Jujulo turned around full circle but could not see anyone. "Who are you?"

"The moment you catch sight of me you will be dead," murmured the cruel voice. "Pray to your gods that you never see me."

The magus intoned a swift incantation. A glowing sphere the size of a closed fist appeared on the palm of his hand. It flew into the dark corners to cast its light.

"So, you think you can find me?" he heard the unknown stranger say. "Look what I can do with your pretty little light!"

Skinny fingers of darkness emerged and moved toward the glowing sphere like smoke, swallowing up every scrap of light.

Is this some rival magus? Jujulo felt that his light-spell was still working, but that the inky blackness had enveloped it, holding it captive. *Does he want to seize my enchanted land? I had no idea. Or . . . could it be a student with a grudge against me?* "What do you want from me?"

A figure stepped silently out of the darkness; the blackness was reluctant to let it go.

Jujulo saw a tall warrior in a metal breastplate with leg greaves and forearm guards in the same material. His clothing was dark, as was his hair, which was held back with a band. Thin black chains encircled his upper arms and a line of long polished rivets ran from the cuirass back over the shoulders. The handles of two swords were visible behind him; his pointed ears were immediately obvious.

So it is an elf, after all. Jujulo's hands were trembling and he tried desperately to remember a suitable attack spell, but nothing would come. Fear was numbing his mind.

The elf stood still and spread his arms, displaying black gauntlets on his hands. "I wish you good evening, Magus Jujulo. As you see, I have not drawn my weapon. I am here to lay claim, in the name of the elves, to your realm. We understand magic, unlike you barbarians. You have abused the forces of enchantment for far too long. It is time to surrender to those who deserve them!"

Jujulo could not believe what he was hearing. And the elf's dialect was atrocious. In all his long life he had only ever met one elf who had come from the Golden Plain and his speech had been most refined and elegant. *This one doesn't sound like a sophisticated elf at all. It's as if he has learned the language of humans from someone with no breeding or education.*

The streets of Duckingham remained silent. The inhabitants must have realized it was better not to leave their houses that night.

"I assume you want all of the enchanted lands? Or did you pick mine because you think I look like a clown?" Jujulo took a closer look at his adversary. The runes on the armor meant nothing to him. This elf was unlike any he had ever come across in Girdlegard. "Which elf realm are you from?"

"Âlandur."

"That's over 400 miles away. You think you can just march straight through Thapiaïn and take over? What about the other kingdoms? What will their rulers say about their new neighbors who don't look so keen on peaceful relations?" *The dwarves were right; the elves are not to be trusted.* Jujulo wondered how he could overpower this envoy. He had to get warnings to the other magi, and all the monarchs, as well. *Those brave dwarves have been protecting us from those on the other side of the mountains, only for us to find insidious treachery within Girdlegard!*

"Staking a claim is a simple procedure when all possible objectors have been removed," the elf said, smiling coldly. "But what good is an enchanted land without its magus and his famuli?"

"Are you *threatening* me?" Jujulo called up a gust of wind to hurl the elf backward against the wall, smashing every bone in his body. *You think I'm a clown, do you?*

The squall threw up a cloud of dust, but the enemy was nowhere to be seen.

"I'm not *threatening* you," the elf murmured into Jujulo's ear. "I'm *killing* you!"

The magus tried to turn around and fling an energy spell, but pain shot through his back and something pierced his lungs. Sinking to his knees, he felt liquid warmth run down his body: his own blood. He collapsed and fell forward onto his face.

"A little bit of a breeze, was that all you could manage?" The elf turned his body over with the tip of his boot, so that Jujulo was forced to look him in the eyes. "So, those little stab wounds have done for you? I expected you would heal yourself and I'd have more of a fight. I thought you'd be more dangerous." He stood up, both swords in his hands, their blades dripping with red blood. "Perhaps your famuli will offer more resistance than their master. Unless, of course, they are even greater fools than you."

A . . . gesture . . . Jujulo made the cautious movements of a healing spell with the fingers of his right hand.

The elf noticed what he was doing. "No, not now, fool!" One sword blade drove down, slicing beneath Jujulo's elbow and splitting the flesh of his forearm and hand. Muscle, tendons and bones were severed.

Jujulo screamed and spluttered, rolling to one side.

"Pathetic," said the elf, his voice full of contempt. "I can see we have been concerned unnecessarily about the trouble you magi might make for our army. Tark Draan will fall more quickly than we had thought."

Jujulo groaned as loud as his damaged lungs permitted. The agony was unbearable and his mind was completely overwhelmed by the pain.

He never saw the final sword blow coming.

His sufferings were quickly at an end.

Tark Draan (Girdlegard), Gray Mountains, Stone Gateway,
4371st division of unendingness (5199th solar cycle),
late summer.

Carmondai headed for the southern gate, taking the risk of traveling through the dwarves' kingdom on horseback. It could not be much farther now.

Caphalor, worried about possible attacks from groundlings, óarcos or other of their allies, had wanted to send four of the Goldsteel Unit with him, but Carmondai had turned down the offer. He liked his own company and did not need a companion.

It's not that difficult to find your way now the älfar scouts have left signs on the walls. Despite this, the number of missing soldiers had recently risen. It seemed that many who had gone off on their own had got lost for good—or been ambushed.

Carmondai took the path to the right as indicated by the arrow on the wall.

He came to an atrium with a gate four paces high, its huge bolts controlled by an intricate system of pulleys and chains. It stood open. Behind it was a second gateway, stronger and more impressive still. Its double doors were shut. An älfar unit of warriors had made camp this side of the second gate. They were there to secure the entrance to Tark Draan.

Made it! Carmondai rode up to them and saluted. In one corner there was a heap of conventional barbarian armor and weaponry.

"Greetings, Carmondai. I have heard and read much about you," said one älf who appeared at his stirrup, wearing a long padded doublet. "I am Armatòn, the benàmoi guarding the gate. Are we going to get a mention in your epic about the victorious invasion of Tark Draan?"

Carmondai noted the same hopeful tone that he heard from nearly all those he came into contact with. It was tiring after a while, fielding these inquiries. "Who knows?" he said with a faint smile. "I'm here out of curiosity. I want to take a look outside and do some sketches." He dismounted. "Will that be in order?"

"Of course. Seeing as it's you." Armatòn pointed ahead where a stairway was hewn into the rock. The steps led up in a spiral through an opening. "This way."

They headed off together.

Carmondai asked about the barbarian armor. "What's that for, if you don't mind my asking? Don't the groundlings think the elves are just as weird-looking as us?"

"If we are up on the battlements by ourselves, I agree. But we do our guard duty with the dwarves, so it looks like our two races have become the best of friends." Armatòn laughed when he saw Carmondai's skeptical expression. "You'll see! I'll wager Dsôn will adore your picture."

They started to climb up past the locked gate.

Carmondai halted and sketched a few details of the locking mechanism on the heavy doors and he grudgingly conceded the previous occupants of the stronghold had done sterling work: cogwheels, thick bolts, chains, pulleys all interconnected in such a way that no one could break in. Normally, that is.

That's what the fellows at the Stone Gateway thought, as well. Carmondai finished off his swift drawing then set off with Armatòn again.

They were on a spiral staircase now; tunnels led off to left and right, but the benàmoi kept climbing until they reached an ironstudded door.

Armatòn levered it open and an icy draft swept in. "We're on the battlement walkway above the gate. Useful for chucking rocks down on uninvited guests. Containers of stone missiles are brought up on hoists from the rooms below. Quite clever."

"I'll have a look at it." Carmondai went outside, meeting cold air free of the taint of stone dust, óarco shit and other unpleasant smells. *Glorious fresh air!* He took several deep breaths.

"It's the same for me every time I come up," Armatòn commented. "Tark Draan doesn't smell bad out here." He laughed and pointed to a dwarf leaning on the stone lintel, one hand shading his eyes from the sun. Occasionally the small figure took his hand down, turned his head, then lifted his arm again. A few paces away there were some more groundlings. "There you are: our new allies."

Carmondai noted the amused tone. "Can I take a closer look?"

"Please do. You can write about how Durùston and I—"

"Sure." Carmondai had had enough of all these requests for mentions in his work. But Durùston's name did prompt him to recall his meeting with the artist on the day he entered the mountain. As he drew closer to the first of the small figures he found his suspicions confirmed: *preserved groundling corpses!*

Durùston had really gone to town—even if these specimens were more practical than aesthetic.

The dwarf's neck had been cut around its girth. Thickened lines running under the skin emerged at the nape of the neck and disappeared under the figure's clothing: strings coated with dried blood and some kind of lubricant. A dull clicking noise could be heard before the right-hand string moved, making the groundling turn its head to one side.

However did he think that one up? Carmondai moved the dwarf's leather shirt aside.

The groundling had been completely disemboweled, leaving only the backbone and ribs for support, strengthened with metal wire; in place of the organs was a mechanism with counterweights and a taut spring, together with the network of colored strings that enabled the figure to move.

There was a very slight, sweet smell of decay but there was no sign of decomposition on the flesh itself.

Carmondai rubbed the skin. *Dry and cold. This weather must have helped.*

"The crows give us a lot of trouble." There was Durùston himself, coming along the walkway in his leather apron. "They're more difficult to deceive than the barbarians are. We have to shoo them off every now and then or they'd hack the flesh away. They must like the taste of the embalming fluid I use."

Carmondai shook hands with him. "This is fantastic work."

"No need to exaggerate; it is *necessary* work, that's all." But the smile on Durùston's face showed how proud he was. "I thought it was boring to just stick heads on spikes and put them on the parapet. Any idiot could do that—even an óarco. We need to show we are capable of higher things."

"It wouldn't surprise me if you'd made them able to talk. Do you have time to sit for me? I'd like to sketch this scene and include you in a picture. It's quite something, you know, to be in my epic. I hope you realize what an honor it is to be asked." With that, Carmondai sat down and started a drawing.

Durùston inclined his head in acknowledgment and knelt down next to the realistic mechanical dwarves, posing as if adjusting a spring.

"There are new ones coming in two moments of unendingness," he said. "We only have eleven for now; the crows get in quicker than we can sometimes. To make the little guys move I had to construct a support and then put in the counterweights and . . ."

Carmondai stopped listening, concentrating on his picture. The compressed charcoal implement he had invented was ideal for the drawing. He would send the picture by the very next messenger to the replica workshop in Dsôn, where art students made themselves a little extra money by copying major works for those citizens who couldn't afford the original. He might even be able to do a whole Tark Draan series. *With any luck, this campaign will make me rich without my having to capture any land.*

His sketch was finished.

". . . even bigger . . ." Durùston's voice droned on. "I hope we can get a dead troll . . ."

A whistle sounded, followed by an alarm signal of a type the älfar did not use. The guards on the battlements ducked down. Durùston did the same.

"What's that?" Carmondai looked around.

Armatòn indicated it was not safe to get up.

I see. Visitors. Travelers from Tark Draan wanting to enter the groundlings' realm. Durùston slid forward to take a quick look down through one of the apertures more usually used for pouring hot oil on attackers.

Carmondai crept over to the adjacent aperture, sketchpad and pencil in hand.

He heard a loud clatter, then some *moo*ing as a heavily laden ox cart rumbled to a halt. Two barbarians in minimal armor were up on the front of the vehicle and a third, dressed in a moth-eaten sheepskin cloak, was riding a plow-horse alongside. A light long-handled ax dangled from the saddle.

The rider waved up at them, "May Vraccas be with you, my good dwarves!" he called, his breath visible in the frosty air. "It's me, your friend Pantako!" He opened his arms wide in greeting.

Armatòn and Carmondai exchanged glances.

Pantako frowned. "What's the matter, my dear dwarves? I've got a cartload of lovely fabrics and silks and have a mind to trade them for barrels of your wonderful beer, as usual."

"No!" shouted Armatòn through the aperture, which made his voice reverberate. He sounded a bit like a groundling. "Not today!" he said, using the barbarians' language.

Any trader worth his salt wouldn't be put off by that. Carmondai was keen to find out how things would develop.

"What do you mean, not today?" howled Pantako. "I've got customers waiting for the beer. They've paid in advance and I'm not going to return their gold to them. You'd be making me look a swindler."

"No!" Armatòn repeated stubbornly.

Pantako spread his arms wider still. "What's your game, friend dwarf? Are you upping the beer price? And what's wrong with your voice? Are you sober?"

"He's a merchant and he's got to have wares to go home with," Carmondai commented. "He won't go away. You'll have to give him a really good reason."

"Like an arrow between the eyes?" suggested Armatòn irritably.

Durùston laughed out loud and Carmondai grinned. "That would be one way, it's true, but—"

"Well, you take over," Armatòn interrupted. "If you're such a master of the word."

"Hey there, friend dwarf," Pantako yelled. "I'm going to wait here until I've got my beer, got it? And if that means you've got to start brewing now, so be it. We've got a deal—"

"Oh no, we haven't," called Carmondai, enjoying the chance to spar with the trader. "You gave us linens of terrible quality last time. The shirts all fell to pieces!"

Pantako looked up, irritated. "Who's that? And why do you all sound foreign?"

Carmondai waited until the dwarf puppet next to him raised its arm. "Here! It's me speaking!"

"What's your name?"

"What's that to you?"

"Go and get me Bendogar Coinstone at once!" Pantako demanded. "I've always done good business with him."

"Coinstone's dead!"

Durùston gave a muffled laugh.

Carmondai continued: "Our deal is over!"

Pantako rode up and down at the gate as if he were trying to wear it down. "So, is that the word of the fifthlings? Is that how you keep—?"

"We can discuss it again when you bring some decent goods," Carmondai broke in. "The latest batch of our black beer is amazing. You'd better hurry up or we'll have drunk it all ourselves!"

"Oh, so that's your drift! Give me thirty circuits and I'll be back again. I'll bring the best linen and thread Gourarga has to offer!" Pantako gave a sign to the cart-drivers to turn the heavy wagon around. "But it'll be pricier—"

"Same price. Don't try that, barbarian!" Carmondai had not been able to stop himself saying that last word. *I hope he didn't hear it!*

Armatòn reached for his bow and notched an arrow.

Pantako was on the point of riding away, but pulled his horse up short. "Did you just call me a *barbarian,* friend dwarf?"

"Beardy, I said," Carmondai called down. Durùston clapped his hand over his mouth so as not to explode with laughter. "I called you Beardy One. There must have been an echo." *What a mess he looks in that filthy coat. And what arrogance!*

"I look forward to our negotiations!" Pantako was angry. "You'll regret what you said. Insults put the price up."

Durùston laughed.

Suddenly a young barbarian girl shot out of the doorway behind the sculptor, leaped on to the parapet and jumped down, shrieking as she fell, but landing safely on the bales of material in the cart. The traders were as surprised as the älfar.

"Where did she come from?" hissed Carmondai. Armatòn had not recovered from the shock.

"Drive as fast as you can if you value your lives!" she shouted, burrowing under the rolls of silk and linen cloth to protect herself from älf archers. "You'll have to whip the oxen! Get going, I beg you! The dwarf kingdom has fallen! There's an army come to wipe us out! Hurry!"

Pantako stared at her in amazement, then he looked up at the battlements. "What the blazes is going on up there? Who is that? And why did she—?"

"Finish them off!" Armatòn commanded.

The guards stood up and took aim, loosing a hail of long arrows straight at the barbarians.

Struck several times over, Pantako and the tradesmen sank down, but the oxen kept going. Carmondai could see that the girl had been spared a feathered death. From the midst of the mountain of cloth rolls, a long rod extended and began to beat the oxen; the animals roared in protest and quickened their pace.

Armatòn muttered a curse. He ordered the guards on the inside of the gate to stand guard.

In the meantime the älfar archers kept up a barrage of arrows. One of the beasts was hit and the cart slowed down. The barbarian girl slipped from the cart, taking a small bale with her as a shield as she ran.

Carmondai bounded down the steps and reached the hall where the warriors were mounting their night-mares.

"Bring the girl back at all costs, even if it means going without your disguises!" Armatòn said. The gate opened.

Carmondai jumped onto his own horse and followed the troop through the gate, trying desperately to keep up with them as they galloped out on much faster steeds, the thunder of their hooves echoing back from the stone walls.

Then they were out, heading into Tark Draan—and way ahead of him.

Carmondai rode past the cart and saw the second ox falter and collapse, stuck with arrows. On the ground he noticed a silver amulet, its chain broken.

Reining in his horse, he jumped down and picked it up. It certainly looked like silver; he could not make head nor tail of the runes inscribed on it, but as he held it in his hand he felt his fingers tingle. *Is it . . . magic?* His kind had certain powers, such as the ability to extinguish light and disseminate waves of fear, but none had the makings of a real magician.

Even so, most älfar would be aware of the presence of magic. This talisman was definitely a case in point.

So, barbarian, who are you exactly? He raised his eyes to where, in the distance, the road wound over the hills. He saw the älfar riders split into several groups, suggesting they had lost track of the girl.

If she managed to reach a town or even a garrison, the news of the fall of the dwarf kingdom would quickly spread and the älfar would have lost the advantage of surprise. *Help me, gods of infamy, let me be the one to find her! It would be a triumph!*

He stowed the amulet in his pocket, mounted his horse and stormed off.

CHAPTER VI

The älfar saw Death coming and did not grasp how serious he was.
They had nearly defeated him once, but he had learned from his mistake.
He would not be cheated again.

Warned by a courageous älf, the älfar armed themselves for the battle with Death to protect their nation, to protect the Inextinguishables and to protect Dsôn Faïmon, their beloved homeland.

Death came rushing in!
More forceful than the mightiest storm, more violent than an earthquake, as incandescent as a thousand fires, Death made his way to the älfar lines of defense.

Epocrypha of the Creating Spirit
Book of the Coming Death
30–50

Tark Draan (Girdlegard), to the southeast of
the Gray Mountains, Golden Plain,
4371ˢᵗ division of unendingness (5199ᵗʰ solar cycle),
late summer.

Morana had been ill at ease ever since first setting foot on elf territory. Now her agitation grew with every mile she covered across the
Golden Plain.

The idyll that surrounded her contrasted with the apprehension she
felt: swallows soared against the sky, one cornfield gave on to the next,
with the occasional deep green meadow for light relief, and scattered
about the landscape were towering trees with huge canopies, shedding
shadows as big as a whole village. Far away there were towns and isolated
farmsteads connected by excellent roads, so traveling was easy. She could
not read the signs at the crossroads; the elf runes were quite different
from älfar script.

Morana kept away from the settlements, not wanting to be confronted with questions about where she was from. She had been more
or less forced to travel by day in order to make reasonable time, and as
a result her eyes—as black as midnight lakes—would have immediately
aroused suspicion. She assumed the elves would remember their enemies' black eyes—even if the älfar had faded to rumor in their lands.

These roads will enable our army to advance very quickly. She decided
to take the eastern fork at the next crossroads, heading deeper into the
elf lands. She was becoming impatient: when was she going to reach
that crater? *Have I miscalculated?*

A town reared up close by. Too close for her liking.

Elves in white attire worked in the fields, gathering the harvest and
tossing corn on to long carts. The sound of threshing came from the
sheds by the mills on the riverbank. Elves who saw Morana passing
raised an arm in greeting.

The älf returned their friendly gestures with hatred in her heart, but
common sense prevented her from drawing her sword and bounding
past the corn to slay as many elves as possible. *The Plain of Gold? We'll be
calling it the Plain of Blood before long,* she vowed.

As the town had no protective wall, she studied its construction as she rode past. It was a strange way of building—senseless, really.

The elves had put all the buildings on stilts. All the houses, streets, and squares were a good four paces above ground level, but the earth was not swampy or particularly soft. *Is it a sign of their arrogance?* Morana looked at the river. *It must be prone to breaking its banks.*

She reined in for a moment, pulled out her record book and made a note to that effect, then continued on her journey. In planning their campaign they might have to contend with floodwater. This natural phenomenon was probably the cause of the fields being so fertile—but an army would come to grief.

She would have to find out what time of year these floods happened so that the nostàroi could take it into account, though she supposed it was most likely to be spring.

The elf houses were round, like tree stumps or mushrooms, and the walls were painted in soft pastels, with decorations and runes in green. Sun symbols were everywhere because the elves worshipped light. Another frequent emblem was a sign for the river: light blue wavy lines.

Morana gave herself a shake. *I look forward to burning down this insult to my eyes; then the river they love so much can carry the ashes away.*

She spurred her horse onward. It was a great relief to know that their enemies did not share their own aesthetic when it came to architecture.

But she should not have been surprised.

She knew many a legend that claimed to explain why the elves were so hated and it was always a question of the deception, treachery, greed and injustice that the älfar had suffered at the hands of the elves.

However, elves and älfar remained physically extremely similar. That was why the elves had to be eradicated, to avoid any further confusion.

You present yourselves to the barbarians as creatures of light, but we know your true nature, thought Morana. *The groundlings were no more deceived by you than we are, but humans are dazzled by you—they'll believe any nonsense you like to tell them. They'll soon see your true colors and how corrupt and devious you are.*

The road she was traveling led due east, passing fields and small groves.

Morana even saw some unicorns grazing at the edge of a wood. She smiled cruelly. *Our night-mares will get the benefit of new thoroughbred blood. It will improve the breed.*

Ever since she had seen the pit, she had had a growing suspicion that the elves in Tark Draan were pursuing their own secret plans. Perhaps it did not entail the conquest of the entire land and the subjugation of all the races living there, but they were following a higher purpose: something to do with their goddess Sitalia, for sure. What sacrifice would their goddess demand? *The death of every creature in Tark Draan, perhaps? It would explain why the elves have permitted the barbarians to breed like animals ready for the sacrifice. They are capable of anything.*

She came up to a crossroad that surprisingly offered only north and south options. She could make out the crater not too far off, but no path to it through the sparse grassland.

The pointy-ears don't want anyone to get there. She urged her horse on and they galloped across open country toward the hole.

The landscape changed and turned into steppe, but nothing was growing in the vicinity of the crater. Morana immediately felt more comfortable.

It's a sign! This region is not permeated by the obnoxious spirit of Sitalia and the elves.

She kept coming across weather-beaten signs, probably warning travelers to keep away. Morana found the aura of the crater was exercising a pleasant attraction.

Approaching the crater, she calculated the huge semi-circular hollow to be about 15,000 paces in diameter and 3,000 paces deep. The edges were black, as if burned. Something vast had crashed into the Golden Plain with tremendous force.

And Morana knew what it must have been . . .

One of our Creating Spirit's tears! She halted her night-mare and surveyed the scene, trying to find clues to affirm her idea.

She discovered a path leading down to the center of the crater and took it, noting the light-colored sand heaped in the center. It looked completely out of place, as if added in later.

The elves have attempted to fill the crater up. Morana dismounted, took out her notebook and pen, sat down at the edge and started to draw the scene, fascinated by what she had found.

This could be the kernel of a new älfar empire—a new Dsôn that our people will use as a base to rule over Tark Draan! When the nostàroi get my report and see my drawings they will want to conquer the Golden Plain first of all and get the Inextinguishables to erect a second palace here. Morana imagined the älfar city growing. *And they will look down on Tark Draan from their Tower of Bones and they will know that it was I that discovered the crater and told them about it. They will give me their blessing!*

She could neither stop sketching, nor stop letting her enthusiasm run away with her.

Tark Draan (Girdlegard), south of the Gray Mountains, 4371ˢᵗ division of unendingness (5199ᵗʰ solar cycle), late summer.

Carmondai felt no fear when he rode through Tark Draan on the evening of the third moment of unendingness. To start with he had followed the faint tracks of the barbarian girl, but now he was following his nose in a southwesterly direction, toward the place where the sun sank each evening.

He did not know why he let his horse go that way. He called it an instinct.

He had split from the älfar riders a while ago and now he looked like a genuine elf on his horse. *On a nice little outing to enjoy the fine weather. Although Caphalor won't appreciate me doing my own thing like this.*

Carmondai took the amulet out to look at. *Where will I find your owner?* Immediately he felt a tingling in his fingers and up along the wrist. "And what are you capable of, I wonder?"

He was not really surprised that the barbarian girl had managed to evade discovery for so long. Hidden in the Gray Mountains, she had miles of tunnels, mine shafts and caves to disappear into. Though it had emerged that the kingdom of the groundlings had not been as secure as the nostàroi had thought. And that represented danger for an encamped army.

Night was falling and the uneven path wound away toward a massive wall. Carmondai presumed it had been built to defend the town behind it; the residents must once have been accustomed to fighting off invasions.

All the better that I found it—I can take a closer look without arousing suspicion. And anyway, he was getting tired. He had been out in the open too long and really liked the idea of a proper bed. Even if it had to be a barbarian bed.

Carmondai reached the town gate. Light fell from two fire baskets and four torches fixed in place on the walls. Two men looked down from the top of the wall, obviously not expecting trouble. "Greetings," Carmondai called, raising his hand. "May I spend the night here? Though I'm afraid I don't know what your town is called."

"You are at the gates of Halmengard, elf," one of them replied. "Welcome, and keep the peace of our town, or we'll trim your ears faster than you can get back on your horse." His comrade laughed.

Carmondai was interested to note that elves were not treated with respect in this region of Tark Draan, but were issued with threats. "I swear to keep the peace. But why are you so uncivil?"

"Do you come from Gwandalur?"

"No, I am from the south."

"Then you are indeed welcome in our walls. May Sitalia be with you," the watchman responded with no resentment in his voice this time. One of the gates was flung wide and Carmondai rode in.

He did not inquire further, not wanting to show his ignorance and appear suspicious. But he made a mental note of the name Gwandalur. *The barbarians don't like the place. Excellent!*

Once inside the town he was struck by the robust and simple construction methods. The flat-roofed houses had no timber frame, and were built from large blocks of stone, as if each dwelling might have to be defended.

Another guard wearing simple, plated armor was waiting on the far side of the gate. His black beard was well kept, making him appear as though he was a relation of the groundlings. "You will be needing somewhere to stay," he said to Carmondai. "Your kind often stay at the Sun Inn. It's on the southern side. Take the first right then keep straight on. You'll recognize the sign."

Your kind. Carmondai suppressed a laugh. *If you only knew*! "My thanks." After a few paces he reined in his horse and turned around in the saddle. "Oh, and another thing, if I need a famula, where would I look?"

"A famula?" The barbarian considered before replying. "I've not seen one in town for ages. We don't have any links with Simin; his realm doesn't overlap much with Thapiaïn, so he doesn't come here and nor do his pupils."

"Thank you anyway." Carmondai took the recommended road, but then turned down an alleyway. The last thing he wanted was accommodation favored by his enemies.

He wandered about aimlessly until he came to a tavern that looked expensive. Two liveried servants waited at the door to greet guests.

Carmondai stopped here. "Greetings. Is the food good here? And the beds, are they comfortable?"

They grinned, taken aback. "We could hardly say anything else, sir," replied the smaller of the two. "It would be an honor for us—"

"I'm not from Gwandalur, of course, if you were worried about that," he continued boldly. He wanted to see how the barbarians would react.

"That is a pleasing circumstance, sir," the man replied. "The dragon worshippers are not welcome anywhere. But if you had been from there the guards would never have let you in."

"And why is that?"

"Our king is a third cousin of the Duke of Wallham."

"And?" prompted Carmondai.

"Sir, Wallham is on the border with Gwandalur," said the servant. "The dragon takes their cattle."

"Of course." Carmondai dismounted, lifting down his saddlebags, then handed the reins to the taller servant. "Show me in."

"Gladly, sir." The small one led the way and took him into a high-ceilinged room where a slim woman wearing a deep yellow dress was waiting at the entrance.

She bowed to the älf. "Welcome, sir. My name is Geralda and I will be delighted to show you our available rooms so you may make your choice. Perhaps you would like to take a bath to refresh yourself after your journey?"

Carmondai was pleased at the courteous reception. He was struck by the symmetry of her facial features and by the way she held herself. *She would do well in Dsôn*, he thought, *though veiled, and as a slave.* Her voice was pleasant, not too shrill like most barbarian women. "My choice is made," he said. "I will take your largest room and that bath."

"Yes, sir. Would you like company when you bathe, or would you prefer just the hot water and fragrant essences?"

The idea of a barbarian woman spoiling the good effect of the water by sitting in the tub with him was repugnant. He had to control his expression. "Just the bath," he responded, aware that his tone was unfriendly and disdainful. He did not care.

Geralda inclined her head. She had understood. She accompanied him up the stairs to the second floor, opening the door of a large chamber with a slim partition wall. "Here you are, sir. You have a lovely view of the marketplace." Her gaze fell on the pocket of his mantle.

Carmondai instinctively covered it with his hand. The amulet had slipped out on its chain. "You know this?"

"Of course, I recognize the seal of Jujulo the Jolly. His famuli carry it with them." She gave him a curious look. "But I did not think an elf would be studying with Jujulo."

"I'm not. The magus gave it to me as a souvenir," he lied, with an ingratiating smile. He put his saddlebags on the floor as if nothing had happened. "See to my bath, will you? I'd like to clean up."

Geralda bowed and left the room.

Carmondai sat down in a reasonably comfortable yellow and white upholstered armchair. He watched as serving girls came in with towels and a copper bathtub, into which they poured blossom essences and several buckets of hot and cold water. He thanked them. When they had all left he undressed and stepped into the sweet-smelling warm water.

Not bad at all. He closed his eyes, breathing in the scent. *Too flowery, but preferable to the smell of the road.*

He slipped down under the water for a short time before surfacing slowly. One thing was for sure: it was better than in the Gray Mountains.

He got out before the water could go cold and dried himself on the towels left out for him. They were not as soft as those in Dsôn because the barbarians did not use silk in their linen goods, but they would serve their purpose.

With one of the bath sheets around his middle he lay down on the bed to deliberate his next course of action. Traveling in Tark Draan was an adventure. He enjoyed meeting the people and knowing his own folk would soon be marching through to take over. *This is how the gods must feel when they visit their subjects in disguise. But if I stay away too long Caphalor will send out a search party. He won't want to lose me. Or my drawings.* He turned his head and looked at the saddlebags. The amulet caught his eye. He had hung it from a hook on one of the beams—and it had begun to glow.

Carmondai got up, walked over to the beam and examined the item of jewelry more closely. The sparkle was not a reflection of any light source within the room—the metal was glowing all by itself. *Why are you doing that?* He took it down, moving it around and watching what happened.

The amulet shimmered more intensely when he swung it toward the south.

So you are showing me a certain direction. Is that maybe where the famula girl you belong to might be? Is that what you are telling me? Carmondai dressed quickly, locked his chamber door and climbed out through the window. A nocturnal excursion over the flat roofs of Halmengard began.

He made his way forward in leaps and bounds. It was delightful to move so freely after that tediously slow ride and he enjoyed putting his stamina and agility to the test.

The amulet led him to a quarter of the town where the inhabitants were less well off. Here filthy water ran through the gutters, and the odor of urine and garbage forced Carmondai to breathe through his mouth. *Disgusting!*

As he leaped across the rooftops, he observed the town. It consisted of several small fortresses surrounded by solidly built houses, reinforcing his idea that they might regularly face invasion. *If we are to conquer this town we will have to be careful and clever.* Poisoning the well seemed a sensible option, as the stone houses would not be seriously damaged by fire.

The amulet was shining so brightly now that it served as a torch, but it was making him visible, too. He cupped it in his hand, checking it every so often to ascertain he was going the right way.

It took him a further splinter of unendingness to find the point where the effect was most intense. He looked up from the amulet to find he was standing on the stone roof of an old building. A trap door led to steps down into the house.

I wonder what I'll find. Carmondai lifted the hatch and climbed down, listening for sounds of occupation. He could hear a woman talking to a couple of men. He followed the voices and came to a door silhouetted against a bright light.

Holding his face against the wooden panel, he found he could see through a gap and into the room on the other side. *There she is!*

The young barbarian escapee was sitting at a rough table with two men in simple clothing; an elderly woman was flitting about the room in quite a state, bringing food and filling their wooden beakers with fresh wine.

Despite the stink emanating from the men, Carmondai picked up the scent of sweet soap. The young woman must have arrived in Halmengard shortly after him and in the meantime had either washed or taken a bath.

"And then?" asked one of the men. "Exactly what happened? Where did they come from?"

She's told them about us. Carmondai found it difficult to fathom why she was not yet in the office of the commander-in-chief: *perhaps she needs local support to gain admittance at court. How else would a simple girl get anyone to listen to her?* He licked his lips in anticipation. He was not too late.

"How should I know where they were from?" she snapped at them. "The dwarves have been defeated, I said!"

"I don't believe you," muttered the old woman, taking a seat. "They have always been there to protect us . . ."

"I bet they've made a pact with the monsters," one of the men hissed. "They've plundered the mountains till there's nothing left and now that there's no more gold and silver in their mines they're looking to steal ours!"

"It must be great to have as simple a mind as yours, Olfson," groaned the other man. "Did you not hear her say the dwarves have all been killed?"

The girl raised her arms, "Uncle Olfson, Uncle Drumann—don't start arguing. Just take me to the governor so I—"

"The king needs to hear about this, Famenia," the woman said. "And then we must send word to the whole of Girdlegard. They need to send an army—"

"Parilis!" Drumann called the woman to order. "Hold your tongue! You know Famenia was always cooking up wild stories like this when she was younger, trying to get attention."

Famenia leaned back in her seat, horrified. "You think I'm making this up?"

"Well," Drumann replied slowly. "I remember, from previous visits—"

"Shall I repeat what the dwarves told me before they sent me to warn Girdlegard?" Famenia stood up and crossed her arms furiously. "The orcs were chasing me through the Gray Mountain tunnels and I only just managed to escape."

Carmondai was listening carefully outside the door. He wanted to learn what the young famula had managed to piece together.

"Orcs!" Drumann laughed scornfully. "Do you know how rare they are here?"

Olfson slammed his fist onto the table. "They were from the other side, you idiot! There are plenty of them over there. And trolls. And ogres and—"

"Älfar," muttered Parilis to herself, tugging nervously at her apron. She was obviously frightened, much to Carmondai's satisfaction. His people's reputation was suitably terrifying. "Ye gods! If Samusin doesn't step in and help us we are lost!"

"It must have been älfar." Famenia took a deep breath. "They looked like normal elves—but in the sun their eyes were black! Black as the night and full of murderous intent." She shuddered and hugged herself in fear. "The dwarves sent me south as soon as they could after the attack so I could get away, but the monsters started swarming into the tunnels. I had to hide until there was an opportunity to escape. I am certain the dwarves were all killed. There are no fifthlings anymore." She gulped down her wine. "The tunnels are full of these fiendish monsters, preparing to invade us."

"But what are they waiting for?" objected Drumann. "If, as you say, they've killed off the dwarves, why haven't they marched in? It'd be harder for them come the winter."

What's your explanation for that? Carmondai would have liked to record what he could see and hear.

Three pairs of eyes were focused on Famenia.

"I . . . They are waiting for something. The dwarves said the creatures were being led by the älfar. The black-eyes will be deciding when to launch their campaign. And . . . the dwarves told me the monsters have a spirit with them," she reported in a quavering voice. "A thing of mist and cloud with lights and flashes and an uncanny radiance—"

"A spirit?" Drumann interrupted her again, laughing out loud. "A load of nonsense, your story."

Olfson frowned.

"But it's true, I say! Every single word!" The young girl had tears of frustration in her eyes. "If Magus Jujulo had not sent me to the dwarves with a message for their king we'd never have known about the danger that awaits us." She threw up her hands in despair. "You are my uncles! You should believe me and do everything you can—"

"To get Famenia an audience with the king!" concluded Parilis with determination. "Your uncles will do exactly that. They were both in the king's private guard for long enough to get themselves heard by their old comrades and their superior officers." She stroked Famenia's blond hair. "The king will listen to you!"

Famenia seized her hand and kissed it gratefully.

No, I don't think the king will ever hear you, little Famenia. Carmondai rubbed the eye he had been using to spy through the gap in the door.

Olfson jerked upright. He had come to a decision. "Someone must ride to the Gray Mountains and take a look!"

"No!" shrieked Famenia. "That's too dangerous. We must send an army!"

"She is one of Jujulo's famuli, she will be believed!" interjected Parilis, her expression full of concern.

"So why not go straight to Jujulo?" muttered Drumann. "A ruler would be more likely to listen to a magus rather than two ex-guardsmen nobody at court can remember."

"Because the älfar are following me and I need your help!" Famenia implored them. "I need the help of fighting men! And you were the nearest, and without my amulet—" She burst into tears.

Carmondai clamped his fist around the medallion. *It's nearer than you think.*

Apart from the girl's sobs the house was quiet. Parilis, Olfson and Drumann were staring at each other; finally Drumann dropped his eyes and stuck his hands in his jacket pockets.

Parilis lifted her head slowly. Her face was ash-gray. "The älfar followed you here?" she whispered tonelessly. "O Vraccas and Sitalia and Samusin, stand by us!"

"They lost my trail, I'm sure," said Famenia softly, wiping her eyes on her sleeve. "I took long diversions along stream-beds and no one saw me." She put an arm around her aunt's shoulder. "You'll be safe, don't worry."

I rather doubt that. Carmondai gave a satisfied smile. So far Famenia had only told her own family and they were not sure if they believed her. He felt a little uncertain about what was to come, but he was not reluctant to undertake it: he knew no pity. But he had to bear in mind that the men used to belong to the king's personal bodyguard.

It's quite some time since I last wielded a sword in earnest. Well, there was that bunch of óarcos, sure, but they were fairly drunk. The fact that nobody in the room had any weapons was in his favor, of course. *And anyway they are only barbarians.*

"Here's what we'll do. Let's get some rest now and we'll set off in the morning." Olfson got to his feet. "I'll warn the guards at the gate to be extra watchful in the next few nights."

Drumann stayed silent, but it was clear from his pursed lips that he still did not believe his niece. Olfson took his cap down from the hook on the wall and Parilis adjusted the collar of his shirt.

She's tidying him up for his death. Carmondai drew his short sword and used his native powers to subdue the lamps.

Twisting wreaths of darkness floated out and insinuated themselves through the gaps around the door as he concentrated on extinguishing the lights. The barbarians would not notice these fingers of black slowly approaching to snuff out the candles flames.

"What's wrong . . ." Parilis looked around in alarm.

"Must be those low-quality wicks they sold me." Drumann searched for a spill to light from the dying embers of the stove. Suddenly all the tiny flames went out. "What the . . . ?"

Darkness had overwhelmed the whole room.

He heard Parilis's sharp intake of breath. "By all the gods!" she squeaked. "My heart! It's going so fast!"

Carmondai put the amulet away and moved silently into the room.

His flat-soled boots made no sound on the floorboards. "You should have believed young Famenia," he whispered into Drumann's ear. "The famula was telling the truth." Carmondai slit the human's throat and then sprang across the room to Olfson while his first victim was still falling to the ground, gurgling and spouting streams of blood. Drumann's broad body convulsed, boot heels hammering on the wooden floor.

"Sitalia, come to my aid!" whimpered Parilis as she sank onto her knees and crawled into a corner, her arms held up to protect her head. "It's the älfar!"

"Famenia, run! Run!" Olfson picked up a chair and was about to whirl it blindly above his head.

"You stay here!" Carmondai aimed a kick and the chair back splintered, bits of wood flying to strike the young girl as she attempted to flee. She stumbled and fell. "Your death, barbarian, is called Carmondai," announced the älf as he slew Olfson with a swift strike to the heart. "It was Famenia that brought me to you." He dealt with Parilis as he strode past, his blade stabbing down behind the collarbone, slicing through arteries and entering the lung, so that she'd choke to death slowly on her own blood. "There's your own niece to thank for that," he said, as he withdrew the blade.

Famenia was groping her way to the door. He grabbed her fair hair and pulled her to her feet.

She screamed and struggled to get free but her flying fists were not powerful enough to have any effect on him.

He pressed the bloody blade up against her bare throat. "Do you realize your own importance, little barbarian? If you had gotten to the king and warned him, you would have ruined—" Carmondai felt a tug at his pocket. *The amulet! She's got it . . .*

A blaze of dazzling light blinded him and the pain in his eyes made him put an arm up to shield his face. He let Famenia go and hit out, punching her. She cried out.

There was a crackling sound and the smell of some unfamiliar gas, then a wave of heat struck him in the chest.

He was lifted into the air and hurled backward through the closed window, shattering the heavy pane of glass and the wooden shutters as he tumbled onto the street in a series of somersaults.

Magic . . . He was unable to move. Every inch of him hurt. Warm liquid ran out of his eye sockets and over his cheeks. It was as if his eyeballs were dissolving. It took him several attempts before he was able to struggle to his feet.

He touched his face gingerly. *My eyes are still there!* But he could see nothing at all. He was terrified he had lost his sight forever. How could he remain a master of word and image if that was the case? *Keep calm! I must get out of here before she can warn the guards on the gate.* He stumbled along the alley.

A strong wind plucked at his clothes before a loud bugle call sounded the alarm.

Carmondai heard doors opening and shutters being flung back, and a buzzing of excited voices out on the street. He squashed himself into a handy niche, enveloped in his own wreaths of darkness to avoid discovery. *Curse that wretched famula!*

His sight returned bit by bit. He could see fiery circles dancing in front of his eyes, but the relief he experienced was quite indescribable. Even he, in fact, was lost for words.

The townspeople stormed past him, some heavily armed, some only with knives or a stick. *They must think their settlement is facing immediate invasion.*

I've got to get out of Halmengard! I have to tell Caphalor that our plan has been discovered! He would not tell the nostàroi that his own attempt to stop the famula escaping had failed, otherwise it would be him bearing the brunt of Caphalor's anger instead of, say, Armatòn.

Jumping back up to roof height, he moved quickly back to the tavern to collect his precious saddlebags with their irreplaceable drawings and notes. He did not stop to collect his horse so that he could slip over the fortified walls and away. In a few moments he was back over the wall and on the road to the Gray Mountains.

The weather was unhelpful. After about half a mile a powerful storm blew up and flying branches forced him off the road to find shelter.

What this failure of his would mean for the whole campaign he could not bear to imagine. This particular chapter of the Tark Draan campaign was definitely not one to be written up.

While he lay in a hollow in the ground, desperate for the violent storm to pass, he consoled himself with the thought that the crack team of älfar scouts had not managed to capture Famenia, either. They had not even found her in the first place. *So the whole älfar invasion plan would have been foiled one way or another.*

But this personal fiasco burned in his soul like fire.

The night had passed and the sun was rising, but the storm had hardly abated at all; the wind was still howling through the trees and raised huge dust clouds that meant vision was restricted.

Now I understand why they've built their houses like little fortresses of stone. If you had a proper roof with shingles you'd be out replacing the tiles half the night with storms like this. Carmondai resolved to continue his journey, storm or no storm. Given the importance of the news, the barbarians would certainly be trying to get a messenger through to their king.

Carmondai bent double and ran along in the ditch beside the road. He had thought the ditches extraordinarily deep the previous day when he had seen them from the saddle. Now he could see why: running along them he had considerable protection from the wind and would be safe from the flying debris.

The wind did not die down until the afternoon.

Carmondai returned to the road and kept up steady progress at a run. That night he stole a horse from an isolated farm and raced it across the miles until they reached the gate into the Gray Mountains. Neither he nor the horse was granted the slightest rest.

The watch recognized him and let him in.

With a fresh horse that Armatòn gave him, he hurried through the groundling tunnels and reached the nostàroi's quarters five moments of unendingness after leaving Halmengard. Covered in dust and dirt and drenched in horse sweat, he barged his way into Caphalor's private tract of rooms to find him seated at supper and alone.

"I've seen her," said Carmondai, not bothering with social niceties. "She is riding south with a troop of armed men. People told me she was going to speak to her king to warn him about a black-eyed threat." *Please don't let him notice I'm lying through my teeth.*

Caphalor, wearing a simple black and red robe that did not in any way reflect his status as a nostàroi, calmly placed his knife and fork back on the edge of the plate and gestured to Carmondai to sit down. "You look tired and hungry." He called the servants to bring more food. "Please, tell me what has happened."

And Carmondai began to tell a mixture of fact and fiction: how he had pursued the magus's young pupil, how he had managed to locate her in Halmengard, but had not been able to approach her without running the risk of revealing himself, thereby confirming her story. He did not mention the amulet at all, nor his own miserable fighting performance. "She will be with their king very soon," he said.

Caphalor had been listening attentively, taking occasional sips of water. "Possibly. They will certainly be sending scouts to the Gray Mountains to check the validity of her story. However fine Durùston's replacement groundlings are, it won't be long before someone smells a rat and they realize the girl is telling the truth." He swirled the water slowly in his goblet and said nothing more.

Carmondai drank and stared at the delicacies on his plate, but he was not hungry. He was too apprehensive to eat. He poured himself some more water and raised the cup to his lips.

"How well do you know Sinthoras?" Caphalor said without warning.

Carmondai put down his goblet. "He's not exactly a friend of mine…"

Caphalor stared at him intently. "That's not what I meant. I want to know if you think you can get inside his head? Do you have a feel for how he moves, and the way he dresses? How he talks?"

"I could do a passable caricature if that's what you want. Why do you ask?"

Caphalor leaned back in his chair, his hands on the table in front of him. "I have to give the order to move off before winter gets here and before the barbarians gather their own army, or we'll be trapped in the groundlings' tunnels, but the army and the demon won't want to contemplate going into battle without both their nostàroi."

Carmondai understood. He felt queasy at the thought. "You're asking me to—"

Caphalor shook his head. "No, I'm not asking. I'm commanding. That way, if, *if* the deception is found out, you can tell the world later you were only following orders. The blame will be mine. But if you do your job well, nobody will ever know that Sinthoras wasn't around right from the very beginning of the campaign."

Carmondai reached out for some strong red wine, filling his drinking vessel to the brim and draining it at one go. *Why didn't I stay in Dsôn?*

"You are the only one I could trust with this. It's too important a secret," Caphalor went on. "If I don't march my troops into Tark Draan in the next few moments of unendingness, we endanger the whole undertaking. The enemy would have the entire winter to hatch a plan of action against us. The magi would be in on things and we'd lose any chance of putting them out of action."

"Nostàroi, I—"

Caphalor leaned forward. His eyes were icy and hard. "You don't have a choice, Carmondai: I am turning you into Sinthoras. Whether you like it or not."

CHAPTER VII

Before winter closed in, the nostàroi gave the order that the army had been so fervently longing to hear.

And a river of annihilation poured out over Tark Draan!
    The whole company of consolidated ugliness—óarcos, trolls and ogres—rolled off in front to strike fear into the hearts of the humans; the barbarian tribes from Ishím Voróo followed. Our own troops marched among the others and were everywhere at once, enforcing discipline. Small units of our warriors were disguised as elves and tricked their way into fortresses and towns, making their conquest in less than half a night.
    And so they ran and so they rode, toward the south, the east and the west.

    No settlement, no citadel could withstand their advance, for our scouts had done their work well and had warned the commanders about potential hazards. There were no secrets kept from the nostàroi, who stormed through Tark Draan conquering the land mile by mile in the name of the Inextinguishables.

The main älfar army arrived at the border of the realm where the Golden Plain elves lived.

    Revenge was close at hand!

Excerpt from the epic poem *The Heroes of Tark Draan*
composed by Carmondai, master of word and image

Ishím Voróo (Outer Lands), Dsôn Faïmon, Dsôn,
4371ˢᵗ division of unendingness (5199ᵗʰ solar cycle),
late summer.

Sinthoras got out of bed, leaving Timanris—who had fallen asleep following their extended bout of lovemaking—to rest. He had an appoint-
ment that was going to be far less romantic.

He dressed in the lobby and put on an inconspicuous mantle over his
simple suit of armor, taking care that the hood hid his features. *Nobody*
must recognize me.

Passing Timansor's collection of weapons, he noted a heavy club that
must have come from somewhere in Ishím Voróo. It had probably once
been wielded in the calloused hand of a stinking green-skinned óarco.

Exactly what I need. He took it out of the glass cabinet and concealed
it under the fabric of his mantle before leaving the house and heading
through the nocturnal streets. He crossed the marketplace and stopped
at the statue of Robonor.

The two watchmen looked at him, waiting nonchalantly as he
approached.

"Excuse me, could you tell me where I would find the artist that
made this? The statue is so . . ."

"The *artist?*" repeated the guard on the right. The two watchmen
exchanged glances. As they were doing so, Sinthoras made his move. He
kicked one of them on the chin, putting him out of action, and smashed
the other one on the helmet with his club, rendering him unconscious.

"You should have let me finish: the statue, I was going to say, is so humiliating, insulting and slanderous that I cannot put up with it any longer."

He shattered the onyx marble statue with violent blows, leaving only
the plinth behind. Taking the piece of red gold that had been used to
represent the wound, he hurried off.

He felt enormous relief. *That was probably not very sensible, but it*
needed to be done.

Of course, he already knew who had made the statue.

After a brisk walk he was standing in front of the artist's house and
pounding hard on the door until it was opened by a veiled slave.

"I am not expected, but that is of no importance." Before the slave could do anything, Sinthoras knocked her to the ground, slamming the door behind him. "Mistress!" he called, in what he wanted to sound like the slave's voice. "You have a visitor!"

"Who, by all the infamous ones, has the nerve to disturb me at this time of night?" Itáni shouted furiously from upstairs. "Get rid of them!"

"I will." *So that is where you are!* It was all Sinthoras needed to know. He glided up the steps and followed the sound of a hammer tapping the end of a chisel. He stopped in front of her studio, took a deep breath and stormed in without warning.

Itáni swirled around with her sculptor's tools in her hands. She had nearly finished a basalt statue of an älf whose face Sinthoras did not recognize. The stone she was sculpting from was supported by a wooden frame to prevent it from toppling. "What are you doing?" she yelled at him. "Who are you?"

Sinthoras brought out the metal wound that had originally been part of Robonor's statue and threw it at Itáni's feet. "That's all that's left of your statue," he said icily, throwing back his hood. "I am impressed by your work, but not by the lies that you are spreading. You have put your gift in the service of the wrong cause."

Itáni lowered her arms and stared at him. Fine black dust covered the light beige robe she wore. She wiped her face. "The nostàroi in person. What an honor that you should come and confess your ill-advised deed in this way. You can't be very bright if you've let yourself be carried away like that."

"Polòtain gave you the commission; it's down to him that your statue no longer exists."

She nodded. "That's what he thought, too. That's why he commissioned four further copies." She laughed at him. "Oh, you should see your face, Nostàroi! You had no idea whom you have made an enemy out of. I assume you have heard the rumors?"

Sinthoras experienced a surge of anger that brought jagged black lines of fury to his face. "Then it's high time to show those friends how dangerous it is to antagonize me," he said in a threatening whisper, lifting the club. "No one will connect me with this weapon, and no one knows that I have come back to Dsôn," he murmured as his hatred intensified—an emotion that really should have had Polòtain as its target. *I'll deal with him next. Death by means of a crude óarco cudgel will be suitably shaming for him.*

Itáni's confidence drained away. She edged away. "You wouldn't dare," she said quietly, feeling for the whistle that hung around her neck.

"Oh yes, I dare." Sinthoras leaped forward, swinging the club straight at the middle of her body.

She sidestepped and the club crashed against the basalt, breaking off part of the statue she had been working on. She shrieked as if the damage had been to her.

Sinthoras whirled around and struck again, missing her once more. She stumbled over the block of basalt and lost her balance, falling onto the dusty floor.

The next second Sinthoras was standing over her, his right foot on her throat to keep her from screaming. "Let your art decide. Your own creation shall be your judge." With his left hand he swept the wooden supports aside, grabbed the statue and pushed with all his might. "I wonder if your art will let you live?"

The block of stone started to tilt and then overbalanced. Just before the statue hit the ground, Sinthoras pulled his foot away from her throat. The stone crashed onto the upper body of the sculptress, breaking her ribs and crushing the inner organs.

Itáni uttered a stifled cry as a gush of blood spurted out of her mouth.

"So, Polòtain's friends have not helped you much, have they?" he mocked. "Your death bears the name Sinthoras. And it comes because you accepted Polòtain's commission." He twirled the sharp-edged metal wound from Robonor's statue in his hand, then jabbed it into her neck. Her eyes clouded over and her gaze broke. Her soul departed into endingness. *That's what you get for your trouble.*

Shocked voices and hurried footsteps sounded in the corridor. Her household servants were nearing the studio. They would know immediately that a murder had been committed. The weapon sticking out of Itáni's throat was a clear enough message.

No other artist will dare work for Polòtain after this. In order that there should not be the slightest doubt about how serious he was, he shattered her beautiful face with a swift blow from his club.

Then he put his hood up over his blond hair and escaped through the window.

He hurried through the streets with a broad grin on his face. His hate had transformed itself into a state of euphoria: Robonor's statue and its creator had both been eliminated.

But Sinthoras had not completed his revenge.

When he reached Polòtain's house he slowed down and concealed himself in a niche in the wall, watching the two guards at the gate.

His immediate instinct had been to smash Polòtain's brain with his cudgel, but he was having second thoughts. *That would cause too much commotion.* The two armed älfar on the gate would not be the only ones he would have to contend with. For the sake of his own safety he would have to act more cautiously than he had done with Itáni. *I will content myself with something symbolic. A really clear sign.*

Sinthoras slipped out of the niche and ran along in the shadow, club raised for action as he neared the watchmen.

His attack took the two dozing älfar completely by surprise. The first clout felled one of the guards and left him groaning on the ground.

The second älfar raised his shield to ward off a blow, but the impact smashed the iron-reinforced wood and the guard crumpled to the floor. A kick to the skull quickly saw him lose consciousness.

That was easy. Polòtain's people are useless. Using the spikes on the cudgel he scratched the word SLANDERER into the gate and under it he wrote YOU WILL GET YOUR JUST DESERTS, AS EVERY LIAR WILL.

I want Polòtain quaking in his boots, terrified for his life. He hurled the bloody club, which still had Itáni's hair and bits of Robonor's statue sticking to it, over the wall and heard it land in the courtyard.

He sped away, making tracks for Timansor's family home.

Satisfied with his achievements, he stole into the house by the back door, took off his mantle and went up to Timanris's chamber.

To his surprise he saw light under the door; she must have woken up.

Curses! A thousand thoughts burst into his mind; foremost was the fear that his recent exploits would be discovered.

After running his fingers through his blond hair to tousle it, he undressed and entered the bedroom, acting astonished to see her sitting up. "Oh! I'm sorry! Did I wake you when I got up?" he said, pretending to be sleepy.

"No. A messenger from Tark Draan woke me," she replied, looking at him inquisitively. "It was some time ago, but the messenger couldn't find you anywhere in the house." The question this posed lay unasked in the air, along with suspicion and silent reproach.

A messenger from Tark Draan? What could that be about? Sinthoras put on a cheerful expression. "I was hungry and I went to the kitchen in search of something sweet. I looked in the pantry as well." He grinned and came over to give her a kiss. "He and I must have kept missing each other. The curse of being able to move silently." He stroked her hair. "Do I still taste of the honey gingernuts?"

Timanris's scowl softened. She put her arms around him and kissed him on the mouth. "No," she said, disappointedly. "You might have brought me some."

That was close. "So, who is this messenger?"

"Caphalor sent him." Timanris released him. "Go and find him. He's in the servants' kitchen. He looked pretty impatient."

There's something afoot in the Gray Mountains, thought Sinthoras, beginning to be very worried. He left the room swiftly, dressed quickly and hurried downstairs where he found the messenger at table.

"Nostàroi! Greetings," he said, getting to his feet. "I have a letter for you that Caphalor handed to me himself." He drew out a leather wallet wrapped in waxed paper. "I was told to give it to you personally, not to anyone else."

Sinthoras sat down, broke open the seal and unfolded the letter, recognizing his friend's handwriting on the parchment. He read the summons to return immediately to the Gray Mountains. The demon, it said, and the rest of the allies, were becoming restless. Winter was fast approaching and the window for a successful sortie into Tark Draan was closing fast. The letter ended: "Give Timanris my best regards, but she is to send you on your way without delay. After a quarter of a division of unendingness you can return triumphant, and she can greet you as a victorious hero in Dsôn."

I've only just got here and I'll have to leave! Sinthoras turned to the messenger. "What else did Caphalor say?"

"He said not to let you write an answer—I have to bring you back with me, Nostàroi."

Sinthoras passed the leather folder back, but tossed the parchment into the stove where it quickly caught fire and disintegrated. "Tell Caphalor that something important came up. I've got to stay and sort it out," he commanded. "It concerns something that could endanger our official function and our reputations as nostàroi. I am sure he will understand that I cannot return to the army yet, though I shall be as quick as I can." He got to his feet. "Finish your meal and get some rest. You should leave at dawn. But remember that you have not seen me here in Dsôn if anyone asks. Nobody except Caphalor is allowed to know."

"Of course, Nostàroi," the älf responded, bowing. "I swear it on my life."

Sinthoras left the kitchen and returned to Timanris. He explained quickly that Caphalor had summoned him back to the Gray Mountains.

"Shouldn't you go at once? The longer you stay here the more likely it is that someone will recognize you," she urged. "If that happened it would put you in a bad light."

Sinthoras was deep in thought. He had wanted to see Polòtain's reaction and he was eager to spend more time with his beloved. *But she is right. If anyone should recognize me, I'm bound to be suspected of Itáni's murder.* He kissed Timanris fondly on the neck. "How wise you are. I'll leave tomorrow night. That way I can spend the whole day with you." He patted the bed. "Right here."

Timanris laughed.

These delightful plans were not to be.

First thing in the morning a servant came in to wake them both and ask them to meet with Timansor.

That does not sound good.

They came down to find Timansor furiously angry—black lines crisscrossing his face in a series of scars. He was wearing a wide white mantle with black embroidery over his night attire. He had clearly not lost not a splinter of unendingness in summoning them. "How dare you abuse our trust in this way?" he snarled at Sinthoras.

"Father, he wanted to see me—" Timanris began. But her father silenced her with a look.

"There was only one reason for his coming to Dsôn," he bellowed, pointing at Sinthoras. "To get his revenge for the humiliation that Polòtain has subjected him to. He needed somewhere safe to stay where he would not be betrayed, so he came crawling to you! He killed Itáni! Beat her to death as if she were scum. Then he went to Polòtain's house and scrawled a warning on the gate so everyone would know what to expect if they speak up against him!"

"But, Father, he was with me all night," Timanris said indignantly. "What makes you think it was him?"

Sinthoras closed his eyes for the space of two heartbeats and upbraided himself for his hot temper. *I should have left it at just destroying the statue.*

Timansor glared at Sinthoras. "Because she was killed with a club whose description matches one that I had in my collection."

"There are plenty of other clubs that look just the same, surely," Timanris tried again to placate her father.

"*ONE I HAD*, do you hear?" he thundered at his daughter. She jumped back in shock. "When I heard about the deed I checked my weapons collection. That one is missing. Somebody took it and went out hunting. And don't tell me it was one of the slaves! Don't you dare lie to your own father just because your heart tells you to."

I can't watch her suffer like this. Sinthoras opened his mouth to reply.

"No, Father, I took it," said Timanris, visibly shaking. "It needed cleaning. Some of the iron had gone rusty so I took it a smith in Ocizûr. He's supposed to be very good."

Timansor stared at his daughter, taken aback. "You?"

"It was meant to be a surprise, Father." Timanris cast her eyes down. "It won't be one now, but I can't listen to you accuse the älf I love of this."

Sinthoras covered his own astonishment with a smile. "So I'm not the murder suspect anymore, I gather?"

It was obvious that Timansor was working hard to take this all in. He did not want to say his daughter was lying, but he certainly could not believe her. "Send a slave to collect it before this smith manages to mislay it," he said quietly, shaking his head in disbelief. Without looking at either of them he left the room.

The door had hardly closed behind her father when Timanris whirled around to face Sinthoras. "You made me lie!" she whispered. "And you lied to me! You were never in the kitchen like you said. What my father says is true!"

"I . . ." Sinthoras did not know what to say. He felt bad for deceiving Timanris while she had defended him so courageously.

"I knew we didn't have any more honey gingernuts. We ran out yesterday," she said frostily. "If you're going to be dishonest, then at least check your facts so your lies sound credible." She flashed her eyes. "Not another word! Get on your night-mare and get out of Dsôn! It's best if we don't see each other for a time." Timanris walked past him and shook off his hand when he tried to catch her arm. "No, Sinthoras. Go off and do your heroic deeds in Tark Draan. You haven't managed any here." She left the room, closing the door quietly to show her deep disappointment.

I did the right thing, Sinthoras thought defiantly. *It may not have been a heroic deed, but it was essential to stop the slander.*

As she had advised him, he prepared for his departure and left the premises as soon as he could. He did not travel with Caphalor's messenger. He did not want company.

He rode through Dsôn at a comfortable speed and could not resist crossing the marketplace.

The scattered debris of the statue was being collected up by a group of slaves.

What are they doing? Curiosity made him ride over, his face hidden in a scarf, to speak to them. "Oh, I see. The Polòtain family has some sad work to do. What's to happen to the damaged hero?"

"The statue's to stay where it is," said one of the slaves, without looking at him directly. "We have been told to put all the broken pieces up on the plinth and to leave them there."

"Why?"

"Our master said there would not be any clearer accusation of the nostàroi. It says a statue can be destroyed, but the truth cannot."

I should have killed the old man yesterday! Sinthoras urged the nightmare to a wild gallop and they swept through the city. *He is too wily a customer to be allowed to stay alive.* He wanted to deal with Polòtain once and for all.

But there was an army waiting for him and they had to get the invasion underway before winter. Without the nostàroi, their own troops and the allies might not even march.

But that doesn't mean Polòtain is safe from me. My arm is long enough to reach Dsôn from the Gray Mountains. Sinthoras was thinking of his personal guards—particularly of Morana, a tried and tested fighter. *I will send her and have the troublemaker killed.*

He was convinced the young älf would not refuse to carry out his commission. *The favor of a nostàroi is worth a great deal—she will know that. Everything she could wish for if she kills the old man for me!*

Sinthoras bought two dozen bottles of good wine from a merchant in town and then headed southeast, to get to the Gray Mountains as quickly as possible.

He left the city as he had entered it—incognito. Riding swift as an arrow through the älfar realm, he reached the same defense outpost he had passed on his previous ride.

The watch on the island fortress were delighted with his gift and promised anew they would keep his secret.

Sinthoras exchanged mounts, taking the benàmoi's fresh night-mare; he was about to cross over to Ishím Voróo when the commander stopped him: "Before you go to the Gray Mountains, can you tell us about these new stories, Nostàroi? They say the dorón ashont have emerged again in the northwest?"

"The dorón ashont?" Sinthoras could tell the question was serious, but he had only heard tell of these creatures in the old legends. They had been defeated for all time, as far as he knew—eradicated. There was only one explanation: *Polòtain's associates must be spreading rumors to make the public frightened! Is this part of his plan to get the älfar to mistrust me? Is there nothing he would not stoop to? I must send Morana off to Dsôn to finish him off. Or Arviû could do it, perhaps?*

"No, this is the first I've heard," he answered. "The dorón ashont are just legend. Forget it! Go back to your men—enjoy the wine, all of you; you have earned it with your loyalty."

Sinthoras galloped over the bridge.

*Tark Draan (Girdlegard), to the south east of the
Gray Mountains, the Golden Plain,
4371ˢᵗ division of unendingness (5199ᵗʰ solar cycle),
late summer.*

Morana placed one page after another down in front of Caphalor. She was showing him the sketches and descriptions of the crater she had discovered. She was so excited; he could hardly read quick enough. "I'm sorry my drawings aren't very good, but I swear by all that's infamous that this location is even more splendid and impressive in reality, Nostàroi."

He took in the content of the pages, focusing on every detail.

They had been conferring in his tent for half a moment of unendingness. He had listened carefully to her report, only interrupting to ask the occasional question.

Morana had not been surprised to see the älfar army marching out into Tark Draan—it was high time they began their campaign, but she did wonder why Sinthoras had not been taking part in the briefing sessions. He had not been at the meeting where the commanders were given their orders and he was not here now. She had been told he had some unspecified malady. *What on earth can it be?*

Caphalor laid the last drawing to one side. "You have found one of the places where the Creator Spirit's tears fell," he said, his voice shaking with emotion. "This is a sign, Morana! A sign that our victory over the elves is nigh! The goddess placed her mark in the earth and the elves have been powerless against her might: they have not been able to fill the crater or reduce the aura. The tear has suffused the ground with Inàste's divinity!" He leaped to his feet and grabbed her by the shoulders. "I can't thank you enough for your courage in daring to explore the place! I knew you were the right choice. That *you* were the one!"

Morana recognized the desire in his eyes. The älf was apparently more than interested in her. In her: a simple warrior, not even from a noble family! *I wasn't mistaken; he liked me from the very start!* She was surprised to find this made her feel nervous. "Nostàroi, I thank you for your praise, but I was only following orders. Any one of your scouts could have completed the task—"

"But it was *you* I sent, because you had caught my eye," he interrupted her. "You among all the others." He realized she might be misinterpreting his words. He released his hold and stepped back. "I meant—"

"I know what you meant," she said with a smile. *Is it him making my heart beat so fast?* Her uncertainty remained. She knew what had happened to his life-partner and that he must have loved her dearly. They had been together longer than any other älfar couple she knew of. *Perhaps his emotions are still confused?* But she couldn't deny the warm wave of pleasure she felt when she looked at him. *Don't get your hopes up. He probably sees Enoïla when he looks at you. He wants a substitute for her, not a new partner.* This meeting was about the Tark Draan campaign and the elves and nothing else. That was why they were both wearing armor rather than sumptuous robes, as if for some social or intimate event.

"Good." He looked more at ease now as he pushed back his long black hair. "Tomorrow I'll give the army the order to march on the elf realm and advance to the crater. We'll raze every single settlement we pass to the ground."

"And when we get to the crater?"

"We offer the elves a target. They will try to drive us out and stop us establishing ourselves there." Caphalor moved the sketches to one side and brought the plan of Tark Draan to the fore. Half of the territory had been carefully mapped out, but there were large blank areas on the other half. The scouts who were covering that area were still on reconnaissance.

"We shall force them to send their army against us. We will choose the battlefield location—one that gives us all the advantages."

Morana perused the figures he had written down.

The list with the heading Marching Orders mentioned around 100,000 barbarians from various tribes, 20,000 Kraggash óarcos, 40,000 óarcos, 4,000 gnomes, 5,000 ogres, 7,000 half-trolls, and 70,000 miscellaneous creatures. Finally, there were 30,000 älfar warriors.

Then the figures had been amended: the army had lost a tenth of its fighting force. Members of their own race had not been affected: the älfar had ensured that it was the other creatures in the army that saw the brunt of the action at the Stone Gateway, thus protecting their own. The barbarians had not suffered too greatly, either, because they had had the óarcos in front of them. The other creatures had heavier losses, but none so bad as to be alarming.

"That's a lot of soldiers," commented Morana.

"It looks that way at first view. I had to split them into smaller units so that we could make quicker progress. 10,000 of our own warriors will be leading these units and keeping them in check where necessary."

Morana leaned forward, took a measuring rule and indicated a point to the north of the crater. "Correct me if I'm wrong, but it looks like we've got 20,000 älfar warriors to attack the Golden Plain?"

"Half of them are archers with a range of a thousand paces, more with a following wind," he added, going on to ask her eagerly: "What would you suggest?"

She circled a small area with the end of the ruler. "There's a small valley here. It looks as if it could be defended against an advancing army without incurring great losses, but with a little preparation . . ." She sensed that Caphalor was staring at her in surprise. *Was I too bold?*

"It sounds as if you know about strategy?"

"I . . . I like to play Tharc with my brothers. It trains my mind." Morana put the wooden rule back down on the table. "Forgive me. I went too far."

He smiled kindly. "No, you didn't! I am glad that you are using your brain. I know the game, but I must admit I was never very good at it." Caphalor placed a hand on her shoulder. "You are just what I need." He left his hand there. "The valley. Good. Explain. Tell me how you would handle it."

"It depends on where the elves gather. We have to pretend we really want them—" She stopped. "Have you not got any trained strategists for this?"

He nodded.

All right. If that's the way of it. Morana drew a deep breath and explained her plan. When she had finished she looked up at Caphalor.

"I am impressed. You have obviously got the territory clearly in mind. You must know it as well as the elves do."

"Better, I think," she said, smiling with relief and satisfaction.

"I have taken on board what you have told me and I'll discuss it all with the strategic advisers the Inextinguishables have placed at my disposal. I mean at our disposal: Sinthoras and myself." He bent and kissed her on the forehead. "For now, you have my thanks. You will receive further rewards later."

"Th-Thank you," she stuttered. *He has feelings for me?* She quickly drained her cup of water with its dash of thujona syrup. *How can I be sure?*

He walked up and down the room, one hand on the pommel of the sword that hung by his side. "As I said: I am very pleased with you."

"Thank you, Nostàroi."

"It would be a waste to send you into battle." He looked at the map. "I want you to head south. Use any trick that occurs to you. Let no one know you are an älf for the duration of the journey. Then, make the barbarians in the south worried—convince them that the elves are their sworn enemies and that we are the ones to save them!" He walked up to her and, with the fingertips of his right hand, touched her cheek. "Find all those who can be talked into joining our army."

"A pact with the scum of Tark Draan?"

"Only on the face of it, Morana. We'll invite them to join us so that we can get to know them properly; it will be all the simpler to destroy them later on. We'll put them in the front line every time we go into battle. They can act as targets for the enemy's arrows. That's what allies are for, after all. At some stage we'll run out of óarcos and gnomes: Tark

Draan's residents will be substitutes for them." His face displayed a malicious grin. "You can always entice a barbarian to do what you want if you offer them gold and land. Promise them riches and they won't fight against us, but go into battle on our behalf." Caphalor touched her dark hair. "I know you'll be successful and I know I can rely on you."

"Of course you can, Nostàroi." She bowed her head. *If he's sending me away, then he can't be interested in me after all. Is that a good thing or not?* "Well, maybe I should get ready to leave."

"Tomorrow is soon enough." He stared intently into her blue-gray eyes. "Would you care to eat with me this evening, Morana? It would be in recognition of your achievements. And I have a gift for you from Virssagòn. Before he left he told me you had given him an idea for a new weapon. He said you'd be able to work out how best to use it."

The invitation to dinner came as somewhat of a shock. "If you will excuse me, Nostàroi, I think it is important I be fully rested for tomorrow's mission, but I am grateful that you have honored—"

"I shall expect you after the benàmoi briefing," he continued, ignoring her objection. "I am sure you will enjoy the meal. It will be a welcome change from the barbarian food you'll be putting up with again soon." He moved to the tent flap and held it open for her. "Until this evening."

I really don't understand. It's impossible to read him. She walked slowly past him and avoided his gaze. She was not sure whether she should be looking forward to the coming evening or not.

Morana headed for the nostàroi's quarters. *My heart is thudding again!*

A servant had come to tell her that the briefing session was over and that Caphalor was waiting for her.

She had secretly been hoping to get out of the dinner invitation. There was no way of knowing what was about to happen within the canvas walls of the tent—and what the consequences might be.

She felt nervous and indecisive.

She had not known how to dress for the occasion. As a member of the nostàroi's personal guard, she could have worn her armor, but Caphalor had emphasized that he was inviting her to join him for a meal, so she thought the uniform would be out of place. Instead, she had selected a long, dark leather dress topped by a deep red bodice. The corsage was decorated with bones set with tionium, between which hung delicate silver chains. She had tied back her black hair and darkened her eyelids with charcoal—she had wanted to keep things simple so as not to give the wrong impression.

What impression do I actually want to make? There was no question in her mind: Morana found Caphalor attractive. But there was something about him that disturbed her.

If he had not been the nostàroi she would certainly have been happy to indulge in a dalliance, but any subordinate who went in for such an arrangement would end up the loser.

It might work until Caphalor finds someone else and then drops me, but the whole of Dsôn would be laughing at me then. Morana sighed and approached the tent hesitantly. *I should have left straightaway. It was stupid of me to agree to come tonight.*

Passing the armed guards, warriors from her own unit, she picked up their unmistakable disapproval and envy.

And then she was standing in front of Caphalor, who had been waiting for her, dressed in a fine black robe. "Good evening, Nostàroi," she said, starting to bow.

But he came up to her and held her arm. "No, don't bow. I'm not your commander tonight," he said gently. "I am Caphalor. Caphalor pure and simple."

It's as I thought! She nodded. "The food smells good."

He laughed. "Yes, the cooks have made something special for us tonight: something you can get in the finest inns back home, but not here in Tark Draan." He stepped aside, letting her see the table.

A veritable banquet of Dsôn delicacies had been prepared. Several different wines stood ready in their jeweled carafes at the head of the table and two goblets had already been filled. There was a casket by the side of her place.

"I told them not to bring the dishes one after another, but to serve everything at once," she heard him say. He was so close to her that she could smell the scent he used: it was heavy and spiced. "I thought it would be better if we were not disturbed."

Of course. I should have known. Morana sat down. "It's nice and quiet; I'm still feeling shaken up after my ride through Tark Draan." Waiting until Caphalor was seated and had served himself, Morana chose some food and started to eat.

"The box is from Virssagòn," he said, indicating the box to her right. "Don't forget to take it with you. He's very keen to know what you think of his new invention. He calls it Sun and Moon."

She wondered what the weapon master had thought up. She ate in silence; the food was wonderful. It tasted of home. She started to hope she would be able to go soon, before . . .

"Do you know what I miss?" said Caphalor wistfully, as he cut the meat on his plate and added gravy.

"Your bed, perhaps?" she joked, afraid of hearing something she did not want to be told; something that would lead to complications.

"Somebody to share my problems with," he said, before he took the next mouthful, chewing carefully and then swallowing before going on. "Take our briefing session just now: I had to listen to the benàmoi telling me that the óarcos and the gnomes are doing whatever they feel like. Some of them are heading off without waiting for orders: the trolls want to go east; there's some mountain range they've heard of they've taken a liking to. The ogres are apparently complaining they won't get the chance to win sufficient land for their needs. And the barbarians from Ishím Voróo are making a fuss about the way we're treating the barbarians in Tark Draan!" As the list grew longer, his voice got louder and louder until he slammed his fist down on the table, making the plates jump. "This is war and the allies are whining and fussing as if we were on some little outing! The only ones conducting themselves properly are our own warriors."

"Does Sinthoras not help you?"

"Sinthoras?" Caphalor gave a bitter laugh. "He keeps to his bed and leaves it all up to me—commanding the chaos that calls itself our army." He hurled his knife and fork onto the table and drained his goblet. He seemed to be looking straight through Morana. "I could talk about absolutely anything with *her*," he whispered. "*She* always had time to listen and knew how to advise me—she would always come up with some idea, some way out." He shut his eyes.

Morana looked at him, uncertain of what to say or do. *Grief is eating him up.* She was torn between sympathy for him and caution. Finally she stood up, walked over to him and put her hands on his shoulders.

Caphalor seized her hands as if he were a drowning man. "I am so glad you are there," he whispered. "I need someone to confide in." He tilted his head to one side, resting his cheek on her hand. A sigh of relief escaped him. "Someone to be close to . . ."

"I know how much it hurts when you lose someone you love, but I am not her," said Morana gently.

Caphalor stiffened. "You think you know how much it hurts?"

"Yes. My brother—"

He gave a contemptuous laugh and raised his head. He grasped her hands hard, hurting her wrists. "You have never been near the depths of despair I have known!" He released his hold and leaped to his feet, staring at her as if she had been at fault—as if she were guilty of murdering his life companion.

I should never have come. Morana avoided his eyes. "Caphalor, I was only trying—"

"You have absolutely no idea!" he roared. "No idea what it is like! No idea what has died in me! No idea what I want!" He turned abruptly, grabbed a carafe of wine and put it to his mouth, drinking greedily. Then he blurted out: "Every single moment of unendingness I long for death, but it has refused to find me: not in battle and not when I tried to starve myself. That's when I rode out to Tark Draan, the land that was responsible for what happened to her. But even here death avoids me. I am not granted any victory that might lessen my pain. The army is advancing mile after mile but the torture never ceases. It never stops burning and burning!" He threw the carafe down and it shattered. "And you have the nerve to say you know how it feels?"

My instincts were right. Morana decided to leave. "Forgive me, I must—"

He strode over to where she was and kissed her violently on the mouth. Violently, but without warmth.

She pulled free and pushed him away so that he staggered against the table. "No, Caphalor! It's not me you want—you want your companion back!"

He was about to reply, but clapped his hands over his face. "What am I doing?" he muttered again and again.

I must not stay a splinter longer! Morana picked up the box, turned and left the tent, hurrying past the guards who were obviously at a loss to understand what was going on. They had been on the point of entering the tent. "He's not well," she told them. "Perhaps it's the same thing Sinthoras is suffering from."

She flew back to her quarters and packed the things she would need for the mission, stuffing Virssagòn's new weapon into her bags without looking at it. *Time enough for that later.* She threw off her dress and put on her armor.

She hurried along to the stables, where she saddled one of the barbarian horses.

It doesn't matter what I feel for him, I cannot give in to his advances. Not as long as he carries the image of a dead love in his soul.

Morana swung herself up into the saddle and galloped out of the camp, ignoring shouts from one of the guards.

Morana did not want to be given any message. She did not want to hear from the nostàroi and she did not want to hear from Caphalor. From now on she would concentrate purely on her task: to win over barbarian monarchs as allies for their cause.

Chapter VIII

All eyes were fixed on the northeast, where the dorón ashont were assembling.

> *But there was a far greater danger in Dsôn Faïmon.*
> *In Dsôn itself, the Black Heart.*
> *Unrecognized but in the very midst of the älfar.*
> *Unrecognized and yet made welcome.*
> *Unrecognized but given everything it needed to live.*

The danger grew and gave birth to new danger.

Epocrypha of the Creating Spirit
Book of the Coming Death
50–72

Tark Draan (Girdlegard), to the southeast of the
Gray Mountains, the Golden Plain,
4371st division of unendingness (5199th solar cycle),
early autumn.

"How do you feel?"

Carmondai could hear Caphalor's voice through the helmet surprisingly well. He had forgotten what it was like to wear the head protection and the heavy armor. He was not wearing it to make himself feel safer but because, in the eyes of the troops, it turned him into Sinthoras. He gripped his night-mare's reins tighter in his gauntleted hands. "All right so far."

The nostàroi laughed quietly. "Try sitting up straighter. Sinthoras loves everyone to see him. He likes to be admired."

"But remember, I'm apparently still suffering from the mysterious sickness. Wasn't that what we agreed?" But Carmondai went ahead and adjusted his posture in the saddle.

"That's why I'm suggesting you stay toward the rear, giving support to the flank with your presence until we have closed our trap around the elves."

Carmondai longed to open his folder and start drawing, but it would look very strange if the nostàroi were seen fooling around with paper and pencil. He turned his head and took in all the visual impressions so that he could use the images after the battle.

Caphalor was wearing armor that was almost identical to his own and only slightly less ornate than his ceremonial attire. The regular älfar troops eschewed heavy protective gear, preferring to rely on freedom of movement and their particular advantages: their agility and the range and strength of their longbows. They wore a simple leather body covering and a helmet and carried a small shield: very few of them even had arm and leg protectors.

The army advanced north at a brisk pace, heading away from the crater. A number of riders bringing up the rear dragged shrubs behind them to increase the cloud of dust their progress stirred up. It was important the enemy should see them coming.

"I wonder how the elves will react?" said Caphalor, not sounding as if he had any doubt as to the outcome of the battle.

Carmondai could smell the earth that was disturbed by their passage, mixed with the smell of the night-mares' sweat and the soft fragrance of the flowers of the Golden Plain. *War and beauty.* The nostàroi had explained his plan: Carmondai's contribution was to sit on his night-mare and stay away from the fighting, inspiring the soldiers with his presence. He was not to intervene and not to give any orders as the benàmoi had been given their instructions already. "What happens if the elves don't do what you have predicted? Won't the warriors near me expect me to give orders?".

"Everything will happen exactly as I have told you."

"You've fought the elves so often that you know how they work?" Carmondai smiled under his helmet. "I am helpless with respect."

"Just do exactly what we've discussed and raise the morale of the troops," Caphalor said curtly. "Make the most of being the focus of admiration and keep your comments to yourself."

"It won't be me they'll be admiring, but Sinthoras."

"You will experience the honor on his behalf." Caphalor readied Sardaî to move off. "Keep to the plan, and remember that you are Sinthoras when you are wearing this armor," he reminded Carmondai. The nostàroi turned and rode off toward the rear guard.

Ye gods of infamy, let me live through the fighting! Carmondai was reassured to know that ten of the Goldsteel troops were by his side, but he knew that in every battle there were unknowns even the sharpest mind could not cater for. Especially given that they were confronting an enemy who had not been tackled for many divisions of unending-ness. *An eternity.* Carmondai did not know of a single älf who had ever fought against the elves.

He was amazed at how confident Caphalor appeared—and how sure he was that glorious victory would be theirs.

Carmondai surveyed his surroundings.

There were around 8,000 älfar cavalry nearby split into equal-sized units. In each of these units there were both archers and warriors trained in close combat, plus a few spear-carriers. The vanguard consisted of around 4,000 älfar and the troops bringing up the rear numbered an unusually strong contingent of around 8,000 älfar.

They had no allied troops along with them, not even to employ as arrow-fodder: it was vital that the victory over the elves should be an undiluted älfar triumph. Caphalor had rebuffed the idea that they might incur unacceptable casualties in their own lines.

Carmondai faced the front.

The valley they were riding through had low hills with sharp rocks on both sides and was gradually getting narrower. Enemy archers could find excellent cover anywhere along the route.

I sincerely hope Caphalor knows what he's doing, or we'll be riding straight into a perfect trap.

A loud horn signal sounded: the enemy had been spotted.

Carmondai's detachment galloped to catch up to the front: the rear guard had their orders and fell back accordingly. They would be taking no part in the action: those 8,000 warriors would be sorely missed when the armies clashed.

When he rounded the corner he saw the elf army waiting for them at the narrowest point of the valley. There was no way around them. Their lines were less than 200 paces apart.

By all the infamous gods!

It was a surprise to see that the elves had heavy cavalry at their disposal. Their lances were significantly longer than the ones the älfar bore and both elves and horses were armored. Long banners of many colors waved in the breeze, swirling in the air and looping around each other.

Nobody mentioned the cavalry when we had that briefing! Carmondai distinctly remembered hearing that the elves fought in a similar way to the älfar. *Perhaps the strategy advisers have overlooked the fact that we are on a plain.* It was obvious that an army in territory such as this would have adopted different fighting tactics, employing heavy lance-bearing troops.

Carmondai tried to calculate how many troops they were facing. He reckoned the enemy had almost equal numbers to their own. *They'll mow us down if we're not careful!*

The enemy horsemen formed a solid block about 500 soldiers wide and there were sixteen rows behind the first line. Then Carmondai saw the infantry behind them: a broad wedge at the exit to the valley with subdivisions of light cavalry in between.

So the elves definitely had the upper hand as far as numbers were concerned and the älfar troops bringing up the rear would not be able to attack directly because of the way the valley narrowed.

Carmondai slowed his breathing inside his helmet. *They've done exactly what Caphalor said was impossible: behaved contrary to our expectations.* He was extremely concerned. It was as if he had been sent back in time to a period he had long forgotten about.

Even before the last of their own troops had moved into the valley, they could hear the fanfares being sounded by the foe. The armored cavalry of the elves rode steadily forward to reduce the gap between themselves and the älfar front line.

The älfar took up the formation they had previously agreed on: a row going from one side of the valley to the other with a spear-carrier next to each archer. But anybody with half a brain could see that a long, thin line of soldiers was not the best tactic when faced with a solid block of the enemy. Behind this line the rest of the archers had taken up positions, ready to shower the enemy with arrow-fire.

Carmondai realized that the enemy infantry was keeping out of the range of älfar archers. *The elves are leaving the decision-making up to the heavy cavalry. They must have total confidence in them.*

The sound of thundering hooves grew louder: the elf cavalry were increasing the speed of their attack while still 1,000 paces away. They began to come in range of the älfar longbow archers.

He remembered a verse of poetry:

> *If sword blades glint in the sunlight*
> *and banners wave in the north wind's breath*
> *The timid one covers his eyes with his hand,*
> *terrified of certain death.*
> *The slaughter and pain that will come before night*
> *Will give no quarter and have no end . . .*

Nobody could have predicted this! Arviû stared at the lines of elf cavalry. The army of the Inextinguishables did not have comparable units, but he did not doubt that his finely trained and well-equipped archers would be able to shoot the enemy out of their saddles.

He turned to his benàmoi. "Tell our archers to use the simple, long three-faced arrow tips. They should be just right for piercing armor." His command was passed down the line.

We have chosen the wrong tactics. Arviû was not deceiving himself on that score: a thin line of troops was not going to offer much resistance to the impact of a block of iron and armored horse. He could see exactly what the enemy had in mind. *They've got the right idea: they're attacking me and my archers to eliminate the long-distance weaponry. Then they will follow through with their infantry and the light cavalry.*

He looked over to Sinthoras, motionless on his night-mare. *He will presumably have worked this out for himself?* The nostàroi's visor was closed, so Arviû could not see what he was looking at. Caphalor was farther up the line and would not be able to see what was happening here.

Arviû was not afraid. He was aware of what would happen if heavy cavalry charged his lightly clad troops. *It would be like crushing icicles with a sledgehammer.*

He reached for his bow, which was three paces in length. Its asymmetric form meant he could fire from the saddle. He used his tongue to moisten the flight feathers. "Fly and bring death in my name," he murmured as he signaled to the archers to make ready.

The nostàroi's command to fire must be imminent. If not, Arviû would lose many fine soldiers, even before battle had actually commenced.

Carmondai could see around half of the elf light cavalry breaking out from the ranks of the infantry and charging over the plain. They quickly covered the distance between them and the heavy cavalry and raised their bows. *They are providing fire cover to their own fighters!*

The benàmoi were just giving the order to loose the älfar arrows when the first enemy missiles hit the front line. At the same time the elf heavy cavalry riders lifted their shields to protect themselves from the älfar arrows. The elves were as efficient with their long-distance weapons as any älfar fighters.

This isn't going to work! Carmondai envisaged the cavalry charge mowing a wide path through their ranks, winning the vital advantage; any conventional maneuvers on the part of the älfar were doomed to failure. *They are concentrating on putting our archers out of action.*

Wounded soldiers were tumbling out of the saddle in front of him, night-mares collapsed bellowing to the ground, kicking wildly about them on the trampled grass.

> *When endingness pursues you*
> *and comes knocking at your heart,*
> *warrior, show death you disdain it*
> *and fear nothing, for your part*

Their älfar archers had responded to the hail of arrows, but were having far less effect on the ranks of the foe than the elves were on them. The armored enemy troops had taken a stand, protected by their shields. Only a small number of elves had fallen.

The elf light cavalry unit came to an abrupt halt, sending another veritable shower of missiles toward the älfar before turning and removing themselves from danger. They had fulfilled their task.

The number of injured and dead among their own älfar people was great, but their warriors were steadfast in keeping their position.

Barbarians would have turned and fled.

Carmondai calculated: another 500 paces and their cavalry will have reached our lines.

Arviû roared out his orders to the troops to prevent chaos from breaking out.

He could feel tension in the air. The nostàroi had still not changed the tactic that was proving utterly unsuitable: the armored riders were charging and would be breaking through their lines exactly where Arviû and his archers were standing. All of them saw disaster approaching fast, and there was no escape.

I shall lose half my troops! At least half! What angered him most was that their arrows were having virtually no effect on the enemy. Their arrows would have pierced the elves' armor satisfactorily, but were useless against the heavy metal-clad shields that absorbed most of the impact.

If the nostàroi doesn't act soon, I will! Arviû ordered his archers to speed up their volleys of arrows, hoping for chance hits. *It was as if the elves had known*, he thought, *exactly what to expect from the älfar longbows.*

All Arviû's battle senses were on high alert.

He danced his night-mare to the side just as two arrows flew past him.

I'll show you how to do things properly. He could see that one of the elves was not holding his shield at the right angle, leaving a tiny gap.

Raising his longbow he notched an arrow, aimed and sent feathered death winging its way through the air.

His arrow flew toward the elves, slid past the edge of the shield and buried itself into flesh through the warrior's shoulder protection. The sudden pain caused the elf to drop his arm a little—quick as a flash Arviû aimed a second arrow through the visor now visible behind the shield and his adversary fell sideways and then back out of view.

That makes one less elf to trouble us. "Watch out!" he yelled, finishing off two further enemy archers. "Don't let up. Shower them with your arrows. You'll need to kill every single one of them if you want to survive!"

Arviû glanced over at Sinthoras again; the nostàroi was still as a statue. *What, in the name of all the infamous ones is the matter with him? How can he just sit there and watch us die?*

Soldier, draw your sword! Raise high your trusty shield
In this fiercest of all fights
Laugh at the threat of death in the field
And your deeds will be honored and your name will shine
In the most glorious of lights

It was becoming impossible for Carmondai to remain aloof. Arviû's fleeting expression had been challenging and full of unspoken accusation. *I am Sinthoras and I shall act like Sinthoras! I don't care about Caphalor's warning.*

He gave the order to break up the line and form a semicircle. "Spear-carriers! Dismount and get to the center, shoulder to shoulder," he called to the bugler who relayed his signal with a blast of notes. "Leave no gaps!"

He sent the mounted close combat soldiers over to the flanks and arranged fire cover, then split up the line of valuable and unprotected archers, hoping to avoid the elves dispatching all of them in one go when their armored troops charged through. He ordered that the riderless night-mares be pushed toward the elves to cause maximum mayhem. *With any luck the animals might be able to break open the elf formation.*

Idea after idea shot into Carmondai's mind and he issued a torrent of commands. "The spear-carriers must resist the onslaught. Tell them to ram the ends of their spears deep into the ground and place one foot against the shaft! I want to see the elf cavalry stuck in a forest of spears!" He urged his steed forward while the troops around him seethed in a hectic dance, taking up their new positions. "Archers, start firing! Stop this plague of elves!"

The sound of approaching hooves almost drowned his words. The elf-riders thundered inexorably closer.

200 paces.

The modified älfar formation meant that the elves were caught in crossfire. Because the angle of attack had changed, more of the arrows were hitting home.

Excellent! The breach in the enemy lines widened at the point the rampaging night-mares were stampeding toward, forcing the elves to scatter.

"Nostàroi!" said one of the bodyguards, indicating the far end of the valley. "They're sending reinforcements!"

The elves' light cavalry was on the move.

"They are afraid of taking too many casualties in the first wave," muttered Carmondai. "They want to make a second push to seal their victory."

There were two elves on each of the horses—they had each taken up a member of the infantry division to get them to the front more swiftly. A good 2,000 were held in reserve at the mouth of the valley.

This is going to get tricky. Carmondai thought quickly about how to counter this new onslaught. If he concentrated firepower on the new wave, he would not be able to continue to reduce the numbers already at the front, and that would have serious consequences for the älfar army.

But there was Caphalor on the left, up on the ridge with the rear-guard soldiers! They had ridden around the valley and worked their way up through difficult terrain in order to attack the elves from the side.

The elf heavy cavalry took more hits from Caphalor's archers—but it was not holding them up.

"Resist at all costs!" shouted Carmondai, readying his troops for the oncoming storm. "Resist or die!"

At that point, the leader of the advancing cavalry charge did the right thing: fifty paces before reaching the first älf he ordered his weakened unit to swerve to the left to avoid the forest of spears.

The elves were now running parallel to and below the ridge.

That's going to make it harder for Caphalor's archers to hit the riders, Carmondai cursed the elf general.

Disaster was on them: the armored cavalry, long lances lowered, broke through the älfar left flank like a battering ram.

With the sound of crashing metal, smashing spears, the whinnying of horses and night-mares and the screams of injured warriors, the noise level was ear-splitting.

It was the sound of war.

"Keep the . . ." Arviû's joyful voice died away.

His longbow archers had finally been making headway, but then the elves had made a sudden turn and swerved to the left—coming directly at him.

At their speed fifty paces was no distance at all. Before he could give the order to retreat, the elves were charging into their ranks, lances at the ready.

"Short bows! Short bows!" Arviû tossed his precious longbow to one side and grabbed the smaller version, but the elves were too close for him to put enough power behind the shots. He still managed to bring down four of them.

The murderous pressure imposed on the älfar ranks reached Arviû and he was forced backward along with his mount, like a piece of driftwood on a raging torrent. He could not control the direction he was going in, but attempted to keep firing. He took his feet out of the stirrups and pulled his legs clear of the crush.

The elf cavalry was unstoppable and eager to avenge their fallen comrades. They charged deeper and deeper into the left flank and had discarded their lances in favor of swords. With precise strikes from the elves, countless älfar were dispatched into endingness.

"Back in formation! You must—" A heavily armored elf appeared in front of Arviû. In his right hand he carried a shield and in the left the remains of his lance that he was using like a cudgel. The elf's polished, gold-colored breastplate reflected the sunlight and blinded Arviû momentarily.

Arviû leaped from his night-mare and landed on the empty, bloodstained saddle of another. He slipped on the blood and lost his balance, then, as he tried to leap again to avoid the fall, a broken spear shaft hit him full in the face.

Time slowed down for him.

He heard wood shattering, splintering into a thousand tiny pieces. The fragments buried themselves in the flesh of the right-hand side of his face. Needle-prick followed needle-prick. The pain increased immeasurably as the splinters pierced deep into his face.

By all the infamous ones! His whole body followed the movement of his head, turning likewise. As he sank backward he saw and heard everything with tremendous clarity: the sounds of the raging battle; weapons sliding through flesh or clanging against armor, bones fracturing, leather tearing, the groans of wounded soldiers. He perceived every detail but was totally unable to change what was happening. His mind and his body had parted company.

What is happening to me?

Then he saw the rest of the lance falling toward him. However hard Arviû tried to raise his hands to protect himself, his arms hung useless by his sides.

No!

"Spear-carriers advance! Right flank: use fire-arrows," yelled Carmondai as he dashed forward. He would have given anything to be able to raise the visor; he was not getting enough air and the heat was unbearable. "Hold them off and kill them all!"

He could not see what the elf reinforcements were up to at all, but he had to deal with the heavy cavalry first, before they could do any further damage.

Carmondai raced over to the left flank like an älf possessed. He heard enthusiastic shouts as he charged past his troops, his sword in the air. "For the Inextinguishables!"

He was in a kind of trance; his identity from his previous life had surfaced and taken control of his actions.

He could smell blood; he urged his night-mare to jump right into the opposing cavalry advance. Dispensing sword blows on all sides he sent half a dozen elves to die under the pounding hooves.

Fire-arrows from his own side whizzed past his head, terrifying the horses with the smoke and flames. The animals shied and backed off, creating havoc with the enemy formation.

Exactly as I intended. "Down with the elf plague!" Carmondai was tireless in his attack. Enemy blood sprayed his face and entered through the slit in his visor, blinding him momentarily.

When he could see clearly once more, the enemy heavy cavalry was in total disarray and on the retreat. *We have fought them off!* A loud laugh echoed in the helmet. *They'll be riding straight into their own reinforcements! Utter confusion!*

And so it happened: the converging elf ranks could not take avoiding action and were falling under a hail of arrows from the intact right flank of älfar. Complete mayhem ensued.

"Nostàroi! Caphalor's mounted troops are finishing off the last of the enemy at the mouth of the valley." A member of his personal guard, his armor slashed and bloodied, had ridden up to make this breathless report.

Carmondai very nearly lifted the visor on his helmet to get some air. He would always have done so in the old days after a battle. His arm and shoulder were painful after all the blows he had dealt out with his sword. "Tell the right flank to pursue the enemy. We will grind them down between us!" He had to rest his head against the neck of his night-mare. *I could do with something for my thirst!*

"Nostàroi!" He heard an angry cry: "Some of the elves are getting away!" He turned his mount and looked toward the southwest.

Nearly 1,000 of the heavy cavalry had charged through a narrow breach in the älfar flank, fleeing from the hopeless butchery. They were heading away and out of sight around a curve.

"After them, Nostàroi?"

Carmondai shook his head. "No. We must ensure we beat the main army. Our left flank is too weakened to be able to defeat them. There will be time enough afterward to send fresh troops after them." He turned back to the battle, where the elves were currently hemmed in on two sides.

Contrary to the old tactics of allowing the opposition a chance to retreat, the älfar now closed up any gap in their own ranks and the elves found themselves caught between two halves of the älfar army.

It is decided. Carmondai thrust his sword back into its sheath; sweat cascaded down his face. When he thought no one was looking he raised the visor carefully and took a draft from his water bottle. The unaccustomed exertion was getting to him.

He had done enough in the present moment of unendingness to gar-ner praise—for someone else. *To compound the misery, of course, it's me that's got to write it all up.* A joyless laugh escaped his lips. *Sinthoras, you owe me!*

Toward sunset, the battle in the little valley was over and done with. The älfar took no prisoners.

Caphalor and Carmondai rode over the enemy corpses, letting their night-mares take gouts of flesh from the cold bodies. Wherever they appeared among their troops, the names of Caphalor and Sinthoras were cheered.

"You fought well. One more little stone in the mosaic of our heroic portrait," said Caphalor so quietly that only Carmondai would hear him. "We'll get those who escaped soon enough."

"I fought brilliantly," Carmondai corrected him proudly. *I shall have to draw all this! All these impressions are still so fresh and just asking to be recorded!* "Better than Sinthoras would have."

Caphalor gave an almost imperceptible nod of agreement. "However, until the very end of unendingness, only you and I will ever know who was responsible for this overwhelming victory." He held out his hand. "You have won my respect and my admiration in the battle today. This will remain forever and you shall have the benefit, as long as I live."

Carmondai shook the proffered hand and felt immediately elated.

He enjoyed hearing the enthusiastic soldiers call out to them both; the sweet taste of victory was his to share. And he wanted to continue contributing to their triumphs. *As far as I'm concerned, Sinthoras can stay in Dsôn.*

"Nostàroi!" An injured archer came up to them. "Come quickly! It's Arviû."

Ishim Voróo (Outer Lands), Dsôn Faïmon, Dsôn, 4371st division of unendingness (5199 solar cycle), late summer.

Arganaï passed swiftly through the streets of Dsôn with a companion on each side. They had been sent by Demenion to collect the brave young warrior who had brought news of the dorón ashont—and given warning about a surprise attack.

I feel awful. Arganaï had to stop and lean against a wall to recover. "Give me a moment," he stuttered, fighting the sickness. He was suffering from the after effects of drinking a concoction the healer had prescribed. His broken thumb had become badly infected: the cost of escape had been amputation of his left arm at the elbow. There would have been little to gain, they decided, by a flesh exchange, and the operation would have been too risky.

"I'll be all right now." He spat, the bitter inti-herb taste on his tongue. They'd given him so many doses of it it seemed to Arganaï that his body was leaking the stuff. "Right, let's get on." He rubbed his brow—it was damp with sweat. His vision clouded and he was not sure where he was. *I am nowhere near recovered yet.*

At last they reached the entrance to Demenion's house. His companions handed him over to one of the serfs.

He was led through the premises, but his vision was clouded and he only got vague impressions of the opulence his host lived in. *I should have stayed at home.*

A door was opened and bright light shone out, hurting his eyes. An älf spoke a greeting to him.

"Thank you, Demenion, for inviting me," he replied, deciding it would be better not to risk bowing and maybe throwing up on his host's shoes. "Please excuse my appearance; my wound is still causing a lot of discomfort. The infection has spread and I'm feverish."

"What are they giving you for it?" Demenion sounded concerned.

"An inti-herb infusion."

"Oh, I've got something that's better. Remind me to give it to you before you go home. If I give it to you now you'll fall asleep, and we need to hear what you have to say."

Arganaï nodded. This was the eleventh invitation he'd had from influential Dsôn families since his return. He had more or less been forced to accept them all. You could not turn these people down if you wanted to avoid any trouble. However, the more he told his story the better known his name became, so his chances for promotion had suddenly risen. Demenion was also a leading light of the Comets faction and their influence had grown with Sinthoras's rise to power. Arganaï had been told he might get a chance to speak to the Inextinguishables.

"You'll have to make allowances if I need to take a few breaks."

"But of course, my guests will understand."

Arganaï was led into another room. He could smell of a mixture of perfumes and hear soft music. The murmured conversations died away as the guests realized he had arrived. His host introduced him to the company so that he could make his report to them.

It feels like I'm here for their edification, not to simply report the facts. Everyone in Dsôn and the radial arms has heard the news by now, anyway. He felt like some artist who people were being polite to, but who was not really being taken seriously. He felt their eyes on him. They must be looking at the stump of his arm.

Without any particular enthusiasm he recounted his story again. He had told it so often now that he did not really have to concentrate on choosing his words.

No one dared interrupt him, and when he had finished, there was applause.

A fresh wave of nausea hit him. "Forgive me if I leave now," he apologized, "but I have this fever—"

"We will let you go, of course. Our best wishes for your recovery," said Demenion, who appeared at his side. "But perhaps you would be good enough to answer a few questions first, if my guests have any?"

Arganaï was aware this was no request. "I'll do my best," he said weakly.

"So you are absolutely sure that they were dorón ashont?" someone asked. The voice was female. "Couldn't they have been half-giants or young ogres or some other monster of that type?"

"I am absolutely certain." He left it at that. *I don't care whether or not she believes me, just as long as the Inextinguishables do.*

"Do you think they can cross the defense canal on their rafts?" a worried-sounding male älf asked.

Arganaï felt his stomach protesting again and had to clamp his jaws together to stop himself from vomiting. His skin was prickling and his belly was making strange noises. "They are huge creatures," he answered quickly, noting that his breath smelled sour. That medical drink had really turned his insides upside down. "But they'd have to cross the open space first, and that would bring them in range of the catapults. I don't think they present a real danger to us." He swayed. "I really have to go, Demenion," he whispered. "I am as weak as an aged barbarian. The wound—" His knees started to give way under him.

Two of the älfar sprang to his side and held him upright, taking him outside while the applause echoed behind him.

"My thanks," said Demenion, who escorted him to the door. "This has been a very successful evening, thanks to you. I shall put in a good word for you if the opportunity arises. You should climb the career ladder quickly." He patted him on the shoulder and disappeared back to his guests.

Outside on the street Arganaï fought for breath.

The fresh air helped a little. He was still being supported but he was starting to feel a little more confident and his vision was beginning to clear. "Thank you," he said to his companions, who nodded at him encouragingly. Pride won through. "I'll be fine on my own."

"You sure?" one of them said, pressing a small vial into his hand. "Demenion said to give you this. Should help with the nausea. Take a couple of small swigs in the morning."

"Thank you, I'm sure." Arganaï moved off, his legs stiff. He wandered through the streets looking at the buildings. If you lived in this part of town you had to show you could afford to and the owners had not held back their creative flare.

The least influential inhabitants only had intricate decorations in precious metals, or murals—where the conquest of Tark Draan was a popular motif. Some house fronts had been completely renovated and already included the downfall of the dorón ashont. Paintings representing älfar enemies incorporated preserved parts of dead bodies. It made for a fascinating mix of culture. There were comparatively few outright sculptures or any abstract forms. Tastes would probably change again in the near future.

Looking at the architecture gave Arganaï something to concentrate on other than his nausea. Even his arm stump had stopped throbbing. He was not aware of these improvements at first, but by the time he had reached his quarters, he was feeling better than he had for a long time.

He found a dozen älfar guards in the room, snoozing in preparation for the early shift.

He got undressed, hung his clothes on the hook by the bed and lay down on the mattress. He took out the vial and looked at it. *But the pain has gone! Do I need it?*

Arganaï did not yet know what would become of him. He would not be able to go on guard duty with only one arm. He was too young to train other warriors and there was no question of taking up an occupation in the weapons store or in administration. Art was not his thing, either, and he did not enjoy speechifying. He did not see himself as anything other than a warrior.

What am I going to do for the rest of unendingness? He stared at his stump. *I'm a fighter and I'm going to drill and practice until I can hold my own with any two-armed warrior!*

It suddenly occurred to him that he could have an artificial limb made. A substitute arm, perhaps in the shape of a weapon . . .

Why didn't I think of that before? This idea improved his general mood tremendously. He took a couple of careful sips of the potion Demenion had sent him to speed up the healing process. Closing his eyes, he waited for sleep. *I'm going to be one of the best soldiers in Dsôn!*

A hot stab of pain went through his belly and his skin suddenly felt as if it had been whipped with red-hot wire.

Arganaï shot upright on his bed and tried to shout—but there was a hard, dry lump blocking his throat. He thought he was suffocating and grabbed at his throat with both hands. It was as hard as iron.

Help! He thought in desperation, looking at his sleeping comrades, but they noticed nothing. He was about to climb out of bed, but his legs had stopped working.

Everything was burning. Enormous pressure built up within his body; his head felt close to exploding.

With a strangled cry Arganaï fell back onto the bed.

CHAPTER IX

My words are as arrows
flying straight and true:
hurting, wounding, killing

My words are as balm
to wounds of the soul:
curing, mending, healing.

My words are as death itself.
My words are as life itself.
For they are
my own words.

Excerpt from the epic poem *The Heroes of Tark Draan*
composed by Carmondai, master of word and image

*Ishím Voróo (Outer Lands), Dsôn Faïmon, between
the radial arms Wèlèron and Avaris,
4371ˢᵗ division of unendingness, (5199ᵗʰ solar cycle),
early autumn.*

Autumn had come to Dsôn. The dark gray leaves of the native black beeches drifted onto the surface of the defense canal, forming small islets that floated serenely this way and that.

On the lateral lookout tower of island fortress one-eight-seven, Téndalor stood watching as nature had its way. It was a pleasant sight that had a calming effect on his soul and gave him the opportunity to let his thoughts wander.

On the other side of the water lay Ishím Voróo. Somewhere to the northwest of the region the dorón ashont waited. The älfar empire expected their attack, but none had come as yet.

I'd never have guessed we'd see their like again. Téndalor would have liked to send out scouts to see what the dorón ashont were up to, but he had been given strict orders to do nothing: the Inextinguishables did not want to tempt fate or provoke the enemy. Instead, the empire put its faith in its defense catapults and the effectiveness of the cleared exclusion zone on the far side of the canal. No enemy crossing that area would escape the hail of arrows, spears, burning missiles and stones that would rain down on them.

Téndalor drew out his dagger and worked on the complex rune he had been scratching in the hard stone of the battlements. It symbolized protection from danger and was, of course, strictly forbidden. Translated, it was something like: *In the protecting hands of Fadhasi.*

Téndalor had come across the Fadhasi cult many divisions of unendingness previously, in the depths of Ishím Voróo. The folk that used to worship Fadhasi were long gone, destroyed by the älfar.

Téndalor had been intrigued by the idea of praying to a god who had only one follower—himself. He used the tip of his knife to chisel away at the grooves of the rune. *A god of my very own. Don't you go letting me down, Fadhasi!*

A horn blast from the Dsôn Faïmon side of the water made him turn his head. *This will be our supplies.*

He gave his soldiers the command to lower the bridge on the city side so that the carts could deliver their freight to the island. The stores included arrows, spears and spares for the catapults in case repairs were needed.

Téndalor blew the dust away from his rune symbol, put his knife back in its sheath and hurried down the tower steps to check over the consignment.

He was not concerned about the quality generally, but something might have gotten damaged en route and he did not want any faulty equipment. If they suddenly had to mend an item in the middle of an attack and opened up a crate to find a load of junk, they'd be in real trouble.

His men were already busy unloading when he got down to the small courtyard. "Let's get these lids off, then."

The soldiers opened the crates and checked the contents carefully. It looked as if everything was in good order, so they packed it all away again tidily. Every square inch of space was required for storing ammunition and space was always at a premium on the island. The news of a possible invasion had only made things worse in that respect.

"What a waste," muttered the female cart driver, not helping at all.

"What do you mean? What's being wasted?" Téndalor looked at her in surprise. He knew she was called Ilinia. She had made deliveries to them before.

"It's a waste of my time." She leaned against the wheel with a frustrated expression. "I earn my money taking cereal crops from the big farms to Dsôn or to the mills." She nodded in the direction of the crates. "But instead I've got to do unpaid war work for the Inextinguishables. And nobody knows if there's really going to be an attack, anyway."

Téndalor raised his eyebrows. "Do you know what you are saying?"

"I do. And I don't mind repeating it."

"We're here to protect you, Ilinia! If the dorón ashont—"

She gave a scornful laugh. "The bogeymen from the nursery rhymes? I know the old myth about how the Inextinguishables tricked them with poisoned wine. All älfar children know the old story of the Towers that Walk, but show me one person who has actually seen them, Benàmoi!"

"An älf named Arganaï. We saved his life."

"He *says* he's seen them. But did you?" She came away from the cart and moved antagonistically toward him. "Did *you* see them?"

"No," he had to admit. "I haven't seen them myself."

"And have we had reports confirming the sightings?"

Téndalor clenched his jaw. "What are you trying to say?"

"I just find it strange, Benàmoi, that we are going along with the word of one single älf, and if we haven't sent a squadron out to verify his story, is it because the Inextinguishables aren't sure they believe him?"

He gestured toward her cart. "And why would they send you from one island fortress to the next with a load of arrows and spears if we weren't expecting an attack?"

Ilinia shrugged her shoulders. "How should I know what goes on in the minds of the Sibling Rulers? Perhaps they just want to make you *think* there's an invasion coming, so that you stay especially alert. We all know a whole obboona unit managed to get over into the empire. They won't want that happening again, will they?"

Téndalor did not want to agree openly. But he had been thinking it odd that he'd been told not to send any scouts out to investigate. *Maybe they don't really believe this Arganaï and they've just brought our supplies up to date with the aim of calming the fears of the populace.* "It's all one to me. I assume—"

There came a shout from the tower: "Benàmoi! There's a groundling on the other side of the water!"

Ilinia looked puzzled. "What do the groundlings think they're doing here?"

Téndalor hurried over to the passage, to make his way up the tower. "You should reconsider your opinion, I think, Ilinia!"

Swift as the southern wind, he raced up the steps to reach the viewing platform where two watchmen were waiting for him. "Are you both quite sure?" He looked over toward Ishím Voróo and did not have to wait for their answer. It was all too true.

On the other side of the river there was a solid little figure: a groundling, indeed, waving a huge white flag.

I don't get it. Téndalor was handed the spy tube. He observed the edge of the forest carefully through the polished lens. *Nothing there. He's come on his own.* "How long has he been there?"

"We saw him coming over the plain. At first we thought it was some small animal that had lost its way," one of the guards explained. "I wanted to let it get a bit closer so we could test out our catapults, but then we noticed we'd got it wrong. He had the flag over his shoulder and then he started waving it like crazy."

Téndalor put the spy-tube down. *My island fortress seems to be where it's all happening.* "He's obviously keen to negotiate. But what about?"

"The Stone Gateway?" suggested the second guard. "Or the other passes? They see themselves as the ones that protect the whole land, I've heard. Perhaps the groundlings have sent an envoy wanting to reach an agreement with the Sibling Rulers."

Téndalor thought that was unlikely, but he couldn't come up with a better idea. "Let's find out."

He turned and gave the order for a troop of twenty älfar to accompany him. He wasn't allowed to send a scout to Ishím Voróo, but if he stayed on the bridge he was not contravening his instructions. He arranged for the catapult team to stand ready. *I'm not afraid of one little groundling, but this looks suspicious to me.*

Téndalor ran down the steps and jumped on to his night-mare. The chains and pulleys creaked and clattered and clanked until the wooden drawbridge linking the island to Dsôn was shut; the watch had ignored Ilinia's furious protests. She was stuck on the island now.

"We're ready, Benàmoi!" called one of the soldiers.

Téndalor gave the order to lower the drawbridge over to Ishím Voróo. The heavy chains unrolled slowly until the wooden structure landed with a bump onto its anchor point on the other side of the water.

Téndalor rode over with his escort and approached the waiting groundling, who took a step forward onto the end of the bridge. Téndalor looked at his light armor and appraised the dwarf's weaponry: he had a crude, ugly knife at his side; the handle of an additional long sword was visible over his shoulder. He was not very much of a threat.

Téndalor had heard about the groundlings' fondness for beards, but this one had shaved his off. His head was bald, too. Then he realized his mistake. *They've sent us a female. They probably thought we wouldn't hurt her.*

She was certainly too big for a gâlran zhadar and not really built like one of them. Téndalor was quite pleased about that. Those notorious Ishím Voróo beings dabbled in the magic arts and always meant trouble.

Téndalor reined in his night-mare shortly before he reached the groundling. His beast could have taken a bite at her if so ordered, but she had an open face and was smiling. His escort surrounded him as well as they could, given the dimensions of the bridge. "Do you understand me?" he asked in the language of the barbarians.

"Yes," she replied happily, placing the end of the flagstaff on the floor. "Your accent is good."

"Then hear this, you insolent upstart: this is Dsôn Faïmon, the land of the älfar." Téndalor was trying to control the anger he felt at her disrespectful remark. "You can count your lucky stars that you are still alive. Normally we would have shot at anything seen on the cleared strip."

"That's what I thought," she said with a laugh. "I hoped you wouldn't and my god helped out a bit, too."

This little groundling doesn't lack courage. Even though she will die for it. "Tell me who you are and what you want from us, groundling!"

"I am Rîm and I'm an Ubari, an undergroundling." She pointed behind her without turning around. "My camp's on the other side. My husband sent me . . ." She thought for a bit and then blinked. "I don't know what the älfar call him."

Ubari? What on earth are they? Ridiculous name. "Call who?"

"My husband."

Téndalor had to laugh. *She is completely insane!* "I don't know him. And I don't care what his name is."

She shook her bald head a little. "I don't mean his name but the name you call his people. He's rather special—"

"I think you have lost your little mind." He turned his night-mare and ordered his escort back in to the fortress, calling out to her as he rode away. "Get off the bridge and go back to your husband. My catapults won't start firing at you until you are one and a half miles away, so the last 500 paces over to the forest should be exciting for you."

"One of your people has seen him, I know," came Rîm's high voice. "It was not so long ago. Near the abandoned cobold village. My husband is much taller and wider than you and wears heavy armor . . ."

Téndalor halted his mount and pulled the beast's head around, at which it protested loudly. "Are you speaking of a dorón ashont?"

"What does that mean?"

"Tower that Walks."

She chuckled. "He'd like that name, I'm sure. It shows respect." Rîm held tight to the handle of her flag. "I've come because he wanted me to bring you a proposal that might prevent the destruction of your race."

Téndalor opened his mouth, but his response was drowned out by the scornful laughter of his mounted escort. "Quiet!" he commanded, studying the ubari carefully. She was calm enough, and did not give any impression that she was afraid for her own life. And she was entirely serious. "How come your husband thinks he could defeat us?" He indicated the defense canal and the island fortresses. "Have a look. We will destroy his followers and him before they even get to the water's edge."

"Do you not want to hear his suggestion?" she asked innocently. "If you hear us, perhaps you will be celebrated one day as the savior of your people."

Téndalor rode toward her once more until his night-mare's head was close to her face. The animal bared its teeth and snorted expectantly. "State your terms, but don't be surprised if my people laugh at you again," he said.

Rîm did not move; she looked past the fiery red eyes of the night-mare and stared at its rider. "What the Inextinguishables did to my husband's kind has not been forgotten, but your actions had unforeseen consequences: the poisoned wine left only the strongest and healthiest alive. These and their descendants have come to exact revenge in the name of the queen. However, the queen will be satisfied if the Inextinguishables surrender to us so that they may be punished. If they don't, we shall destroy your whole empire."

Téndalor was lost for words. He could not even laugh. His escort had fallen silent as well. "You really are out of your mind," he said finally, staring hard at her. "How can you—?" It was impossible to find words to express his indignation. This proposal was absolutely unacceptable for both the Sibling Rulers and for every single älf in Dsôn Faïmon. "Take her," he ordered, turning his steed and thundering back over the drawbridge to the island.

His escort followed, driving the ubari in front of them. She still looked quite unconcerned. She probably thought she was being taken to the Inextinguishables.

They all rode back into the fortress. The bridge was raised again and the way out to Ishím Voróo was blocked once more.

"Bring her over here!" Téndalor dismounted and went over to one of the catapults.

Rîm followed him, her white flag over her shoulder. "This isn't the palace. You are not taking me to your leaders?"

"No, and you won't be seeing them." He gave the order to remove the heavy boulder suspended from the catapult arm. "But I'll help you get back to your husband." The soldiers grabbed her and managed to place her in the net despite her violent struggles. Téndalor came up close to her. "If you survive this, I have a message for your husband: tell him that we will fight anew, but this time we won't leave any survivors."

"You're trying to intimidate me, aren't you?" She was still confident, still sure she would be released any second now. "I'm just the negotiator—"

Téndalor gave the signal.

The retaining lever clicked upward and the counterweight crashed down, releasing the throwing arm.

Rîm shot, screaming, into the air, describing a high arc before reaching the edge of the forest and beginning to fall.

Ubari have a good range.

Téndalor followed her flight through his spy-tube and watched her crash down on the trees at the edge of the forest. For a short time she tried to free herself from the branches that had pierced her, but her blood ran too quickly from her body and her energy drained from her. Her head fell back as she died.

"What a shame, she won't be able to pass on my message after all."
Téndalor handed the glass to one of his troops. "But I think her husband
will get the idea." He told the crew to load the catapult again. He sent an
alarm signal to the soldiers on the other islands to warn them that an attack
was imminent. What had been a possibility was now a definite threat.
Unless, of course, Rîm was completely off her head and making it all up.

Téndalor went back to the courtyard where he found Ilinia climbing
back on to her cart. The bridge toward Dsôn Faïmon was down and the
draft horses were straining to get underway. "What do you say now?"
He asked. He assumed she would have seen the whole spectacle.

"I haven't changed my mind just because some nutty groundling or
whatever turned up and spouted a whole load of nonsense, Benàmoi."
She leaned down with a sneer. "Her *husband*, eh? Did I hear correctly?
That would be like a night-mare mating with a puppy."

"That's what she said, and I—" Téndalor fell silent. Deep down he
was trying to make sense of what Rîm had told him. "Well, whatever . . .
There *are* such things as the dorón ashont. And we're ready for them."

Ilinia looked at him pityingly. "You'll see—nothing will happen.
And all this is just wasting my time—"

Shrill alarm tones issued over the water. *An attack.*

"There you are, with your made-up story!" he hissed at her furiously.
"Go, if you're leaving. We will be pulling the bridge up shortly." Téndalor
ran back up to the platform. "What's happening?"

A dull hum filled the air and something large landed in the water,
causing a huge wave to drench the älfar.

They've got catapults. Fadhasi, take me in your hands! Téndalor wiped
the canal water out of his eyes. "Find out where they're shooting from,"
he ordered, sending two soldiers to the top of the bridge, now in its
upright position. "Hurry!" *That's what we get for not having sent out
scouts.* He would never have thought the dorón ashont were capable of
constructing such powerful catapults.

"Benàmoi! Over there! At the edge of the forest!"

Téndalor took a look through his spy-tube.

Had he ever needed proof of the existence of the Towers that Walk,
here he had his evidence: a heavily armored dorón ashont wearing a

black martial helmet shaped like a skull stood where Rîm had crashed to earth. He tenderly lifted her body from the branches; blood trickled from her wounds, painting red lines on his armor.

He really is her husband!

As if the impressive creature could feel he was being observed, it suddenly turned and looked straight at Téndalor with great big violet-blue eyes.

Téndalor felt his throat constricting and his hands began to shake. The shaking soon took over his whole body. *That intense shade of blue . . .* He had to look away or the fear would engulf him. He could not look at those eyes a second longer.

Tark Draan (Girdlegard), six hundred miles
south of the Gray Mountains,
4371ˢᵗ division of unendingness (5199ᵗʰ solar cycle),
late summer.

"Ha! There, you see! I'm winning!" Ossandra was sitting by the village fountain with the other children. With twigs and pebbles, through which water flowed, they had made little courses in the sand. Colored flakes of wood served as little boats for their races. The prizes were pieces of honey caramel. Ossandra wiped her wet hands on her light brown dress.

"No! No! I'm much quicker!" squeaked Mollo, hopping up and down in excitement. Gatiela and Sarmatt laughed and clapped their hands.

"In your dreams!" Ossandra had already won two races and the early evening was promising another triumph. She turned her head and noticed Mollo dropping sand on to her little raft. "Stop cheating!" she said, and pushed him.

The sound of splashing coming from behind her made her look around. A tall slim lady wearing a simple white linen dress was standing at the fountain, sprinkling water over her face. Ossandra had been concentrating on the game so hard that she had not noticed the stranger approaching.

"Ooh, isn't she pretty!" she murmured. Ossandra was a bright little girl of eleven cycles and she always studied newcomers when they turned up in Milltown, trying to deduce where they were from and work out what made them different from the villagers. She was the burgomaster's daughter and as such she considered this her duty.

Getting to her feet, she went over to the woman and stood with her hands behind her back, observing closely, but not really able to believe that anyone could be quite so beautiful. The lady's white hair had a special shimmer to it and Ossandra felt ugly and clumsy in comparison, even if her parents always said she had a nice little face.

It was quiet around the fountain. Her friends had gone back to their game and the market stalls had all been packed away by midday. With most of the inhabitants working in the mills down by the river, or in the fields, bringing in the last of the harvest, the black and white half-timbered houses were all pretty much empty at this hour. Nobody was paying any attention to her.

"Are you a goddess?" she blurted out.

The woman ran damp fingers through her hair, which had ornaments of gems and fine bone carvings in it. Her ears, occasionally visible between the strands of hair, were pointed. She was carrying a shoulder bag with her belongings. "No, I'm no goddess, little one. My name is Horgàta and I am—"

"Oh, look! It's an elf!" Mollo shouted. The others abandoned their game and came over. "There's an elf sitting on our fountain!"

"Shut up, idiot!" Gatiela snapped. "You'll frighten her off."

Ossandra saw there was no dust on the stranger's dress, or on her travel bag. "You can't have come very far. You're all clean, not like the other visitors who come to Milltown." Her friends gathered around like a flock of nosy lambs.

"Well observed, little barbarian."

The others pointed at Ossandra, laughing.

"I am not a barbarian," she retorted. She no longer found Horgàta pretty at all. There was a hard, cruel line around her mouth and her eyes were cold. "I am Ossandra and I am the daughter of the burgomaster. If you wish to speak to my father perhaps you should be politer to me. He does not make time to see just anyone, you know."

"Oh, forgive me," the elf replied, bowing. "There was no way I could have guessed that I was in the presence of a noblewoman." She surveyed the group. "How many children live here in Milltown?"

"Loads of us," said Mollo. "Why?"

"You got presents?" probed Sarmatt. "There'd be enough for just us, wouldn't there?"

Ossandra studied Horgàta carefully and deduced that the boots poking out from under the white dress were not those of someone who did a lot of walking. She had seen that shape of shoe on the king's mounted brigade when they rode into town now and then to get food for the fortress. "Did your horse die?"

"Why would you—?" Horgàta looked down at the tips of her boots. "You really are a clever little thing." Her laugh was clear and friendly. She stretched out her arm and touched Ossandra's cheek. "Yes, I lost my horse on the journey. I wonder if I'll be able to get a new one here?"

Her voice sounded cold and Ossandra did not like it. Horgàta was not like the elves she had imagined. In all the old stories elves were magnificent and radiated kindness, warming human hearts with their presence. Despite this, Ossandra found her completely fascinating.

Mollo piped up: "My father has horses for sale, but the burgomaster hasn't!"

"Don't you ride unicorns?" Gatiela put her head on one side, her brown braids slipping over her shoulder. "I thought elves and unicorns were friends?"

"I'm afraid I couldn't find a unicorn," said Horgàta, putting on a sad face. She opened her bag and took out a little black and white flute with wires connecting to small flaps. The mouthpiece was silver. "I'll let you in on a secret: this is what we use to attract unicorns."

Ossandra had never seen an instrument like that before, but she could see it had been fashioned from a piece of bone. "What animal has bones like that?"

"Perhaps it's a unicorn bone." Horgàta put the flute to her lips and played a tune.

The very first tones mesmerized the fair-haired young girl. Her thoughts stood still and the world around her disappeared. All she could do was stare at the elf and listen, listen, *listen*.

The song had no words, but it told a story of a man and a woman who loved each other. Then a terrible warrior turned up with a dragon, demanding the woman follow him. He took the woman, but her lover collected as many men as would support him and they set off to storm the evil warrior's castle . . .

The song finished with a vibrato sound that had Ossandra weeping.

"No!" The girl was disappointed. "Tell me how the fight ended! They've got to live happily ever after and have lots of children and—" She heard voices and looked around.

The market square was full to bursting with townspeople. The elf's playing had enticed them all away from the fields and the mills. Their faces showed trance-like expressions as they stared at Horgàta, but Ossandra could see them coming slowly back to reality. And they all seemed just as upset as she was.

Horgàta put the instrument down. "I am glad you liked it." She scooped up some fresh water and sipped it out of the palm of her hand while the audience, young and old, applauded her performance. Leaping gracefully up onto he wall of the fountain so that everyone could see her, she addressed them. "Kind barbarians of Milltown," she called, sounding like one of the royal heralds. "My name is Horgàta and I have come a long, long way to ask for your help with a special task." She pointed at the quarry with her flute. "My people have an army that needs to hide in your cavern up there. It has to be kept a secret. They can't be seen by anyone—man, woman or child— who is not from your town."

Ossandra thought it was time to go and get her father. She pushed her way through the crowd and hurried through the alleyways.

"Father!" she shouted as soon as she got to the door. "Father, come quick! There's an elf!" She located her father in the council chamber with a stack of papers and pile of coins in front of him. He had been working out the tithes due to the king. "Her name is Horgàta and she's been playing her flute—"

He raised his finger and she stopped speaking. Ossandra knew this gesture well. It meant "Just a minute, I'll be with you soon."

It was hard for her to keep quiet, so she danced around on the spot. This earned her a warning look.

"What have you thought up this time, Daughter?" her father asked in his soft, calm voice.

"I haven't made up the elf. She is there at the fountain! And she plays the flute. It's really lovely, and all the people—" Ossandra went over to the window and opened it. You could hear the elf addressing the crowd and the sound of footsteps hurrying past the house to get to the marketplace.

Ossandra's father stood up and came over to where she was, looked out and saw how many people were there. "Why didn't they come and get me?" he grumbled, giving his daughter a kiss on the forehead. "What a good thing I've got you!" He unhooked his burgomaster chain from its place beside the door and put on his feathered cap and ceremonial black robe.

He walked to the fountain with Ossandra, where Horgàta was still making her speech. People made way for the burgomaster and his daughter.

"Here's my father!" Ossandra called out, pushing him forward.

The elf turned her gaze on him. "Ah, so you are responsible for what happens to Milltown and its people?"

"I am Welkar Ilmanson. I am honored and at the same time surprised to see an elf in our town. The Beings of Light have never visited us before."

She stretched out her hand and pulled him up to stand next to her on the edge of the fountain. "I was just telling everyone that the elves need your help." She swiftly repeated that the cavern had to be completely emptied so that the army could move in and make camp there. "It is a great task."

"I'm afraid I haven't quite understood why this needs to be done," Welkar admitted. He did not look very pleased to hear the stranger's message. "Why would your army need to conceal itself?"

Horgàta lowered her voice, but it was still audible to every ear in the square, "There is a storm coming. A terrible force will explode over your land and no one will be able to stop it. But we, the elves, want to protect you. We are taking up secret positions everywhere in the land so that we can fight back when the invasion comes."

The square fell silent as the people absorbed what the elf had told them.

Ossandra looked at the elf and then at her father. She could see he was struggling to make a decision.

"How will this work, Horgàta of the Elves?" he asked. "Am I to keep this secret even from my own king?"

She nodded. "It must be kept secret from everyone outside of Milltown. Evil will have sent out spies and they will move secretly among you, crushing any resistance." Horgàta placed a hand on his shoulder. "You should count yourselves lucky that we have chosen to come here. We will keep you safe from the clutches of darkness."

Welkar turned to the townspeople. "You have all heard what the elf has to say, but I'll make no bones about it: it is treason to deceive our king in this way. The king ought to be told about this threat. The council will meet and if I am alone in my opinion I shall give in to the majority view. Otherwise," he said, addressing Horgàta apologetically, "I shall have to decline your request, or at least seek royal permission to accede to it."

Ossandra observed the elf's face. She was smiling, it was true, but her eyes were cold as ice. The burgomaster's words had angered her.

Here and there in the crowd, people began to call out in support of Horgàta.

Horgàta raised her hands. "Humans! Listen to me. The situation has become urgent: evil is on its way and there is no time to waste in holding council meetings or sending messages to the king. If I can't find a secret campsite for my army, we'll lose the advantage of surprise. Even we elves," she said, running her eyes over the heads of the townspeople, "are not capable of confronting and defeating this danger in open battle."

Ossandra shuddered. Elves were known to be pure beings, the best warriors in the whole of Girdlegard—nothing could hold a candle to them. But here was Horgàta, admitting that their army would find victory difficult to achieve. "What is this threat you speak of?" someone called out. "Who is it that wants to invade our land?"

"Yes!" shouted another voice. "The orcs and other monsters out there in the wilderness cause trouble occasionally, but there aren't enough of them here to do us real harm. How is this Evil going to get here with the dwarves protecting us?"

Horgàta placed her hands on her narrow hips. "A gap has opened," she said darkly. "You have to be told, so that you'll understand."

"Where?" Ossandra wasn't happy with the answers they were getting. "How did the gap open up? Didn't the dwarves notice? Why haven't they sealed it?"

The elf pointed north. "It happened in the Gray Mountains. The Stone Gateway fell to the enemy and Tion's monsters took over. The dwarves have been defeated and eradicated. Nothing will hold back the dark wave of terror that is about to pour into our native land."

The crowd were speechless with horror.

Ossandra was reluctant to believe what the elf was saying, but Horgàta seemed utterly convinced of the truth of her news. The girl wished fervently that she could hold her father's hand.

Welkar Ilmanson kept his cool, as might be expected of a burgomaster. "This is terrible news. But . . . why are the elves remaining silent? Why not spread the word throughout Girdlegard and assemble a fighting force big enough to repel the invaders?"

"As I said before, there are spies everywhere, even at the royal courts." Horgàta cast another glance over the crowd. "If you help us, people of Milltown, you will be celebrated as those who helped us defeat evil. Your names will be in the history books!"

The market square fell quiet again.

"Are you telling us that our king—?" Welkar started to say.

The elf nodded. "It is not safe to speak of this to anyone except you. Help us!" She pointed west with her flute. "A group of óarcos is about seven moments of unendingness from here. We will protect you if they come, but it would be better if we took the children and any vulnerable old people with us to the cavern. They'll be safer there."

The crowd became restive. Ossandra recognized fear in the murmuring voices of her friends and family.

"Don't delay, Welkar!" called a young woman urgently. "Think of us and of our children!" Similar calls were heard on all sides.

The burgomaster lifted his hand for quiet. "I hear what you are all saying." He lowered his hand and offered it to Horgàta. "I swear in the name of Milltown that we won't tell anyone about your army."

The elf shook hands with Ilmanson and the people cheered.

Ossandra looked at Horgàta. There was malice behind her smile.

"Take the children and old people up into the cavern immediately. I'll have my elf-warriors move in overnight to protect them," she said. "Don't forget to organize food for them." Horgàta jumped down from the fountain, landing at Ossandra's feet. "Well, my little one? Are you glad we came?"

She knew it would be better to nod and pretend she was relieved. So that is what she did. But she would not join the elves, because that cavern was starting to sound like a prison.

*Tark Draan (Girdlegard), south east of Gray Mountains,
4371st division of unendingness (5199th solar cycle),
early autumn.*

Morana stood before King Odeborn of Ido, biting her lip so as not to say anything negative about the appearance of the court. It was a miserable dump, the air tasted of stale smoke and rancid candle fat and the frescoes might have been painted by a blind barbarian with absolutely no understanding of form or color. *I wouldn't even expect my night-mare to put up with this.*

There were four men and women to the right and left of the king and everyone was staring at her with intense curiosity. These were, she had been told, the richest and most important nobles in the land: the king's closest advisers.

I think their main concern is to see that they do well out of things personally. Morana's black leather armor felt slightly out of place. As long as she was abroad on the roads of Tark Draan she chose not to wear it, but it was more or less essential for the kind of negotiations she was conducting: she needed to show she was no ordinary elf.

And the barbarians had obviously fallen for it. People trusted her, even to the extent of allowing her into the throne room carrying the weapon Virssagòn had created for her: Sun and Moon.

Morana appreciated his gift hugely and had practiced with it on her way to the king. The moon part of the weapon was two curved sickle shapes fastened on to a central stick. The blades of the other part were as straight as the rays of the daystar. The inner and outer edges were honed as blades, and her fingers were protected by metal basketwork. The weapon was intended for close combat; used with speed and precision it would be lethal and unique in its efficacy.

I could kill them one by one. She swept the room with her eyes, taking in the guards. *They look pretty slow. They wouldn't stop me.*

She played with the idea of wiping out the entire leadership of the kingdom. They would be directionless and confused. Then the älfar would take this realm easily.

She noted some of the crude rings and chains the nobles wore over badly made garments. *If they fight the way they make their metalware we'd be better off without them.* But the nostàroi had ordered her to forge an alliance with this man and she could not disobey. She placed her hand on her midriff and sketched a bow. "Nobles of Tark Draan, King of Ido, you have my greetings and my thanks for agreeing to receive me."

King Odeborn, a broad figure with a thick nose and drooping eyelids, sniffed audibly. "I just wanted to see what an elf was like," he said baldly. The nobles gave titters of false laughter, and some of them rolled their eyes at his comment.

Morana knew that the king had inherited the throne—he had certainly not been awarded it due to intelligence or wisdom. *That should make things easier for me. It'd be better if I included these nobles when I address the king.* "Do I look like an elf?" she asked.

Odeborn waved a servant over and got him to refill his goblet. The wine slopped over the rim leaving fresh stains on the bright blue robe he was wearing. The stains were not without company. "Well. You look a bit . . . *dark* for a Being of Light," he said, sipping his drink noisily. "Maybe you are a moon-elf? One that only goes out at night?"

"Your Majesty has a quick mind," she smiled. "I am indeed different." Morana saw fear in the faces of the nobles. Not fear of her, but fear of Odeborn. "And I am about to talk about something that may well affect us for longer than one human life span. Could we include the king's successor in our discussions?"

"Successor?" roared Odeborn. "If there is anyone eyeing my throne I'll have his guts for garters!"

"You don't have a son or a near relative, who could—"

"Our king had most of his family executed immediately on seizing power," a woman said quietly—one of those who had rolled her eyes at the king's previous remarks. "He has never married."

Odeborn emptied his goblet in one long draft and threw it at the woman. "Stop telling the elf my secrets or you'll be joining my family, you daughter of a whore!" he snarled.

That's why he needs so many guards. Whoever kills him will rule. Morana indicated the armed men at the entrance and dotted around the hall. "Perhaps I can help you secure your throne? I offer a pact between the Kingdom of Ido and ourselves."

"Pact?" he growled. "What do I need with a pact?"

"The elves of Lesinteïl and Âlandur are planning to extend their borders at the expense of the human realms—and that includes your own." Morana was aware of the surprise on the barbarians' faces. "We can work together to prevent this." *It's not going to be easy to talk them around.*

"Are you from Gwandalur or the Golden Plain?" asked the man at the end of the line on the right. Morana's attention sharpened on him—he looked quite smart for a barbarian. *He might be harder to convince.*

"And how do you know about these plans?" the woman asked. "Have you any proof?"

Odeborn ignored these questions and addressed Morana. "They're so rude, aren't they, these advisers of mine?" He gestured down the line. "Why don't you introduce yourselves to our *guest*?"

One by one they gave Morana their names.

"Now that you know who they are, you may as well understand that these are the few of my relatives I allowed to live." He sank back in his throne with a malicious smile and called the servant over for more wine. "I hope you can give me a good explanation for your claims."

"I belong to a tribe that has remained separate from the other elf races because we know how untrustworthy they are. For a long time we stayed in the south, hidden away from all eyes, watching them. They have been deceiving humans for as long as the two races have lived next to each other."

"They have been *deceiving us*?" This was Starowig, a well-groomed noble with the neat beard. "If that is the case, perhaps you can tell us what their true intentions are?"

"They want the entire territory. They plan to conquer the human realms and assassinate the wizards. Then, when everything is under their control and they have divided the land among themselves, they'll eliminate the dwarves. They pretend to be creatures of light, but they are creatures of pure greed!

"You have little time: their numbers were once insufficient to risk declaring war, but now they are ready. Haven't you heard the news from Quarrystone?"

Odeborn's jowls quivered as he shook his head, but the woman sitting on his left, Sagridia, nodded. She looked more frightened than any of the others. "Some traders told me the town had been wiped out by the elves. Just like that. Only one little girl survived. She's got a mark on her forehead that protected her, they said. I thought it was all a fabrication."

"It is the beginning of their war," Morana announced gravely. *Convincing them may be easier than I thought, but I'm going to have to do something about the power structure here. There are more than enough candidates for the succession.*

"So what?" said Odeborn, not bothering to suppress a belch. "Let them come! I'll pull their pointy ears off and shove them up their asses!" He laughed. "My army is loyal to me and I have many men. I don't need a pact with *you*."

Judging from the expressions, he was the only one of this opinion.

"I understand." Morana looked at the nobles. *Let's try something different.* "Which of you is wealthiest and the most popular figure with the people, apart from your wise ruler here?"

There was a little muttering among them and eyes flitted anxiously hither and thither, before most settled on Starowig.

"So be it." As quick as lightning, Morana pulled out the Sun and hurled the weapon with all her strength at the king.

The steel blades struck him in the middle of his fat chest. The impact was so violent that it tipped him back and overturned his throne. His carafe smashed on the floor and red wine and blood flowed together.

No one moved. Not even the guards.

Morana put her hand to her belt and nodded to Starowig. "Congratulations, *King*. How do you feel about forming a pact with us? Or do you think I should name *your* successor?" She grasped the steel Moon in her right hand.

Starowig, not over the shock, but manifestly pleased with this turn of events, got to his feet and said loudly: "You have your alliance."

CHAPTER X

And that is how the nostàroi achieved their victory over the elves of the Golden Plain.

Using cunning and courage, they overwhelmed their mortal enemies, led their own troops from battle to battle and took the first of the elf realms at the speed of the wind.

By the onset of winter the Inextinguishables' army controlled whole swathes of land in the north of Tark Draan.

Plans were underway to conquer Gwandalur, Álandur and Lesinteïl.

Gwandalur was part of the Golden Plain, a minor adjunct, small but dangerous.

The elves there served a white dragon worshipped as the incarnation of their goddess. The nostàroi knew that they would have to use subterfuge if they were going to defeat this creature. The next strike was to be on Gwandalur before the dragon had a chance to attack the älfar.

But the alliance was disintegrating.

However hard the älfar tried to keep the allies together, the different groups acted independently. This, together with the bad weather, brought the cleverly planned strategy for the advance to a halt.

It was some time before a certain absence was noticed.

Excerpt from the epic poem *The Heroes of Tark Draan*
composed by Carmondai, master of word and image

Ishím Voróo (Outer Lands), Dsôn Faïmon, Dsôn,
4371st division of unendingness (5199th solar cycle),
early autumn.

Polòtain was giving a dinner for all those whose opinions the Inextinguishables would listen to—his own voice was not sufficient. *I want to*
bring a whole chorus together.

He scrutinized the room where twenty of the most influential älfar
left in Dsôn would soon be gathering: male and female, Comets and
Constellations alike. This was to be a unique event where political
adversaries would come together around the same table. *And they will*
come because I have invited them. Everything must be perfect.

The guests soon began arriving and by the appointed time all of them
were there, seated at the table with Polòtain at the head, visible to all.
None was younger than thirty divisions of unendingness.

"Before I open the proceedings I'd like to thank you all for attend-
ing," he said, standing to address the company. "It is a great privilege
to have members of opposing political camps coming here in peace. I
must ask for your tolerance and understanding regarding tonight's
revelations: there are some painful truths that have to be confronted.
But it is for the good of our nation that I bring up these uncomfortable issues. Terrible events have been set in motion and we must inform
the Inextinguishables of them before they become imminent. If we fail
to do this there will no longer be any Comets, nor Constellations." He
sat down again and ordered the wine to be served. *That should have*
aroused their curiosity . . .

"In the past, when you were more in the public eye, you were always
feared by your Comet colleagues, Polòtain," said Ratáris with a smile,
breaking the tense silence. "But now you are a burned-out star rising
again, and you want to take over both factions? I wonder if it will work?"

She looked at the other dinner guests. "We, the Constellations, are eager to hear your plans, but we are . . . *suspicious* of them."

Nobody from the Comets wanted to speak. They preferred to bide their time.

"There are several hot topics being discussed in the streets and squares of Dsôn," Polòtain began. "We have the situation in Tark Draan, for example. My sources—"

"What sources are these?" Ratáris interrupted.

"Benàmoi of the smaller älfar units who are unhappy at how the war is going," Polòtain continued. The easier he made it for them to understand, the readier they would be to believe the truth. His truth, at any rate. "The nostàroi have sent small units out to accompany the barbarians, óarcos, trolls and ogres so that the älfar can keep the allies in order. That's how it was supposed to work. But there is a snag." He grabbed the edge of the cloth in both hands and yanked it off the table, leaving plates and cutlery undisturbed, to reveal a huge map of Tark Draan painted on the wooden table. Polòtain took up the pointer at his side. Nothing had been left to chance this evening. "I have no wish to detract from the victories Caphalor and Sinthoras have won. These are excellent warriors and they have led our troops to a glorious triumph in the Golden Plain. But the way they are deploying the allies, or the scum of Ishím Voróo, as I refer to them privately," (at this point there was polite laughter on both sides of the table), "puts them at the end of a chain—and the chain is no longer holding. Greed is responsible for the disintegration of the alliance. They all want the land they were promised, and of course, they are squabbling over who gets the best bits. My sources"—he went on, looking particularly at Ratáris—"say that the barbarians are starting to quarrel among themselves and the Kraggash óarcos have put the half-giants' noses out of joint. Our warriors often have to face the resistance from Tark Draan on their own. As soon as the local kings have got over their initial shock and have their armies sorted, it will be even more difficult for our soldiers."

"You are saying that the nostàroi are not up to the task?" Demenion, of the Comets faction, said. "Their mission was to conquer Tark Draan for the Inextinguishables and establish a vassal state—but judging by what you have said, it looks as though they are awarding the whole place to the scum!"

"I thought this campaign was about destroying the elves?" objected Ratáris. "And that's surely what the nostàroi are working toward. Or have I misunderstood?"

"It is wrong to send our soldiers to Tark Draan in the first place," said Landaròn, who was sitting next to her. "So far our catapults on the island fortresses have managed to hold back the dorón ashont. But where are our forces if, by some incredible mischance, the Towers that Walk effect entry into Dsôn Faïmon? We're left with nothing but raw recruits led by a handful of veterans, plus the slaves we could use in an emergency. But can we depend on their loyalty? What if our serfs turn against us and join forces with the dorón ashont? At first sight it may seem that we are secure enough, but if you dig a little deeper you have to admit that the älfar empire has never been in such danger." He shook his head and stared over at the Comets. "Say what you like, this campaign has proved a disastrous mistake."

Polòtain was delighted that the discussion had gone this way. "Even if I belong to the expansionist camp, I find myself agreeing with you, Landaròn," he said, for all to hear.

Every head turned toward him in astonishment.

He addressed the other älfar. "The nostàroi talked the Inextinguishables into using tactics that were created in arrogance and over-confidence. Sinthoras and Caphalor were working on the assumption that they had made the borders of Ishím Voróo secure as they had enticed all of our enemies to Tark Draan under the guise of new alliances. It was thought the nostàroi would be returning in triumph by now, with the whole of Tark Draan conquered. Not least because of the demon, who they said would be able to break any last pockets of resistance." Polòtain crossed his arms. "The reality is that they have hardly made a start. Winter will soon call a halt to the whole campaign and Dsôn Faïmon will be left weak and vulnerable. Look toward the northwest where the dorón ashont are up against our borders!" He raised his right forefinger. "I am not saying the war was a mistake—but the way they are going about it will bring disaster. The nostàroi have got things wrong and they've put us in grave danger." He took a mouthful of wine and waited for his guests' reactions.

They were all looking at the map with worried expressions.

Polòtain was convinced that the views of the two opposing factions were starting to draw closer. *That is exactly what I wanted to happen.*

"I cannot fathom where you are going with your speech," said Ratáris after a while. "Do you intend the Comets to support the Constellations in trying to get the troops recalled?"

There was lively dissent, but the reaction was less extreme than it would have been before Polòtain's presentation.

"I am merely pointing out that we find ourselves in a situation where our differences pale into insignificance." Polòtain placed his wine cup back on the table. "I have a proposition to put to you all. I think it is a reasonable suggestion that will be acceptable to both factions and at the end of the day it will be Dsôn Faïmon that profits from it—and that means us, of course. If you hear me out we can discuss it together."

Ratáris signed to him to go ahead. "You have us on tenterhooks."

"In order to protect our people we need to recall a large contingent of our soldiers from Tark Draan; some will remain to hold their position over the winter and keep the allies under control. Our soldiers will defeat the dorón ashont upon their return and make their way back to the front with the coming of spring, when they can join the attack on Tark Draan once more. But, in my opinion, the war should be under different management. Caphalor and Sinthoras have botched their opportunity through their conceit, and it will not serve us in the future. My way, the interests of both the Comets and the Constellations are served and each faction can see one of their principal demands being met." Polòtain's mouth was dry, not only from speaking, but also from the tension. Polòtain took a few deep breaths. He had done his part. Now to see how convincing he had been.

The Comets and the Constellations put their heads together.

A servant came up to him and whispered, "Master, you have a visitor. It is Timanris."

"Timansor's daughter?" *The traitor bitch?*

"Yes, master."

"What does she want?"

"She did not say. She wants to speak to you urgently. Straightaway, she said."

"Get rid of her."

"Master, she looked very upset. It must be important."

Polòtain was unsure. *Does she want me to forgive her for betraying Robonor? Or might it be something I can turn to my advantage? I can't miss that.* He got up. "Please continue your discussion, my dear friends and valued opponents. I shall be back shortly."

The servant took him to a small reception room where Timanris was waiting. She was wringing her hands nervously. When she saw him approach she stood up.

"My dear," he said kindly. He concealed his distaste behind a mask of feigned courtesy. "To what do I owe the honor of your visit?" He indicated to the servants that they should leave the room. "Have you come to apologize for sleeping with my great-nephew's murderer?"

Timanris stared at him, then dropped her gaze. "I—" she said quietly, taking a deep breath. "I heard that you have called all the leading members of society together. Everyone in Dsôn knows you are attacking Sinthoras because you believe he is responsible for Robonor's death. But you are wrong! I wanted to ask you not to—"

Polòtain snorted, then gave a cold laugh. "I have proof, Timanris! And I have a witness whose evidence clearly incriminates Sinthoras. He has sworn on oath that Sinthoras was implicated in a conspiracy targeting Robonor!"

"But that is impossible!" she cried. "He swore to me."

"You know what people say about Sinthoras and how he came to gain his present office!" he cried. "He is a Comet and his trail could not burn more destructively. If there is something he wants or something that gives him some advantage, he will have it, come what may." He stepped toward her. "He saw you, he wanted you. That sealed my great-nephew's fate. His death had to happen. Such a convenient *accident*, wasn't it? But I'm not giving up and I'm not going to be lulled, like you, into believing his protestations of innocence."

Polòtain realized that it was sheer desperation that had forced her to come and plead her lover's case. *You know that I am plotting to bring him down and it's driving you crazy.* He looked at her face and wanted to strike her. "He is also responsible for the death of the outstanding artist Itáni—"

"No!" she exclaimed, seeming relieved to be able to contribute something toward clearing Sinthoras's name. "No! That's utterly impossible! He spent the night with me!"

Polòtain froze. "What did you just say?"

Timanris winced. "Nothing. Only that he spent the night with his troops in—" She swallowed hard and her face went as white as samarkit dye. "Tark Draan. He—was in Tark—Tark Draan . . ."

Polòtain stepped forward again so he and she were close enough to touch. "The nostàroi has been in Dsôn?" he hissed, holding her gaze. "By all the infamous ones, Sinthoras was here! Here in Dsôn!" he exclaimed with a laugh. "Betrayed by his partner after she'd betrayed my Robonor for him. O god of the winds and of justice, Samusin, that is priceless!"

"No, I said nothing of the sort!" Timanris said. "You must have misheard!"

"It doesn't matter what you said or how much you deny it. I shall seek an audience with the Inextinguishables and lodge a murder accusation against Sinthoras. I'll interrogate your father and his whole household. I'll cross-examine all the neighbors and all the island fortress teams. There'll be someone else who will have seen him. You have given me a good tip." Polòtain kissed her on the forehead. "This almost makes amends for what you did to Robonor." He turned away from her and left the room. *Samusin, this is true justice indeed.*

"No!" she cried. "No! Don't do that. I beg you, Polòtain!"

He halted and looked at her again.

She stopped short on the threshold, clinging to the doorframe for support, sobbing; her body was trembling "Please—"

"You have no right to ask any favors of me. You have given shelter to a multiple murderer and that is enough to bring you and your entire family down, Timanris. But because Robonor loved and worshipped you until the very day of his death, I shall spare you and your father. I shall find the witnesses I need to confirm that Sinthoras was in Dsôn and then my revenge will strike him! He will lose everything! *Everything!* That includes you. If you don't want to be sucked down into the maelstrom of his downfall, then wash your hands of him. For the sake of your father and your family. Prove that you have not abandoned all your senses!"

Polòtain returned to the hall, his heart thudding with excitement. There would be no problem getting the hated nostàroi recalled from the army. It would be quick. It would be dirty. Every citizen in Dsôn Faïmon would hear about his deeds and they would repudiate the one-time hero out of hand. *This is for you, Robonor!*

Elated, he re-entered the ceremonial room where the Comet and the Constellation supporters had been debating their next course of action. They were now being served supper. Nobody else had left.

Polòtain took this as a good omen. "Forgive me. I missed our discussion." He made his way back to the top of the table and stood waiting. "So, what is it to be?"

Tark Draan (Girdlegard), in the Gray Mountains,
4371st division of unendingness (5199th solar cycle),
early autumn.

The trio gasped and wheezed their way up the steep side of the Split Anvil, a peak half a mile away from the uninterrupted chain of mountains to the west of the Stone Gateway.

"Vraccas, according to the dwarves, was supposed to have forged the rest of the mountains on this very peak and then he split it down the middle so that other gods would not be able to use it," said one of the women. When she spoke, little white clouds accompanied her words. "The Anvil seems to me to be both a warning and a greeting at the same time. Wanderers are told: this is where the dwarf realm begins and if you don't know your way around here, turn back and stay on the path."

Famenia leaned forward with her hands on her hips and looked down. The mountain was flattish on top and had a vertical fissure that ran to its base, creating a narrow gorge with a path leading through it. They had come off this narrow road and climbed up to get a better view. Famenia's lungs were hurting as badly as her legs, but she did not want to let on. The couple who had brought her here were older, but coping better—and that was embarrassing.

Having escaped from the broken remains of the fifthling kingdom and the älf who had attacked her in Halmengard, she had gone to Simin the Underrated, a good friend of her master's. Simin, for his part, had consulted Ortina the Omnipresent. Then the three of them had decided to investigate for themselves and get an accurate picture of the situation before alerting the various monarchs.

Famenia had the impression that there was one particular item in her report that had concerned everyone and so, to prove her story, she had had to accompany Simin and Ortina, even though she was convinced the undertaking was nonsensical. *What good are two magi and a famula against the enemy hordes? We need a whole army! It would be better to speak to the rulers and persuade them to act.*

She certainly could not understand why they were struggling to the top of the Split Anvil. There was nothing to see but sheer cliffs, a perilous platform and a million ways to kill yourself. The terrain was so difficult that not even the dwarves had tried to post a lookout point.

"Nearly there." Simin held fast to a boulder and took a look back. "What a wonderful view! We must be at least 800 paces high!"

Famenia did not bother to look down again. She was getting exceedingly impatient. "Forgive me, honored magus, but what are we doing up here?" She was panting hard. "I'm no mountain goat and not used to hopping from rock to rock."

Ortina gave a cheerful laugh. "You'll see in a moment." She made her way carefully behind a jutting rock and disappeared around the corner with Simin following.

"Ye gods," murmured Famenia, doing her utmost not to lose the others. As she struggled to keep up, she thought over the little she knew about her two companions.

They were both at least one hundred cycles old and were well liked by their subjects in the neighboring enchanted realms of Siminia and Ortinaland. Simin spent his time doing research on human senses, experimenting particularly with optimizing hunting skills and farming techniques: the magus was keen to make people's lives easier. Ortina, on the other hand, was involved in work on speed, trying to see if it were feasible to travel swiftly without a horse. Apparently she was able to make certain objects fly, from carpets and broomsticks to larger items such as benches and coaches.

If that's true, why on earth do we have to walk and clamber about like this? Famenia rounded the jutting rock and saw the two of them standing on an outcrop from where they might well have been able to see the entrance to the dwarf realm if it had not been so very far away.

"Over here!" cried Simin.

Famenia was convinced her next step was liable to be her last. The wind was dragging at her clothing and the sudden gusts made her unsteady, so she was hanging on to the cliff wall for dear life. It took her ages to reach the others.

"Now look at the entrance and tell me what has happened." The magus pointed in the direction he wanted her to look.

"But how—" She felt his finger touch her right temple and in the blink of an eye her eyesight had improved so much she could see all the way to the entrance. "By the gods!" she exclaimed. She could see the battlements, the gate, the path . . .

"A little spell to sharpen your vision, that's all." Simin's voice did not betray any special exertion on his part. "Our sight is as good as that, too. Tell us what happened."

Famenia retold the story of her escape, about the óarcos that had found her, about the false elves and the doll-like stuffed dwarves that had been placed on sentry duty on the walls. She could see the mechanical things moving on the battlements. They were nothing but empty shells. It was sheer abuse of the dead.

"This means that the demon has not yet used his power," said Ortina, when the famula had finished her narration. "Otherwise they would not need that performance with the dwarf corpses."

"Or perhaps it's not that kind of demon, after all." Simin removed his finger from Famenia's temple; she blinked and found her sight had returned to normal. The gate was gone. "There are so many possibilities."

"We've come because you want to find out what this mist-demon is really like?" Famenia asked. "But you'll need to get into the mountain, and I can't tell you where he is to be found—"

"You told us the dwarves you spoke to mentioned strange events, child," Ortina broke in. "Where did these things happen?"

Is that what's worrying them so much? This horror story? The famula had to think hard to reconstruct the exact words she had heard from the dwarves. "They said that when they were fighting the älfar at the Stone Gateway, the dead would come back to life if their heads were not severed from their shoulders. But this was not a widespread phenomenon, it only occurred in that area." She tried to remember more details. "Oh yes, they also said that the moss on the walls had gone gray and died."

The magi exchanged meaningful glances, communicating without speech.

Simin tightened the scarf around his neck. "That indicates that the demon did not join the big push into Tark Draan. If he did—or does in the future—we would be dealing with enemies who could not be truly defeated unless we incinerated them."

"Or beheaded them," added Ortina.

"So . . . you think the dwarves were telling the truth?" Famenia was horrified.

"More or less," said Simin. "I presume the demon changes the land that it conquers, altering the characteristics of the place and the creatures that live there, but I would have to study him more closely with my magic to be sure."

Famenia was at a loss to understand. "So, there really are beings as awful as that?" Simin and Ortina laughed. It was not meant scornfully, but the young famula was upset by it nonetheless. "It's not my fault that Jujulo did not have much to do with the powers of darkness. He was—"

". . . more cheerful by nature, I know," said Ortina soothingly, laying her hand against Famenia's cheek. "I know, child. We all treasure his memory."

"The question we're faced with is this: what does this demon look like?" Simin stepped back out of the wind. "I think we should seek the advice of Grok-Tmai the Worrier. He never talks about his research. Who knows what powers he experiments with?"

"He's not the right person to go to!" Ortina objected. "He's forever philosophizing about the world; he's not happy around other people and is certainly not one for danger. It's Hianna the Flawless we should consult. She pretends she's only concerned with her own beauty, but I don't believe it. She has a hidden secret, I'm sure."

"What about Fensa the Inventive?" Famenia suggested. "Jujulo thought a great deal of her, even though she shrouds herself in an aura of mystery—"

"He meant an aura of alcohol, child," commented Ortina drily "She likes a drink. It's said her magic is at its best when she's downed a bottle of wine."

Simin chuckled.

"Oh," said Famenia. *Great.* "Then we'll have to discount her."

The magus focused on the distant gate once more. "How shall we proceed?" he asked Ortina. "We must keep the demon from leaving the mountains to join the army of evil or there'll be no way of stopping them."

"There's no point thinking about destroying him, but we could use our combined power to stop him or trap him." Ortina turned to Famenia. "It is only thanks to you that we have learned about this threat, child."

The famula shook her head. "No, it was Jujulo who sent me to the dwarves."

"Your modesty becomes you." Simin graced her with a fleeting smile. "We will leave it up to you to decide who you wish to complete your studies with. Any magus or maga in Girdlegard would be happy to take you on without the usual selection process. It is no more than you deserve."

Jujulo would not have wanted that. Famenia bowed. "With your permission, I should like to walk in the footsteps of my master. I was his most senior famula and had nearly qualified." She took her amulet from under her thick winter coat and held it out to them. "He named me as his successor. I never thought that I would be assuming the office so soon."

Simin and Ortina looked surprised. "That is a heavy burden that you are taking on," said the maga slowly. "You are still very young."

"And you won't yet have developed any one particular character trait to use as your magic name," added Simin. "But something tells me that it will be happening in the not-too-distant future. Perhaps you will be the Brave One or the Courageous, but certainly not the Optimistic." He winked at her. "We will discuss it at our next assembly."

"Until then you'll have to put up with my calling you *child*." Ortina laughed.

"I wouldn't want that as my extra name," Famenia said. She had been afraid that her youthfulness would disqualify her for Jujulo's office. *I wonder what will happen at that assembly.* "So, what is to be done?"

Simin placed one foot on a boulder. "I'm going in," he announced. "I'll find a way to get past the monsters, secure the exit point and, with any luck, prevent the demon from leaving if he tries to invade." He registered the concerned expressions of the two women. "Oh, don't worry. Remember I am the Underrated One, not the Overrated. I am perfectly aware of what I am capable of. If I come to the conclusion that the demon is too powerful for me I'll come straight back." He looked at Ortina. "You two let the others know what's happening and bring them to the northernmost part of Hiannorum. Send out messengers to all the high rulers of Girdlegard. They must assemble an army, recruiting every single man capable of bearing arms. We"—he said, drawing a circle in the air around the three of them—"will take on the demon."

Famenia was pleased to be included, even if she did not show it. *Jujulo would be proud of me!*

Ortina was skeptical. "The humans will never manage to assemble an army; the monarchs are always at each other's throats. The south will say it's not their problem; the Lake Lands in Wayeern never get involved in anything."

"Leave that to me," said Famenia. "I'll be best at explaining what happened in the Gray Mountains and describing the army that threatens us. And I can warn them about the awful power of the mist-demon."

Simin nodded. "So that's settled: I'll keep the demon occupied, Ortina will contact the rest of the magi, and Famenia will warn the kingdoms and persuade them to work together before it's too late. May the gods protect us!"

They all shook hands.

As she clasped the hands of the other magi, Famenia thought she felt a tingling sensation through her leather gloves: a certain strength flowing through her. It was an exhilarating and unforgettable moment. Up there on the heights of the Split Anvil she felt she had become a real maga. *I have yet to earn my magic name. I intend to work hard for that honor.*

The wind blew colder now, cutting icily at the exposed parts of her face.

"Let's waste no time!" said Ortina. "Evil won't wait for us. We all know what is at stake—" But as she spoke she coughed suddenly and staggered forward, frowning. Blood spurted from her mouth and she sank down between Famenia and Simin—a long, black arrow stuck out of her back.

"Get under cover!" Simin pushed Famenia so that she fell backward just as a third arrow passed close by her own neck, slamming into the rock face.

Where are they? She looked over to the other side of the narrow gorge and saw an älf with a longbow in his hand. Several orcs were arrayed around him, staring at her. Four of them were starting to climb down. *They will try to cut off our escape!*

The älf took aim and fired once more. The arrow's flight was strong and true despite the buffeting wind.

Famenia attempted to warn Simin, but his hands were raised to begin a spell and he could not break off in the middle of the incantation.

The arrow struck him in the throat. At the same time a flaming blue sphere the size of a cow's head appeared from between his fingers and hissed its way across the gap toward their enemies.

"Master!" Famenia sprang over to Simin and caught him as he fell. The arrow had pierced his larynx, but had missed the neck vertebrae. His eyes were wide open and he tried in vain to speak.

A clap of thunder sounded from the opposite side of the mountain.

Famenia glanced back over her shoulder and saw blue flames where the älf and the orcs had been standing. Fire danced over the rock, growing in intensity; their enemies turned to ashes in its wake or tumbled into the depths. *They can't hurt us now!*

She pulled the bloody tip of the arrow off and then attempted to remove the shaft. She concentrated on the only healing charm that Jujulo had taught her. Simin's blood flowed warm and red from the wound on his neck.

The amulet on her breast grew warm, releasing energy. Magic could not normally be stored unless it were in the body of a magus or maga, but Jujulo had dedicated his life to finding a way to instill magic power into certain alloys. His research came to Simin's assistance now.

As Famenia watched, the wounds stopped bleeding and closed over. *Keep it up! I have to be sure!* She redoubled her efforts, although it caused her to feel slightly giddy.

Four heartbeats later the magus spluttered and took a breath. He grabbed Famenia's arm. "Thank you," he said, sitting up. "Jujulo was correct in choosing you." His fingers brushed the healed wounds in his throat while he stared at Ortina's dead body. "Ye gods, how could they?" His voice was thick with fury and grief. Rubbing his eyes, he wiped away tears.

"What now?" Famenia was at a loss. She felt sick to the stomach. Numbness overwhelmed her. All her strength had dissipated. The spell had taken its toll.

"We can't . . . take her with us." Simin got to his feet. "Help me to cover her body with stones—we will make a grave for her. When we have won the battle against evil we can return and bury her with all honor." Simin looked over toward the gateway that led into the Gray Mountains. "They will have noticed my spell. We'd better be quick."

"What will happen now?" she repeated. "I mean, to our plans?"

Simin worked quickly in creating the grave, the wind making his robe flap about him. "We stick to what we discussed. I'll head into the mountains." He looked at her with a serious expression. "You now have two tasks: call the magi together and then go to the leaders of the king-doms." He removed a ring from his finger and pressed it into Famenia's hand. "Keep this and show it when you enter my enchanted realm. You will be given everything you need. Take the best horses—you'll need a spare and one for your luggage." He placed a final stone on Ortina's resting-place. "Let us go."

It took a breath or two for Famenia's legs to start obeying her. She stepped past the grave, hoping she would not share her fate.

The famula had become a maga, with a heavier burden on her shoulders than she could ever have imagined. *I should call myself Famenia the Tested.*

CHAPTER XI

Do you know the Walking Towers?
With their deadly floods and toxic showers!
Come on! Come on!
Fight however you can
so THEY don't win
Don't let THEM in!
They have wild and crazy plans
to put us in their pots and pans
They want us for meat!
They want us to eat!

Nursery rhyme *The Towers that Walk*
2nd verse

Ishím Voróo (Outer Lands), Dsôn Faïmon, radial arm Wëlèron,
4371ˢᵗ division of unendingness (5199ᵗʰ solar cycle),
late autumn.

"What are you saying?" Arviû had to pull himself together. Rage sent fine black lines zigzagging across his face; he could feel the pull of them on his skin. He sat there unable to see anything at all. Except the dark.

"You are lucky to be alive," a female healer said. He had forgotten her name, just as he had forgotten most small facts since being hit on the head. His memory had functioned excellently up until the Golden Plain battle—but after that point . . . "We opened up your skull and were able to take out lots of shrapnel. We were able to save your eyes—"

"So why can't I see anything?" he yelled, digging his fingers into the sheet. "What use are my eyes if they won't show me anything?"

"We don't know the answer to that," she said. "It could be that a fragment entered your brain and is still lodged in the part that is the seat of vision. We are afraid that if we undertake a further investigation you could suffer more serious damage."

"Or maybe it's the after effects of the blow to the head." This voice was a male. "To be honest, you can see that we—I mean, we are at a loss."

Arviû had noticed the älf backtracking in the middle of the sentence. He uttered a loud, long cry, as if to drive away the darkness that enveloped him. There was no pain or weakness—the only thing was this blindness. He wanted to get back to Tark Draan and punish the elves for what they had done to him—but a blind archer? *What use am I now?*

He tried to relax. He lifted a hand to touch his face, located his eyes and discovered that they were open.

But when his fingertips touched them he could not feel anything. The eyelids did not even close instinctively.

Arviû gave another shout of anger and helplessness.

"We'll give you a potion to calm you," said the female. He felt her put her hand on his chest. "Give yourself some time. You have time enough to spare. Maybe your sight will return."

A drinking vessel was placed at his lips. He swallowed the sweet liquid and after five breaths he felt in less turmoil.

In place of fury came implacable hatred: hatred of the elves. Hatred such as he had never known before: destructive, deep-seated, demanding. "Where am I to be taken?"

"You are still in Welèron, in Ertrimar's infirmary."

Arviû turned his face away. "I keep forgetting," he whispered. *Ye infamous ones, those splinters have bored into my memory and made it like a sieve!* "Leave me."

"As you wish," said the male älf. "There's a bell on the table next to your bed. If you need anything, ring."

He heard their steps retreating and a door opening and closing, then it was silent. *If I need anything . . . Of course I need something! Can't they give me some new eyes?*

Arviû knew the healers were good at what they did, but apparently his case was beyond them.

In his mind's eye he saw the armored elf swinging the broken lance and striking him. He heard the sounds of battle, the horses and nightmares neighing . . . He could remember all those details—but now he was staring into a dark abyss.

I must have my revenge, or I shall have no peace until I enter endingness! Arviû clenched his fists. *I shall make the elves pay. I'll slaughter them!*

And it suddenly occurred to him how he might achieve this end.

The Inextinguishables had sightless confidants who had volunteered to be blinded so they would not go insane upon beholding the Sibling Rulers. These älfar were held to be the best warriors; they used their hearing to find their way about. The slightest rustle or clink told them where their adversary was standing—they could defeat sighted soldiers.

I wonder if I can achieve that same perfection with my archery skills? Arviû was doubtful about applying that same standard to himself. He would have to train his sense of hearing to the utmost degree if he was going to detect a potential target at a distance of 500 paces, let alone the 2,000 he had been able to cover before. There would be distracting sounds from the environment, wind, voices . . . *No, I'll never be able to do it!*

That's over with. That's the past. His hatred of the elves boiled up again, negating the beneficial effects of the potion he had been given.

They have taken what was most precious to me: what made me unique. No one in Dsôn Faïmon could rival my archery skills. Nobody in Dsôn and no creature in Ishím Voróo or in Tark Draan!

A strangled cry issued from Arviû's throat, but it gave him no relief. The urgent wish to bring cruel death to the elves grew and grew.

I will blind them! I want them to suffer what I suffer. I'll blind them and turn them out into the wilderness as target practice. I'll enjoy hunting down that quarry. All the fairer if huntsman and prey alike have no sight!

The idea settled firmly in his mind. *The Inextinguishables' coterie must teach me how to fight without sight.* He felt for the bell and rang it. He would achieve what the blind bodyguard had—mastery over the darkness.

Something else struck him as he was ringing the bell.

The door opened. "You rang, master?"

A slave! So I could try. Quick as a flash he hurled the bell in the direction of the voice.

The slave grunted; the bell tinkled as it fell to the floor. "What did I do to deserve that, master?"

"Where did I hit you?"

"On my nose, master."

"Curses! I was aiming at your mouth." But Arviû was pleased with himself. He had not lost much of his accuracy. *I shall have a set of knives made. Virssagòn can do that. They'll have blades sharp enough to give my victims slashing wounds if I even catch them with a glancing throw.* "Help me get dressed. I don't know where they've put my clothes. We are going to Dsôn. To the Bone Tower."

"Yes, master."

He swung his legs off the bed and felt a sudden surge of confidence. "And bring the bell."

"Of course, master."

The slave helped Arviû into a silken robe. It was apparently one of his own that his two daughters had brought in.

He felt the ornamental border on the sleeves. The fabric bore a perfume he recognized as his elder daughter's, Parnôri's. It touched him to think she had been looking after him although she lived so far away.

Both daughters had chosen the life of rural estate owner in Shiimal and had nothing to do with the military life. At first this had been a source of regret to him, but now . . . *I could go and live with Parnôri until I—*

"Forgive me, master. But have you not heard about the mysterious sickness? The whole of Dsôn is in upheaval. Many of the citizens from the capital have fled to the countryside. It may not be a good time to travel."

Arviû's train of thought was interrupted by the slave's words. "Since when have the älfar ever feared illness and disease?" he asked patronizingly.

"I know your race is particularly resistant to disease, master, and I am full of admiration," the human replied as he helped Arviû into his boots. "There seems, however, to be a new illness that leaves the healers puzzled."

Arviû would not normally pay any attention to barbarian rumors, but the man sounded genuine in his concern. "It's only älfar getting sick?"

"Yes, master."

Arviû stood up and walked toward the door with his hand on the slave's shoulder. It was humiliating to be led in this fashion, but it was unavoidable. When the warriors in the Bone Tower had trained him, he would be independent, of course. "Tell me what has been happening."

"It began forty moments of unendingness ago. An älf by the name of Arganaï was the very first victim. He had been taken captive by the dorón ashont but managed to get away to warn Dsôn. He was found one morning in his quarters. It's said his whole body had burst open. His intestines were completely destroyed, as if they had been sprayed with acid. Some other älfar died soon after that, in exactly the same way."

"These others, where were they from?"

"They were guards like he was and they had shared rooms. Then the illness spread. There seems to be no stopping it."

They had arrived at the stables, as Arviû realized from the smell and the noises.

"Wait here, master. I'll put the horse in the shafts."

"But carry on with what you're telling me." Arviû removed his hand from the slave's shoulder. He abhorred this feeling of utter helplessness. *I was the best archer in the land and now I'm no better than an infant.*

"I'm afraid that's all I know," the slave said as he put the horse in harness. "I only know that Wèlèron's healing experts remain confused. As slaves, of course, we don't get told the details."

"So it began with that älf . . . ?" *This confounded memory problem.*

"Yes, Arganaï. He lost an arm during his escape, but still managed to fight his way across Ishím Voróo and past enemy lines. And then to pass into endingness like that . . . Nobody deserves to die that way. He must have suffered terribly." There came the sound of wheels turning.

"He can't really have suffered much, or wouldn't his comrades have come running?" objected Arviû. *This slave could be pulling all kinds of faces and making fun of me and I wouldn't notice.* "Or perhaps it attacked his lungs first, so he couldn't cry out." Hearing the name dorón ashont reminded Arviû of what the two healers had been talking about at his bedside: monsters that had attacked the border between the radial arms of Wèlèron and Avaris, but he had forgotten how the rest of the story went. "And what's happening in the north?"

"You mean where the dorón ashont attacked, master?"

"What else could I mean?"

Steps approached him again.

"The empire is safe, but in Wèlèron three of the defense islands had their fortresses badly damaged by enemy catapult fire. They were taken by surprise. No one had thought the dorón ashont capable of building such powerful machines." It hadn't escaped Arviû that the slave sounded quite glad about these events. Either he was not able to conceal his feelings or he did not want to.

Arviû was concerned. *Could this be the seed from which rebellion might grow?* "I am blind, but not deaf," he said coldly. "Don't think that you will profit in any way if we lose. And, of course, we won't lose."

"But I would never think like that, master," the slave said indignantly.

"What is happening at the northern part of the defense canal?"

"The Inextinguishables have had the damaged fortresses repaired as far as possible, but they are still being bombarded. The enemy hasn't made it as far as the canal yet. They are kept in check at the edge of the cleared area by the älfar catapults."

Arviû was pleased to hear that. "They will never get over to Wèlèron," he said. "Are you nearly ready? I'm keen to leave today."

"I'm nearly done, master. May I take your hand to help you up?"

Arviû stretched out his arm and his hand was grasped. He was soon seated in the wagon: a small one with a seat for two passengers and one for the driver.

Their journey began.

Arviû pulled the curtains at the side window shut to prevent anyone seeing him. *I won't show myself until I'm a champion warrior again.*

He thought about the dorón ashont. He cursed his loss of sight—when did one ever get the opportunity to witness the second downfall of a race? He only knew about the first defeat from the old legends. *Poisoned.* He smiled. *They were so easy to defeat. This time it will be more difficult.* The älfar only knew about danger because of . . .

"What was his name?"

"Whose name, master?"

"The älf who escaped!"

"Arganaï, master."

"A true hero." In his thoughts he was already in the Bone Tower and talking to the blind bodyguards about some training.

After that, Tark Draan was waiting for him!

I shall practice and practice until I drop with exhaustion, and as soon as I wake up I'll practice some more. There is no time at all to lose if there are to be any enemies left for me to slay!

"Master, I'll let you know when we are near Dsôn. Because of the sickness, you know."

Burst open and putrefying. "You would think, perhaps, he caught something in the dorón ashonts' prison. Perhaps it was that," mumbled Arviû. He tried to discover as much as he could about his immediate environment, listening carefully to any sounds that arose. His hearing was to become his most vital sense.

Tark Draan (Girdlegard), far to the southwest of the Gray Mountains,
4371ˢᵗ division of unendingness (5199ᵗʰ solar cycle),
late autumn.

Doghosh of Ligard stood on the battlements of the highest tower of the
third and outermost defense wall of the town of Sonnenhag.

The commander surveyed the incredible army encamped at his walls
with some concern. The troops were composed of monsters in numbers
he had never seen before. The humans would never be able to sneak out
alive, and there was no way to bring relief troops or further supplies in.
They were under siege. *But we've got enough to keep us going through
the winter.*

"I've never seen an orc army that large." Endrawolt, his deputy, stood
behind him, looking down at the enemy who remained just out of range
of their catapults. "Up to now we've only ever had to deal with the odd
band of greenskins." He beat his gloved fist against the stone balustrade.
"How can they dare to take arms against us like this?" Endrawolt shook
his head. "Look how many they are!"

"They know we are in charge of defense for the entire region. If the
town falls, they can do whatever they want." Doghosh saw the ugly banners fluttering over the orc camps. "These monsters must be from several
different tribes, but I don't recognize any of the devices on those flags
out there." He stepped back so he was next to Endrawolt. "If I didn't
know any better, I'd say they were from the Outer Lands. But that would
mean one of the passes had fallen."

"Unthinkable! Utterly impossible! I'd say they must have been
breeding here in secret—letting us think there were really only a few of
them so that one day they could spring something like this on us!"

Doghosh's silence indicated that he disagreed.

Sonnenhag had had the good fortune to receive warning of the
invading force: an orc scouting party had been spotted early, so they had
barred the gates. It had just been a precautionary measure, but less than a
quarter of an hour later the army had turned up to storm the town walls,
failing at the outer ring. Now nearly 30,000 inhabitants were quaking in
their beds with a mere 2,000 soldiers responsible for their safety.

"They'll have to defeat us if they want the land for fifty miles around us." Doghosh drew the cool air into his lungs. "They're taller and broader than normal orcs, their tusks are painted and their armor and weaponry are different." He pointed to the siege ladders the town defenders had destroyed. "Even the way they've fixed the rungs to the uprights is new."

"You're quite sure they're from the Outer Lands?"

"Tell me how they could possibly have kept their growing numbers secret if they were breeding so quickly," said Doghosh. "There must be about 20,000 of them. And then there are the others, the smaller ones. We'd have been bound to notice what they were up to if they'd been local! They can't make themselves invisible." He looked past Endrawolt to the rings of town walls behind them. "Do our men know we're giving up the outer ring at the next surge?"

"Yes."

"They are making preparations?"

Endrawolt nodded. "We'll need another seven days. Even nine." His hand caressed the stone of the battlements. "It's an outrage to have to surrender the walls our ancestors built."

"But it'll kill many more than the catapults can." Doghosh had given the command that all the male residents between fourteen and sixty cycles were to report for digging duty. The idea was to undermine the foundations of the ring wall so that at the crucial moment—and given encouragement—it would collapse outward. The wall was tall enough that it would crush the orcs along its whole circumference. With enough impetus, the blocks of stone would roll down the hill and take out plenty more.

There will be a few thousand fewer to fight if the gods are with us. Doghosh had never had to think in numbers like this. The most dangerous bands of outlaws might have been fifty strong, and a horde of orcs perhaps up to a hundred. Even if there were skirmishes along the border with troops from rival kingdoms, you would not usually get more than 500 warriors on each side.

How should he proceed in order to save his town? Sonnenhag had, in the times of peace, lost its importance as a bastion and was now nothing more than a large fortified town that owed its prosperity to trade with nearby Ido.

The commander still had 2,000 men under him, but he had no idea if they were really up to repelling further attacks like the one they had repulsed eleven days ago. Chasing a robber band through the woods or running down a gang of pickpockets in town was absolutely not the same thing. He had seen naked fear in his men's eyes following the attempted storming. Some of the younger guards had had the trembles ever since.

"Right," he said, starting down the tower steps. "Let's get the second ring sorted. We'll need stones up there to throw at the enemy."

"We've started to pull down the oldest buildings."

"Remember to tell them the blocks must be small enough for even the weaker ones—women and boys as well—to heave over the side. Who knows how long we'll have enough trained soldiers doing the job?"

Doghosh and Endrawolt made their way down the spiral stairs and strode alongside the ditches at the foot of the first wall, where substantial wood supports prevented the walls from falling backward onto the workforce hacking away with their shovels. Straw soaked in pitch and petroleum had been piled against the wall.

They looked up at him with a strange mixture of fear and loyalty. Doghosh tried to display as much confidence as possible and keep his men's spirits up.

But by the time he and his deputy had arrived at the second wall he could not help sighing deeply. "It's going to be hard, Endrawolt. We won't have any more walls in reserve if the orcs bring up reinforcements. What are we going to do?"

"Pray. Our safety lies in the hands of the gods."

"Our safety used to lie primarily in the hands of the dwarves." Doghosh looked north, to where dark clouds were gathered on the skyline. *What can have happened for the dwarves to let us down like this?* He turned around abruptly. He needed to get to the council meeting at which he was expected to report his progress.

He got on his horse and rode through the gate of the innermost wall. This one was not as substantial as the two outer rings of fortifications: time and weathering had allowed fine cracks to develop on the northern face. The inhabitants had always been able to rely on the strength of the outer walls. But it was about to be sacrificed.

Men and their sons were busying themselves with cartloads of stones. Ammunition. There was no complaining. It was life or death.

Originally from the south, Doghosh had made Sonnenhag his home when he was forced to leave his birthplace due to plague. He had promised his dying wife he would go. He liked it here: the half-timbered houses with their carved balconies and murals were how the townspeople had demonstrated a hard-won prosperity. Now their peaceful life was under threat.

He acknowledged every greeting with a silent nod.

He would not have to speak much; he would only explain, yet again, that every single person was doing everything they could. The old councillors would be glad to hear this and would congratulate him and then they would all say a prayer to Elria. It had been the same story every day since the beginning of the siege. The goddess did not seem to be taking much notice.

He reached the citadel that housed the council chamber. This was where the weakest inhabitants would take shelter when the next attack came. There were bunkers underground where people could be safe even if the houses burned or collapsed. A secret tunnel led out of the catacombs into the open air, but it did not go far enough to evacuate the whole town without the orcs noticing.

Maybe they will be the only ones in Sonnenhag to survive the siege. Doghosh reined in his horse and was about to dismount when the alarm sounded.

The North Gate! He turned his horse back through the narrow streets, racing through the exits to the outer wall. "What's happening?" he shouted, springing out of the saddle and running up the steps to the walkway. "They're coming!" Endrawolt pointed to the broad road that led toward Sonnenhag. Before the siege, merchants and tradesmen in coaches and on carts had regularly used this road, but now it was a throng of orcs trundling their crude but functional siege engines along. He could see three battering rams heading their way and then catapults for spears and arrows. "I can't see any catapults. That's one good thing."

Doghosh wondered what instructions he should give. "How far along are the excavations?"

"The towers will stay standing, but we can topple the walls right and left for a distance of just over a hundred paces. We haven't been able to get any farther yet. We had expected the attack to come from the south—" Endrawolt uttered a curse. "They're coming really fast! They've got new siege ladders, three or four dozen, it looks like."

Doghosh watched them approach. They had impressive-looking ladders on rollers, which had shields to protect the climbers from bolts and arrows fired down on them. Infantry in various formations brought up the rear. *This is not going to be easy. They've got lots of tricks up their sleeves.* Doghosh was convinced that these monsters had come from outside Girdlegard.

The enemy started firing arrows, many of them falling short and crashing into the stonework, but others flew in far over their heads.

"They're testing the aim. Another couple of salvoes and they'll be around our ears." Endrawolt yelled down at the men in the ditches, telling them to get out. The ditches were to be filled with water to make things go smoothly. "Take hold of the supports," he called. "Listen out for the order."

Doghosh realized that the falling wall would only take out half of the enemy front. "Endrawolt, send word for the best horsemen: those who don't have family! They must be sent out with messages for our king. He has to know what is happening in Sonnenhag. He must assemble an army to defeat the orcs when we are gone. We will do all we can in the meantime. The messengers should be given the best of our horses and must set off as soon as some kind of gap appears in the enemy ranks. Warn them they may well lose their lives in the attempt to get word out."

His deputy nodded and spoke crisply to one of his officers, who ran down the steps to carry out the order.

"Get down!" came a shout from the nearby tower.

Endrawolt and Doghosh ducked, narrowly avoiding incoming fire.

The second salvo had been accurate. Anyone up on the battlements was at risk of being hit if they were spotted in the open embrasures. The Sonnenhag defenders could only reply with archers and crossbowmen. The council had never dreamed their city would be confronted with dangers such as these.

Nobody had. Doghosh was not apportioning any blame to the city elders. Once he had thought that the stars would fall to the earth before the orcs would turn up with a force like this one. He peered cautiously around the edge of the protective crenel. "They'll be here any minute! Their siege ladders are only forty paces off! Withdraw now!"

The command was passed down the line without a bugle sounding. A handful of the bravest stayed up on the battlements, showering the attackers with arrow-fire to make it look as if all the defenders were still in position.

Doghosh and Endrawolt made their way down to the foot of the walls where the men stood ready with their long poles.

There was only a distance of thirty paces to be covered before they reached the safety of the second wall. If the worst came to the worst, the surviving orcs would catch some of the slower humans. The archers up on the second wall would do their best to prevent that from happening.

"The masonry will kill them all," Doghosh called, climbing up into the saddle. "Take heart! Sonnenhag is our bastion against the monsters of Tion. We will stand firm until the king arrives with an army to liberate the town!" His words echoed back from the town walls. There were no answering cheers from the townspeople.

Water steadily filled the ditches, softening the ground and allowing the pitch-sodden straw to float to the surface.

The din the orcs were making got louder and louder; their tinny instruments squeaked and their drumrolls urged them on. The walls amplified the noises so that those waiting by the ditch felt that the enemy army must be getting bigger all the time.

Elria, protect our people and our town! Help our children!

One of the archers up on the wall called out, "Ten paces to go."

"Get down!" Doghosh ordered before turning to the men. "Right! All of you, push hard against the wall. As hard as you can! We'll crush these vermin when the walls collapse. As soon as the wall starts to fall, drop your staves and run for it!" He rode along the line repeating his orders so that everyone could hear him above the gruff orc shouts. It was vital their own losses were kept to an absolute minimum at this stage. *Ideally, we won't lose a single man.*

The last of the archers came running down the steps, taking up their positions behind the men with the staves who were shoving with all their might.

Cracks started to appear and mortar crumbled away; some sections of the wall were tilting, but the whole construction was still intact.

"Push harder still!" Doghosh yelled. "And start the burning!"

Some orcs had managed to scale the walls, weapons raised, looking in vain for someone to fight.

The straw on the water-filled ditch was ignited with a fire arrow and the pitch and petroleum mix burned strongly, sending up clouds of thick black smoke to make the invaders' eyes water.

"Shoot them!" Endrawolt cursed. "Those triple-damned—"

Archers on the ground and on the battlements of the second wall sent their arrows flying at the enemy, killing one orc after another as soon as they appeared around the sheltering armor of the siege ladders.

But for each monster killed, ten new ones arrived. Some were already running down the steps wielding terrifyingly large clubs, axes, morning-stars and swords. Doghosh could smell the rancid fat they smeared their armor with and their war shouts were ear-shattering.

"Start shoving again!" Doghosh shouted. The stones continued to put up staunch resistance to the softness of the ground and the muscle power of the humans.

He stopped near where the wall was weakest. *Oh, ye gods, give me your blessing and aid!* Covering his horse's eyes, he dug his spurs sharply into its sides and forced it into a charge, muttering, "Forgive me." At the last moment he threw himself free.

The horse leaped the barrier of the burning ditch and crashed into the wall, which yielded under the impact, bringing down the other sections of the fortifications as it collapsed with a thunderous noise. It fell straight down onto the besieging orcs.

"Yes!" shouted Doghosh in relief as he struggled to his feet. His right leg was painful, but he had sustained no other injury. "Thank you, gods!"

A 300-pace portion of the town wall had gone. Those orcs who had already stormed the battlements found themselves hurtling down onto their own ranks. Some jumped clear only to be shot down by the Son-nenhag bowmen or to fall onto the burning pitch.

It's worked! Bellows of terror came from the other side of the wall as the enemy force saw their vanguard pulverized by the stone blocks. Siege ladders crashed down onto the enemy lines and the careering stones rolled back through the mass of horrified monsters.

Doghosh exulted as the last sections of the falling masonry smashed down, squashing the throng of beasts and sending up clouds of dust.

Endrawolt cantered up and pulled his commander up behind him. "The men are running back, sir. Let's not give the orcs a target for their anger!"

The two of them rode straight for the gate, men running before them, away from the rubble they had created. Archers on the second wall gave covering fire.

I wonder how our side have fared? Doghosh risked a glance over his shoulder.

The first orcs who had escaped the collapsing wall were leaping out of dark brown clouds and thick smoke. Some had injuries seeping green blood where smaller stones had gashed them. They looked horrific with their painted tusks, fat-smeared armor and enormous crude weap-onry. They no longer had any discernible battle plan; snorting and snarl-ing, they were hunting down the humans like animals.

They are so set on killing us they've forgotten about our archers. As long as none of his own men tripped and fell, they should all reach safety. Nobody need be left behind.

Endrawolt was riding through the gap between the opening gates.

I am the commander. Doghosh slid down from the horse and stayed back, sword and shield at the ready, until every single one of his men had run through. *Now I can go through!*

"Commander!" Endrawolt shouted. "What are you doing? Get in here!"

"I'm coming!"

The orcs stormed nearer.

Doghosh took the scene in. He wanted to remember every detail for his report to the king.

The beasts forged a path to him, fixing him with their beady little eyes, their muscular legs pumping tirelessly as they covered the ground, sharp, predator teeth on display as their broad mouths hung open. One of the monsters was struck three times by arrows before it keeled over, but its fellows marched straight over the obstacle of its carcass without a second glance. Their armor rattled as they sprang.

There's no way these orcs are from Girdlegard!

One of the beasts hurled an ax at him.

He dodged and the ax embedded itself deep into the wood of the gate. If he had tried to take the ax on his shield it would have gone straight through and he'd have lost an arm.

What creatures! His heart pounded suddenly with fear and he hurried in to safety. *Tion has sent his worst creations to attack us!*

The gates closed on the orcs, leaving them on the outside.

For now.

Chapter XII

The Inextinguishables stood on the highest part of the Bone Tower.

They turned their faces toward the northwest, to the land between Wèlèron and Avaris.

They came to the conclusion that they and their people were safe.

And so they laughed at the threat of attack by the dorón ashont. They mocked them and sent wine barrels as the payload of their strongest catapults to remind them of their previous humiliating defeat.

The tears of joy the Sibling Rulers shed as they laughed made them blind to the dangers they would face.

The Epocrypha of the Creating Spirit
Book of the Coming Death
72–95

*Tark Draan (Girdlegard), south of the Gray
Mountains, Enchanted Realm of Hiannorum,
4371st division of unendingness (5199th solar cycle),
late autumn.*

Morana finished the piece she was playing on her death's head flute and put it away. She was riding downhill along a broad valley toward an oddly shaped building—her destination. To her right a high waterfall cascaded into a river. Clouds of spray floated in the air, dampening the blood-red roof tiles so that they shone like gems under the setting autumn sun.

This looks like the sort of house you would find in Dsôn! Its three elegant towers of various heights were connected at a number of levels by delicately carved bridges. Staircases wound around the outside, protected from the elements by glass, and the walls were covered in ivy and climbing roses. The daystar sent the last of its golden rays over the brow of the hill, bathing the three buildings in warm, shimmering light.

Morana had to admit that it appealed to her.

The valley itself had been expertly transformed into a delightful garden. Every bush, every shrub and every tree had been precisely trimmed and decorated with strips of bunting and ribbons that wafted prettily in the breeze.

Statues were displayed picturesquely. Small fountains and burbling streams adorned the scene.

She saw stone benches and garden tables where women were seated, reading or talking, while others played ball. The resident enchantress was living up to her name: Flawless.

By all the gods of infamy! This is almost classier than our royal palace! Morana admired how clean and tidy everything was. But she did find it . . . cloying. *Too much honey, too much decoration and not enough real art. When you think what they could have made of this valley! I should ask the nostàroi to let me redesign it.*

But the mere thought of asking Caphalor any favors went against the grain. She had not forgotten his behavior at their last meeting.

People had noticed her. The ladies put down their books and stared. A man up on the highest of the three towers banged a gong. Its round, rich tone rolled across the valley to announce the visitor.

Morana did not mind. On the contrary, it suited her plans.

She was already wearing her black armor and knew that she stood out in the midst of all the frippery. But her own native gracefulness trumped any barbarian.

She rode across the valley floor, heading straight for the towers.

As she drew closer, she began to make out the mosaics on the walls. They all showed the same female form: a woman carrying out various activities; brushing her hair, looking at herself in a mirror, handing out gifts of food to the poor. She could see labels in elegant writing by each of the pictures.

She did not understand everything, but they were all praising Hianna the Flawless for her beauty, wisdom and generosity.

How very modest. Morana's mouth curved into a small smile and she slowed the horse to a walk as she approached the nearest of the towers. *If she were stupid, would they praise her for that as well?*

A woman stepped out. At first glance Morana thought she might be an älf; she was tall and slim, with finely chiseled features and long blond hair that fell over her high-collared red dress. She wore gold filigree at her throat, golden rings on her fingers and a silver coronet studded with diamonds in her hair.

"Greeting," she said warmly. Her outspread arms and her smile would have melted the heart of a rampaging óarco. "I am Hianna the Flawless, mistress of Hiannorum." She placed her hands together, "You are welcome as my guest, a welcome happily extended for one so graceful."

Morana was itching to draw one of her weapons. She studied the maga's ears suspiciously. *Round, not pointed. So she's not an elf.* She sketched a slight bow. "My name is Morana and I have come a long way to see you." She halted her horse and jumped lightly to the ground in front of Hianna.

The first of the ladies from the garden hurried up, but kept a respectful distance while they stared at the visitor in her dark and warlike attire.

"Oh, a messenger?"

"More of a negotiator."

Hianna was still smiling. She raised her linked hands and pointed both index fingers at the älf visitor. "You have piqued my curiosity, Morana. You are no elf, though you have their grace and elegance." She looked Morana directly in the eyes. "Black. Strange, but attractive in its own way." She passed her tongue over her lips. "You will be tired after your journey." The maga moved aside and invited her into the tower. "I'll have you shown to a room where you can bathe and be given fresh clothes. We can talk at supper."

That sounded more like a command than an offer. "Very kind of you." One of the girls came over and took her horse's bridle.

Morana entered the tower, taking her surroundings in watchfully, wary of danger. A cautious nature was the mother of a long life.

A famula in a deep yellow dress walked past her to a narrow shaft bathed in shimmering blue light.

"You may follow Iula to the guest room," Hianna said.

"Come," said Iula. "It's quite safe. Don't worry. We would never hurt a guest."

It may be a trap. Despite her unease, Morana let the famula lead her into the circle of blue light. She felt a tingling all over her body as invisible forces took her up through the shaft. "Magic!" she exclaimed although, of course, in an enchanted land this was only to be expected.

"Yes, kept in permanent readiness by means of the mistress's spell," Iula explained. "The spell is fed by our force field, so there is no reason to worry it might lose energy and drop us." On the way up, Morana saw doors set in alcoves with platforms to step onto; markings on the walls helped to identify the rooms beyond. "If you place one foot on a platform you'll stop going up and can step out safely." She demonstrated and Morana followed suit. "This is the guest wing." The door opened onto a corridor. "I'll show you where everything is."

Morana had noticed Iula studying her features. Iula was, herself, striking enough to break the heart of any barbarian with a bat of an eyelid, but in comparison to an älf she was only tolerably pretty. "Thank you."

Maids brought a tub to Morana's room and filled it with fragrant warm water. A long black dress was provided for her to wear after her bath.

"Would you, perhaps, like someone to help wash you?" Iula gave the impression she would be more than willing to carry out the task.

"No, thank you. I would rather be alone."

The famula clapped for the maids to withdraw. "I'll come back for you later. The mistress will be looking forward to dining with you." She left the room.

Another cozy tête-à-tête. Morana was reminded of the supper with Caphalor that had gone so very wrong. *If I'm not careful I'll be fighting off the enchantress, too.*

She put down her weapons and armor and laid her clothes on a chair before climbing into the water. A selection of fine-scented soaps and soft sponges had been placed by the tub. *Hianna has good taste.*

Morana closed her eyes and permitted her thoughts to roam, wondering what the evening held in store.

Her task had been to win new allies for the älfar campaign and she had already secured undertakings from several nobles, barons and earls. Barbarians were easily won over with the promise of gold and the prospect of a share of elf riches, fertile land and good hunting grounds. *Humans are so predictable, but some of them still surprise me.* She remembered the instance of a barbarian fighting off five robbers intent on seizing his wife. Morana had been riding fifty paces off and had followed the action with interest. Outlaws had ambushed a group of travelers and all but this couple had been killed. The man was quite badly injured, but he still tried his best to beat off all comers in order to protect his wife who was cowering at his side, sobbing with fear.

The älf-woman had found this quite memorable: barbarians making sacrifices for love, not payment.

In the end the man had been killed and the robbers had grabbed the distraught woman.

Morana had intervened, slaying the outlaws.

She could still see the blood-smeared features of the woman when she had pressed her partner's sword into her hands with the words: "Learn to fight. Defend your next lover or die with him, but don't you dare cower uselessly at his feet!"

Any of that would have been unthinkable with our people. I could never have stood idly by if someone were attacking my companion. Morana took a sponge in her hand, soaked it and squeezed water over her head, indulging in the pleasures of the warm bath.

She had come to Hiannorum in search of new support for the cause. It had struck her that a maga known for perfection in all things ought to be easy to win over because her motivations were already known: it would be easy to find something to tempt her. *I'm sure I could entice her by saying the elves know the secret of beauty. Or I could say we hold the secret and would share it with her. Share it later, of course, after the war.*

Slowly, Morana became aware that she was no longer alone. A slight of touch of air on her damp skin betrayed the presence of someone else in the room.

A trap? She jumped up and catapulted herself out of the tub in a single movement.

As intended, she landed next to her weapons and seized hold of Sun and Moon, ready for action.

She could not see anyone, but someone was there. *I can hear you breathing!* She raised Moon.

"That won't be necessary." A familiar voice came from the shadows. An älf in black studded armor stepped forward into the light and bowed without averting his eyes. "I should have realized you would know I was there, but I had no idea it was you when I entered the room." His eyes scanned her body. "And no idea you would not be clothed." He tossed a towel to her.

Virssagòn! Morana caught the towel and wrapped herself in it. *I did not hear them sound the gong like when I arrived. Either he's been here all the time or he's just slipped in.* "What are you doing here?"

"No, that's what I get to ask *you*," he countered, leaning against the four-poster bed.

"I'm here to win Hianna over to our alliance." She threw her wet hair back and wrung it out. Water coursed down her back to form puddles on the floor. "Having a maga on board would be useful against the elves."

"That was not your mission."

"The nostàroi will be pleased—"

"The nostàroi have sent me to Tark Draan to remove all the barbarians who deal in magic. They are a danger to us and their powers far outweigh our own."

"That's why we need at least one of them on our side," she insisted. *He just enjoys killing.*

He pointed to the window. "How did you think you could induce her to join us? She already has everything she could possibly want. Jewelry, power, magic—"

"She is obsessed with perfection. The barbarians might have thought her flawless, but when they saw me their smiles froze on their faces." Morana knew she was stretching the truth somewhat, but she wanted to ensure that Virssagòn did not wipe out a potential ally. "If I tell her she could be made as beautiful as an älf—"

"And how would that work?"

"I don't know yet. We're to have dinner together tonight. I'm positive I can reel her in." Morana looked the warrior full in the eyes. "Give me this chance! If it doesn't work you can always go ahead and kill her."

Virssagòn considered this, his eyes sweeping over her body, concealed somewhat under the towel but still visible enough. "Agreed," he said after a slight hesitation. "I shall be there when you talk to her. She won't see me, of course." He smiled. "You received my gift. Do you know how to use it?"

"I still need practice." As she spoke, she put on the black dress, placing her armor over the top, and fastening Sun and Moon to the belt on her hip.

Virssagòn smiled. "You can go anywhere dressed like that: out to dinner or off to battle. You look like the pride of the älfar." He made silently for the door. "I don't know whether or not to wish you luck. It might be good for our campaign if you win, but it would derive me of my fun." He opened the door and disappeared.

Morana admired her reflection in the mirror. *A good mix: beauty and danger.* She painted a light smudge of soot around her eyes and on the lids to make herself look more sinister.

*Ishím Voróo (Outer Lands), Dsôn Faïmon, between
the radial arms Wèlèron and Avaris,
4371st division of unendingness (5199th solar cycle),
late autumn.*

"Another one! From the west!" The alarm signal rang out across the courtyard.

Téndalor looked out and caught sight of a black speck arcing down through the air, about to hit the ruins of island fortress number one-eight-four. The workforce attempting to repair the towers began to run.

"It's spot on," he muttered angrily. *They've got the range exact now.*

The missile thudded home, sending the repair towers crashing down. This had been the forty-eighth attempt to get the support platforms up.

In the name of infamy! How could this happen? Téndalor and his crew were now the only älfar defending the section between the radial arms Wèlèron and Avaris. All the other island fortresses had been razed to the ground or were too badly damaged to function. The island under his command, bastion number one-eight-seven, had had its fair share of strikes, but at least the walls were still intact, and in the intervals between bombardment, supplies arrived via the Dsôn bridge, so they had plenty of ammunition.

One of his female comrades, Daraïs, appeared at his side. "Benàmoi, the troops for the decoy attack have arrived. When the sun is overhead we are to let down the bridge to Ishím Voróo."

Téndalor turned to the Dsôn side of the river, where the army the Inextinguishables had sent were assembled. He had expected warriors on night-mares and fire-bulls, but judging by their postures and the size of their mounts, it was obvious these fighters were only humans disguised as älfar. "Where on earth did they drum those up?"

"Slaves wanting a bit of advancement with their masters," answered Daraïs.

So we've got armored slaves and they're sitting on horses and oxen in war paint. The Inextinguishables did not want to risk genuine älfar lives on a frontal attack on the dorón ashont. He could not control his amusement.

Daraïs smiled with him. "I'd like to bet they won't reach the other side of the cleared strip. Or the enemy catapults."

"Just as long as they win a bit of time for our own warriors." Téndalor signaled for the bridge to Dsôn Faïmon to be lowered. The sorry crowd of pretend warriors trooped onto the island. There were fewer than fifty real älfar among them driving the barbarian slaves on, encouraging them to believe they might actually survive the mission they had volunteered for.

But they won't, of course. Téndalor looked toward Ishím Voróo again. *None of them will come back.*

The dorón ashont had set up camp on the banks, out of range of the heavy älfar catapults. After the island fortresses to the right and the left of one-eight-seven had been put out of action, there was nothing to deter the enemy from entering the tree-free area.

Téndalor was proud of the accuracy of his catapult crews, which had ensured that his own fortress had not shared the fate of the neighboring islands. He put his trust in his god, Fadhasi. "We shall be granted the sight of our mythical adversaries being defeated for the second time in history."

He had heard that the Inextinguishables had ordered a foray. The main body was in the west, marching into Ishím Voróo and circling behind the dorón ashont, while the barbarian troops here provided a distraction. Téndalor would give the barbarians covering fire, but that was all he was prepared to do. *They're only slaves, after all.*

He watched the false älfar troops ride over the first of the two drawbridges. He could hear their laughter and could see the smiles on their ugly faces. *They really do think they're going to be victorious.* "Get the catapults ready and lower the second bridge," he commanded.

The chains clattered as they were slowly released, allowing the wooden platform to swing down.

The odd collection of soldiers advanced, sweeping through the courtyard and stepping onto the bridge even before it was completely level with the ground.

"Death can't come to them soon enough, it seems," said Daraïs cheerfully.

"Who knows what they've been promised?" Unobserved, Téndalor touched the Fadhasi rune he had carved. *Give us the strength to destroy this enemy once and for all!*

The body of human soldiers were now in Ishím Voróo, dividing in two with the intention of attacking the enemy camps to the right and the left of fortress one-eight-seven. With almost childish enthusi-asm they raced off at a gallop with weapons drawn. The genuine älfar warriors among them fell back and remained near the drawbridge. They had done their duty and had no wish to go down in a hail of stones.

The dorón ashont had long since seen the attack coming and had put their defense lines of huge warriors in place. Their catapults hurled stones the size of óarco heads at the attackers. The salvoes came in waves, tearing great gaps in the slaves' ranks. Barbarians, horses and oxen died in the bombardment.

They're only concentrating on one direction. Téndalor looked west where the authentic älfar army was scheduled to appear. There was a dust cloud in the distance. *That'll be them! This will be the end of the dorón ashont!*

At that point something strange occurred: the giant creatures, who had so recently formed a protective phalanx to counter the mounted troops, all pulled back. One by one they turned tail and sought shelter in their camp.

"We've taken them by surprise! They weren't ready for us!" Téndalor clenched a fist in triumph and took out a spy-tube to watch their destruction.

Daraïs laughed. "We'll give them something to be afraid of!"

The true älfar warriors charged through the opposition's camp, showering the canvas shelters with arrows before overturning the tents or setting fire to them.

Then the earth swallowed many of the night-mares and their riders.

The advancing army hastily came to a standstill.

Téndalor hastily placed the spy-tube to his eye. "The dorón ashont have excavated." Téndalor told Daraïs what he could see. "They must have known what was coming—" He heard a loud noise and then the clatter of weapons, quite close to where he stood.

"Benàmoi! They're on the drawbridge!" yelled Daraïs. "They're on the bridge!"

"Who's on—?" Téndalor put down the tube and turned.

Not ten paces from the bank a hole had opened up in the earth. Dorón ashont were surging out of it.

The älfar warriors who had been waiting at the end of the drawbridge lay dead next to their slaughtered mounts. The hate-fueled enemy had trodden them into the ground with their iron shoes.

"Catapults, fire!" Téndalor could not grasp the fact that the enemy were already so close to the fortress, running swift as the wind in spite of their size and the weight of their armor. It looked as if the ground were giving birth to this teeming throng. "Get the drawbridge up!"

Daraïs had gone white. "By all the infamous ones! They've dug a tunnel!"

A salvo of arrows flew toward the dorón ashont, but could find no purchase on their long, studded shields. Not a single enemy soldier died. The timbers of the bridge groaned under the stampede.

The winches jammed and the drawbridge stopped rising.

Another ten paces and they'll be here! "Keep turning! What are you doing?" Téndalor shouted to the bridge crew.

"It won't budge!" Daraïs reported. "Look over there!"

The weight of the dorón ashont forced the bridge downward. The älfar could not possibly close off access to Ishím Voróo. *No!* His gaze swept the battlements. "Get into the courtyard!" he ordered those manning the catapults. "Hold the gate and get the second drawbridge up. When you've done that, destroy the capstans so they—"

A sudden draft touched his hair and something heavy flew overhead to land with a thud just behind where he stood. Purple light exploded around him and a deafening thunder set all his limbs aquiver. Ice-cold fear overtook him.

Daraïs screamed and drew her swords.

Fadhasi, don't forsake me! Téndalor turned and drew his own weapon. All he could see was a wall of iron: an excellently forged set of armor covered with ornaments and symbols—and a metal gauntlet wielding a mighty war hammer aimed at his midriff.

Téndalor bounded back and tried to ward off the blow, but he had underestimated both the force and the range at his adversary's disposal: his sword was struck out of his hand by the shaft of the hammer and the weapon's head struck him on the side of his body, hurling him against the parapet as if he had been a cloth doll.

Téndalor felt a sudden pain in his chest as he struggled to breathe. He slipped down onto the floor, his left hand reaching for the Fadhasi rune on the stone wall. *Where is the support I prayed for?* The walkway was teeming with dorón ashont. His own men were being slaughtered piecemeal. The älfar armor might as well have been made of paper.

A vertical sword-strike split Daraïs from the helmet down. One half of her toppled over into the courtyard while the other fell onto the walkway. A blow from an ax took off an älf's right side; another älf lost his face to a spiked gauntlet.

No army can defeat the dorón ashont! Fighting for breath, Téndalor lifted his head to examine his own injuries. The hammer had crushed his left side, halving the size of his chest. There was blood splattered all over his protective harness and his shoulder had been totally destroyed.

I must . . . Téndalor tried to get up, but his feet kept slipping on the stone floor. *Warn Wèlèron . . .*

A blackened helmet filled his vision, and from behind the death's head visor, a pair of purple eyes stared at him fixedly. Téndalor could hear a growling noise, directed only at him.

Rím's husband?

"I don't understand you, you freak!" he groaned, desperate for breath.

He was grabbed by the nape of the neck and held up in the air, so that he could see that the bridge to Dsôn Faïmon remained lowered.

"What are you doing?" he groaned. Then he was swung around and forced to look in the direction of Ishím Voróo. The älfar warriors there charged toward island fortress one-eight-seven. *Fadhasi, I beg you: send a miracle!*

All of the attacking dorón ashont had crossed the bridge and now they pulled the drawbridge to Ishím Voróo back up.

Téndalor realized that the dorón ashont had managed to acquaint themselves with the island's catapult mechanisms. They sent showers of arrows down on the älfar, killing dozens.

The älfar were forced to retreat. The division manned by slaves in disguise was long gone. His dying eyes took in the sight of the bridge to Ishím Voróo, still standing vertical. No one could cross. "In the name of Fadhasi, I curse you—" he gasped.

The dorón ashont hurled him away.

Téndalor followed a high arc. For a moment the flight was peaceful, then he splashed down in the defense moat and he realized that, for the first time in many hundreds of divisions of unendingness, an enemy foot had touched the soil of his homeland.

And he would not be in any position to prevent Dsôn's defilement.

Tark Draan (Girdlegard), Gray Mountains,
4371ˢᵗ division of unendingness (5199ᵗʰ solar cycle),
early winter.

Have I been here before? Simin had only been able to penetrate the complex tunnel systems of the Gray Mountains because the älfar had put some idiot orcs on watch. He had only needed to use a smidgeon of magic to escape the orcs' sharp eyes. But now he was wandering fruitlessly through the underground passages.

The magus had been struck by the orcs' build: the ones he had seen here were broader and taller than the local version. They would present quite a challenge to the soldiers of Girdlegard.

How do I go about finding a mist-demon in an underground kingdom when I have absolutely no idea how big the place is? The dwarves might have permitted travelers to pass through, but had never given away their secrets and had certainly never made a map he knew of.

Simin's only hope was to find some clue as to the whereabouts of this demon and follow a trail.

Have I been this way before? He looked carefully at the junction he had arrived at. *No.* There were dwarf runes scratched on the wall, but other symbols had been painted over the top in yellow. Simin supposed the new markings were intended to help the occupying force find its way around. For him, it was getting more and more like finding his way through an ant heap.

He was despondent and very alone.

You'll have to think of something! He looked down the separate tunnels. Perhaps this way?

He had found out that the various creatures were kept strictly isolated from each other. The main contingent of the army was already in Girdlegard proper, but many small units had remained behind to secure the conquered territory in the mountains.

He had quickly lost all sense of how time was passing. He rested whenever he felt tired and carried on his search as soon as he woke.

In many of the deeper-lying areas of the old dwarf kingdom the temperatures were nice and warm. He would not die of cold and he would not starve to death because he stole food along the way. Most of it was tolerable enough—a kind of ground meal that he mixed with water. He had not touched the dried meat.

You know what? I have been here before. He stopped, hearing steps coming toward him.

Swiftly he started to climb the wall, pulling himself up by handholds in the carvings. He found a cleft in the rock he was able to squeeze into and hide.

Before long a whole division of human soldiers marched past. They had weapons and knapsacks and their furs had a fresh layer of snow on the shoulders.

More returnees. Simin had already noticed some of the tribes going back to their homeland. He understood enough of what they were saying to work out that a lot of them had not exactly volunteered of their own free will. More and more of these groups were sloping off, disappointed by what they had seen of Girdlegard. *This group looks like they're doing the same thing.*

Simin waited until they were far enough away before he crept out of his hiding place.

He wiped the dirt off his hands. *I've been cleaner. And I know I've smelled better before now.* But he realized that the scent of soap would instantly give him away.

He sighed. *I've taken on far too much. I'm never going to find the demon like this.*

The humans did not seem to be talking about the demon at all, he could not understand what the orcs were saying and he did not dare grab someone and force the truth out of them. *Too dangerous.*

He jogged on, thinking about his next course of action. He remembered that the dwarves had told Famenia about "undead" creatures at the Stone Gateway. *I must make my way there.*

Simin had reached a further junction. *But how do I know where north is?*

There was nothing for it but to guess. He took the passage to the right and from then on, he chose the way that led up rather than along or down, hoping to check the position of the sun at some point. When the air felt chilly he took this as an indication that he was near the surface.

He caught a sudden whiff of cooking.

Something smelled delicious, like a meat broth. Simin's stomach rumbled. *I hope it's suitable for humans, whatever it is.*

After climbing some stairs he came to a door that was not completely shut. The aroma was irresistible.

Simin crept forward, hearing voices behind the door conversing in a language he did not understand. When he glanced inside the bright room he was utterly horrified.

It was an old smithy. Bones were simmering in a foaming grayish liquid in buckets originally intended for molten metal. Skins of various sizes spanned the glowing forge to dry out. Millstones meant for grinding soft rock were producing coarse bone meal and the tiny white pebbles were then poured into sacks. Simin could imagine whose bones were being processed.

Ye gods! Simin felt sick. *What are they doing with the dwarf corpses? This is worse than disgusting! Unforgivable!*

There were elf-like creatures in long leather aprons in the workshop, holding and examining the bones in their gloved hands; others were working at long tables, cutting up hair and lengths of beard. Two of them were stirring a red substance in little pots.

Dried blood? Simin did not really want to know what the dyes had been fashioned from. *This is a workshop of death.*

He could not stand the sight any longer. He turned and ran away, the nausea nearly getting the better of him.

He would never be able to eat goulash again in all his life.

CHAPTER XIII

None doubted the nostàroi.

None that saw them ride into battle.
The älfar troops revered their commanders and would have followed them
through Tark Draan to subjugate even the next empire.
Oh, älfar! If only you could have seen Caphalor and Sinthoras!
Oh, Constellations! If you had only kept faith with them!
Oh, Comets! If only you had not left the path!

And so winter arrived.

Excerpt from the epic poem *The Heroes of Tark Draan*
composed by Carmondai, master of word and image

Tark Draan (Girdlegard), far to the southeast of the Gray Mountains,
4371st division of unendingness (5199th solar cycle),
late autumn.

Doghosh of Ligard ran to where the enemy's nearest siege ladder was
being placed against the walls. He hardly noticed the pain from his

wounded right forearm, so great was the exertion of the moment. "Bring your poles over here! Push the ladder away and send them to their deaths!" Steadily repetitive thumps came from the battering ram currently attacking the gate.

He watched four young boys attempt to push the ladder away from the battlements, but they were not strong enough; the ladder was securely anchored at the base, and the combined weight of the metal shield and the orcs on the rungs made their task impossible. "Sir, we can't do it!" came the frightened cries.

"I'm coming right over!"

Doghosh muttered a curse. The picture was the same all along the second defense wall: men, women, boys and girls were all doing their utmost to defend the town. They sweated and struggled with heavy stones, which were toppled over the parapet onto the beasts attacking tirelessly from below; they fought for breath as they shoved ladders away, or repelled individual invaders with a courage born of desperation. Their own dead and wounded lay ignored at their feet. There was simply no time. Every hand was needed to fend off the fifth wave of attack, or to douse the fires breaking out in the narrow streets where orc firebrands had lodged in thatch.

Ye gods, let it get dark soon! If the enemy pull back for the night we can get some respite. Doghosh reached the four boys just as an orc heaved itself over the top of the battlements and loosed a bolt from a small crossbow, hitting the first boy in the belly. The other three kept up their vain attempts to thrust the ladder away.

"To Tion with you!" Doghosh slammed his mace straight into the orc's face, but the spike lodged under the helmet's nosepiece, forcing him to let go of the handle. He kicked the orc in the chest with his armored boot.

The orc staggered back with a roar and plunged backward over the parapet. The next orc's face appeared around the edge of the ladder-shield.

"Is there no end to your numbers?" Doghosh took a run up and leaped, his feet crashing onto the topmost rung. By adding his own weight to the boys' muscle he had pushed the ladder away—while he was still on it.

The orcs stared up, open-mouthed. One of them hurled a sword in his direction, but missed.

Doghosh was carried farther and farther away from the battlements, swaying as he tried to retain his balance. He finally managed to leap back onto the walkway.

Not a grain of sand too soon: the ladder reached tipping point and fell with its cargo of orcs, slamming into their own besieging troops on the ground.

Endrawolt grabbed Doghosh by the leather cuirass to steady him. "You are urgently needed here, commander," he said sourly while the defenders applauded him for his stunt. "In the future, please leave stuff like that to the acrobats."

"I promise. I mean, I *swear* I will." Doghosh ducked to avoid a salvo of incoming arrows and sprang up onto the parapet to inspect the scene.

Nothing had changed: a throng of orcs at the base of the wall were climbing over their fallen comrades, ramming more ladders into the soil and climbing up. At the same time the battering ram was getting the better of the wooden gates. It was a toss-up as to which of the enemy would get in first.

"What can we do?" muttered Doghosh. His vision blurred and the enemy became one dark green mass, their screams and yells merged to a monotone punctuated by the thuds of the battering ram. *Bizarre music.* "We may have killed a few thousand, but there are thousands more coming at us."

Endrawolt stood speechless at his side, shaking his head.

Because they had not been able to send out messengers, there was no hope of rescue, but surrender was not an option. The monsters would surely massacre the population. Or do worse. There was no mercy to be had from enemies such as these. No question of decent treatment for women and children.

I need a miracle, you gods! You must stand by us, even if the dwarves have let us down! Doghosh took a deep breath.

The splinter of wood and screeches of triumph accompanied the final thud of the battering ram.

"They're through!" Endrawolt exclaimed with a curse. "Fall back to the last wall, Commander?"

"Yes. Sound the retreat." Doghosh glanced up at the sun, setting now. But the night would still be a long time coming. "Are the cauldrons heated?"

"Yes."

"Then call everyone back in." Doghosh planned to swamp the orcs with boiling excrement and hot urine. He had already ordered the lead to be taken out of all the windows and the gold of the wealthy to be collected and melted down to pour on the attackers' heads. The choice of substance was immaterial. *Gold, lead, shit—the only thing that matters is, can it kill? I never thought they would keep up these onslaughts, wave after wave.* "Leave—"

His words were drowned by a bugle signal announcing that friends were coming to their aid.

"What?" Doghosh and Endrawolt looked around to see where help could be coming from.

A double row of heavy cavalry with lowered lances thundered toward Sonnenhag, breaking through the hindmost orc ranks. A second double row followed, weapons still held vertical. Banners fluttered in the wind: the runes they bore had not been fashioned by human hand.

"Elves!" exclaimed Doghosh. A warm wave of relief flooded his body. "It's elves!" he shouted, slamming his clenched fist up into the air above his head. The men on the walkway yelled with glee and the orcs screamed in horror. He gave the order to repel the orcs at their walls. "Drive the beasts back into the lances of the elves!"

"Armored cavalry from the Golden Plain, I think," said Endrawolt. "The princess must have sent them! It looks like there's about 800, maybe even 1,000."

"That's plenty!" Doghosh felt a surge of optimism. "We'll wipe out this scum and then we'll find out where they're from. Then we can send word out to the whole of Girdlegard." Fired with renewed energy he paced along the walkway encouraging the defenders, helping out where necessary and keeping an eye on how the elves' battle was going.

The elves were sweeping mercilessly through the ranks of the orcs. It was wonderful to behold.

The lances they wield must be reinforced in some way, otherwise they would not withstand the impact. The elf cavalry met little resistance and stormed through the enemy's undisciplined stragglers, dispensing death generously. Suddenly the orc catapults were burning, and with that the hitherto constant stream of arrows and spears ceased.

There were no more beasts on their siege ladders; they had all turned to face the greater danger. The town's defenders rejoiced at the unexpected arrival of allies.

"Keep up the barrage of stones!" Doghosh shouted as the attack on the town diminished. *All-merciful gods and Elria in particular, bless you!* "Don't let up now!"

When the orcs noticed the danger at their backs and saw that they had already lost thousands of their troops, they scurried together at the foot of the walls, directly under the hail of rocks and missiles from the town, attempting to present a united front to the elves.

Doghosh called for a heavy-duty wagon shaft to use as a lever and beckoned some men over to him. "Right! The orcs wanted to shelter up here. Let's send the battlements down as a gift, then they don't need to make the effort of coming to us!"

Before the orcs had fully regrouped, around 500 elves had assembled in a long line, and were charging the enemy, horse pressed tight against horse, lances at the ready.

The air filled with loud crashes and thuds. "Down with the parapets now! All of them!" Doghosh shouted. "Push!"

As the second wave of elves followed the first, bringing yet more mayhem and destruction to the orcs, the top ring of the defense walls crashed down on the unsuspecting enemy beneath them.

Endrawolt congratulated Doghosh with a slap on his shoulder. "That'll see them off! Look! By all the gods, look! The green-skinned plague! They're beginning to run!"

Doghosh leaned over the broken wall and wept with joy: orcs were running in all directions, chucking off their armor to be able to get away faster. Small groups of elves set after them, mowing the fleeing soldiers down. Only a handful escaped with their lives.

Doghosh gave the order to push the stilled battering ram away and get the gate open. "Our warriors must go out and finish off any of the wounded orcs. I want justice for my town."

Endrawolt nodded and grinned maliciously. "It will be a pleasure." He strode off.

In the light of the setting sun the elves rode back from all directions, most having lost their lances.

They approached Sonnenhag in a loose formation, their horses splashed liberally with enemy blood. Many of their warriors were on foot, having lost their mounts in battle. Their losses were within reason; Doghosh could see dead elves among the heaps of slaughtered orcs.

Fine figures! Doghosh realized he would never be able to express adequate thanks to the neighboring elf sovereign, Princess Veïnsa, for the help his town had been given.

He raced down the steps to greet their friends at the gate and sent a messenger to announce to the townspeople that they had been rescued. A grin stole over his face. *They won't enjoy spending the night in a town that stinks of boiled shit and simmered piss.*

He wondered how to deal with the heaps of orc cadavers. To burn that number of corpses he would need timber from an entire forest. Could they just dig an enormous pit and shovel the orcs in? Or cart them down to the river, maybe? He rather liked that last idea. The bodies would be carried down to Ido on the current. His country and the Ido realm had been at loggerheads for ages. *A splendid warning to our dear neighbors. Yes, that would be the thing.*

The first of the elves had ridden up. They entered through the gate amid the cheers of townspeople standing on the old walls. They were a splendid sight, ablaze with grace and nobility.

Their leader, a brown-haired elf with two long swords attached to his saddle, approached Doghosh and inclined his head. Orc blood trickled off the armor elf and rider bore and there were traces, too, on his face. "Greetings, human. You are the leader of the bold band of men who stood firm against the orc army?"

"I am Doghosh of Ligard, commander of the town guard for Sonnenhag," he said and indicated Endrawolt, who was issuing orders at the gate. "That man is my deputy . . . You are warriors from the Golden Plain?"

"That is so. We come from a battle raging not far from here. We have been keeping an eye out for these beasts so that we may destroy them. Will you permit us to rest in your town?"

"Of course! You are most welcome."

The elf gave his troops instructions to ride into the town while he remained with Doghosh and examined the state of the walls. "Your citadel would have fallen if we had not arrived in the nick of time. Why were the orcs so keen on taking this town? Surely they would have done better to bypass you and occupy the hinterland?"

"Not at all. Our town is strategically important, a vital crossing-point for several trade routes. It has been growing, cycle for cycle. It's only garrisoned in times of war, which is why we had such difficulty when the orcs attacked."

"You humans!" laughed the elf. "You make your fortresses far too small and you've nowhere near enough soldiers to protect you."

Doghosh did not appreciate this patronizing comment, even though he personally bore no responsibility for the town's defense policy. "It is not my fault—"

"Forgive me, I did not mean to hurt your feelings. You fought courageously, all of you." He swung himself elegantly out of the saddle.

All the elf cavalry was now in the town and had dispersed. Only those left without mounts were still gathered around their leader.

"And you fought equally bravely," responded Doghosh, appeased. "When did a human last have the opportunity to observe elves in battle, I wonder?" He did not dare to offer to shake hands with the elf commander, thinking this was unlikely to be good manners.

"Did you notice anything untoward? Any different beasts?"

"No. Just these ones. They suddenly turned up, but I have a feeling they're not from Girdlegard."

"What makes you say that?"

"Because of the way they are built. Their armor is different, too. There are quite a few clues. Endrawolt was going to check out some of the corpses and report back." Doghosh registered the elf's pensive expression. "You don't agree?"

"You are extremely observant. They came from a land on the far side of the Gray Mountains. And they did not come on their own. I fear that many of the kingdoms to the north will have been conquered. Among them, my own homeland, the realm of the Golden Plain."

"*What?*" Doghosh's eyes were wide with disbelief. "How could that happen? I've just witnessed your 1,000 mounted troops defeating far superior numbers."

"We were able to take them by surprise, Commander." The elf smiled. "Surprise and speed are our allies. With these two qualities it's possible to beat the strongest enemy." He whipped out his dagger and slashed it across the man's throat.

The cut went deep, slicing through arteries and severing the larynx.

"Do you see what I mean, barbarian?" asked the elf with a malicious glare as he stepped nimbly aside to avoid the jet of blood. "If you had known my true nature it would not have been so easy to kill you. Or to take over your town. The name of your death is Carmondai."

Doghosh felt the burning slash and the air on his opened flesh. *He has . . .* His legs gave way beneath him and he fell onto his knees, blacking out as he tipped sideways to the floor.

Carmondai was sitting on the second wall, his face turned to the town, his feet dangling over the edge. He had a goblet next to him and a bottle of fruit wine that Caphalor had included in his luggage for special occasions.

Taking Sonnenhag was just such an occasion.

My head is still spinning from the triumph. He had spread out his drawings and weighted them down with fragments of masonry to stop them blowing away.

Since dispatching Doghosh, he had done nothing but let his fingers fly over the paper, charcoal in hand. He was aching to put all his impressions from the battle, the victory and deaths he had witnessed down on parchment. He had taken off most of his armor because it got in the way when he was drawing. He would bathe and change his clothes later.

Below, in the open space between the innermost town wall and the defense mound, the captured residents—men, women and children—had been herded together. Caphalor was off somewhere in Sonnenhag with the guards, inspecting the houses.

From time to time Carmondai heard a shout from the huddled captives demanding to know what was to happen to them. He did not respond.

Spilled blood—you serve my pen
Thwarted soul—you serve my edification
Broken eye—you serve my astonishment
Razed city—you serve my reputation
But: fame and glory—what is it that you serve?

He had soon filled the next sheet of paper and it joined the others beside him.

He gave a satisfied smile and sipped his wine, then leaned back and studied the stars. They were the same ones seen back in Dsôn Faïmon, of course. *What a good decision, to come along with the troops.*

His right hand was starting to ache and his left shoulder was tense and uncomfortable from overuse in battle. The elf lances were nicely balanced, but heavy because they were reinforced. The impact of crashing into an armored orc took its toll on one's joints and he could still feel the jolts he'd taken on his shield in his forearm. Carmondai smiled. *And it was such fun!*

Caphalor appeared on the walkway having apparently completed his inspection of the town. He cast an eye over the pages strewn around. "Drawings and poems in excess. I take it the day provided inspiration?"

"It did." Carmondai collected the sheets of paper to make room for the nostàroi to sit. "And you? What decision have you come to?" He gestured at the captives with the end of his pen.

"Sonnenhag will provide building materials: it will be our quarry. The stone blocks are more or less regular, so we won't have much work to do. Some of the barbarians can transport the stone to the crater on the Golden Plain. And we can use the beams from the houses as fuel: nicely seasoned firewood." Caphalor sat down at his side. "Those with the best physique we can send to Durùston in the Gray Mountains. He'll get the best out of them."

Carmondai knew he meant exactly that. "Yes, and he was telling me that back home the people will give anything for souvenir jewelry made from the bones of barbarians. He can scarcely keep up with demand." He swung his feet to and fro. "Do we keep the citadel in the center of town just as it is?"

"Yes. It will be an excellent base for us. We can keep the surrounding territory under control from there." The black-haired älf looked at the goblet and the wine. "May I?"

"Help yourself. It's yours, anyway."

Caphalor drank, surveying the town in the evening darkness. With the inhabitants gone, there were no lights in the homes. From a distance, you would not be able to see the town at all.

Carmondai was more impressed by this city than by most barbarian settlements they had seen along the way. Humans did not set store by aesthetics: they just seemed to care about having a roof, some walls, windows and a door. They paid no attention to delicacy and sophistication in their buildings; any filigree work or playful additions they did use tended to look effeminate or fussy. True, the royal cities were more impressive and had columns and domed roofs and so on, but no älf was going to think much of the carvings on the balconies here in Sonnenhag. They were skillfully executed, but childish.

"You have trained the troops excellently." Caphalor said. "Without your help we would never have beaten the óarcos."

"They are good soldiers and took to the new fighting style right away. And, of course, we practiced every single splinter of unendingness."

"Of course. But we did need someone who knew the forgotten military techniques. Our people have not been using these strategies for a very long time." Caphalor was still addressing him, but he looked dead ahead. "The Inextinguishables have no idea of the caliber of soldier they lost in you."

"I'm not a soldier anymore." Carmondai did not want to return to his previous existence. *Those feelings and those thoughts have no place inside my head!* "My life is my art now. What I've done here is an exception for the sake of our nation." He gave a little sigh. *But I did enjoy it.*

Caphalor stayed silent for a while. "Will you be Sinthoras this evening for the troops? They will be expecting to see the two nostàroi to appear together."

Carmondai glanced at him. "How long do you intend to keep this charade up? How long before the pretense is exposed?"

"We keep it up until Sinthoras gets back. There's no other choice. The troops need him and they need to see him. They worship him now after the battle of the Golden Plain." He gave a bitter laugh. "If they only knew they were risking their lives for an älf who's back home romping in the bed—"

"That's not what I'm doing," came a voice from the other side of the walkway.

Carmondai swiveled around and saw their missing nostàroi. *How did he manage that?*

Sinthoras was wearing the black armor of the älfar with a cloak slung over it; shadows played around him. He was thinner than usual. "I have come back," he said quietly. "My apologies for taking so long, but there were things happening in Dsôn . . . I have enemies there, determined to bring me down, and they want *you* to fall with me, Caphalor. I had to act."

He's not looking well. "You two will have matters to discuss that don't belong in my writing, I imagine." Carmondai stood up to leave.

"Stay. We have no secrets from you." Caphalor held him gently by the shoulder. "It may well be that we have enemies, Sinthoras, but your soldiers need you. They love their dazzling nostàroi, his rousing speeches of glorious victory and the confidence he instills in them on the eve of battle." He turned to Carmondai who was feeling awkward. "Oh yes! The Sinthoras who inspires them in battle—here he is, sitting next to me!" Caphalor joked, then grew serious once more. "Without Carmondai the pretense would have failed. And without that pretense we would never have conquered the Golden Plain."

"I heard that I had been quite a presence. I seem to have been just about everywhere while I was back in Dsôn." Sinthoras's response was cutting. "Someone took my place."

"That's the last thing I wanted—" Carmondai began. He was aware that the blond älf was jealous of his success. A deadly rivalry had sprung up out of nowhere.

"You have no right to feel affronted, Sinthoras," Caphalor's interruption was a cool rebuke. "He was acting under my orders. He did extremely well. But now you can prove that you are big enough to get over the setback." He stood up. "You have been away too long and you are in debt to us, friend. We took care of your reputation while you were away having a fine time in Dsôn."

Carmondai could not help noticing the reproachful tone, but there was another layer of meaning he could not quite identify. *It's as if some ancient antipathy had surfaced.* He stayed quiet. Whatever he said would be wrong.

"Can one of you tell me why we killed thousands of óarcos?" Sinthoras wanted to know. "Even if we can't stand them, aren't they supposed to be our allies? Not that I feel sorry for them, but we need them. Especially the Kraggash." He was obviously trying to distract them from his absence.

Caphalor drained his cup, unperturbed. "Toboribar's group took off on their own initiative. They thought we were taking too long and they wanted to get in quick and grab their share. This was unacceptable. Anyway, because of our false armor, any surviving óarcos will swear blind it was elves that slaughtered Toboribar's troops. That exonerates us and should make Toboribar more compliant in the future. This incident will have shown him that it's not worth going it alone."

"I understand. A good move." Sinthoras was having difficulty admitting this. "Where is the demon?"

Carmondai had been asking himself the same question. *Our most important ally in the Tark Draan campaign is off in a sulk somewhere.*

"Carmondai is my witness to that: he turned up demanding to speak to you. Said you were in his debt. He said he would take his ever-so-grand powers away and that he would not come back unless you begged him to. And then he had the gall to threaten me." He exhaled sharply. "I thought you would have seen him at the Stone Gateway on your way back."

"We didn't." Sinthoras looked worried. "He can't have disappeared?" Carmondai could not help staring at the blond nostàroi. *First he goes home and has a good time in Dsôn and when he eventually comes back he does not even bring the demon with him.* It was getting too difficult to praise him in the epic. *Here I am doing his work for him and I'll get nothing for it! Well, hardly anything.*

"We don't need him and his undead dwarves," said Caphalor, placing his empty cup on the remnants of the battlement. "I suggest you go and collect your applause and enjoy your moment of glory."

"I'm back now," was the cold reply. "No one has to wear my armor for me any longer. It is too big for anyone else, anyway."

You conceited . . . Now Carmondai felt his honor had been sullied with this offensive remark. He leaped to his feet and confronted Sinthoras, the aches and pains forgotten. "Let me tell you this: you would completely disappear inside my armor! I never *want* to wear yours again, even if all the stars were about to fall on my head and it was the last thing left to shelter beneath!" He stomped off.

I should never have gone back to warfare. I'm an artist. My weapons are pen and words. And that's the way it's going to stay from now until endingness.

But a certain feeling told him this might not be the case.

Carmondai hated the idea.

Tark Draan (Girdlegard), many miles south of the Gray Mountains 4371ˢᵗ division of unendingness (5199ᵗʰ solar cycle), early winter.

Famenia shivered, threw a log onto the dying fire and pulled her mantle tighter. Her bed that night would consist of a deep layer of moss and foliage with a horse blanket on top. *That's about as comfortable as it gets if you sleep in the open.*

To make matters worse, she kept thinking about the stories Törden used to tell: tales of monsters who clambered out of their dens at full moon, ugly maws and long teeth ready to attack and eat humans. They were invisible until they fell on their victims, but you could always hear them howling like a pack of wolves.

That's quite enough of that! There's nothing like that here or anywhere else! Exhausted, Famenia laid her head down on the blanket and thanked the gods for their support so far.

Grok-Tmai the Worrier was the next person she had to visit. She was a little apprehensive. *The Worrier.*

The moon shone silver bright, throwing strong shadows of thinning foliage onto the ground. There was a smell of cool, earthy damp and the crispness of the coming winter.

She grew melancholy thinking of her home. She remembered her friends: the evenings spent together baking, the laughter and happiness.

Famenia gently touched the amulet. She was not sure what she was: no longer a famula, but surely not yet a maga. She no longer had a mentor to advise her, but she bore more responsibility than most would be able to cope with.

On her journey she had gotten to the point of giving up several times. She wanted to crawl away and hide under a fallen tree trunk until everything was over.

A breeze blew through the grove, lifting dead leaves and making them rustle. The branches swayed and creaked as they rubbed against each other. The flames of her campfire juddered and danced to the wind's melody.

Famenia found herself shivering again, and this time it wasn't the cold, but fear. At first the forest had looked a good choice for shelter: the occasional carved rune indicated that the place had been dedicated to Elria, and the places where gods resided were apparently protected.

But she could not get to sleep.

Sometimes the moon was too bright, sometimes it was the noises of the night that disturbed her: the sounds of animals calling, the memories of Törden's ghost stories, the shadows . . . She was used to sleeping in a bed with a warm coverlet to snuggle up under.

I'll have to face up to it: my carefree existence is over. Famenia shut her eyes and tried to drive away the worrying thoughts. But hardly had her lids closed than she was tortured with the image of Ortina dying, the sight of Simin with an arrow through his throat and the metallic smell of blood . . .

I'll never get any rest like this! She opened her eyes.

The fire was flickering, providing a little warmth, but it did give her a certain feeling of safety. Then the wind died down and something rustled in the undergrowth.

There's someone coming! O ye gods! She grabbed hold of the amulet and called up a spell that could . . . that could make a human laugh. That was all she could think of, her mind had blanked everything else. *Not ideal for warding off a hungry wild animal.*

Her magus Jujulo had not been keen on battles and destruction and that was why he'd always appealed to her, but at that moment she would have been very glad to have been taught at least one spell of defense— or attack.

She heard a soft groan. It sounded as if someone was in the bushes, possibly wounded or dying.

Whatever you are, please pass by and spare me. Törden had talked about beings that pretended to be humans. Humans you felt you had to help. In that way, harmless wanderers could be enticed into the bushes to have their blood sucked from their veins.

Did these creatures walk abroad at full moon?

Famenia fought down the urge to jump up and run. *Fire! I'll scare them off with a firebrand. Or . . . no. How about that spell where you call up a gust of wind?* It was intended just to ruffle someone's hair or make their clothes flap about a bit, but if she concentrated hard and put enough energy into it, it should be enough to topple objects. Or monsters, even.

She concentrated on the formula.

The groan was repeated and she heard shuffling steps through the undergrowth. The noises were much closer now.

She sat up in her bed and pointed her thumb and little finger toward the creature. "For—" She broke off her incantation, unsure of what to do.

The monster was a little girl with a dirty face and filthy clothing. She raised her left arm plaintively and stretched out her hand; the other arm hung uselessly at her side. She was obviously starving, all skin and bones, and her hair was matted. This was an image fit to melt the stoniest of hearts.

"Help me!" whispered the girl, sobbing bitterly. "Please!" She staggered closer, fighting her way through the overhanging branches. The twigs broke under her grip and the girl tumbled down by the fire with a scream, then fell motionless.

You must help her! But Famenia remembered Törden's story about the bloodsuckers who liked to pretend they were humans in distress.

"Hey, you!" Famenia pushed the girl with the toe of her boot. The little one sobbed again and begged for mercy. "Who are you? What has happened to you?"

The girl did not move and remained on the ground with her face buried in the dead leaves. "Please . . ."

Famenia looked around, but there was no one else to see. She decided to risk it.

With one hand quickly shielded with a spell, she drew a burning log out of the fire to protect herself, and with the tip of her right foot she turned the girl's body over, expecting to catch sight of enormous fangs.

But instead she saw the ravaged face of a young girl whose sunken cheeks and feverish eyes were witness to her having gone through great trials. The girl's eyes met her own. "Please," came the barely audible plea. "Go to the king . . . my father . . . burgomaster of—" Her eyes rolled up inside her skull.

She's dying! Famenia put the log down close at hand, knelt next to the young girl and concentrated on a spell that would prevent her spirit from fleeing her body. She put one hand on the girl's solar plexus, keeping her other hand on the amulet, and pronounced the spell. Magic flowed through her and into the girl, whose tortured face started to relax. The broken bone fragments in the girl's arms creaked as they healed; the scratches and cuts on her face and body disappeared or scabbed over. The frantic heartbeats calmed, slowed and grew stronger and her breathing normalized.

That will have to do. I'll need the rest of that energy later. Famenia released her hands and studied the girl.

The effect of the spell was to send the person into a deep slumber so that, fully rested, they would awake restored to health.

But Famenia was unwilling to wait that long. *What has happened to you?* She shook the girl's shoulder gently.

The girl shrieked and sat up with a start, flailing about her; one frantic hand caught Famenia in the throat and made her cough. "Oh, I'm so sorry," the girl cried, quite distraught. "Forgive me, by all the gods, forgive me." She covered her mouth with both hands and noticed that her arm was mended. "What . . . How did you—?" The girl scanned the immediate vicinity: the woods, the campfire. "Where am I?"

"You're safe. You're with me." Famenia cleared her throat again. "You were feverish and your arm—"

"It was broken!" The girl raised her arm and waggled it. "How—?"

Famenia sat down. "My name is Famenia and I am Jujulo the Jolly's successor. Perhaps you have heard of him?"

"The *magus* Jujulo? You are his famula and . . . It was a magic spell! You've healed my arm with magic!" She crawled over and seized Famenia's hand, covering it with grateful kisses. "The gods have sent you! My father, the others . . . the elves have shut them away in the cavern and—"

"Take it slowly, little one." Famenia put her arms around the child. "Tell me your name."

"Ossandra. I am . . . My father is the burgomaster of Milltown, and the elves . . ." The story came tumbling out, although her voice was croaky and weak. "They came to set up camp in our cave in the hill. Up in the quarry, hidden from view and from the evil that's rampaging through Girdlegard. That's what they told us. But they demanded so much from us all, and then they insisted on taking my friends . . . on taking all the children. They wouldn't let them go—" She drew a rasping breath. "Help me! You can help me with your magic and your spells, can't you? Drive the elves out from our town and do something bad to the terrible Pointy-Ears!"

Famenia stared at Ossandra. "Are you sure they are really elves? Could they be other creatures who look similar?"

"What . . . How do you mean?"

"Tell me about their eyes: do they go black in the sunshine?"

Ossandra thought for a second then nodded. "I . . . yes. Yes! I thought I was imagining it, but their leader, a female . . . Yes, I saw her eyes go black."

"What is she called?"

"Horgàta. She is very beautiful, but cruel." Ossandra put a grubby finger to her own mouth. "When she laughs, that's the worst. I'm scared of her. We all are."

Famenia had a horrible feeling she knew what kind of creatures were responsible for this. "How many are in the cave now?"

"About 5,000. And they all have black horses with red eyes and—" Ossandra started sobbing again. "Once we were trapped, she told us they would do awful things to us if we betrayed them. They're not really elves, are they? Elves would never do that! Elves are creatures of light." She dissolved into tears, clinging to Famenia.

"I'll see what I can do to save your friends." Famenia stroked the young girl's forehead.

But in truth she had no idea who might challenge an army of 5,000 älfar.

Chapter XIV

Have you ever heard tell of the Walking Towers?
They go on the rampage for hours and hours!
Armored with steel,
They'll hurt you for real!
They're no good as a friend
And it's best in the end
To kill them quite dead.
When all's done and said
If we don't, there'll be trouble, triple and double.
They'll put an end to my rhyme: They'll win every time.

Nursery rhyme *The Towers that Walk*
3rd verse (forbidden)

Tark Draan (Girdlegard) far to the south east of the Gray Mountains,
4371ˢᵗ division of unendingness (5199ᵗʰ solar cycle),
late autumn.

Carmondai strolled through Sonnenhag wearing his warmest clothes, notebooks and pen in hand. The town had changed since his forces had captured it.

The houses had, for the most part, been removed and the foundations demolished and carted away by slaves. Caphalor had wanted what was left of the town walls strengthened, and the barbarians were working to reinforce the ramparts. Sonnenhag would become a secure base for the älfar. It already had a new name: Kòraidàdsôn.

Carmondai paused where there were still a few barbarian homes scheduled for demolition. The slaves were being made to work in cruelly cold conditions. The women and children had already been sent away to the Gray Mountains and the menfolk had been told their families were hostages to ensure their own good behavior. That kept them docile. *They will be dropping dead of cold and exhaustion soon.*

Since the conquest of the town, the älfar had also made prisoners of several travelers and traders who had tried to travel through Sonnenhag, unaware of what had happened. They took the place of any slaves that keeled over.

Carmondai opened his folder and looked at his preparatory sketches for a big mural. *It will have to be at least ten paces long and eight high. At least! Otherwise it won't have the desired effect.*

A group of armored cavalry soldiers had created a grove of bones by taking óarco cadavers and opening them up to retrieve the skeletons. They had boiled some of the bones in huge troughs to produce glue and had carved the rest to look like branches, twigs and trunks. All of this had been joined together to make a forest circling the newly renamed town: a forest of bones of utter perfection—it was a magnificent work of art. Black beech, blood pines and arrow thorn bushes—many of Dsôn's plants—had been replicated, with the leaves formed from the tanned and dried skin of the óarcos. Óarco teeth provided the thorns. The carved branches shimmered dull white. Carmondai had never seen anything like it, it really was unique.

I think I'll take a little walk through the grove later. It's exquisite.

Carmondai sat down on a low wall and did some sketches of the laboring barbarians. He was not of a mind to stay in Kòraidàdsôn much longer because he wanted to find out where the heroes had gone.

It was the fate of the blinded Arviû that concerned him most. And he had heard no word of Morana, Virssagòn or Horgàta since they had been sent out on the Inextinguishables' missions. He needed to include their deeds and experiences in his epic. This meant he would be riding out soon and thus would stop training the troops. *It's probably better that way. After all, I'm an artist and a poet and that's the way I'd like it to stay.*

His quarters were with the nostàroi in the citadel, which had received a decorative overhaul to bring it more in line with älfar tastes, but Sinthoras and Caphalor would soon be returning to the main army so that they could attack Gwandalur before winter set in.

Those left behind will thank us. Roughly 900 älfar would remain in the citadel to hold the fort, while the forges in the town would produce new armor to replace what was lost when they took up the elves' battle-dress. But, until that was ready in sufficient quantities, they would have to make do with what they had, its metal blackened and the elf runes obliterated.

Shouts at the gate made Carmondai turn his head. *So, we have visitors!*

An impressive horde of óarcos entered the town on heavy work-horses painted green and black. They held tattered óarco banners aloft and the procession was accompanied with kettledrum thunder and ear-shattering trombone blasts.

The barbarian workers stopped and either stood glowering at the beasts, or ran to hide.

Carmondai recognized Toboribar's insignia on the banners; he was the undisputed óarco leader. *He has probably come for negotiations.* He closed his folder quickly and ran over to the citadel, where the column of óarcos were pushing their way through the doors.

I don't want to miss this! Carmondai hurried up the steps, slipped past the green-skinned beasts and headed in the general direction of

Toboribar's angry shouts. They were being held up by älfar guards at the doors of the hall and the óarco prince was going berserk, throwing furniture around and hurling objects at the walls; he was certainly giving vent to his displeasure.

Trying to remain inconspicuous, Carmondai slipped from the hall through a side door, but stayed at the back. Soon, the furious Toboribar burst through and began haranguing the two armored nostàroi and some of their bodyguards. *Does he suspect that we tricked him?*

The óarco's fists were clenched at his side and his huge biceps flexed beneath ruddy gray skin. He was clearly having a hard time controlling his temper, but he took a deep breath before thundering: "You damnable pointy-eared Black-Eyes! You have wiped out my army and blamed others for your treachery!"

"Ah, Toboribar," Sinthoras said warmly, as if greeting an old friend. "We have not seen you for ages. I thought you and your óarcos had gone—absent without leave, I might add—to carry out your own private incursion." His smile was false. "It doesn't seem to have gone too well for your army. I assure you that your loss is my own, because we had a sound alliance, but as you see by our bone grove, we have found a use for your fallen. So your dead soldiers have served a purpose, after all."

"You slaughtered 10,000 Kraggash! You ambushed them while disguised as elves!" Toboribar roared, hands dangerously close to the handles of his weapons. "It is an outrage! And you've been using their corpses for—" Words failed him. "We had a pact!"

"But you did not keep to it," Caphalor broke in, his quiet voice all the more effective after the óarco's roaring. "So it's no good coming to us and complaining—"

Toboribar stamped his metal-soled boot down on the floorboards. "I was promised the south, and I wanted to secure it."

"You will be given the south *after* we have subjugated Tark Draan. We can only win if our orders are followed to the letter—as your warriors had to learn to their cost."

He's not going to let that go, thought Carmondai, taking notes.

"Nonsense!" yelled the óarco. "My army was on the point of victory when yours ambushed them from behind. Now we have suffered huge losses and the survivors are badly injured!" He snorted angrily. "I absolutely demand that you have the hideous forest outside taken down! You have desecrated the bones of my Kraggash. I want a proper burial for them."

Sinthoras marched up to him, standing firm. "You countermanded our express instructions. Tell me, óarco princeling, how you would handle your own mutinous troops? Shower them with riches and rewards? Praise them to the heavens and give them medals?"

"No, of course not—"

"So why do you think we should put up with it?" said Sinthoras. "Insubordination cannot be tolerated! The Ishím Voróo barbarians who think they can head home whenever they feel like it will be getting the same treatment as the blockhead trolls who have suddenly discovered a deep attachment to the Eastern Mountains. This is war, not a day trip."

Carmondai watched to see how the óarco would react. *Will he lunge at the two commanders, or will he obey them?*

Toboribar stood firm under Sinthoras's challenging gaze. "Then it is true." His tiny yellow eyes glittered with danger. "You did attack my Kraggash, älf. It would have sufficed to give me a warning. There was no need to kill them."

"That *was* your warning." Sinthoras spoke in velvety tones. "The punishment will be much harsher should mutiny occur again." He pointed to the door. "Return to your people and explain to them that 10,000 had to perish because of your own greed and stupidity. I'm sure they'll understand."

The óarco prince's biceps flexed again and a ferocious roar issued from his throat.

Sinthoras looked at him with disdain. "You know, it wouldn't take me long to designate a successor for you, and your bones will have pride of place at the top of the tallest tree in the bone grove."

Carmondai completed his rough sketch of the furious óarco—his tusks plated in gold. He was truly a terrifying figure, but he did not seem to intimidate the nostàroi at all. *I can't think of anything that would frighten Caphalor, judging by the way he saw off the demon that time.*

"I won't do you that favor," growled Toboribar. "You'll be begging my forgiveness soon enough." He stomped out, crushing imaginary älfar at each step. He brushed past Carmondai, ignoring him completely.

"Ah, our artist!" Sinthoras said warmly. "I hope you enjoyed my performance?" He came over with Caphalor at his heels. "That's the only way to deal with these beasts."

Sinthoras was in dazzling good humor, but Caphalor looked displeased. His friend's return had not improved things. Carmondai did not bother to contradict Sinthoras. "If you say so," he responded. "I'm just grateful you did not tell him it was me in command when his beasts were massacred." He lifted his folder and pen. "My favored weapons might not have been appropriate."

Sinthoras laughed heartily, but Caphalor's laughter sounded distinctly hollow.

Carmondai grinned and was about to think up another witticism when an älf accompanied by ten armed officers and wearing the robes of an envoy to the Inextinguishables appeared at the door. *Since when does the voice of our rulers need armed reinforcement?*

"What an honor!" said Sinthoras in his inimitably condescending manner. "Welcome. Word has quickly spread about our whereabouts, I see."

"Indeed it has." The gray-haired älf bowed. "Congratulations on the capture of the fortress. Honored nostàroi, my name is Verànor and I bring tidings from the Inextinguishables that concern only yourselves."

Caphalor dismissed his guards, but asked Carmondai to stay. No one objected.

Verànor took the Inextinguishables' seal out from under his cloak and showed it to the nostàroi to substantiate his credentials. The words he spoke had the status of the rulers' own voices and were to be obeyed as if Nagsor and Nagsar Inàste were standing directly in front of them. "Listen and obey: I must insist that you, Sinthoras, accompany me back to Dsôn Faïmon."

But he's just come from there. Carmondai had to bite his lip to stop himself laughing. *At least this time it'll be official and I won't have to pretend I'm him. Thank you, Samusin!*

"For what reason? I've got a war to fight. I'm needed here," Sinthoras countered frostily. "I would think it could wait."

Caphalor lost control of his features for a short moment. It was not clear to Carmondai whether this was due to Sinthoras's defiance, or his contemptible arrogance.

"It's only *you* I need to bring, not both nostàroi," Veranor said firmly. "You and two-thirds of the älfar troops you have here."

"I agree a respectable escort is demanded by my status, but the number you cite seems a little exaggerated," Sinthoras replied. "Surely your ten guards—"

"The Inextinguishables need the soldiers for the defense of Dsôn Faïmon," Veranor interrupted. "The dorón ashont challenge our borders and the defense moat is weakened. The threat they pose has to be eradicated. We need more warriors."

Carmondai was horrified. "*The* dorón ashont?" *This must all go in my epic! How am I going to cover it all?*

Veranor nodded. "They have returned. It is worse than the first time they came."

"That is certainly not good news," Caphalor said. "But surely our homeland has enough forces to defend it? We need to keep as many troops as possible here to destroy the elves. We want to conquer more of their terrain before the onset of winter—"

"The Inextinguishables have decided that there are sufficient allied forces with you here in Tark Draan for the purposes of achieving the agreed objectives." Veranor was inflexible. He showed the Inextinguishables' seal once more to emphasize that any haggling about troop numbers was out of the question. "It is not important who wipes out the elves. If they are destroyed by the crudest of our allies then the enemy's disgrace is all the greater. The security and safety of Dsôn Faïmon takes precedence. The dorón ashont will be defeated by the spring, then your forces can return to you." Carmondai thought of the thousands of óarcos slain in the Kòraidàdsôn siege. *If this news had filtered through a little earlier, they'd all still be alive.*

"I understand. I shall lead our warriors against the dorón ashont and save Dsôn." Sinthoras was reconciled. "And Caphalor will hold the conquered territory and work on the plan of attack for the spring."

He gets to be Savior of Dsôn Faïmon and *Destroyer of the Elves—
you can't ask for more,* thought Carmondai. *He'll be happy enough
with that.*

But Verànor shook his head. "No, Sinthoras. You have to stand
before an inquiry. Accusations of murder and incitement to murder
have been laid against you. Aïsolon will be leading the troops against the
dorón ashont."

"*What?*" Black lines of fury broke out over his face as Sinthoras took
this in. "That confounded Polòtain! He's behind this! *Isn't he?*" he yelled
in the envoy's face.

"I can't comment," Verànor replied.

"Samusin is my witness: I shall ram his slanderous accusations down
his throat. How can the Inextinguishables have been taken in by the
nonsense he spouts?"

"There are witnesses, Nostàroi." Verànor remained relatively unimpressed by this outburst and Carmondai admired his calm demeanor.
"Their testimonies have led to the Sibling Rulers' decision to recall
you. The public is very keen to see the law being observed. Murder of
a member of one's own kind is a very serious offense. Until the matter
has been clarified in a court—"

"No," whispered Sinthoras, sensing the worst. Carmondai was agog.

"I must—" Verànor continued.

"*No!*" barked Sinthoras, his eyes black as lakes in the moonlight.

He made to draw his weapons, but Caphalor stopped him with a
restraining hand on his forearm. The ten soldiers accompanying the
envoy drew their swords in response.

Verànor went on as if he had not noticed this upheaval, "—suspend
you. You are relieved of your office as nostàroi."

Sinthoras opened his mouth and shut it again. His voice failed completely and he staggered, saved from falling by his friend's arm.

Carmondai could only guess what was going through the ambitious
älf's head: a moment ago he had been expecting to enter Dsôn Faïmon
as a victorious hero and now he was plunging toward destruction. *A true
Comet.* Everything he had worked for was in jeopardy: his reputation in
the army, his successes in Tark Draan, his newly acquired social status

in Dsôn . . . *What drama! Losing his commission must be like being struck in the face with a cudgel.*

Verànor turned to Caphalor. "I am to tell you that you must also resign from your post as nostàroi. It can be arranged to look as if you are leaving at your own request, in order to spare you any disgrace."

"For what reason?" Carmondai thought Caphalor looked strangely relieved.

"We have heard that the alliance is beginning to fracture. Word has got around Dsôn that the campaign has been disrupted and the people are unhappy. The Sibling Rulers cannot afford to have problems on two fronts and they must be seen to take action. This is why you will be downgraded to benàmoi with a unit of your own. Another nostàroi has been chosen to take your place."

"I understand." Caphalor gave a faint smile.

Carmondai could not believe it. *How am I going to word this in my epic? It's outrageous!* He worried that Verànor might make him quietly disappear for fear he might publish what he had heard.

The envoy's bodyguard sheathed their swords and surrounded Sinthoras, who was now no more than an ordinary älf in an extravagant set of armor—and a murder suspect. His past services to the state were overshadowed and eclipsed.

"You should know that there is . . . an ally here in Tark Draan that only obeys Sinthoras," Caphalor warned.

"How could it be significant enough to merit disobeying the wishes of the Inextinguishables?" Verànor asked, seemingly implacable.

"The mist-demon will only fight for us if Sinthoras is here."

"Why is that? I thought you had both negotiated with the demon to get him to join the campaign?"

"He . . . likes Sinthoras better." Caphalor gave the envoy a steadfast look. "Please tell the Inextinguishables this and I am sure they will find a solution for the inquiry. Otherwise, disaster is assured. The demon has been quite clear about it: he insists on speaking only to Sinthoras."

"I am tied to the orders I receive from the Sibling Rulers." Verànor looked at Sinthoras. "You will have to explain to the demon that you are unavailable for the present, and the creature can take its wrath out on Tark Draan."

Sinthoras shrugged. "It is a demon, Verànor! How am I supposed to make him understand that? I can't force him to do what I say."

"But he'll listen to you, I thought?"

"I—" Sinthoras stood up straight, but now had an air of defeat where arrogance had existed before. "I hope so."

We all hope so. Carmondai knew that the mist-demon was utterly unpredictable. It had terrified him to the depths of his soul and Carmondai knew that nobody could constrain him if he were to turn against the älfar. He represented the greatest danger to the whole campaign, much greater than the threat of insurrection among the other allies. *Samusin and all infamous powers, protect us!*

"I hope so, too, for your sake." As far as Verànor was concerned, the matter was settled. "My guards will accompany you from now on, Sinthoras. Get your things ready for the journey." He turned to Caphalor. "As of now, you are benàmoi to the armored cavalry and you will take orders from the new nostàroi, who is currently with the army encamped in the Golden Plain, inspecting the crater. The plan subsequently is to tackle Gwandalur."

Caphalor nodded briskly then turned to Sinthoras and embraced him. "We shall meet again," he said reassuringly. "And you will be appointed nostàroi once more, as you deserve to be."

"Thank you for your faith in me," Sinthoras replied despondently, returning the embrace. "My enemies in Dsôn will learn what it is to go against me. And in spring we will conquer Tark Draan. The two of us will make it happen, as no one else can." They shook hands. Then Sinthoras left the room together with Verànor and the escort. As he left he gave Carmondai a curt nod of acknowledgment.

Ye infamous gods! I did not expect any of that! He opened his folder and started making notes. *No one could have predicted it!*

"It is said that Samusin is responsible for the direction of the wind and for dispensing justice," Caphalor said thoughtfully. "I wonder what Sinthoras has done to merit such punishment?"

"Murder and incitement to murder?" Carmondai blurted out.

"The accusation of murder will be connected to Robonor's accident, I presume. As far as I know, Sinthoras had nothing to do with it." Caphalor sat down on one of the benches and propped his feet up on the table. "I investigated the events of that night because I wanted to know what had happened."

Carmondai stopped writing. "But why didn't you—"

"Because it is not my place and because I have no proof." He looked at the poet. "The stones on the roof had been levered off, it is true, but not at the nostàroi's request."

"Whose then?"

"The Inextinguishables themselves."

Carmondai felt as if he had been struck by a lance. The pencil snapped in his fingers. "What are you talking about?"

"There were blind älfar on the roof that night. They waited until Robonor's crew were beneath them. A blind älf could not aim a stone with complete accuracy—unless he had come from the Bone Tower."

"That's insane! Why would they give an order like that?"

Caphalor sighed deeply, a sigh of resignation. "It is not our place to try to understand their motives. Perhaps they even thought to do Sinthoras a favor by disposing of his rival. Perhaps they were making secret preparations for accusing him of murder should he become too powerful." He leaned forward. "I am sure of what I say. Proof or no proof."

"How do you know the älfar up there were blind?"

"Two locals saw them up there. Their movements were a peculiar mixture of caution and confidence at first, as if unsure of where they were. That's why I think they were testing their immediate environment, getting to know it. The blind bodyguards are used to doing that." Caphalor pointed to the door. "Sinthoras made the mistake of quarreling with Polòtain. Polòtain is a fine politician: ambitious, very powerful and with a strong network of important contacts. He *wants* to believe that his great-nephew died at Sinthoras's hand, and the Inextinguishables can hardly admit their own involvement. The fact that they have not intervened now shows that they are not averse to having Sinthoras cut down to size . . . I am a simple benàmoi and consider myself lucky." His tone was cynical.

Carmondai's head was buzzing. "And that is why you did not object when they said you had been demoted?"

"What use would it have been? I can bring my destructive hate raining down on Tark Draan just as well in the capacity of benàmoi; there is no need to be in supreme command. Besides that, holding the office of nostàroi is chiefly to blame for the loss of my . . . life's companion." Carmondai noted that Caphalor was musing to himself now. "Supreme command or Tark Draan—I don't give a damn about either. If it weren't for Tark Draan and the elves I could be sitting at home with Enoïla right now, doing wonderful things. I could be defending Dsôn Faïmon against the dorón ashont like a proper warrior. I—" He shut his eyes and gulped back a sob. "I am full of hate," he whispered flatly. "I hate Tark Draan and all that live there."

Carmondai felt a surge of sympathy. *A broken älf, trapped in grief and trying to obliterate his pain by inflicting suffering on those he holds responsible.* He composed a few lines on the topic, which was difficult because of his pencil having snapped in half.

From an author's point of view, Caphalor was the most interesting character in the epic: complex and driven by his emotions, but a hostage to his own pain, incapable of breaking free. Carmondai had heard that Caphalor had argued with Morana. She had been off on missions ever since—no one had seen her. *And yet, I thought they were attracted to each other. It would have been wonderful if she could have released him from his deep distress.* The figure of Sinthoras paled in comparison; his motivation was simple: pure ambition. *What justice have you planned for Caphalor, Samusin? He deserves better.*

The black-haired älf sat motionless, tears running down his cheek. Black fury-lines formed in their wake, slicing his face into segments.

Heart-rending, and so poignant. Carmondai made a quick drawing. With every line he sketched, his sympathy for the nostàroi increased. He would never be able to show the picture to anyone lest the commander's military reputation be called into question, but the scene was crying out to be captured on paper.

Shortly before he had completed his sketch, steps approached the door. An älf came in and stood blocking his light. "Move aside. I can't see what I'm doing." From the corner of his eye he saw it was a female.

She stepped aside obediently.

At the final flourish of the pencil Carmondai stood back a little from his work and looked at it critically. *It is . . . exactly right! Anyone seeing it would immediately be on the commander's side.* Enthused by his own skill, he smiled and sighed before turning aside and looking at the female älf waiting patiently at the door, watching Caphalor. "What do you want?"

"I heard," she said in a warm, low voice, "that Carmondai and Caphalor were to be found here." Her light-colored eyes were fixed on Caphalor, who had not noticed her presence.

"You have found us." Carmondai looked her up and down. "Another envoy with a message from the Inextinguishables?" He did not care what she made of the comment.

"No. I wanted to meet you both. I've been told you are important." She moved to study his face. "My name is Imàndaris."

"Ah, the daughter of Yantarai the artist!" Carmondai could smell trouble. *Are they getting rid of me, too? Replacing me with her?* Then he remembered there had been some rumor about Yantarai and Sinthoras before he took up with Timanris. *No coincidence then, that she's the one they sent. Yet another humiliation for Sinthoras.*

She inclined her head and then tossed her long red gold hair back. "I am honored that you have heard of my family."

"It is delightful that you have come to flatter us," said Carmondai, pointedly raising his open folder. "But I am the one who is recording the events and the battles in Tark Draan."

"And nobody is better qualified, Carmondai." Imàndaris bestowed a brief smile on him. "But I can see you have the wrong idea: I have come here as the new nostàroi."

Carmondai's mouth fell open.

Tark Draan (Girdlegard), south of the Gray Mountains,
the enchanted land of Hiannorum,
4371ˢᵗ division of unendingness (5199ᵗʰ solar cycle),
late autumn.

Morana sat opposite Hianna the Flawless and managed to suppress a shudder. It was not that she was frightened, nor was she finding the room unnerving. It was merely that she was finding Hianna's icing-sugar sweetness hard to take.

The maga was fond of prettiness. In fact, the entire realm of Hiannorum consisted of adorable things. Even the crops in the fields and the cemeteries where they buried their dead were charming. Add to that the delicate embroidery, nicely decorated towers, the neat garden . . .

Morana was desperate to see something dark and unpleasant. The barbarians called it Death Art. *What do they know? Their brains are tiny. They have no concept of true beauty.*

She looked down at the table. The gold design on the plates was repulsive and the cutlery, in the form of rose bush stems, was hideous. The wine goblets were fashioned to look like climbing plants and the brocade cloth on the table was covered in patterns sewn in metallic thread . . . The list of abominations was endless.

I am surrounded by horrors. Morana, dressed in her black dress and armor, felt safe knowing she was not to the maga's taste.

"The soup is . . . spiced." She could not bring herself to be more specific in her judgment and laid her spoon down after the fourth mouthful. To her it tasted of old meat, badly stored spices and vegetables harvested long past their best.

"I'm glad." Hianna emptied her own plate and clapped her hands.

Young women in flowing robes with light-colored trains cleared the soup bowls away and brought a mound of something yellow out; it stank of burned butter.

Morana smiled politely. *She's torturing me; that's what she's doing. I wish I'd stayed hidden as Virssagòn did.* "What is this delicacy?"

"Boiled semolina topped with toasted cheese and butter," Hianna explained proudly. "The cook has grated some fine pi mushroom over it, as well. It's very good for the complexion. Though yours is absolutely perfect already, I must admit."

Am I supposed to rub it on my face? Morana lifted her fork and had to force herself to spear some of the food. It tasted even worse than it smelled. She laid her cutlery down and asked for some bread instead. "I'm not feeling terribly well. I think my stomach will be best with just bread today," she said, by way of apology.

"Oh, that is a pity. There are several courses still to come." Hianna signed to the young serving women to clear the table. "But it does mean we can get to the purpose of your visit." She asked for several carafes of wine and liqueur to be placed on the table and then some small glasses. "Now, Morana. I'm all ears."

Morana told her the same story she had told countless dignitaries, princelings and local luminaries. She told her about the elves and their greed and how they were intent on extending their territory. Then she mentioned the only remedy. "We offer you the same conditions as all those who have gathered under our banner," she said, winding up her presentation. However hard she looked, she could not see Virssagòn. *He is far too good at this.*

Hianna had listened intently. "You claim to be elves from the south, then?" She laughed delicately. "Oh, my dear Morana! How stupid do you think I am? I've been around for a long, long time and I know Girdlegard like the back of my hand—the land and all of its creatures, humans and monsters." As she patted her mouth with her napkin, her movements could almost have been described as graceful. Almost. "In my search for perfection I have traveled to every corner of this land, and if there is one thing I did *not* find it was elves in the south." She placed her elbows on the table, the long sleeves hanging down like banners, and went on: "Am I hearing the truth from you, my dark beauty?"

Morana did not know how to react. She was afraid that Virssagòn would suddenly emerge from the shadows and slice the maga's head off.

Hianna misread her silence. "Shall I tell you what I think?" She took a sip from a small violet-colored glass. "You are from the Outer Lands and you hate the elves. You all long for their complete eradication. When I look at you and the unusual weapons that you carry and the dark armor that you wear, there is only one conclusion I can draw: you are an älf."

What will she do now? Morana prepared to have to evade some magic assault and readied herself for a counterattack. *If Virssagòn and I work together we should be able . . .*

Hianna beamed at her. "And as such, I bid you heartily welcome!"

Did I hear that correctly? Morana twisted slightly to face Hianna. "You're *pleased*?"

The maga downed the rest of the liqueur. "You have no idea just how pleased I am." She reached for another glass. "The elves are the most arrogant creatures I know. I have stayed with them, in their lands, in their groves, on the plains, everywhere. I went to inquire politely about physical perfection and how I might achieve it." She put a hand to her own face. "I am known for my beauty. *Beauty!* And they laughed in my face! They said I was nothing but a human and so was uglier than the plainest of their kind." She scowled. "The humiliation! I shall never forget it. I prayed that Samusin and Tion would give me an opportunity to take my revenge." She stood up, and stepped around the table to embrace the älf-woman. Morana was taken by surprise. "My dear friend, you are most welcome! Samusin and Tion have brought you to me! And naturally I shall join your pact against the elves. My famuli are at your disposal."

"That is . . . amazing." Morana pushed the enchantress gently to one side, almost overcome by Hianna's strong perfume. *She reminds me of an obboona. She wants to be just like us!* "My leaders will be glad to hear it." She saw Virssagòn appearing briefly before disappearing into the shadows once more. "Could you detail what arts you can bring to the campaign?"

Hianna adjusted her clothing and returned to her seat. "If you think all I can do is a few charming incantations, please think again. I can read your looks, my friend." She gave a mischievous smile. "Did you know I consort with demons?" she whispered. "Yes, that's right! With demons! I thought they might lead me to perfection: a big mistake, but I learned the strangest things from them."

"Which are?" Morana was hoping Hianna would not see how excited she was. *We could only dream of an ally like this!*

"A sample? How would you like to speak to a demon?" Hianna closed her eyes and murmured a formula. Her whole body began to tremble until the air around her sparked. When her eyes opened again they were bright green orbs emitting tiny flames that did not harm her. She raised her left arm.

Everything in the room that had not been fixed in position—apart from the chairs the two women sat on—started to float upward. Objects circled them, turning ever faster. Virssagòn was sucked into the spiraling eddy. He had to hold fast to the wall to avoid being seen.

When she spoke, it was with many voices simultaneously, "I can extend this particular trick to cover a circle with a radius of half a mile . . . there's no way to combat it. Buildings and armies would all be affected." She lowered her arm and everything was restored to its proper place. By dint of landing softly, Virssagòn managed not to reveal his presence. Hianna shut her eyes and after speaking a short spell, they returned to normal. "Are those arts enough to serve your alliance against the elves?"

"Extraordinary!" Morana was proud of herself. *And this barbarian might have been murdered by Virssagòn! What a loss to our cause.* "Now it is *my* turn to bid *you* heartily welcome!"

The maga laughed happily. "Not so fast. Tell me, is it possible to get the secret of perfection for me? Your people must have spells for that?"

Morana did not know.

She had never been inside any of the academies run by the very few älfar magicians that there were. And she assumed that none of the älfar wizards could match a Tark Draan maga for skill. She was, herself, mightily impressed by what Hianna was able to do.

"Of course," she lied. "We have recipes for everlasting beauty, just like the elves. But we would be happy to share our knowledge with you. You and your famuli will be worshipped for your beauty." Morana noted how well her speech was going down with Hianna.

"I am so happy," she exclaimed jubilantly, throwing her hands in the air, her sleeves following gracefully in an arc that imitated the tails of comets. "I've even worked out a plan to help you and your army."

"With magic, I hope?"

"Yes. But the thing about magic here in Girdlegard is that it is restricted to certain regions where the ground is saturated with it. Here my power is immeasurable, but outside my magic would soon be used up and I would not be able to do very much." Hianna ran her fingers through her hair. "But I know a way around it. Listen carefully . . ."

The more Morana heard, the surer she became that Hianna was completely insane. And so Morana was not surprised to learn that Hianna's plans were already well advanced.

All she had been waiting for was someone's army.

Chapter XV

Winter of destiny.

It brings death on the wind,
sowing seeds of vanished trust
and harvesting betrayal.
Malicious slanderous tongues
sang the song of false assertions,
found their audience
and found favor.

The favor needs its tribute
from all sides.
Once seen, once heard,
all faith is lost.
The hardest time:
enforced isolation
when company is craved.

Loneliness brings insight.
Insight becomes action.
Action makes heroes.

Winter of destiny.

Excerpt from the epic poem *The Heroes of Tark Draan*
composed by Carmondai, master of word and image

*Ishím Voróo (Outer Lands), Dsôn Faïmon, west of the radial arm Avaris,
4371ˢᵗ division of unendingness (5199ᵗʰ solar cycle),
early winter.*

"I've heard the derren eshant are gaining ground." Jiggon stole a glance
at the others, but nobody else commented. They were concentrating on
dipping wooden spoons into the communal pot of broth. Plates were
not used and there were a lot of stains on the rough table: souvenirs of
previous meals. "They're winning against the black-eyes! Just think
of it! We—"

"Hold your tongue!" his father Hirrtan snapped. "What happens if
you're overheard?"

Jiggon rolled his eyes and tried to get a spoonful of soup. "The black-
eyes won't be hiding under the table."

His elder sister Elina shoved his hand aside and collared the big-
gest piece of meat: revenge for his bold talk. "Slaves have been put to
death for less," she said. "How about thinking of *us* for a change?" She
swept crumbs to the floor with her sleeve. The food would get trodden
into the bare earth and every week or so someone would take a broom
to the mess.

"Cowards!" Jiggon glared at his family.

"Will you keep your mouth shut?" growled his father. "And anyway,
these Dirron Asharnt will want to see us off as soon as they've finished
killing the älfar."

"You are being unfair," Grandfather Rodolf said. "He's only seven-
teen and he's got the fire of youth in his belly." He turned to his grandson. "I know how you feel, though it is pronounced dorón ashont."

Jiggon smiled gratefully at him.

Soon the broth was finished and the family left the table. It was
his turn to clean out the pot, but he'd leave it until the next day. He
was tired.

There were nineteen of them living and sleeping in the tiny hut—it was always overcrowded. Some days Jiggon felt he couldn't move at all, especially if drying laundry was hanging from the beams.

He headed for the little alcove where he would sleep for the night; there were not enough beds for everyone. Their master, Yintaï, was not known for caring about his serfs' welfare. He gave them work. They had to do it. He had no further interest in them.

These cowards. Jiggon had been born into slavery, but had heard that in some places in Ishím Voróo you could live in freedom.

He was not put off by the idea of having to deal with monsters in the wilderness or having to fight other humans if only he could do it on his own account. Anything would be better than getting up every morning and going to work to make someone else prosperous—someone who did not even appreciate it. To Yintaï a human was chattel, as good as a chair or an animal.

What I would give to be able to fight in the war! Jiggon had long dreamed of serving as a soldier in one of the human divisions, but Yintaï had laughed at his request saying: "You? You don't even know how to use a knife! How could you hope to manage with a sword in close combat? Carry on swinging your pitchfork and make yourself useful in my fields! That's your calling."

It should be me who decides what my calling is. Jiggon sat up to look out of the window just above him, pulling aside the coarse jute curtain that was supposed to stop the wind howling through their hovel.

The trees had lost their leaves and an early frost lay on the meadows and harvested fields. His breath formed in clouds in front of his face. Winter was coming. *The nights will be cold again.*

He pulled his threadbare old jacket tighter, having no blanket or animal pelt to keep him warm. He thought about their village, Evenlight. It had a population of around 800 souls, guarded by a score of älfar. In his mind's eye, he could see the hut where Irhart the smith lived; Irhart with his serviceable metal tools that were never good enough for his master. Next to his hut was Salisala's place, the wise woman who looked after any injured slaves, although she was forbidden to use her healing arts and had often been whipped for doing so; then came Güldtraut's shed, where four lovely young girls had lived—until Yintaï had taken them off. They had never come back. It was said that the jewelry Yintaï's wife wore around her neck—carved bone set with gems and inlaid with silver—had something to do with that. Yintaï's young son had also been given a miniature sword and some new carved bone toys.

So many human lives would have been better without the black-eyes. Jiggon felt impotent fury rise in his guts. He was so isolated. It seemed he was the only one in the village who wanted to rebel.

Steps approached. It was his father. Hirrtan crouched down at his side.

"You are being unfair to us," he said, spreading a thin blanket over his son's shoulders. "It's just that it is impossible to defy the master. He would simply have us killed. Or would find a worse fate for us."

"Would it not be better to risk death trying to gain your freedom?" Jiggon said, still staring out at the night.

"It would be a fatal attempt," replied his father, running a hand over Jiggon's head. "The älfar are cruel in revenge. I am no coward. I don't want you or your brothers and sisters to suffer." Before Jiggon could respond, Hirrtan had got back on his feet. He always avoided arguments.

The young man kept his gaze fixed on the world outside. He shrugged the blanket off. He did not want it. *This way, nobody will ever get free. The älfar have no right at all to keep us as slaves.* There were some älfar masters who were kinder, *but that doesn't change the fact that we are not at liberty to come and go as we please and are not free to make our own decisions. They even control the number of children we are allowed to have.* Yintaï had often taken newborn babies away. They were never heard of again, either.

If the dorón ashont—the Towers that Walk—were enemies of the älfar and strong enough to challenge them, it must be a good omen that they had turned up again. The gods were trying to show the humans that there was a way to throw off the yoke of slavery.

But not as long as there are people like my father who won't take any risks. Whether from cowardice or fear for others; it's all one. Jiggon let the coarse curtain drop, closed his eyes and fell into a deep sleep. The day spent heaving corn sacks and threshing had been exhausting.

But in the middle of the night he woke with a start without knowing why.

Father and grandfather alike were snoring away, someone else moaned in their sleep, and in another corner there was a noise of grinding teeth. The wooden floor creaked and the wind whistled. He knew these sounds. They would not have woken him.

Jiggon listened, then slowly sat up and pulled the jute curtain back.

An icy breeze hit him as wind seeped into the room through the cracks around the windows; black smoke blew into the room from the still-smoldering chimney. Stars shone in a clear sky. Cows in the stables mooed from time to time, sheep bleated—nothing unusual. *I'm just uneasy.*

Out of the corner of his eye, Jiggon saw light reflected on metal and turned to look: an älf with a drawn sword was prowling past Irhart's hut, cloaking himself in shadow. He held a long dagger in the other hand.

What is he doing there? Jiggon did not dare move. *Is he looking for someone? Has one of us tried to escape?*

The älf sprang up onto the wall of the well; from there, despite his leather armor, he launched himself with ease onto Salisala's thatched roof. He knelt down, obviously waiting and watching.

A second älf appeared with a longbow ready in his hands. He remained on the ground below his companion, keeping a lookout.

Perhaps a slave has escaped from one of the neighboring villages? Jiggon was excited by the thought that one of their people had got away. *He can't be far away or they wouldn't be searching here.*

Jiggon kept watching the älfar closely.

The one on the roof sprang down to floor level without making a sound; his armor did not even clatter or creak. They made dangerous opponents, these älfar; they had made a pact with the dark. The two älfar exchanged a few quiet words and then they went their separate ways: the swordsman headed in Jiggon's direction while the archer moved out of view.

Jiggon could not move. He watched the älf come closer.

The älf suddenly stopped, looked to the right and opened his mouth to shout. Violet light fell on his face.

A gigantic cudgel slammed down, smashing the älf's helmet in as easily as if it had been paper. Fatally wounded, the älf collapsed.

Jiggon jerked back but could not tear his eyes away from the scene. *What is happening?*

The archer appeared again by the well, loosing an arrow against a target the young man could not see.

The arrow whizzed by and hit home. A metallic groan was followed by a deep roar of fury: a sound that Jiggon had never heard before and which made the hairs on the back of his neck stand up.

Just as the älf was about to attempt a second shot, a round object flew at him, smashing the bow and striking him in the middle of his chest. The impact sent him hurtling backward to fall a few paces behind the well. A third of the flying object was buried deep in the älf's chest cavity. Sudden moonlight revealed that it was a shield, the edges honed to a razor-sharp edge.

That shield looks so big and heavy, that I doubt even Irhart the Smith could lift it. Jiggon risked leaning forward to see where the unknown assailant was.

A colossal, heavily armed figure approached the well. Animal skins slung over the armor made its appearance even more unsettling and a purple glow came from behind a helmet, which had been shaped into a skull. He held a massive cudgel at his side. With his free hand the creature gripped the arrow lodged in its side and yanked it out. Blood spurted, brilliant yellow under the moonlight. The creature let out a roar of pain and fury.

It's one of the Towers that Walk! But . . . the canal is miles and miles away! I thought they were being held at bay there! His heart thumped in his chest—not from panic and fear, but hope and exhilaration. *Perhaps the älfar have all been defeated?*

Then he recalled his father's warning words. *"These Dirron Asharnt will want to see us off as soon as they've finished killing the älfar."*

I wonder if they will? Why has this one not attacked us already? He could simply have set our huts on fire and killed all of us.

He watched as the dorón ashont pulled the shield back out of the älf's body. Using the edge of it, he sliced through the cadaver, severing it in two, presumably to ensure his enemy was really dead. A heap of steaming entrails flopped out and blood flooded the dirt-covered ground. Then the giant creature stomped over to the älf whose head he had shattered. The dorón ashont dragged his first victim up to the other one and cut him in half in the same way, slicing through at navel height. When he had finished he stood up, snorting like an angry bull.

If they wanted to kill us they could have stormed through our huts by now. They've got something else in mind. Jiggon was keen to find out more. He mustered all his courage, pushed the window open and climbed out of it.

"Wait! Tower that Walks!" He avoided using the name the älfar gave these creatures and ran toward it. He stretched out his arms shakily. "I'm not an älf, we're not like them!" He pressed his wrists together to signify chains. "We are their slaves, prisoners! Do you understand what I'm saying?"

The vast creature turned its purple gaze on him and snorted again, more quietly. It went down on one knee, but was still as tall as Jiggon. With one hand it reached into the pile of steaming älfar innards, wrenched them out of the body cavity and held them out to Jiggon as an offering.

Jiggon was unsure what to make of the gesture.

The dorón ashont uttered a roar that went through the young man like a knife. It was answered by similar shouts from all around the village.

Ye gods, it's not here on its own!

The sheep in the barn began to bleat in fear, the village dogs started barking, children began crying and grown-ups called out to each other in alarm. Light appeared in the huts as people lit the lamps.

The armored creature stayed on one knee and threw the guts down at Jiggon's feet. He tore off an arm from the älf body and showed Jiggon the broken bone.

Jiggon thought he understood. "You want to prove that they are only flesh and blood; that they are not unbeatable?"

The first of the villagers came out, but did not dare approach. Fragments of talk such as "beast," "killed the masters," "all of them slaughtered" and "an end to us" were heard.

"Come back to me, Jiggon!" Hirrtan shouted, his voice full of fear. "By all the gods, he will kill you!"

The vast creature pulled the älf's sword out of its sheath and growled.

"No, he won't." Jiggon was still quaking, but slightly less violently now.

The weapon was tossed at his feet.

What . . . ? Jiggon bent down to pick up the sword. It was surprisingly light in his hand and the grip and blade were well balanced so that the weapon could be spun.

The dorón ashont raised its bloody gauntlet to the skies.

Is that a signal?

There was a chorus of roars from the periphery and another dorón ashont lumbered into view: the humans scattered to let it by. This one was carrying a wounded älf that it held by the nape of the neck as one might carry a rabbit. He chucked the captive down in front of Jiggon, who soon grasped what was expected of him.

Slowly he lifted the sword.

The injured älf writhed, turned over and struggled to his feet. There was a broad gash in his hip that had gone through armor and clothing to expose the bone. His chest had been crushed. Torchlight fell on his face: it was Heïfaton, one of the overseers. He was related to Yintaï.

"Slave, do not dare to touch me!" he threatened darkly even as he fought for air. "If you harm me, the whole village will be brought down. Fight the thing!" Heïfaton nodded toward the dorón ashont. "They are enemies to you and us!" Blood trickled out of his nose and mouth as he spoke.

"Jiggon!" yelled his father. "Throw the sword down! You don't know what you might be doing to us."

"What *I* might be doing to us? The dorón ashont have killed the black-eyes. If Yintaï hears about it, he will blame us anyway for not helping the guards." He laughed. "Slaves saving their guards' lives! I don't think so!" Jiggon placed the tip of the sword at the älf's throat. "We should free ourselves from our oppressors. The gods have sent us allies. And they have sent us hope."

"We will kill you," whispered Heïfaton and his eyes went black. Jiggon was suddenly beset by fear and staggered back. "After that we shall wipe out the whole village as punishment for your insurrection. Simply by considering the possibility of helping our enemies you have sealed your fate."

It seemed to Jiggon that an invisible hand was crushing his heart. *If I don't stab him straightaway I shall find myself running!* He yelled to give himself courage and rammed the blade into the unprotected throat.

Heïfaton's eyeballs went white and then a dark blue color surrounded his pupils. The expression on the älf's face was somewhere between surprise, pain and disbelief.

The crowd in the square had gone silent. The älf's death rattle could be clearly heard.

I . . . actually did it! Jiggon felt invincible, free of the alien pressure on his heart and his thoughts. He drew the sword back and struck the overseer on the side of the neck. "That is for all of us you people have killed."

Talk broke out among the crowd.

Jiggon did not quite manage to sever the älf's neck. He was unused to handling such a weapon as he held. The head was still attached by flesh and tendons and hung down sideways like an ill-fitting hood. Blood pumped out of the cut and onto the ground. The body of the älf fell forward onto the ground.

Jiggon struck the älf once more, driving the sword in through the back of the armor encasing the älf's chest. Blood spurted again. "That is for everything you have stolen from us, and for the children! I am not frightened of you any longer!"

This time the villagers' shouts of approval merged with the dark roars.

Tark Draan (Girdlegard), many miles to the south of the Gray Mountains, 4371ˢᵗ division of unendingness (5199ᵗʰ solar cycle), early winter.

Famenia had reached the outskirts of Milltown and was observing the valley from the branches of a red-barked pine, taking care not to be seen from below.

She could see the stone quarry and the entrance to the cavern where the älfar army had their secret camp. The mills on the riverside were busy and people were walking about as usual. Everything seemed normal.

They are going along with the pretense because they are frightened for their children imprisoned in the cave. Famenia noticed a small group of figures in light-colored robes. They stood out from the humans because of their height. *Those will be the älfar in charge, watching out for any untoward behavior.*

Satisfied, but not happy with what she had seen, she climbed down from her vantage point to where Ossandra was hiding at the foot of the tree. "It all looks quiet."

"That means nothing," Ossandra said, sounding worried. She had put on the clean clothes that Famenia had acquired for her on the way and looked more rested than she had on that first day. "They told us that if anyone left they would kill one of the children and put the body on display. I . . . It would be awful if they killed one of my friends."

"I didn't see anything like that." Famenia stroked the girl's hair. *And I hope, too, that it hasn't happened.* "I want to go and see what they'll do if a visitor arrives."

"And what about me?"

"You stay hidden. I've got to get into the cavern somehow to find out what they've done with the prisoners. Then we'll find a way to get them free." She set off.

For the first few steps Ossandra kept up with her, but when Famenia left the trees the little girl went back into the undergrowth. "May Elria protect you!" she whispered as Famenia left the forest.

The famula strode forward. The state of her clothes would help her story: she looked like she had traveled a long way on foot and could pretend she needed rest.

Milltown was situated in an isolated valley overshadowed by the mountain, with plenty of fields for agriculture and the nearby forest to provide winter fuel. The town's location had made it ideal for hiding.

What excuse can I think of for needing to get to the cavern? And if I get in how am I going to get out again, alive? The closer the famula got to the town, the less sure she became about her idea. *Perhaps I should not be so exposed? Shall I check it out after dark?* She slowed her pace.

It was too late to turn around now: a rider was heading in her direction, lance in hand. It was a man in simple leather armor wearing a black sash across his body. This signified that a dangerous infection was raging in the town.

That's a clever way to keep people out, of course. "Greetings," she called while he was still some way off. She raised her hand to show that she was unarmed.

The rider reined in his horse. He looked anxious. "May Sitalia be with you. Where are you headed?"

"Is no one allowed in?"

"The people are sick. Give Milltown a wide berth," he said, emphatically. "I can't let you pass. It's for your own protection."

Famenia tucked her thumbs under the straps of her knapsack. "How dangerous is this illness? Perhaps it's one I've already had, then it would be fine for me to rest here."

"No," he insisted. "You can't. It's . . . the plague."

"I see . . . the plague." Famenia looked him up and down. *How can I talk him around?* "What sort of plague would that be?"

"Why do you ask?" He was getting more and more uncomfortable and so was his horse. The animal wanted to be off and was pawing the ground with its hoof.

"There are different types of plague and I'm a healer." Famenia waited, keen to hear what his next excuse would be. "Shall I see if I can help your sick?"

"Thank you for your offer, it is brave of you, but we have already called in the best healers. The king sent them." He glanced over his shoulder at the älfar in disguise behind him. They had taken their bows from their shoulders and were pretending to be deep in conversation. "Now, go your own way and warn everyone you meet not to come to Milltown. It would be fatal to come."

Famenia was well aware that she was being closely watched and that she would not be able to enter the town. *They will shoot if I stay talking too long.* "Thank you for your warning. I pray the gods will help you and liberate you from the evil."

He nodded at her, relieved she had taken the hint. He rode back into the town and the gate was closed again behind him.

Well, that didn't work. I'll have to carry on being a hiker. She went around the outside of the town and headed for the mills. She would try to talk to somebody there.

She approached the first of the mills.

A man wearing the costume of his trade opened a door. Again, he wore a black sash across his traditional whites.

He spotted her and his eyes widened. Famenia raised her arm. "I know, I know. The plague. They told me at the town gates," she said quietly, thinking fast. *I'll try to get a coded message across.* "Is it safe for me to take water from the river? I heard the source of the infection is up in the cavern?"

He looked startled and pretended to scratch his nose, putting a finger to his lips. He pointed to the mill. "The cave is full of filth, that's true. We hardly know what to do about it. We won't be able to deal with it on our own. How did you know about it?"

"Oh, I met someone who told me." Famenia understood that there were älfar watching from the mill. *These dark abominations, is there no escape from them?* "Well, then, I'll turn around and try to find a source elsewhere."

"Yes, do that. Anywhere is better than here." The man waved and gave her an imploring look before walking back inside.

Famenia made her way along the river, passing the clattering mill-wheels that scooped up the water and churned it into foam. She could not imagine what was being ground. She could not see any sacks of corn. And there were no carts.

I've got no choice but to try again at night. With any luck the älfar won't be expecting anyone to be so bold as to enter the cavern. The idea was not pleasing, however keen she was to do something to help. She felt a bit like a chicken trying to break into a fox's lair.

Famenia left the mills and returned to the forest. "Ossandra?"

There was no answer.

"Ossandra! It's me! Where have you got to?" she called quietly, plunging into the undergrowth to search for the young girl. *Has she got lost? Or has she been hurt?*

Her mind raced as she fought her way through the brambles. She rejected her original plan of trying to get into the cave. It was simply too dangerous. One of the älfar was sure to see her. And even if she managed to get in and actually find the children and the old people, she would not be able to shepherd them to safety, let alone free Milltown from its occupiers.

And she had a mission to fulfill that could not be delayed.

But she could not just carry on with her journey; she had to help the people. And presumably the älfar had more in mind than just hiding out—they could be planning an attack on Girdlegard from there!

"Ossandra?" Famenia wiped the sweat from her brow and turned to look behind her. *There's no trace of any path. I'm completely lost!*

The forest was not dense here and none of the trees was taller than four paces high—not like the trees farther back—but it was enough to keep her from seeing where she was.

She would have to keep going until she hit a road. *I only hope Ossandra hasn't tried to get into Milltown on her own!*

As the sun started to go down, Famenia reached a familiar-looking part of the forest planted with red-barked pines.

My thanks to the gods! Now all she had to do was to find Ossandra.

She cursed the dark that spread more quickly in the woods than on open ground. She carried a lantern in her knapsack, but to light it would have meant alerting the älfar.

Famenia suddenly heard a sharp cry. *Ossandra!*

Horrified, she ran in the direction of the sounds: horses snorting, men's voices, metal on metal. *They have found her! Oh, dear gods!*

She was determined at least to rescue this child, even if she could not help the townspeople. Her right hand closed on the amulet and she rehearsed the spell for conjuring up gusts of wind. As she broke through the lower branches of the trees, she jumped down onto a road, her hand raised, ready to hurl the magic formula.

Ossandra was eleven paces from her; behind the girl were four heavily armored riders holding reinforced lances. Rune-inscribed shields hung at their sides.

The leading älf pushed up his visor and frowned, first at Ossandra and then at the famula.

"You won't have her!" Famenia released the spell with two hand gestures and a short incantation, hurling a gust of wind in the direction of the riders.

The intense stream of air skimmed the top of Ossandra's head, only ruffling her hair, but it hit the riders with full force. The branches of the fir trees bent backward and the horses shied, whinnying with terror. Two riders were thrown and the third fell with his mount. The leader battled to control his nervous horse.

It worked! "Come with me," Famenia shouted, stretching her hand out. "Get into the trees!" The child ran to her and grabbed her hand. They ran together.

The famula quickly recognized their danger: in a pine wood there is no undergrowth. One or two of the branches hung very low and would impede a rider's progress, but the älfar would certainly be able to ride after them. On her own Famenia might have managed to cut across to the other little wood and get into cover, but with the little girl . . .

The riders' shouts and the dull thud of hooves on a carpet of pine needles came ever closer.

I must turn and fight. Out of breath, Famenia stopped and lifted Ossandra up into the branches of a tree. "Climb up and wait for me to come for you," she gasped. "If they get me I want you to try to get a message to the king about the älfar." Then she sped off some distance before turning to face the enemy, her right hand grasping the precious amulet. *I won't manage more than three or four spells.*

The four älfar were nearing fast, their lances down so as not to catch them in the low branches.

The leader had seen her; he closed his visor and gave a silent signal to the others.

They fanned out so as not to be all swept away if she tried another wind-gust. They approached Famenia in a wide semicircle.

I need an illusion spell to make their horses shy again. Perhaps one of the älfar will break his neck? Gods! Help me now against this evil! With three swift hand movements and a single word, Famenia created an instant display of brightly colored lights and sent sparkling spheres whizzing through the trees accompanied by entertaining whistles and shrieks.

Even though the animals had been trained for warfare and could tolerate the sounds of clashing blades and battle noise, these fireworks were too much for them. They stopped abruptly and swerved from the path, lashing out with their hooves at the balls of fiery light; two of them crashed headlong into tree trunks and fell, crushing their riders under them.

Famenia was impressed with her own performance. *If Jujulo had known how successful his tricks are in battle he would never have shown us how to do them!*

When she turned around to see where the remaining two älfar had got to, she found only their riderless steeds.

Suddenly one of the älfar lunged toward her. She ducked under his arms and dodged behind a pine tree to prepare another spell, but found herself confronted with the second älf who had sword and shield in hand. Whirling around, she fell into the clutches of the first one.

"No! Hands off, black-eyes!" She struggled and lashed out, twisting her head to escape their hold, inadvertently smashing her forehead against her opponent's helmet. Stars danced in front of her eyes and her legs started to give way. The steely grip on her arms intensified. Her flight was over.

As the dazzling shapes cleared from her field of vision, she saw a sword blade pointing at her throat. The weapon belonged to the leader of the älfar unit, half-hidden behind his shield. "Who are you?" he demanded, his voice threateningly persuasive.

"Kill me, black-eyes, and I will turn into a ball of fire big enough to incinerate you and the whole town!" she declared, hoping her words sounded convincing. "I am a maga and only one of the many who will come to liberate Milltown. Hurt one hair on the heads of the townspeople and we will torture you, let you recover, and then torture you again until you lose your minds! You will see that we can be just as cruel as you!"

She was astonished to see the älf lower his sword. "This is obviously a regrettable misunderstanding," he said courteously.

"No, it's nothing of the kind! I know that you've a whole army concealed up there in the cave. Everybody knows! Girdlegard is ready and waiting. Your secret is out. There's no point in using the humans as hostages. And spare me your polite lies!"

He gave a nod and released his hold. *That seems to have had the right effect.* She scanned her surroundings for a gap she could escape through.

The älf looked her up and down. "I think we could find a use for a maga."

"What are you talking about? I certainly won't—"

He came up close. "We aren't black-eyes at all, if that's what you called us. We are elves from the Golden Plain."

Famenia was confused and her thoughts were whirling. "Why should I believe a word you say?"

"Because we will help you to destroy the älfar in your cavern." He put his sword away. "My name is Narósil. If you follow me to where my warriors are, I can explain everything that has happened. By first light at the very latest you will see the difference between Tion's scum and our kind. For we are Sitalia's children."

CHAPTER XVI

Thus Sinthoras and Caphalor lost their status as nostàroi.

> *Because of intrigues,*
> *short-sightedness.*
> *lust for revenge.*
> *To satisfy the demands of a handful of bedazzled älfar.*
> *Many have to walk through a deep, dark valley in order to return in glory.*
> *Some remain in the depths and never return.*

Hear now what next befell the Heroes.

Excerpt from the epic poem *The Heroes of Tark Draan*
composed by Carmondai, master of word and image

Ishím Voróo (Outer Lands), Dsôn Faïmon, Dsôn,
4371st division of unendingness (5199th/5200th solar cycle),
winter.

The long trek through Tark Draan and Ishím Voróo was nearing
its end.

Throughout the journey to Dsôn, Sinthoras had hardly said a word to his companions, keeping communication to a bare minimum. Verànor would not be able to give him any more information than that already imparted back in Tark Draan and Sinthoras preferred to use these moments of unendingness to work on the arguments for his defense. He had done things in the past that had often made him unpopular, even within his own Comets faction, but he had had no involvement in Robonor's accident.

Polòtain's denunciation had played into his enemies' hands.

It all fits. I can't really blame them all for suspecting me.

Sinthoras certainly blamed Polòtain for pursuing his revenge. He must have paid out a great deal of money to get witnesses to sign statements against him. *For that I shall kill him! He has robbed me of my high rank and of my war, but it will take me half an eternity to get compensation for the loss of my reputation.*

Sinthoras tried to pacify himself with the thought that he would be acquitted at the hearing. Nobody could prove a thing. His honor would be restored—of that he was convinced.

He was particularly sorry that his loyal Timanris would be bearing the brunt of malicious gossip. *She is strong and I am so proud of her.*

The only good thing about his enforced return to the Black Heart was that he would be seeing his beloved once more and would be able to spend time with her. Openly.

The group moved on to the broad Bone Tower approach, a continuation of the radial arm Shiimal they had been riding through. This was where Caphalor was from. Sinthoras was surprised to see that although plenty of slaves were about, only very few älfar were to be seen. They were all holding cloths over their noses and mouths and some of them swung small smoking incense holders.

"What's wrong?" Sinthoras asked Verànor. "Are our people not allowed to be out in the open?"

"I expect the sickness has spread," was the response. "Didn't I tell you?"

"What sickness?"

"It started with the arrival of the dorón ashont. People think they have something to do with it. An älf who escaped from them in Ishím Voróo came here to warn us and was the first to get sick and die. After him, it was the guards who had shared his quarters in barracks." Verànor tied a scarf around the lower half of his face. "They must have infected him with something and deliberately allowed him to come back to Dsôn."

That will be their revenge for the poisoned wine the Inextinguishables sent them. Instead of poison they have sent a plague. What a perfidious response! "If the enemy is currently stationed in the old fflecx territory, could it be possible that the älf who returned had been in contact with their toxic potions?"

Verànor thought for a while. "Possibly, but I think it's more likely that this is a cunning enemy plan. I don't think it's coincidence." They had arrived in front of Sinthoras's house. "You can stay here, but we'll be posting guards as long as there are charges against you."

Sinthoras was aware that he had been allowed the privilege of house arrest because of his services to the state. A suspect accused of a major crime would normally be placed in the cells.

"I shall let the Inextinguishables know that you have arrived. The date of your hearing can then be set."

"Tomorrow," said Sinthoras firmly. "I must get back to my army. There's a war on. This whole procedure is a sheer waste of precious time. You saw how the troops revere me." He felt it right to stress his status and his military importance to Verànor. His rank had been the second highest in the land and he wanted it back. *Polòtain is going to wish he had never started this!*

Verànor nodded. "I'll tell them. You should use a mask, too. Otherwise you'll be taking the sickness back to Tark Draan and infecting our troops." He turned his night-mare and headed for the Tower.

A good idea. Sinthoras entered his house, accompanied by the guards.

He was surprised to see the door opened by his slave Wirian and not by his steward Umaïnor. Wirian bowed in greeting, keeping her face veiled because she was not particularly pretty. Compared with Raleeha, most human females were disappointing.

"Master! It is so good you have come back!" she exclaimed, heartily relieved. He assumed she had not meant the comment maliciously. Her slim-fitting gray dress outlined her slim barbarian figure. She had obviously lost weight.

"Where is Umaïnor?"

"He is dead, sire. This terrible sickness killed him." She broke down in tears as Sinthoras dismounted. Together they walked in; the älfar guarding him kept three paces behind.

Sinthoras heard nothing at all. There was no chatter, no clattering of pots and pans from the kitchen, in fact no signs of anyone else in the vicinity. "Where is everybody?"

"The household ... Umaïnor died first. We found him in the hallway, his body burst open and his guts exploded. It was like he had been hollowed out." Wirian shuddered. "It took me a long time to clean everything up, I can tell you."

He shouted at her: "Where are the slaves?"

"Master, it's not my fault!" she whimpered. "Don't be angry with me! I'm the last person you should be angry with. I stayed here and have always been loyal, but the others all ran away. They went one night. They slipped out of Dsôn and went to join the Army of the Ownerless."

What powers are conspiring against me? "And what in the name of all infamy is the Army of the Ownerless?" he barked, marching off to his private quarters. "Bring an herbal infusion and come to my rooms at once. I need to know everything that has been happening." He dismissed her and went to the relaxation room, slamming the tall double doors behind him. *Has absolutely everyone gone crazy?*

Sinthoras threw himself down on the upholstered couch and looked out of the long windows: the gray grass lawn and dark red and black foliage was subdued and beautiful. But what caught his eye were the weeds disfiguring the white bone-gravel paths. Nobody had been tending the garden.

Slaves running off! In the old Dsôn that would have been unthinkable!

The dark blue of the room calmed him and he gazed on the unframed works gracing the walls. His own. *When did I last stand at my easel? Perhaps it might ease my troubled soul.*

He became aware how much he had missed painting. His style was not the same as Carmondai's; Sinthoras preferred to give his hand free range over the canvas with his mind selecting colors at random; his work was always powerful.

His thoughts were circling around the imminent hearing when Wirian returned with a tray; she poured out some of the drink for him and knelt down on the floor. "You asked about the Army of the Ownerless?"

"Yes." Sinthoras gave an almost imperceptible smile. "And don't be afraid. You won't be punished."

The slave was relieved to hear it. "After the steward died, no one knew what would happen. I wanted to ask your relatives to appoint someone, but the others were against that. They said they would leave Dsôn. They said it was going to be easy because of the sickness. They wanted to join the Army of the Ownerless. They locked me in the cellar. By time I had managed to get free they had gone."

"The Army?" he urged, taking the cup.

"Yes, yes, of course, the Army! It's made up of escaped slaves and a handful of soldiers from the vassal nations. They have a camp near—"

"A *camp*? We're letting a bunch of runaways set up camp in Dsôn Faïmon?" Sinthoras stared at Wirian in astonishment, trying to read her veiled features. "How can that be? A single one of our rawest recruits would suffice to deal with a hundred barbarians!"

Wirian was equally surprised at his reaction, but remained silent.

"What?" he snapped.

"You...haven't heard? The dorón ashont have thrown up a barricade at one of the island fortresses and are holding it against all älfar attempts to oust them." Wirian fussed with positioning the teapot correctly over the heated coals in the metal container. "Some of the dorón ashont have got to the sections around Wèlèron, Avaris and Ocizûr, inciting the slaves to rebel. Many of your people have been killed, master. Whole settlements have been razed to the ground and the Towers that Walk have led this Army of the Ownerless into countless battles. They seem to be invincible."

"How...?" Sinthoras did not know what to say. "This cannot be true," he said. "I've been riding through Tark Draan conquering one kingdom after another and back home neither Constellations nor Comets can deal with a few scum insurgents?" *The dorón ashont are cunning. First they weaken us, then they set the barbarians and vassal nations against us.* He placed a hand to his brow. "By Samusin! I've arrived just in time!

Before I go back to our troops I must save Dsôn Faïmon. Tomorrow, straight after the hearing."

Sinthoras noticed that Wirian was trembling with fear.

"Go and make me something to eat," he said, more kindly. "Then go over to Timanris—"

"Master . . . I-I . . ." Shaking violently, she stammered, "I can't do that. For the same reason that I could not consult her about a new steward."

He felt sick and there was an ice-cold knot in his stomach. "What's happened to her?" he whispered. "The plague? In the name of infamy, if she—"

"No, master, it is not the sickness."

Sinthoras felt his heart might burst. "Tell me! Out with it, you wretched thing! What's happened to Timanris?"

"She will have nothing to do with you. She has renounced you, master." Wirian bowed her head humbly. "Please do not punish me!"

Sinthoras was transfixed as if struck by a bolt of lightning. He was numb. He had no heartbeat. He was as if dead. He had even ceased to breathe. He forced himself to inhale. "What?" he whispered incredulously, although his instincts told him to bellow.

"She has publicly renounced you and has severed all connection," Wirian expanded, head down. "She had it proclaimed in the market square. The reason given was your involvement in the death of her previous partner, Robonor."

Sinthoras heard the words, but could not take them in. The room started to turn, the pictures on the walls merging into one long smear.

This is the cruelest trick Polòtain could have played. He has deprived me of what is dearest to me. I . . . He was unable to think, so badly affected was he by the news. *Timanris! She must say it herself to my face! I can't simply . . .*

"NO!" He leaped to his feet, hurling his cup aside, and ran from the room; the guards followed hard on his heels as he headed out through the empty alleyways and streets of the capital city.

Sinthoras was so distraught that it did not occur to him to place a handkerchief over his mouth and nose for protection.

Tark Draan (Girdlegard), to the southwest of the Gray
Mountains, the area formerly known as the Golden Plain,
4371ˢᵗ division of unendingness (5199ᵗʰ solar cycle),
winter.

Caphalor appeared, fully armored, in front of a house that had been
newly constructed inside the crater they had discovered by the Golden
Plain. He surveyed the progress with satisfaction.

The fortifications were taking shape and would soon reach a stage
capable of holding off an enemy onslaught. Buildings had been swiftly
erected to house those älfar troops still in the town. They, like him,
refused to accept any accommodation the barbarians (let alone elves)
had used. These quarters would serve for the snow-rich winter months.

The huge crater held a strange fascination for him.

Behind him, the new nostàroi left the new accommodation and
joined him. "It's all looking good," said Imàndaris. "We hadn't seen all
the details in the dark."

"The barracks won't be in use for very long," he replied. "But the craftspeople will be delighted to hear their work praised by their nostàroi."
Caphalor let his gaze wander over the labors of stonemasons and carpen-
ters, busy trying to make the älfar warriors feel at home in Tark Draan.

On top of the pleasant change their efforts had brought about, there
was also the comforting atmosphere exuded by the location itself. The
crater's aura recalled the mood in Dsôn Faïmon.

But the atmosphere here is more intense, more authentic somehow.
He squatted down and dug his fingers into the soft earth. *It's as if the*
place were glad to welcome us here; there's a special energy.

"I can feel it, too," said Imàndaris from behind him, her tone formal,
almost ceremonial. "This is indeed an extraordinary spot and it deserves
to be blessed with a city that will outshine Dsôn."

Caphalor smiled to himself and stood back up, pressing the crumbs
of soil between his fingers as if to preserve the essence. "It's unlikely the
Inextinguishables will commission anything like that."

He watched her closely. The early morning light illuminated her features and darkened her eyes. Caphalor's interest in her was growing. As

the daughter of a renowned artist, her career path had been quite different; she had moved in the realm of art, but had walked a path of death. She was extremely unusual.

The episode with Morana was still in his mind. Caphalor had been strongly attracted to her from their first meeting, but when she was so outspoken that evening at dinner, the scales had fallen from his eyes: Morana had understood him and his emotions so much better than he had done himself.

"Penny for your thoughts?" Imàndaris looked at him quizzically. "What is worrying you?"

"Nothing." He answered lamely. "Nothing to do with the crater or the project."

She gave a kindly smile. "Then it must be me! That's why you're staring."

Caphalor decided to seize the moment. "Well, now that you mention it: I was wondering why the daughter of an artist would choose to take up the sword rather than a sculptor's chisel or a painter's brush. You are sure to carry your mother's talent within you."

"Who knows? I prefer handling weapons. That's all." Imàndaris looked up at the crater's edge, where a unit of cavalry were heading out on their rounds. "They're going to hunt down elves, I see?"

"Yes. I have sent them to search for elves and do their arms practice at the same time. If Tion and Samusin are favorable, the soldiers will get to try out their new lance skills." His laughter was dark. He went on: "We were lucky at Sonnenhag because the óarcos weren't expecting us, otherwise Carmondai would hardly have carried off the victory against Toboribar, but what he managed to teach the troops in that short time is amazing." Caphalor walked on, accompanied by the nostàroi. "And how is it that the Inextinguishables came to select you for this high office? Please don't think me rude; I have never been one for politics and I don't know who is advising the rulers now. You may have many sponsors. But I had never heard your name until very recently."

"You were well known for not being interested," she said. "You had your estates, your family and you preferred life as an . . . outsider. You went into battle when you were needed, but then you went back to your farming." Her tone remained amicable. "You and I were never on the same campaigns, Caphalor. That will be why you had never heard my name."

"You must have been good." He pointed to the silver nostàroi emblem on her black mantle. "Or you would not have been awarded that badge."

"My mother never understood me. Sometimes she said she doubted I was really her daughter. She did not disown me, but she never invited me to come home. I'm her guilty secret. Her other children turned out better, to her way of thinking." She looked around. "Where are we heading?"

He pointed to the center of the crater. "Over there. The elves attempted to have the hole filled in, but they could not finish it. I want to take a closer look. That hill would be a good place for the governor's palace. Excellent vantage point."

Imàndaris nodded. "We ought to get the slaves straightening up the edges. That gentle curve wastes space. We'll need more room."

"More? There's plenty of space for thousands here. What numbers are you thinking of?" Caphalor grinned. "Dsôn's citizens won't want to emigrate."

"That's true. But . . . I don't know. What we create here today we don't have to worry about tomorrow." She tossed back her reddish blond hair. "Will you join me at dinner? I'd like to discuss our plans for the other elf regions. Our scouts are back from Gwandalur and they've got news about the dragon. It could prove more dangerous than we'd thought."

"Oh?" He was pleased that Imàndaris was interested in his opinion, although he was well aware that her goals were different from his own: consulting him would help her strengthen her reputation with the troops. He was still a popular commander and if she were on good terms with him the soldiers would accept her. *A clever move.*

"You can answer later." She indicated the massive heap of earth and strode off. "Let's have a good look at this first."

They arrived at the foot of the hill. Composed of loose sand it now had a light frosting of snow, making it look like icy chalk.

Caphalor cautiously scaled the slippery slope. Grains of sand and crystals of snow crunched under the thick soles of his winter boots. He trod heavily, testing the composition of the ground. "I've always wondered why they started building this mountain in the center of the crater," he called to Imàndaris. "It would have been easier to tip all this sand down the edge rather than build up in the middle."

"That's true. Almost any other method would have been simpler." She bent down to pick something up. "Is this glass, do you think? Have they been trying to melt the sand down?"

Am I imagining it? Caphalor felt the atmosphere changing. The energy he had noticed before was ebbing away as he climbed. He turned to the nostàroi. "Do you feel it?"

"It's fading," she said, bewildered. "Can it be to do with this sand?"

The sand is blocking Inàste's aura! Caphalor suddenly understood why the hill had been constructed in the middle of the crater. He stabbed his heel into the frozen layer of sand.

Imàndaris, eight or nine paces behind him, started clearing snow and sand away with her boot. She had gotten the same idea. "What's this?" She crouched down.

Caphalor hurried over to her, sliding on the white surface. He saw something black where she had exposed the ground. *It's stone! Just as I thought.*

Brushing the pale sand to one side, Imàndaris was surprised to find a rock underneath. "What have the elves done here?" All at once her puzzled frown gave way to a dazzling smile. "Can it be . . . the fossilized tear of Inàste?" She closed her eyes in rapture. "Oh, Inàste! How wonderful if we have truly found a holy relic!"

"We should get the whole stone uncovered." Caphalor kept his excitement under control, but inside he was as joyful as his companion. *How inspiring for our people if we have found some genuine portent from our creating spirit—something that can grace us with its powerful aura.*

Imàndaris laid a hand on the precious stone. "Oh, in the name of all infamy!" she murmured, her eyes tight shut. "Come here, Caphalor! Place your hand here! It is—"

He knelt at her side. As he touched the black stone his fingertips tingled. The aura, the energy that filled the entire crater, was streaming into his body, permeating every fiber of his being and filling him with incredible warmth.

Inàste's fossilized tear! There was no longer the slightest doubt in his mind. He quivered with joy. By chance he caught Imàndaris's eye.

Their glances melded, as did their thoughts and their emotions, it seemed to Caphalor. His heart was racing and his head refused to turn away from her. *What . . .*

Everything around them disappeared—only her face existed in his mind. The place near the heart, the solar plexus, woke explosively and flooded his body with heat from head to toe.

Caphalor gasped as the feeling tore through him. It grew more intense yet and made his whole body quiver and shake. His teeth chattered wildly. Suddenly he understood that this was not happening within him, but was coming from the ground under their feet.

His thoughts and his senses returned abruptly to the present moment.

Imàndaris was kneeling at his feet and he could tell she was as shocked as he. The hill beneath them bucked and rocked like a rearing night-mare, eager to throw them off. Snow and sand slid down, slowly revealing the black stone.

"Inàste's tear has felt our presence!" she cried joyfully. "It has been waiting for us to find it and touch it."

Caphalor was having trouble keeping his balance. Now he could see that they were standing on a sharp ridge, no broader than two sword blades. The pleasant vibrations emanating from the stone grew stronger as more of the rock was revealed, but jumping down would have been unwise as more and more sharp rocks appeared. One false move might see their death—or serious injury.

"Wait until the rock has settled down." He said to Imàndaris. He held her by the arms and she placed her hands on his shoulders. In this way, each could help the other to remain stable on their precarious ledge.

Caphalor saw slaves staring up at them and other älfar running up to the crater from all directions. But there was nothing anyone could do but wait until the hill had stopped moving.

He glanced at Imàndaris and she returned his gaze. Something had changed. He remembered this from the time he had spent with Enoïla. *Has the power of the stone locked us together?*

The quaking did not lessen. In fact, the vibrations were growing stronger and the summit of the hill started to move upward with a deep rumbling sound.

More multi-colored stone came to the fore and the hill became a mountain, higher and higher, and broader at the base. Great clumps of earth crashed down to the floor of the crater, making the waiting älfar scatter in fear.

Caphalor and Imàndaris were carried up and up, almost level to the crater edge, then farther still.

By all that's infamous, what is happening here? Caphalor scrutinized the plain. Gusts of wind threatened to topple him, but Imàndaris held him fast.

At long last the vibrations ebbed away and the astonishing growth of the rock halted.

Imàndaris looked around excitedly. "What just happened?" she asked, joyously, as a flight of birds went past them. Gray wisps formed beneath them and they were surrounded by light fog—they had reached the clouds. "What a splendid gift the Creating Spirit has given us. We are so high above the crater!" With a laugh she released Caphalor's hands.

Caphalor nodded. The recent splinters of unendingness had brought so much that was new and unusual he could hardly keep track. Strangely, he was thinking about how difficult the descent was going to be. *One false move and we die.* He leaned over and looked down.

The mountain reared up, sharp as a needle within its coat of cloud and mist. Pieces of earth slipped down its sheer sides, breaking up as they plunged to the crater floor. The rock was wet in places and jets of water could be seen emerging.

"The Creator Spirit's tear is pretty sharp and pointed, isn't it?" he commented.

"But it has to be one of her tears. How else can we explain what has just happened to us?" Imàndaris also risked a look over the side. "Is it a sign? Does she want us to find our future here? Does she want us to leave Ishím Voróo?"

Caphalor was doubtful. "I reckon the mountain may explode or slip back down again," he said. "But if it does remain, it would be a good site for a palace," he added cautiously. "We will need many slaves to hew steps into the rock." He imagined a new Bone Tower up here on the mountain as a symbol of his people's superiority over the elves. *Truly! Can there be any greater fate in store for me than this?*

Imàndaris stretched out her arms and laughed, her bright red hair and the edges of her robe lifting in the breeze. "We are blessed, Caphalor!" she exclaimed. "The Creating Spirit has chosen us!" She turned abruptly toward him, eyes bright with enthusiasm and he could not resist: many paces above the floor of the crater, their faces touched by the wind and clouds, he took her chin gently in his hands and gave her a long kiss on the mouth. She responded passionately.

Tark Draan (Girdlegard), in the Gray Mountains, 4371st division of unendingness (5199th solar cycle), late autumn.

By now Simin was having no trouble at all finding his way about in the labyrinth of tunnels—as long as he stuck to the main paths, which would let him traverse the Gray Mountains quickly in his search for the demon.

Three times now he had narrowly avoided bumping into orcs. One of the monsters had got wind of him and had followed his tracks, but a masterly shove had sent the screaming greenskin plunging into an abyss. It would not be coming out again.

But then he had seen Hianna the Flawless escorted by a troop of älfar and she certainly did not look like their captive—more like their ally.

Famenia was too slow. She did not explain the true nature of the älfar to Hianna in time.

Unfortunately Simin had found no opportunity to speak to the maga alone. There had always been several älfar around her and he could not risk discovery if he wanted to carry out his original mission.

Who knows what kind of promises the älfar have made her? If they've got Hianna on their side, it will make everything harder for us. His disappointment ran deep.

At least his mission was proceeding. He was now fairly sure he had reached the northern part of the mountain and the place where the dead had risen again, according to what Famenia had said. But as yet he had seen no indication that the demon was near.

Where has it gone? Simin did not want to think about the demon being in Girdlegard, using its unholy powers. *It's essential that Famenia has succeeded in warning and winning over the other magi. Otherwise...*

A shadow unfolded from the wall and lunged at him and Simin sprang backward as an ax just missed his head and shattered upon meeting rock.

In front of him was an orc nearly the same size as himself, staring dumbly at its broken weapon in dismay.

That's all right by me. Simin kicked his enemy in the groin, making him double up with pain. The magus then aimed his boot at the creature's face. Snorting, the orc lurched to the side and fell against the tunnel wall.

The fact that the orc was in that area of the mountain was strange. *This region is under human control.*

He sprang forward, pulled out the orc's sword and placed the tip of it against the creature's neck. "What are you doing in our region of the mountains?" He hoped the orc would fall for the trick and assume that he was a human ally.

The beast looked at the edge of the sword and then at Simin. He groaned. *That kick was effective.* "I got lost," he grunted, his tiny eyes glittering with fear.

"Why were you trying to kill me?"

"Thought you were a dwarf."

"Look how tall I am!" Simin kicked him in the belly. It did not have much effect because of the armor, but the blow was intended to give the message that he was willing to inflict more damage. "I want the truth!"

"I will whisper it in your ear!" The orc tried to get around the sword and attack the magus.

Alarmed by the sudden movement, Simin stuck the blade deep into the creature's throat and let go of the sword. The orc fell and foolishly pulled the sword out of the wound, causing a sudden hemorrhage; he ended his life in a pool of his own blood.

The magus strode over the cadaver and crept forward. *Perhaps he was guarding something?*

He soon found himself in a small cave where the dwarves had transformed stalagmites into cleverly carved columns. Lighting was provided, as in the rest of the tunnels, by luminous moss.

In the center was a naked orc. Chains leading from four of the pillars were attached to a ring around his neck; he crouched on the floor, head on chest, his body covered in cuts and dried blood.

That is . . . quite revolting! A large clump of flesh had been cut out of the orc's right shoulder and the wound had not been dressed or covered. Thick crusts of scab had gone putrid. *What had he done to deserve that punishment, I wonder? And why is he alone?*

Punishment had to be *seen* in order to be an effective deterrent, but there was no one else in the room and it was quite far from anywhere else. Perhaps this one had led some kind of rebellion. He might have been tortured and was perhaps awaiting execution.

I don't have to put myself in their place. He was about to withdraw when he saw a long dagger sticking out of the creature's side. *By Elria! How is he not dead?*

The orc took a shuddering breath, raised its head and looked directly at him. A long wound that ran under his chin from one ear to the other was clearly visible. The monster snorted aggressively, displaying long teeth as powerful as the fangs of a wolf.

It should surely be long dead! Then the appalling truth struck. *Is this one of the dead come back to life?* Cautiously he approached the captive. *Perhaps the demon is close at hand?* He looked around again.

The beast stood up and the chains clattered. A roar came from its muzzle, accompanied by the smell of drains.

"Are you an Undead?" Simin asked, stopping just out of the range of the filthy claws. Then he moved swiftly, pulling the dagger out of the creature's side and plunging the blade into its heart.

At least that was what he tried to do. He had little experience in combat and had made the mistake of inserting the knife at the wrong angle, so that it did not slip between the ribs as he had hoped.

The orc roared and aimed a blow at him.

Simin managed to avoid the long talons, but tripped on the rough ground. Before he could help himself, he fell and was grabbed by the orc's right forearm and dragged into range of the horrific fangs.

I am an idiot! Simin wanted to preserve his store of the magic energy so he drew the dagger out again and rammed it into his enemy's throat from below.

The orc did not seem impressed. He continued in his efforts to get at the magus's face, ready to strip it of flesh.

I'll have to use magic . . . Simin could see the dagger point sticking up through the monster's lower jaw and piercing the tongue. He conjured up a dazzling ball of light, blinding the beast for several heartbeats; then, using the confusion that resulted, he thrust both feet against the orc and pushed with all his might, ignoring the pain in his belly to pull himself free.

Simin landed in a pile of shit, and slid away from the monster, who flailed wildly at the end of his chains, making the stalagmite pillars shake.

"Ye gods!" Simin watched the orc roar and thrash about in spite of the new injuries. *Thank you, Sitalia!*

<There are no gods here.> he heard a persuasive, whispering voice inside his own head.

"What?" he looked right and left. "Who . . . ?"

<In these mountains it is I who decides who lives and who dies. And death, of course, can mean eternal life, as you can see in this disgusting example.>

"The demon!" Simin exclaimed.

<Yes, the demon.> The voice whispered. <But I wouldn't describe myself as a demon. Look up and you'll see me.>

Simin tilted his head back and saw a cloud of fog floating just under the cave roof.

Chapter XVII

The smell
of endingness
recalls the taste
of foul words
which lie on the tongue
and then pour, stinking, over the lips.

So, when you speak,
speak pure,
and clear
and only what is true.
So your mouth may remain
untouched by decay.
Be aware: evil words
bring evil in their wake.

Excerpt from the epic poem *The Heroes of Tark Draan*
composed by Carmondai, master of word and image

Ishím Voróo (Outer Lands), Dsôn Faïmon, Dsôn,
4371st/4372nd divisions of unendingness (5199th/ 5200th solar cycles),
winter.

Sinthoras ran across the white bone gravel of the main thoroughfares, his breath coming unevenly. He knew full well his guards were finding it difficult to keep up, but the urgency that drove him to find Timanris would not let him slow down.

Polòtain can take everything else, but he mustn't take her away from me. Not her! He felt an icy rage that spurred him on to revenge and bloodlust. He wished he could confront Polòtain, who had caused him all this upheaval and distress, so that he could repay it all in kind. *I would murder him and be glad to answer for it in a court of law. That way I'll be condemned for an offense I'd actually committed.*

No one had ever been as important to him as Timanris; she fascinated and encouraged and, in so many ways, completed him. He wanted to be near her and to lay Dsôn Faïmon and Tark Draan at her feet.

I would have named cities after her and erected temples in her name. Despair burned in his soul. *And now she disowns me without telling me the cause!*

A few paces ahead a solitary älf stumbled along, then collapsed, grabbing his belly and his chest. He rolled from side to side. Moaning, he tried to drink from the puddles, before tearing at his robe.

Sinthoras slowed down as he reached the figure.

"Stop!" called one of his guards in a panic. "Don't touch him, whatever you do! He has—"

With a sound like the breaking of a fresh loaf the älf's belly burst open. Intestines and inner organs flowed onto the street and a warm rain drenched Sinthoras. The älf died with a loud groan.

"Get back!" came the warning again and Sinthoras was dragged back by the shoulders. A horrified exclamation followed.

Sinthoras could not take his eyes off the corpse. He could see the älf's shriveled organs on the road. *They look as if they were boiled.* Then he saw something moving in the entrails. "What is that?" He moved a little closer.

Purple threads the length of his little finger pulsated in the dead älf's guts, breaking through the stomach wall in hundreds and swarming off to disappear among the pellets of the road. *It's not a sickness that has struck our nation! It's parasites!*

Sinthoras took out his coin purse, emptied it and turned it inside out, then used the bag to pick up some of the worms, flipping it back the correct way when he had a handful. He fastened the top tightly so that none of the little worms could escape.

Getting to his feet he turned to one of his guards. "Take this to Wèlèron," he instructed him. "It needs to go to the älf Bolcatòn—he needs to study this. Tell him exactly what you saw."

But the guards drew back and one of them laid his hand on the hilt of his sword.

"Are you—" Sinthoras noticed that something was dripping down his face. Wiping his brow with his index finger, he saw that he had blood on his hand. Someone else's blood. *They think I've become infected.* "It's not in the blood! It's the worms that bring death—" Then he realized that with the force of the exploding guts, it was very likely that some of the parasites had reached him. *Well, then, I'll go myself.* "You go to Timanris and tell her I want to see her." He pointed to the other älf and continued, "And you, come with me. I'll need a night-mare."

At first no one moved, but then one ran in the direction of Timansor's house, while the other followed the one-time nostàroi, keeping a safe distance away.

They went back to Sinthoras's house and collected a night-mare. Together with an escort that was nervously trying not to get too close, he galloped out of Dsôn toward Wèlèron, where the communities of academic älfar resided and where the schools of higher learning had been established. All known älfar wisdom was gathered in that place.

Is that the solution? He had not put down the purse, which smelled badly of blood and excrement. *The dorón ashont must have introduced these parasites to their captive and then let him escape, knowing he would bring them to us.* He shuddered to think of the number of worms that had eaten their way out of the dead body. *There must be many thousands of them in Dsôn already.* The mere idea made his throat tighten with fear. *The worms are multiplying all the time under our feet.* There could be no escape, if his understanding of the situation were correct: the worms could be anywhere; searching for all of them would take hundreds of moments of unendingness.

After a strenuous ride they reached the town of Arrilgûr in Wèlèron's outskirts.

This was an alien world for Sinthoras, one in which academic life was at the heart of things. He could not remember when he had last been there. Scholars held no sway in politics and thus had never been of any use to him. The only person he could approach was Bolcatòn—a high-ranking scholar specializing in medical matters. He chaired the civil research committee.

Sinthoras stopped the nearest älf and was soon directed to the main building: an imposing semicircle built of bone marble. The façade was shimmering white and the polished stones showed the lines that recalled their origins.

Let's hope he's good at his job. I don't know where else to go. Time is of the essence. Sinthoras stormed noisily through the hallowed halls with his escort, brushing slaves and älfar servants aside until he had reached Bolcatòn's rooms. This was not the proper way to approach an älf of Bolcatòn's standing, but now was not the time to stand on ceremony.

He found the expert at his modest evening meal of bread and fruit; an opaque liquid filled a clear goblet next to an empty carafe. Bolcatòn seemed distinctly old, which was unusual for one of their kind. *I wonder how many dawns he has seen?*

Sinthoras approached and sketched a small bow. "I must apologize for dispensing with the normal niceties," Sinthoras said swiftly, halting five paces back from the table. He lifted the grubby purse. "I think I have found the cause of the sickness that is carrying off so many of our people in Dsôn."

Bolcatòn, in his fiery red gown, was an august figure. His gray hair had been twisted into a complicated knot at the back of his head. Disgruntled at being so rudely disturbed, he addressed Sinthoras gruffly. "I thought you had come to arrest me," he said. He removed the lid from the carafe. "Put it in here. Tell me why you think *you* have the solution to the crisis facing our people. Soldiers are not known for making scientific discoveries."

Sinthoras undid the cord on the bag and dropped the purse of threadworms into the transparent jug.

Bolcatòn closed the lid carefully before turning the carafe this way and that and shaking it gently until some of the worms wriggled out of the cloth purse.

"Purple phaiu su," he stated, seemingly unsurprised. "They are quite choosy about what they eat, but we seem to be quite high on their list of delicacies."

Sinthoras was taken aback. "You've seen them before? Why didn't anyone know what was happening in Dsôn?"

Bolcatòn tapped on the glass with the tip of his finger, irritating the little creatures. "And exactly who are you?" he asked. Sinthoras introduced himself briefly. "Ah, I see. The disgraced nostàroi." Bolcatòn's tone was scornful. "Aren't you supposed to be obliterating the elf race? But it turns out we're the ones being wiped out. They will survive us."

"Those are the words of a traitor," Sinthoras said.

Bolcatòn was angry now, his eyes glinting. "It's you warriors, all you Comets and Constellations, that have brought us down with your eternal rivalries, arrogance and ambitions. All these accursed political intrigues and tricks, exerting your influence on the Inextinguishables and insisting upon a senseless expansionist campaign! Who is the traitor here? You will find it is not I." Bolcatòn paused. "The war served one purpose and one purpose only: to get rid of the demon you brought."

"What?" Sinthoras was at a loss. "Why should we have wanted to get rid of him? He has helped us."

"That's another topic entirely. Let's deal with this one. The purple phaiu su here represent an acute danger. I have known for a long time that they are the root cause of the apparent infection raging in Dsôn. The Inextinguishables have been fully informed."

"And what has been done about it? An älf just exploded on a public thoroughfare in front of me! The solution in place can't be all that effective."

"So I see," said Bolcatòn, staring at the distraught älf's clothes. "I am acquainted with these parasites. They decimated the troops that were sent south to suppress the nations there. That was in the time of the old gods: Shmoolbin, Fadhasi and Woltonn. The worms crawl in at night through nose or mouth, make their way to the stomach and lay eggs; the hatchlings eat the flesh and the blood of the host, secreting an anesthetizing substance so that the victim is unaware of their presence. This substance eventually comes into contact with the stomach, and reacts so strongly with the acids there that the host more or less explodes. As indeed you saw. With the end of the southern gods the purple phaiu su were forgotten about."

How old is he if he can recall those past wars? "Is there no remedy?"

Bolcatòn indicated his supper. "This is a food combination the phaiu su are not partial to. It gives some protection, and taking a loffran infusion helps to prevent them from entering the host. If you are already affected by the parasites the loffran encourages them to leave, but if the intestines are already too damaged, the victim will, of course, quickly leave unendingness."

I must let Timanris know at once! Sinthoras stared at the expert. "But surely everyone in Dsôn should be told? We should provide the loffran infusion to the whole population, put containers of it out in the streets—"

"You would have to saturate the entire city with it if you want to eliminate the worms entirely," Bolcatòn argued. "The bone particles the roads are made of provide the ideal habitat for the creatures. I told the Sibling Rulers this, too. But there is another problem."

"Which is?"

"Loffran is not much cultivated, nor is it a respectable method of treatment—we have moved on. In Shiimal it's not grown at all. It's only found growing wild in the area between Wèlèron and Avaris. I've had it planted there, but now the dorón ashont hold that land. Half the fields have been destroyed and the others can't be harvested because they're within range of enemy catapults."

Fear fastened its grip on Sinthoras's heart. "What can be done?" Sinthoras asked.

Bolcatòn took a sip of the cloudy liquid. "The city needs to be burned down and built anew. The phaiu su are unlikely to flourish outside of Dsôn. They are at home in Ishím Voróo's south, but they will bring Dsôn to a standstill. The Black Heart will cease to beat."

Sinthoras looked at the carafe where the worms were coiling and wriggling. They were slowly dying, exposed to the remains of the loffran infusion. *It would be so easy to save Dsôn. Curse the dorón ashont!* "Where do you get the loffran roots?"

"Before the uprisings I took in a reasonable harvest. The roots were dried and ground into powder. This works just as effectively as the fresh root, but we don't have enough to save Dsôn." Bolcatòn wiped his mouth. "One might almost think a time of knowledge and research, not war, is upon us. Only we had the foresight to study and find answers, while the Comets and the Constellations—so busy with power and influence—were unaware of the danger." He gave a quiet laugh and tapped his forehead. "Knowledge is power. And since I know more than you do, I am obviously more powerful. I'm sure you will agree."

I'm going to need this remedy for Timanris and myself. "How much can I buy from you?"

Bolcatòn smiled patronizingly and spread his arms. "You were a nostàroi and a hero of the empire. And you have shown initiative and presence of mind in coming to me with the parasites. For this reason I am prepared to give you a small container of it; eat a spoonful once every moment of unendingness. The purple phaiu su will not come near you." He pushed the carafe to the edge of the table. "Look."

The worms were all dead at the bottom of the glass jug. "So simple," he murmured.

"So simple, indeed." Bolcatòn sent a servant to fetch the remedy. This was handed to Sinthoras. "May I wish you luck at your hearing. If Samusin is on your side he will have sent a few worms to your accusers and nobody will be able to pursue a case against you."

Not a bad idea! He bowed to the scholar and withdrew, clasping the small box—its contents more precious to him than all the gold in Tark Draan. He was not inclined to express any thanks to Bolcatòn after the insults he had been offered. But really, it was not important any longer.

I could have some of the parasites sent to Polòtain and I'd be free of him. He won't have heard about the effects of the loffran root. He felt his guards' eyes on him; they were well aware that he carried the only effective treatment against the ravages of the phaiu su. As they walked back through the corridors of the academy he dipped his moistened finger into the yellow powder and licked it.

It fizzed on his tongue and had a slightly soapy but sharp, refreshing taste. *No wonder the parasites don't like it.* He went on dipping his finger and licking it until he thought he had probably got the dose right. He closed the box firmly without having offered any of its contents to his escort. *Who cares if they die. I'll be needing all of this for myself and Timanris.*

Sinthoras lost no time in leaving Arrilgûr.

He returned to Dsôn at first light and galloped straight to the Timansor residence, but he was refused entrance. Neither Timanris nor her father could be seen. The fact that his way to Timanris was barred by watchmen bearing Polòtain's emblem only increased his hatred of his arch enemy.

Having no idea what to do, he went back to his own home, where he found a summons to his midday hearing. This left him no time to collect sufficient parasites to smuggle into Polòtain's presence.

In spite of his lack of sleep, Sinthoras concentrated on preparing for the court appearance. The speech he was rehearsing would not have had its equal in Dsôn's history. *I shall emerge vindicated and victorious and then Timanris will come back to me.*

Tark Draan (Girdlegard), to the south of the Gray Mountains, enchanted land of Hiannorum, 4371st division of unendingness (5199th solar cycle), winter.

". . . and that is why I am leaving it up to you, Grok-Tmai the Worrier, to decide whether to surrender voluntarily with all your famuli, or whether you would prefer to be subjugated by force. Expect no mercy, if you push me to . . ." Hianna the Flawless broke off and paused, the quill pen hovering in midair over the paper. Unnoticed, ink drops ran slowly down the nib to splash onto the page.

"Curses!"

Obediently, the quill pen wrote the word "curses."

Infuriated, Hianna crossed the room in two long strides and grabbed hold of the pen, canceling the dictation spell. This new technique of air writing, as she had termed it, was still in its infancy.

"I'll have to work on that one," she mumbled to herself, dipping the writing implement back in the little pot of black liquid. She tore the spoiled page in two and took a fresh sheet of paper out of a drawer, sitting down to write it all anew by hand. She formed the individual words with grace and care. As with everything she did, the calligraphy was aesthetically pleasing. It did not match the threatening content.

Her message would be sent to and understood by every maga and magus in Girdlegard. They would know what to expect.

Her trip to the Gray Mountains had given her wings. That massive assembly of monsters was unparalleled and the military efficacy of the combination of human warriors, beasts and älfar had already been proven. Winter would hold them back for now, but in spring Girdlegard would experience a second storm.

Hianna composed her missives in one of the topmost rooms of the tallest tower, a place she also enjoyed working in when she was thinking up new spells. Woven tapestries in glorious hues hung on the walls, depicting landscapes and towers, the Valley of Grace and various other motifs that gave an overall impression of harmony. The room was bright and welcoming and she always found it stimulating, even when her task was less pleasant.

Morana had accompanied her to the Gray Mountains and had introduced her to the älf Caphalor and the commander Imàndaris. There had been long talks between them all, but the maga had realized that these two high-ranking älfar did not particularly trust her. *As soon as the enchanted lands have agreed to my demands, I'll see what I can get out of these black-eyes.* She blew gently on the wet ink and strewed a little sand over the page. *They need me because they can't rely on the demon's power.*

Satisfied with her work, she folded the page, sealed up the edges and pressed her signet ring into wax. She called her best famuli and sent them out to deliver her message to the various enchanted lands.

Now I must wait. She rose from her desk and went over to the window to look down at the Valley of Grace, which was slowly disappearing under a veil of snow. It was extremely picturesque. The white powder dusted the statues and the trees wore bright crowns; the fountains had transformed themselves into delicate glittering ice sculptures.

Some of her young protégées were having a snowball fight, their tinkling laughter rising up to her window.

Hianna rested her forehead on the glass as she watched the young women at play. *My sweet ones, so innocent . . . But you must be ready for what is to come. It will come as a shock to you when everything changes so radically. Your carefree times will soon be over.*

Soon the intense red sun sank behind the hills at the end of the valley. Darkness was falling more swiftly than usual. The room lost its welcoming appeal.

Hianna shivered, but she still pushed the window open to call down to the girls in the garden. "Come inside, my dears! It is cold and dark and your tea is waiting. Read through the notes about the spells I showed you and then off to bed with you all!"

"Yes, mistress!" they chorused, hurrying in from the snow.

The cold wind spread through Hianna's chamber, stealing the warmth from the walls and the color from the tapestries.

She closed the window sharply and reached for the fringed stole she had placed on the back of her chair. Her light dress was not enough in this cool air. But the shawl was not there. Hianna looked around. *I'm sure I hung it on the chair? I must be getting old. Oh well, as long as I can still remember all the spells . . .*

"I did not trust you, right from the start," said the darkness.

An älf! Hianna smiled. "Are you trying to frighten me? That might work with small children, but it doesn't scare me. I'm used to dealing with demons and worse. I know you älfar and I know what you are capable of."

"You're wrong. I'm not *trying* to scare you at all."

The tone of voice was, at once, amiable and lethal and Hianna shuddered. Fear crept into her heart and it began to race. She broke out in a sweat. Perspiration ran down her back and gathered in beads on her brow. She slumped, moaning, half onto the chair, half onto the small table she had been writing at.

Where is he? Thoroughly weakened, she spoke an incantation that filled the room with dazzling radiance.

An älf she had never seen before was standing next to the cupboard. His riveted armor absorbed the shimmering light.

As soon as she could see where to aim, she launched a fire-lance.

The force surged out of her hand and nearly reached the älf, but he managed to spring nimbly back out of the way. The flames struck the curtains, setting them alight.

At long last the terrifying fear released its icy hold on her heart and her mind. Hianna instantly created an iridescent protective sphere around herself. "What do you think you are doing?" she said. "We are supposed to be allies!"

"You are better at this than that idiot Jujulo. All he could do was pull faces." The bright light floating in the middle of the room started to flicker and fail. He was attacking it with his own power. "He tried to knock me out with a puff of wind." The älf laughed. "At least you will give me some challenge!"

The älf disappeared again as the light died. "Why do you want to kill me?" Hianna fed the light with the magic energy she was able to call upon everywhere in her enchanted land, but it remained weak. *I wonder if he, too, is able to draw on the magic power I use.* "Your people need my art. Who else could control the demon while Sinthoras remains behind in your homeland?"

"The nostàroi commanded me to kill all the magi in Tark Draan before the offensive is launched, so that they cannot harm us," he said, his voice mild as warm rain, as if he were her best friend and he was telling her a story. "Jujulo was the first, and then there was an enchantress near the Gray Mountains who was eliminated, too, I understand. I'm sure she'll make a splendid example of subjugated art. And you, Hianna, are already halfway to the other world: your death has borne my name ever since Morana saved you from my sword."

Hianna looked around and saw him standing by her desk; he had her original rejected missive to Grok-Tmai in his hand.

"You are able to deceive an älf like her. She is nothing more than a simple bodyguard who was keen to gain esteem by winning you over as an ally." He tapped his own armor. "I am a virtuoso killer and I celebrate death by inventing new methods and sophisticated weapons forged by my own hand. They allow me to break the will of my most powerful enemies, and to gain access to the truth." He dropped the torn paper. "I saw through you straightaway. You don't tell lies very often. Or rather, you don't tell many good ones."

"That's where you are wrong!"

"Is that so?" His lips twitched. "But what if I have proof of your duplicity?" He placed one foot on the discarded scraps of the letter. "After I had killed that ridiculous figure Jujulo and his useless crowd of followers, I took the trouble to explore his home a little. Did you know that Jujulo wasn't able to remember the code you have been using for your correspondence? I found his notes. Why you had to make it so complicated I really don't know." He smiled when he saw her shocked expression. "Ah! I see you have caught my drift?"

Hianna sent out a second fire-lance. He dodged it elegantly again.

The magical shield that she was using to protect herself gave a shrill sound of protest. She had not noticed the älf's attempt to stab her with his sword, but his attack had been foiled.

"You know nothing about demons and you never intended to join our campaign," he said, stepping back. At that same moment her magic light went out. The stars in the night sky provided the only illumination in the tower room. Her uncanny visitor melted into the shadows. "I can read what you have written in these letters, Hianna. Your message said that you wanted to win our confidence and that you had received news from the Gray Mountains. Famenia, famula and successor to Jujulo, got to you before Morana did. She told you about us. You were only pretending to want to be on our side."

Hianna swallowed a curse: curses and perfection did not go well together. *Jujulo, you hopeless incompetent! Why on earth did you not hide the code key?* She increased the light again, but the älf had disappeared. She saw that the tower door was slightly open. *Where has he gone?*

"Your death bears the name Virssagòn," came his words from outside the room. "I'll leave you till last, Hianna. First I'm going to see to your sweet little famuli. Their deaths, too, bear my name. I'm going to make you live with that knowledge for a while and that will be far worse for you."

I won't let you! She ran after him, thrusting the door open and hurling a ball of flames along the corridor. In the orange light she saw his silhouette as he escaped out of the window. The ball of fire dissolved on contact with the stone wall, leaving a scorch mark. *The next one will get you!*

Hianna darted off—and was brought to a halt by stabbing pains in first one and then the other foot. Sharp metal objects had pierced the thin leather soles of her shoes.

She looked down. The älf had strewn metal barbs over the stone floor and with every step she tried to take she drove more of them into her feet.

The . . . She groaned and sat down in a window alcove, calling out for her maids. She wanted to send them to warn her female students about the älf while she used her healing powers to enable her to walk again.

Nobody came in answer to her call, so she opened the window and cried out in warning to the other towers. "Watch out, everyone, there is an enemy here in the valley! Stay exactly where you are until I tell you it is safe. Lock your doors and remember the spells I have taught you all!" Hianna turned to extract the wire barbs from the flesh of her feet, but suddenly she realized she could no longer move her legs.

The paralysis spread with lightning speed, affecting her entire body

She fell forward, helpless. Her face landed in the midst of more sharp metal. The sharp edges cut through her thin clothing and barbs pierced the unprotected flesh of her face, puncturing nose and cheeks.

Hianna tried to scream, but could only produce a pitiful whimper. Without the ability to speak or move, she could not weave any magic to help. *Virssagòn set a trap for me. He knew perfectly well that I would chase after him.*

The maids did not come.

The triangular metal barbs were swept to one side with a clinking sound and a pair of black boots came into her field of vision.

"You thought you were so clever, didn't you? You thought you could trick us," Virssagòn said, like a parent gently disciplining a child. "But now the great maga has run into trouble of her own making." He knelt at her side and gently turned her in order to study her face. "I have never seen a victim's face lacerated like this. Mostly, they will just tread on the barbs, not lie face down in them," he said maliciously. "I shall wait here with you for your death, Hianna the Flawless—the death that already bears my name."

Someone shouted from the corridor. "Get away from our mistress!"

No! Did they not hear my warning? Hianna could only whine in distress, although her whole being was urging her to leap to her feet to defend her students. She was plunged into despair at the thought that she would not be able to help them at all.

Swift steps approached her and the älf.

"If you listen very carefully," he whispered, drawing his sword slowly, "you can work out what it is I'm doing to your girls. Mind you don't die till I've finished!" He jumped to his feet and leaped over her.

No! Ye gods, no! Protect them! Protect my dear ones! Hianna wished that she were unconscious. That would have been preferable to lying there, helpless, on the cold floor and having to witness the death of her protégées.

This wish was not granted.

Instead she found herself forced to listen to the death-throes and dying screams of her young pupils. She had to hear the sound made by a blade as it tore through fabric, skin, flesh and bone.

Tark Draan (Girdlegard), many miles to the
south of the Gray Mountains,
4371ˢᵗ division of unendingness (5199ᵗʰ solar cycle),
early winter.

"I should like to offer thanks to fate for bringing you to us," said Famenia. "You could kill 5,000 älfar in battle. I couldn't."

"Killing the älfar in the cavern would be initial compensation for the
destruction of the Golden Plain." Narósil was outwardly calm, but his
eyes betrayed how fervently he wished to see his enemies dead.

Famenia nodded.

It had been quite a day. She had waited patiently with the elf for sun-
up so that she would be able to look him in the eyes and determine what
kind of creature he was. She was inordinately relieved to note that the
whites of his eyes did not turn black in the revealing light of the sun.
The same held for the rest of his unit. Upon ascertaining this, she had
fetched little Ossandra down from her perch.

And now they were all gathered in the leader's sparsely furnished
tent. Narósil had told her he was an elf noble, related to the princess
and that his unit was the monarch's guard of honor.

The elves had not taken it amiss when Famenia insisted on waiting until dawn before speaking to them. They told her what had happened in the Golden Plain and how the älfar had destroyed Princess
Veïnsa's army. Tears rose in Famenia's eyes: this did not merely signify
the demise of a noble and admirable race—it showed that evil had
taken hold.

Narósil and his warriors had broken free of the ring of death in order to
mobilize the elves in other lands and beg for their support in trying
to fight back. But wherever they went, they came across älfar troops or
their allies. They had been forced to go south to avoid them. The noose
around Lesinteïl and Âlandur was being pulled ever tighter. Famenia
gathered that they had a long-established antipathy toward the elf land
of Gwandalur. They did not want to go in that direction. Narósil had
thus decided to join with the army of humans in Hiannorum and to
march against the enemy in the spring.

But beforehand we must liberate Milltown, or those men and women will be the next victims. Famenia had told the elves about Horgàta and her army. "We need a really clever plan to bring down the älfar without endangering the lives of the vulnerable." She looked at the elf leader. "There is only limited space in the caves. There would not be enough room for your cavalry," she said on a note of caution.

Narósil rapped himself on the breastplate. "We are just as capable as the älfar of moving in complete silence and we can fight on foot if necessary. Can you give me any more specific details?" He took out some paper and drew a map according to what Ossandra could tell him about Milltown, its immediate surroundings and its cave system. Famenia added anything she could, but Ossandra supplied the most useful information: there were two further cave entrances, invisible from the outside, one of them on the very top of the hill.

"I don't suppose the townspeople will have told the älfar about it," Narósil said pensively. "I suggest I send in a hundred of my people with firebrands to create an acrid smoke screen. The älfar will be forced to seek the open air if they don't want to suffocate." He indicated the free area around the town. "What is the terrain like here? Is it soft going, or will we be able to let the horses run fast over this part?"

Ossandra shrugged. "The meadows are normally quite wet."

"So the ground will be difficult. Not ideal for cavalry." Narósil studied his map.

"Can't we lure them away?" suggested Famenia after some thought.

"I don't think so. The älfar are anything but stupid, as we've all learned to our cost. I'd be surprised if they failed to suspect an ambush." Narósil's slim gem-adorned finger tapped the paper plan, indicating the meadows. "We'll have to proceed through here. We won't be able to make our normal swift progress, but we should still have enough impetus to do away with half of their troops. Our latest battle showed that they don't have much in the way of defense against heavy cavalry." He looked worried; he was not completely convinced by his strategy.

"What about the älfar already in Milltown itself?" Famenia put her arm around Ossandra's shoulders. The young girl was obviously very concerned about her friends and family.

As Narósil placed his hands together, the jewels in his rings sparkled. "A hundred of my people will go into the cavern to look after the children, the sick and the elderly. A further 200 will go into Milltown and engage the enemy there. After that we'll have our archers up on the city walls shooting as the älfar come streaming out of the caves. That should be enough to confuse them until our cavalry can attack. We should cause a good few casualties among the enemy."

Famenia approved of the plan, even though she was no tactician herself. "The city will be eternally grateful to you."

"That won't be necessary." Narósil stroked Ossandra's head, a smile on his comely features. "We may be of different races, but we are united in our war against evil. It is a matter of honor for us to help others. And it is what the goddess wishes us to do." He looked at Famenia. "I have explained what I and my warriors can do. What about yourself?"

"Me?"

"You are a maga, aren't you? I recall you threatened to annihilate us with a fireball. So I'm assuming you'll have some spells at your disposal. That should give us a major advantage over the älfar." His blue gaze rested on her. "Or is there a problem?"

How can I tell him without making myself look a fool? "You must forgive me, but . . . I was lying to scare you. I thought I could get you to leave me alone. My master Jújulo, who taught me everything I know, was always more for entertaining rather than warfare."

"Meaning?"

"Meaning that, no, I can't hurl flames and no, I can't magic flesh off bones. The spells I have are mostly to make people laugh, but I'm quite good at healing." She stared at the floor, feeling totally useless. She was a good messenger, of course, but her magic skills, compared with those of a Hianna the Flawless or Grok-Tmai, were childish in the extreme.

Narósil laughed. "I was quite impressed, though, back there in the forest. That wind you conjured up made things quite awkward for us. That kind of thing should be more than adequate to create a bit of mayhem among our adversaries." He placed his slender hand on her sleeve. "Famenia, please, we do need your help. They outnumber us five to one."

I'd hate to be held responsible if we fail.

"I'm sure we can bring their numbers down to 2,000 before they realize what's happening. But then things will be tough for us. If we were fighting orcs or humans"—he said, looking apologetic—"those odds would not be a problem, but the älfar are dangerous foes."

In the face of the urgent pleas from Narósil, she racked her brain to think how she might contribute, but she was struggling to meet this challenge.

She knew she could not escape her destiny; she was preordained to play a leading role in the fortunes of Girdlegard.

For your sake, Jujulo, I'll do whatever I can to set Milltown free. "I'm in, Narósil." She held out her hand.

The elf took the proffered hand and shook it firmly.

CHAPTER XVIII

And thus I sat with Caphalor, now deprived of his office.

And I asked: Tell me, how is it with you?

And he answered: Never better!

And, surprised, I spoke: How is this possible? Did you not lose everything: honor, fame, office and authority? How is it that you can be of such good cheer?

And Caphalor smiled and responded; I just am. My soul was touched in a place I had thought lost. I lived for this once and it was torn from my grasp.

On suffering that loss I wanted to leave unendingness.

But now that I am truly alive, awoken from the stubborn rigidity of heart, I shall fight with renewed vigor.

For my own sake.

For the sake of unendingness.

For her sake.

Excerpt from the epic poem *The Heroes of Tark Draan*
composed by Carmondai, master of word and image

Ishím Voróo (Outer Lands) Dsôn Faïmon, Dsôn,
4371ˢᵗ/4372ⁿᵈ divisions of unendingness (5199ᵗʰ /5200th solar cycles),
winter.

"We have heard your report. Do you still insist you were not in Dsôn on the night Robonor was killed by the falling masonry?" Polòtain was sitting directly in front, staring him in the face, fury and hatred in his eyes.

Sinthoras faced him down. He had dressed carefully in ceremonial armor to make the best possible impression in court, to remind everyone of his previous high position and recall his glorious past, which was surely to become his glorious present once more. *May the phaiu su enjoy consuming you, Polòtain!* "I already told the court that I spent the night in my studio with Timanris. Do you need to know all of the detail, old älf?"

This was met with quiet laughter.

The hearing was being held in the western part of Dsôn, in the foyer of the temple of Samusin. In this way, the god would keep his eye on proceedings and ensure a fair and fitting ruling.

As well as the god, around forty representatives of the Comets and Constellations were present, acting as the jury and making decisions on behalf of the Inextinguishables, who preferred not to deal with the minutiae on difficult cases—such as those concerning high-ranking officials.

The jury belonged to the Dsôn elite—their extravagant formal attire emphasized their importance. Polòtain was the sole exception, having chosen a simple white garment that stood out in stark contrast to the black that Sinthoras wore.

Comets and Constellations faced each other in rows four paces apart. A paper-strewn table and two chairs, where Polòtain and Sinthoras were sitting, stood between these opposing benches. The priests were in the temple itself. Otherwise, no one else was allowed in and the guards on the doors guaranteed the hearing would not be disturbed.

Sinthoras had planned to make as many personal attacks on Polòtain as possible in order to irritate and unsettle him, but he knew he was not at his best after the all-night ride and he was finding it difficult to keep his thoughts in order. "Say what you like—I am not responsible for the death of your favorite nephew. Perhaps we need to accept that a loose stone was nothing more than that: a loose stone." He pressed down on the armrests of his chair as if about to stand. "The committee will be wanting to send me back to Tark Draan where my task is of greater importance." *Audacity may yet save the day.*

"Of course the committee will send you away, it is only a matter of deciding where to send you to: Phondrasôn, perhaps? Exile would be a suitable punishment." Polòtain pointed at him accusingly. "Keep your seat, disgraced nostàroi! You owe this chamber due respect! Gathered here are the noblest of our race and you are acting as if they had merely come to judge you innocent." He turned his head and let his gaze sweep over the company. "But we are meeting on a more urgent matter: we need the truth!"

"The truth people tell each other is only one version of events. Interrogate ten witnesses and you will hear ten different versions. This does not change the fact that on the night in question I did not leave my home." Sinthoras sat down. "But you are right: I should not have tried to rush the committee in their findings." He took a deep breath. There was an overwhelming fragrance of incense in the hall. Light from the high windows illuminated statues portraying Samusin in his role as protector of justice. These symbolic representations showed the god either as a strong wind disturbing foliage and sending up high waves, or as a set of scales. Fairness: equality before the law. Sinthoras found the environment reassuring. *It will all end well.*

His accuser lowered his outstretched arm and then picked up and held out a rolled parchment. "I have here a witness deposition made under oath stating that Sinthoras commanded the guard Falòran—the man walking behind Robonor—to hold his shield in such a way that Robonor's leg would be cut, preventing him from stepping out of the path of the falling masonry."

If I had known about that witness I would have dealt with him. "There can be no such witness because I had nothing to do with the whole thing! This must be a lie!"

Polòtain savored his triumph. "He could not bear his guilt any longer, so he confessed his part in it to me. He told me he had been acting on your orders."

"It's a lie!" Sinthoras repeated. He had wanted to say something different, but his mind was numbed and dull with tiredness and he had been taken by surprise. *You can't let them get away with this! Pull yourself together. Contest this claim.* "No such orders were ever given."

"No *such*? Perhaps you gave other orders?" snarled Polòtain.

"No!" *O god of justice!* He was hoping wildly that a statue might speak out in his defense, but the Samusins were silent.

Polòtain unrolled the paper. "I, Falòran, confess that I was paid by Sinthoras to remain close to Robonor at all times to enable a certain incident to become a fatal accident." Having read out the confession he raised his eyes and addressed the members of the chamber committee. "I can have Falòran appear before you. He will give his statement under oath once more."

He must have blackmailed the guard. Or he'll have bribed him. Sinthoras shook his head. "This is utter nonsense—and badly conceived nonsense, at that—all thought up by a very old älf whose mind has been eaten up by grief," he said scornfully. It was time for the counterattack. "I can produce witnesses for my part that show that Polòtain is responsible for introducing the sickness that has befallen the capital. It is easy to buy tongues willing to bear false witness." *I'm finding it really hard to organize my thoughts.*

The members of the committee whispered to each other and then insults started flying between the benches occupied by the opposing factions.

Sinthoras presumed things were going in his favor. "Dismiss the case—not proven!," "Unsubstantiated accusations!" and "The witness was paid!" were among the phrases being mumbled.

"Before you acquit him," Polòtain called out into the hubbub, "I want you to listen to a further deed that he committed. This is why he has been summoned back to Dsôn. This time he won't be able to deny the truth." He whirled around to face Sinthoras and pointed at him accusingly. "He murdered Itáni!"

All fell quiet. It was as if Samusin himself had called for silence. All eyes were on accuser and accused.

Sinthoras laughed. "Old fool! So I have the gift of being in two places at the same time? In Tark Draan and here in Dsôn?" Even he noted that his laughter sounded false and shrill. "I was with the troops fighting the elves. I had no time at all to think about some would-be artist you had commissioned to produce scandalous nonsense and erect it opposite my house!"

The room was still. The committee waited with bated breath.

"I call these älfar as witnesses." Polòtain called out several names in quick succession.

As the doors opened up, a group of soldiers marched in. They looked uneasy and avoided Sinthoras's eyes.

To Tion with him! That is the crew from the island fortress. The ones I sent the wine to. All at once he felt sick.

Polòtain pulled a box out from under the table, opened the lid and took out a decorated cudgel with hair and dried blood on the points. "Please tell the chamber," he said, addressing the soldiers quietly, "who it was you saw crossing the bridge into Dsôn and then on a second occasion going out again. Don't forget to mention the gifts he sent and the promise he extracted from you in order to hide his misdeeds."

Sinthoras sat as if thunderstruck. *I . . . thought . . .* He was suddenly furious with the island unit. *Traitors!* Lines of anger shot across his face although he attempted to smile. It was clear he was presenting a ridiculous picture.

While the soldiers were giving their evidence, the black lines on his face were obvious to all in the room. There was more whispered discussion and this time the drift of the comments went against Sinthoras.

The fortress soldiers finally trooped out of the hall.

Polòtain got to his feet and took up a stance in front of the committee, holding the cudgel in such a way that everyone could see. "This is the weapon used to destroy Itáni's sculpture and which was then used to *murder* the artist herself. There can be no doubt about this: the implement was thrown into the courtyard of my home and an openly threatening message had been scratched into the wood of the gate." He slammed the club into the wooden uprights and there it remained, bathed in a stream of light. "At first I thought Sinthoras had sent some of his retinue to carry out the deed, but it appears that he was arrogant enough to commit the murder with his own hands! What greater hubris could there be? Who does he think he is, to kill an artist for having created a sculpture that was not to his liking?"

Sinthoras stared at the weapon. *What a fool I am.* "Lots of people have clubs like that. War booty from Tark Draan," he said slowly. "You can be sure I would never use something as clumsy as that."

"That's what makes it the *perfect* weapon." Polòtain placed his fingers around the handle. "No one would ever assume a high-ranking älf would dirty his hands with it." His smile could not have been bettered for the malice it showed. "When I learned that the nostàroi had indeed been in Dsôn on the night in question, I thought it probable that he had visited his mistress—and I was proven correct!"

The committee members followed his account eagerly. Nobody spoke. The faces of the Comets grew dark as they listened to the evidence and the witness statements.

"I went to see Timansor and interrogated him. At first he denied that the nostàroi had been there, probably for the sake of his daughter's reputation. But he finally admitted it. This cudgel," he said, standing aside so that all eyes were on the implement, "was taken from Timansor's own collection of weaponry."

Cries of "Shame!" started to be heard. They came from his own faction, the Comets, in whose eyes he had once been the great hope. Their dazzling star was losing all its splendor.

Say something, he kept telling himself, aware of the jagged lines of anger on his face. He felt as if an enemy army outnumbered him and he was cornered in a narrow gorge with no way of escape. *He has got me now!*

He saw the steely expressions on the älfar faces. No one was kindly disposed toward him now. They might perhaps have doubted the testimony of simple warriors from the island fortress, but they would not call into question the evidence of a respected artist such as Timansor. And then, of course, Timanris had deserted his cause. There could be no more telling indictment.

More shouts of "Shame!" were heard.

Sinthoras made a mental note of those älfar who were shouting the loudest. Again it was his faction, the Comets. *We appear in the heavens in the blink of an eye and fall just as swiftly.* He exhaled slowly, his head down on his breast. He had given up. *It is impossible to catch a falling star without burning your hands, but don't you dare convict me!* He sought out Demenion, Khlotòn and Rashànras, in whose homes he had been made welcome and who had acclaimed him as a protector of their race. *The celebrations you laid on in my honor, the speeches you made, your fine words of support—don't forget them now! Don't forget your vows of loyalty, or—*

"There is only one conclusion to be drawn: Sinthoras was in Dsôn that night. We have evidence that he visited Timanris. He then removed the cudgel from her father's weapon collection, destroyed the statue of Robonor and committed the heinous, unthinkable crime of killing Itáni before leaving a warning on my gates and tossing the murder weapon into the courtyard!" Polòtain perched on the table. "Let the committee now determine their verdict. Unless, of course," he said, addressing Sinthoras, "you have something to say in your defense? But you seem to have gone quiet. Does the truth make you too angry to speak?"

"My anger is directed against you, Polòtain, for attacking my honor in this way. You have been lying," said Sinthoras, but his words sounded hollow and unconvincing.

"So are you accusing Timansor, Timanris and the entire crew of the island fortress of lying under oath?" Polòtain shook with laughter. "You can see no way out. Who else do you want to blame for fabricating evidence? I assume you will be alleging the whole of Dsôn has been telling lies to bring you down!"

Hold your tongue! Sinthoras wanted to launch himself at Polòtain and strangle him as he stood. He saw Timanris's face and longed for her support but she had abandoned him. *They have forced her. Polòtain and her father made her denounce me. Otherwise she would have stood by me, I know.* He opened his mouth, but closed it again. *There is nothing I can say now. I underestimated the old fool, and I was so careless; I've given him all the ammunition he needed to destroy me.*

"The rest is silence." Polòtain bowed briefly to the court. "I await your decision and I rely on you to come to a proper decision. Justice will win out."

Demenion, the Comets' spokesman, and Ratáris, the spokeswoman for the Constellations, rose from their seats. It came as no surprise to Sinthoras that the word *guilty* was pronounced twice. What else was said or what reasons were given was all of no interest to him.

He could not bring himself to look at Polòtain. *Enjoy your victory. I shall find a way to get my revenge. I shall hurt you as badly as you have hurt me!* He directed his gaze and his unbounded hatred at Demenion, Khlotòn and Rashànras, who all lowered their eyes to avoid his. They knew they had betrayed him. *And I shall not forget your treachery today.*

"... it will be left to the Inextinguishables to formulate the sentence," said Ratáris.

Sinthoras started to pay attention. *Nagsor and Nagsar Inàste! They won't forget the service I have done them!*

Polòtain leaned forward over the table. "What?" he barked, acute disappointment and incredulity in his voice.

"'Sinthoras is a former nostàroi, a commander in the campaign against Tark Draan,'" Ratáris went on. She was reading from a letter. They say: "'He has achieved much for us, for Dsôn Faïmon and for his own people. His name is revered by young and old alike.'"

"That is indeed so," Sinthoras echoed the words to himself. Hope began to blossom. He might well be pardoned after all, not sent into exile to Phondrasôn, the appalling underground realm of cruelty and horrors beyond anything known in Ishím Voróo.

"'Due to this, the deeds of which he has been found guilty are multiplied a hundredfold.'" The spokeswoman's voice faltered; she was having difficulty reading. "'For this reason, we hereby exile Sinthoras from Dsôn Faïmon. Though he is not to be sent to Phondrasôn, he is under our orders to march west and to keep going until it is not possible to go any farther. He should not return before forty divisions of unendingness have passed, or before he has slain 10,000 of our enemies in our name.'"

Sinthoras gave an empty laugh of utter hopelessness. *Forty divisions! The war will be forty times over by then!*

Ratáris made a sign and the doors opened up to admit the Inextinguishables' guards, who surrounded Sinthoras.

"'He is to leave immediately, with no opportunity to make any arrangements,'" announced Ratáris. "'He may take armor, weapons and a nightmare. That is all. This is our will.'" She lowered the paper and nodded.

Two guards pulled him to his feet and the unit marched out, leading him off.

Thrown out of my own homeland. Banned. Exiled to Ishím Voróo. The words echoed around and around his head. He was seeing stars. He started to shiver with shock. *Forty divisions of unendingness. Forty . . .*

"That is your deserved reward!" Polòtain yelled after him. "Worse than endingness: solitude!"

Sinthoras did not look at anyone. He did not want to see his enemies' triumphant grins, or the guilt on the faces of his one-time colleagues and supporters.

"Loneliness and more loneliness!" Polòtain thundered, beside himself with hatred and delight. "None to admire you! You will be totally forgotten! Go and die in Ishím Voróo. Do you hear? Go off and die!"

You will all regret what you have done. Unprotesting, Sinthoras let them take him to where his night-mare was waiting. This was not the time or place to rebel against the decision.

He rode to the radial arm Wèlèron. From there his route would take him past the dorón ashont, over the bridge and off to Ishím Voróo.

But for Sinthoras one thing was clear: he would return.

At some time in the future, some splinter of unendingness, he would face those that had betrayed him.

Tark Draan (Girdlegard), in the Gray Mountains,
4371st division of unendingness (5199th solar cycle),
late autumn.

The amorphous cloud of mist with its glittering sparks neared the cave floor, encircling Simin. <You are quite different from the humans who came to Tark Draan with the älfar.>

The magus was hearing the demon's voice inside his own head. *Just so long as the demon can't read my thoughts . . .* "You are the . . . the creature people are talking about!"

<Oh, do these people sound awestruck or full of fear when they talk about me?> There was a laugh that would have suited some rogue trying to convince a group of little children that he was harmless. <Who is it that is speaking of me?>

I'll try a bit of flattery. "A good friend. She told me you have the ability to overcome death itself. That's why I've come here to meet you." Simin was being very cautious. He was watchful, not only because of the demon, but also on account of any orcs that might be in the vicinity. They could turn up at any moment to see how their prisoner was faring. Then they would find the dead keeper in the corridor . . . Or the demon would bring the dead keeper to life . . .

<No, I can't overcome death, but since Sinthoras was kind enough to make me what I am now, I have had the power to reanimate the dead: their soul remains dead, but they move as if living. I also have the power to transform the land around me, whereas previously I only rendered it ashes.> The cloud had reached the floor and was hovering between the orc and the magus, making it difficult to see the greenskin. It was as if it were caught in a bubble. <You say you came here for my sake? From where?>

"From the place you call Tark Draan. Girdlegard is my homeland."

<I see: you are from my future realm!> The mist glowed in greedy anticipation. <Then regard this as an initial audience. What are your wishes, my subject?>

"They are conquering Tark Draan to give to you?" Simin indicated the orc. "I thought evil was randomly attacking my land, devoid of any plan."

<Not at all, my good . . . what is your name?>

"Suchandsuch," the magus answered, his instincts warning him to be wary of giving his true name.

<Right, my good Suchandsuch. The älfar and their vermin allies are subjugating Tark Draan for me. That is my reward for getting them

access in the first place. The älfar want to destroy the elves, and the other monsters are desperate for more land to rule over, but at the end of the day they'll all be paying me tribute. As will you.>

"And Hianna the Flawless? What agreement have you come to with her?"

Who?

"The maga—the one who does magic stuff. She was with the älfar in the Gray Mountains. I thought she had met up with you."

<Nope. One who does magic stuff, eh? How interesting. I must find out why nobody introduced her to me.>

Simin paid careful attention. Apparently the älfar were not letting the demon in on everything. Perhaps it would be possible to drive a wedge between the different elements? "They will doubtless get around to it. But say, can't the two of us do some kind of a deal?" He kept an ear open for any approaching orcs, but heard nothing.

<What do you mean?>

"The älfar have won Hianna over as a friend. How about the two of us becoming friends as well?"

The mist giggled. <I don't need any friends like you. The land already belongs to me, for the most part.>

"Maybe the land itself is yours, but not the humans who live there: they may obey you out of fear, but they won't belong to you."

<As soon as they die, they will. That's perfectly sufficient.>

Simin watched the shimmering cloud and felt the uncanny atmosphere that oozed from it. "What do you mean by that?"

<Take a look at this órco. Its own people slayed it so that I could show them what I am capable of. I kill any land I travel on and I transform it at the same time. Everything that lives is subject to change and all the dead shall rise again.> The demon gave another snort of laughter. <Maybe you'd like to try it, too?>

"So the orc is immortal now?"

<In one sense, yes.>

Simin needed certainty so that he could warn the humans of the danger they would be facing. "But presumably he'll decay eventually? Isn't that so?"

<If I move away and the land is no longer saturated with my incredible powers he'll grow weaker and then he'll die, but why should I leave?>

What he and Ortina had feared might actually happen. In his mind's eye Simin saw hordes of the undead overrunning Girdlegard. *I must stop the demon invading my homeland.* It was bad enough to know that the dead lands were spreading throughout the Gray Mountains already. *That is the right expression: dead land.* "If you stay, you'll soon have double the number of troops in your army."

<Yes.> The cloud drifted over, wider now. <Do you think I should show myself to the humans in Tark Draan? I was going to wait until Sinthoras had won the last of the kingdoms for me, but it would be nice for my soldiers to get a glimpse of me.>

"I'm sure that would motivate them to greater things!" *Curses! I hadn't wanted to suggest that.* Simin was intent on finding out exactly what sort of being they were up against. Unnoticed, he formulated and released a spell to discover the demon's true nature, while keeping up a steady patter to distract the mist's attention.

For an instant his identifying spell turned the cloud an intense black with a scant admixture of red and yellow. This told Simin that the demon was pure evil, but that he had once been neutral enough. He remembered that the demon had said Sinthoras was the one to effect this change. This must mean that the mist-demon could be influenced from outside. *By magic perhaps?*

Simin made sure that his thoughts and his words were completely separate; he kept up a stream of superficial platitudes while his mind worked feverishly.

With his newfound knowledge he could design a banning and barrier spell, but this would take more time than he had at his disposal.

I must keep him occupied so that he stays here for a bit. Simin looked around for inspiration.

<You have talked a lot, Suchandsuch.> The mist-demon floated over to the orc. <Did you think you might get to be my friend if you heaped praise on me? That would be making life far too simple. You'll have to come up with something a bit more special if our friendship is to be worth anything to me.>

Simin thought fast. "I should be honored if you would allow me to demonstrate my artistry, for I, as well as Hianna, am a magus, and might be of use to you."

<Perhaps I can use your services after all. Perhaps you'd like to be my very own magus?>

Simin knew his energy was at a low ebb and that he would not be able to produce many spells, but he could use it wisely and it might be sufficient. "Will you spare my land if I work for you?"

<Spare it? No. But I'll settle minimal payments for you to meet,> the demon countered mischievously as he enveloped the orc in his cloud. The orc snapped, trying to defend itself. Every time it bit at the glittering sparks they only glowed more strongly, but that was all that happened. <What do you say?>

"That seems fair enough. Let's seal our contract with a friendship ritual." Simin raised his arms and started to pronounce the magic wording. With intense concentration he invested the spell with the last of his strength and hurled it toward the demon.

A bright blue ribbon of light surrounded the mist-demon and orc, tying itself tightly and binding the demon to the orc. The cloud was absorbed into the creature.

Orc and demon shrieked at the same time and Simin blocked his ears. The brute pulled wildly at its chains; one of the stalagmites cracked and broke, but the remaining three were still sound.

That's not quite what I had planned. I wanted to tie him to the orc, not force him inside it. Simin could only think that since its transformation, the undead beast had probably carried some of the demon's power and that was why the absorption had occurred. *Now I seem to have created a demonically possessed orc.* Simin really could not care less. The result was what counted.

But he did not try to deceive himself. *This new prison probably won't hold him for long. He'll find a way to free himself, or he'll manage to take control of the orc and will break out somehow.*

Before that happened, Simin wanted to plan his next major piece of magic to halt the demon's progress into Girdlegard. *If we all pull together . . .* Simin remembered that there were not many magicians left who would be able to work with him. Ortina and Jujulo were both dead and Hianna had changed sides.

First he would go to the Valley of Grace to do away with the traitor maga. She was a danger, because her powers were great and she might turn entirely to the side of evil. He would need to gather his remaining friends and colleagues and take them to Hiannorum. Hianna must be killed as soon as possible, before news got around that another magi had been in the Gray Mountains.

If the gods are on my side and all goes well, I'll still have Grok-Tmai the Worrier and Fensa the Inventive on my side. And then there's Famenia, of course, but she doesn't have a magic name yet. Simin glanced over at the orc, which was hurtling around like a crazy thing, fighting against its iron collar, and foaming at the mouth. He knew the demon was trying to get free. *I'll have to be quick! The spell I wove was not a strong one. He might break out of his prison tomorrow. Sitalia, come to my aid! Help me to be in time.*

He raced off through the tunnels that led south and to the outside.

He had run out of magic energy and that made things particularly challenging, but it was not for nothing had he been given the name Simin the Underrated.

Ishím Voróo (Outer Lands), Dsôn Faïmon, between the radial arms Wêlêron and Avaris, 4372ⁿᵈ division of unendingness (5200ᵗʰ solar cycle), winter.

Jiggon swung the sword forcefully against his target: a wooden stave jammed in the ground and covered with leaves. "Like this?" There were a dozen other structures surrounding them for the serfs to practice their weapons skills on. The noise as they worked was like a mixture of the sounds of threshing and wood chopping.

"No. You wouldn't even cut your enemy's skin like that." Ataronz—an óarco who had come to them from one of the vassal settlements—had taken it upon himself to help with training the new recruits. "Try it like this." He showed Jiggon how to put his whole shoulder behind the blow. "Don't just use a wrist action. And let the weight of the weapon work for you."

"Thanks. I'll give it a try." Jiggon raised the blade once more.

He had soon been promoted within the human Army of the Ownerless because of his eagerness and commitment to the work. He was in charge of a small unit of thirty, and one of the Towers that Walk accompanied them on every sortie. They destroyed serf settlements in Wèlèron and Avaris, liberating other slaves, and set fields alight, but as yet they had not dared attack any älfar cities. And it had not really been necessary: they were able to keep the älfar occupied with these irritating needle-prick assaults so that the acronta—the name the humans gave the Towers that Walk—could prepare their invasion on Dsôn.

Jiggon dealt a fierce blow to the dummy and his blade cut through the straw surround to sink into the wood. Ataronz gave a grunt of approval. "That's the way!" he said before stomping off to supervise the next recruit.

Strike, jump, strike, duck, strike . . . Jiggon's day was filled with the monotonous rhythm of training movements.

By the time evening fell and he finished his practice, his shoulders were protesting loudly. He arrived back at the tent he shared with twenty others—mostly the same age as himself—exhausted but pleased with his progress. He stretched out on his hard mattress. The tent was nearly empty. The men were all off with their women, or were still training.

The inside of the canvas tent did not smell too good, but that did not matter. There would be time enough later to see about clean clothes and washing every day and shaving whenever you wanted to. This was war. A bit of stink was all part and parcel of it.

I shall kill a few älfar, he thought, as his stomach rumbled. There would be food soon—even if they were surrounded by bad smells, dirt and garbage, the food still tasted twenty times better than what he had been used to. They were getting proper nourishment, taken from the älfar overseer's house. And he was eating it as a free man!

Next to him Khalomein sat on a low stool, sharpening his sword. "What do you hope for?" he asked dreamily.

"What do you mean?"

"What are you hoping to get out of what we are doing?"

"I want freedom for all slaves and vassal nations. And the end of the älfar," replied Jiggon, surprised at the question. "Isn't it obvious? What else are we fighting for?" He sat up to look his comrade in the face. He knew that Khalomein had two children. His wife lived in the camp next door.

"I'm not sure we have been too clever in our choice of allies. I think the acronta are just using us." He kept passing the whetstone in regular strokes along the edge of the blade.

"But they gave us freedom!"

"Because they needed us to fight with them against the black-eyes. So they're using us." Khalomein tested the blade with his thumb and inspected it closely. "They don't care what happens to us after the uprising. Perhaps they'll kill us if they think we're in the way."

"No, they won't." Jiggon took a seat opposite him. *What makes him think that, I wonder?* "They'll leave us the älfar empire. Well, that's what I've been told."

Khalomein laughed dismissively. "Of course: you understand them."

"I don't understand their language. They drew us a picture. The acronta that liberated our village drew the defense canal and the radial arms and then he scrubbed out Dsôn itself. Then he pointed to the rest and pointed to me and the others who were standing near me." Jiggon could hardly believe that Khalomein's opinion of the acronta was so low. *He doesn't get to see his family often enough. It'll be that.* "They are practically gods! Look at them! No other race could have done what they have done. They are the only ones to challenge the älfar and we're helping them. But we're doing it for ourselves, not for them."

"So you can promise me, on your honor, promise me that we won't be serving the acronta as slaves when this is over?" Khalomein pointed the tip of his sword at Jiggon. An obvious threat. "I don't want to risk my own life and the lives of my family, only to be thrown into another set of chains."

"They're not like that." Jiggon firmly believed what he was saying. "And wouldn't we regret it forever if we didn't make the effort now?"

"I'll take you at your word." Khalomein lowered the weapon and resumed his sharpening. "It's difficult to trust someone if you don't understand their language. We haven't got any promises, any contracts, treaties, nothing to build on." Khalomein glanced at him. "I trust *you*, Jiggon. Don't disappoint me, will you?"

Jiggon found it strange that he had been given such an elevated status. He sank back on his camp bed and stared at the flapping tent wall.

The winter wind blew cold through their meager canvas shelter. Jiggon found himself thinking of the cramped corner he used to sleep in. *It was drier and warmer, but I was a slave: the property of an älf.*

He had not been able to be servile any longer and he knew he might one day have been done away with at the whim of Yintaï or Heïfaton. There was no reward for loyalty or for hard work in the fields.

Jiggon had previously met slaves who spoke well of their owners, but it became apparent that their masters' acts of cruelty and the frequent disappearances had been made light of; these serfs were not admitting, even to themselves, the dire truth of their situations. *The gods have not given bravery to all of us.*

The gong sounded for the evening meal.

Taking his simple wooden bowl and spoon, Jiggon left the tent. Khalomein did not follow; he continued to work on his sword. *I don't understand him. I won't be surprised if he goes off back to his master.*

A few steps brought him to the waiting line of hungry recruits. Sometimes there was the odd scuffle when the food was distributed, but people were trying their best to stay disciplined.

Jiggon was given his ration of cereal broth, some pieces of sausage and a ladleful of cooked vegetables. It smelled delicious.

Making his way to his favorite place, the lookout tower, he climbed a little way up the ladder and sat in the narrow gap between the rungs. He liked being able to look down on the whole camp while he was eating.

It's grown since yesterday! Jiggon shoveled his food in quickly. He reckoned, judging by the number of new tents, that the army must have around 7,000 men by now. In the camp next door, where the women, children and old people were housed, there would be, at a rough guess, a further 15,000. They were kept separate from the soldiers as a precaution in case of attack. So far the acronta catapults at the fortress had kept the älfar at bay.

The acronta had completely demolished the island fortress and moved the stones to a new site farther forward on Dsôn Faïmon territory. Using these materials, together with the timber they had felled in Ishím Voróo, they had managed to erect a circular barricade capable, Jiggon assumed, of withstanding conventional catapult fire. This protected reserve was where the Towers that Walk were encamped; they had installed their own catapults next to those they had confiscated from the enemy. If you fell foul of one of those missiles you would end up a messy, bloody mass.

They are nearly gods, these creatures. Jiggon chewed on a piece of sausage; he relished its juicy flavor.

He did trust them, of course, but he would have loved to know what the acronta were up to in their camp. He wondered what they looked like when they had taken their armor off, what kind of thing they liked to eat. But nobody was allowed to see in.

Occasionally you could hear the odd rumble behind those ramparts. It was a bit like an earthquake. Then there would be a screeching sort of sound. None of the humans could make head or tail of it.

Jiggon was convinced they were building new assault equipment in readiness for the onslaught on the Black Heart of Dsôn.

I want to see Dsôn with my own eyes. And then I want to raze it to the ground so absolutely that nothing is left of it. After that I shall really be free. We shall be free—every single one of us!

That very instant the warning bugle sounded from the lookout tower, calling the Army of the Ownerless to arms. The älfar were attacking: a new attempt to destroy the acronta and their allies.

Jiggon jumped down from the ladder and ran back to his tent. Khalomein was just leaving, newly sharpened sword in hand. *I'll kill the next älf I see!* Jiggon grabbed his own weapon, put on his armor, which was far too big for him, planted his helmet on his head and ran out into the open. He was looking for his own platoon, to get them to the assembly point.

CHAPTER XIX

The power no one withstands.

It was obvious to all beholders.
The past had practically eradicated it,
the present called it back to life,
and thus the future was lost for all time.

The power no one withstands.

The Epocrypha of the Creating Spirit
Book of the Coming Death
95–101

Tark Draan (Girdlegard) southeast of the Gray
Mountains, formerly the Golden Plain,
4372nd division of unendingness (5200th solar cycle),
winter.

Caphalor continued to watch Imàndaris as she brooded over the news.
Her bright red hair played around her face and her black mantle was

unfastened, revealing a flowing stone-colored robe with black metallic wire decorations.

His heart raced when he looked at her. Every morning he begged his conscience for forgiveness. Each morning he begged Enoïla's forgiveness, too. *But she is . . .*

"What shall we call this älfar realm here?" Imàndaris laid aside the paper she had just been handed by the messenger. "Dsôn . . . and then what?"

"Surely we should leave the decision to the Inextinguishables." He grinned. "You're impatient because no news is reaching us."

"Do you call this no news?" She indicated the papers strewn around about. "I have no idea how to deal with all this on my own. Being a nostàroi is more administration than fighting. I hadn't realized."

"That's because Sinthoras and I had already fought the great battles before you arrived." Caphalor enjoyed winding her up. He adjusted his clothing: a slim-fitting black robe with a white fur surcoat.

"They should have brought in a supervisor from Shiimal's corn stores," she complained, tossing back her wonderful hair. "I came here to win battles. Now I have to deal with provisions, rations for the soldiers and fodder for the night-mares."

"That's how it is on campaign." Caphalor walked over, placed a hand on her shoulder and planted a kiss on the top of her head. "Let me see what I can do." He saw at first glance that there were problems with equipment in the Âlandur and Lesinteïl elf regions. "They need support over there. As soon as the elves realize how few of us—"

Imàndaris interrupted him with a muttered imprecation and shuffled her pile of papers, from which she retrieved a further bundle of communications. "Here! These are all from Dsôn. They are replies to my requests for more troops. I suggested they at least send us their óarcos or some vassal soldiers for the time being, but I'm getting nothing but refusals and objections! Those Comets and Constellations never used to agree on anything, but they are together in this. Sitalia and Elria take their cowardly souls!"

She's irresistible when she's angry! Caphalor remembered full well why he had never wanted anything to do with politics: every single project made you a plaything in the hands of other people's interests, right down to how one conducted a war. He untied the string on the bundle of messages and scanned the responses, each more arrogant than the previous one. The main thrust was that the Tark Draan commanders already had sufficient forces at their disposal. After all, one älf warrior was worth 1,000 barbarians. "Idiots! They've ignored the fact we're up against elves."

"They've also forgotten that our once impressive army is steadily falling apart at the seams. Two-thirds of my forces have been ordered home—" Imàndaris broke off and gave him an apologetic look. "Forgive me. It was *your* soldiers they recalled . . ."

"I'm glad to be free of the responsibility. I'm just sorry that you were given the command at such an unfortunate juncture. It's almost as if someone wanted to dent your reputation."

"That's how I see it, too." Imàndaris studied the numbers again. "I must summon Horgàta. Even if we could use the 5,000 cavalry remaining secret, it's too much of a risk not to have them here. It's vital we keep the elves under control." She pointed to the map. "I've been thinking we might attack Gwandalur in winter." She swiveled the map around on the table to give Caphalor a better view.

"Because?"

"Because my scouts report that not only do the elves worship a dragon, but that there's a hollow mountain in Gwandalur that is full of the creatures. Dragons are cold-blooded and will be slow in the winter. We ought to be able to penetrate the mountain and kill them all while they are asleep."

"The elves or the dragons?"

"You're trying to irritate me, aren't you?" Imàndaris glowered. "The dragons, of course."

"How many are there?"

"The report says there are three adults and eleven smaller ones. The elves like to ride the small dragons so they can attack their enemies from the air."

Caphalor grimaced. His mood was thoroughly spoiled.

He had expected any number of difficulties, but had not reckoned on elves having scaly, winged transport. They would be at a hopeless disadvantage faced with such opposition.

"Yes, you're right. We're in urgent need of reinforcements." He looked at the map and worked out the distances involved. *Horgàta could easily reach us.* "What a good thing these dragons can't take frosty conditions."

"We'll be hard pushed to withstand attacks from a dragon unit unless we get them while they're hibernating. Winter is on our side, not Tark Draan's. If you had started the offensive in summer we'd all have been lost." Her expression changed. "And that would have been terrible, because you and I would never have met."

She is amazing! But his guilty conscience assailed him even as the thought passed through his mind. He turned his attention deliberately to the charts. "As far as the elf realms are concerned, I suggest—"

"Caphalor?"

He raised his head and saw her knowing smile. "What?"

"Don't worry. It's all right. I'm not trying to make things difficult for you."

She has seen through me. "It's complicated," he said, despairingly. "I was with Enoïla for such a long time that it seems like a betrayal to even stand at your side."

"You are a very special individual, Caphalor. Any other älf, male or female, is in the habit of swapping partners every few divisions of unendingness, but you and Enoïla spent so much time together." Imàndaris came over to him, hands outstretched. "I can't replace her in your affections and I don't want to. I am Imàndaris. No more. No less."

He nodded. "I know. I tried once before to find a replacement. It was a mistake. Her name was Morana and she was—"

She placed her forefinger on his lips. "I don't need to know. I can see you are upset every time you look at me, but you must get over these feelings. If you are not ready to say goodbye to Enoïla, tell me. I can wait. But I can't see you suffering like this. Do you understand?" She seized his hand and pressed it gently.

"Yes." He took a deep breath. "It's as if I can hear Enoïla speaking when I hear your words. She would have said exactly the same thing." Caphalor kissed her on the forehead and smelled her hair. "You are my life-partner, but I shall carry her in my thoughts. Not all the time. It will get less. But she has a constant place in my heart and in my soul. When she died part of me died with her. Do you understand?"

Imàndaris nodded and pressed his hand once more. "Yes. What remains of you is good enough for me, Caphalor." She kissed him tenderly.

A warm feeling stole through him. He pressed his lips to hers.

Someone knocked.

The couple moved apart as the door began to open. Carmondai hurried into the room, his notebook and pen at the ready. "Pardon me for barging in, but we have news of our friend Toboribar."

"To Sitalia and Elria with the wretched óarco," muttered Imàndaris, making Caphalor laugh out loud. "You would think he would have learned his lesson by now, wouldn't you?"

Carmondai handed her the message. "The letter wasn't sealed, so I took the liberty of reading it. He has revoked our treaty and has left for the south!"

"Very clever; he knows we can't pursue him. We don't have enough troops." Caphalor looked at the map. "Who else has gone? Just his Kraggash, or all the óarcos?"

"All those from Ishím Voróo; he has killed the few Tark Draan óarcos that had joined him to ensure we don't profit from their local knowledge." Carmondai sounded extremely bitter. "It began so gloriously and now it looks like it'll end in catastrophe."

Caphalor said nothing, casting his mind over their remaining options. *The óarcos have gone and so have half the barbarians. We're left with few of our own warriors and fewer trolls and ogres. It'll be a miracle if we can hold onto the Golden Plain when spring comes.* He glanced at Imàndaris; her face showed that she was thinking along the same lines. "When the snow starts to melt and the dragons wake up, we'll be faced with a third front. Your proposal, Nostàroi, is absolutely the right one: we attack Gwandalur now. That should relieve some of the pressure."

"And after that we will undertake a few decoy forays into Âlandur and Lesinteïl to make the elves think we have enough troops to go on the march even in winter." Her eyes were shining. She had finally been given the opportunity to operate as a warrior. "The dorón ashont will be defeated by spring and then we'll have the reinforcements we need to finish off the elves."

"We must demand more forces from the monarchs and nobles of Tark Draan. We can use them to defend the territories we have already won, but we will defend the crater ourselves." Caphalor was pleased with the strategy. "I suggest we send Virssagòn to Gwandalur with a few älfar. He can't carry out his other mission because the mages know what's happening. A master killer like Virssagòn will find some way to kill the dragons."

Imàndaris indicated her agreement. Carmondai was making a faithful record of the details of their discussion. "I'll go with him," he announced. "I could do with a bit more in the way of adventure for my epic. If I'm not going to be allowed to write about—" He broke off, reacting to Caphalor's warning look. "The defeat of Gwandalur will be excellent material."

"Why don't *you* command the cavalry?" suggested Imàndaris. "Caphalor tells me you are excellent. Take the mounted troops and Virssagòn."

Carmondai shook his head determinedly. "I have opted for the life of an artist."

"But you used to be a warrior?" Caphalor was keen to learn more about this älf, who kept his head in the heat of battle and knew how to lead and command, but refused his right to lead. *Without him we would never have won.* "How is it that you know so much about cavalry combat? I can't remember the älfar ever really deploying heavy cavalry. Our race has always depended on the use of bow and arrow."

"We are a race dedicated to death and to art," Carmondai corrected him courteously. He sat down and laid his notebook and his pen on the table. He seemed to be happy to talk. "How we use both is entirely up to each of us."

Imàndaris took a seat and pulled Caphalor to the chair next to hers.

"In a time when the älfar fought in Ishím Voróo, on terrain as flat as the Golden Plain, we came up against enemies who moved too fast for our archers: the cûithones. They were annoying creatures, a bit like humans to look at, but they aged twice as fast. They moved twice as fast, too. They would make it to our forces and cause incredible damage before our first arrows had fallen."

Caphalor had never heard of the cûithones. And he could not think where this territory was that Carmondai had been describing. "Where is this land?"

"A long way to the south. We traveled many miles over land and then took a ship—"

"You went by ship?" Caphalor exclaimed. "In the name of infamy! There's no sea anywhere near Dsôn Faïmon."

Carmondai smiled. "You just have to keep going south, Benàmoi. In those days the Comets exercised a strong influence on the Inextinguishables, and the älfar empire eliminated all potential enemies within a range of 1,000 miles."

"But that must have been ages ago!" Caphalor was impressed. *I feel quite ignorant.* He glanced at Imàndaris, who gave an almost imperceptible shrug.

"Not everyone knew about it. The unit I belonged to was thought to have been lost." Carmondai looked out at the horizon, his thoughts reaching out to the far past. "The cûithones had fortresses they attacked us from. We racked our brains for the right tactics. Pikes were good for an initial line of defense, but the cûithones squirmed past us like rats through the undergrowth and we lost a lot of good soldiers. I saw that we needed to run them down en masse, as the cûithones had no archers; they always relied on their speed. It seemed to me that heavy cavalry would be the best method. We came up with more resistant armor and made longer lances for our mounted troops. I planned maneuvers and invented signals to steer the cavalry quickly and reliably, to make full use of their combat skills. After that we beat the cûithones every time we met in battle. We razed their fortresses to the ground."

Imàndaris was hanging on his every word and Caphalor was equally fascinated.

"When we eventually returned to Dsôn after five divisions of unendingness, we'd been as good as forgotten. The Constellations accused us of ignoring all the messages we'd been sent, but I swear we never received a single one." Carmondai looked out of the window at the mountain in the middle of the crater: it rose, black and massive, throwing its shadow across them. "They deployed us in a defense role against the cûithones, farther to the north, near Pataiòn."

"That's all forest up there. Cavalry would be useless," commented Caphalor.

Carmondai nodded, a sad look in his eyes. "They wanted to punish us for our apparent refusal to follow orders—and because the Comets favored us. We lost half our fighting force in the first attack on our position. In the second we only managed to escape total annihilation by the skin of our teeth. I quit the service and abandoned military life. That was the beginning of the period when Dsôn lost so much territory to the óarcos, the barbarians, the fflecx and other scum from Ishím Voróo. Our heavy cavalry belonged to history." He turned to Imàndaris. "Can I have some wine? The past is in need of it."

"Don't you think it would make a good epic?" Imàndaris said, moved by what she had heard.

"No. I . . . I don't want to bring it up again. Nobody needs to know about it."

Now I understand what made him such an excellent warrior. Caphalor looked at Carmondai differently. Much had been rumored about this älf, but no one had guessed that in reality he had been a consummate cavalry warrior all those divisions of unendingness ago. He was also surprised to learn how great the extent of Dsôn Faïmon territory had been. *I have never bothered to find out about our own history. I really should have.* This story explained Carmondai's somewhat arrogant and disrespectful attitude when they had first met: he was understandably unimpressed by anything to do with politics and the status games—games Sinthoras was master at. *It must be so distasteful for him to hear history twisted and turned into lies . . .* "Politics serves only to satisfy the vanity of certain individuals," Caphalor remarked soberly. "To think what the cavalry could have achieved if they had been allowed to!"

"I'll tell you this for free: the Constellations in Dsôn won't be pleased to hear the unit has been resurrected, particularly as it was me . . . I mean, particularly as it was Sinthoras who suggested it." Carmondai hurried to correct himself and swallowed the wine Imàndaris offered him. "I hope the Inextinguishables will bring both factions to reason." He pointed to the new mountain. "What's going to happen with this?" he asked, deflecting any further attention.

"We have decided to keep the real story secret. We'll pretend the nostàroi caused the mountain to be built to demonstrate how superior our race is to the elves. Only the Inextinguishables will be told the truth."

Carmondai moved to face Caphalor again. "Then I'll have to cut a whole section of my poem!" he exclaimed in horror. "It took me a whole splinter of unendingness to write all that."

"I am sorry." Imàndaris refilled his beaker with wine, but did not offer to change her mind on this subject.

"And what about the älfar who were present?" asked Carmondai. "You were seen raising Inàste's tear from the ground. They'll have spread the news of the miracle."

"I know. We'll have to manage that somehow. Your verses will, we hope, reinforce our version of events, said Caphalor."

"But . . . why?" Carmondai drank more of the wine. "It would only increase your reputation—" He looked intensely at Caphalor. "So you *don't want* the glory." He turned to Imàndaris. "And you feel the same?"

"You are correct. That kind of miracle should be reserved for the Inextinguishables," Caphalor admitted. "And I am afraid that, back in Dsôn, some would gladly make use of myself and the nostàroi's 'miracle' for purposes of their own. Imàndaris and myself are warriors first and foremost; we do not wish to be put on a pedestal and admired. My friend Sinthoras would not share this view. I'm sure he'd appreciate a few statues in his honor, but that's where we differ." He hoped he had been able to make his position clear.

"I understand. At least, I think I do." Carmondai took up his notebook and pen. "I could describe the incident less dramatically. Would that be in order?"

"It was not anything special we did. It would have happened anyway, whichever älf laid his hand on the stone," said Imàndaris. "It may have looked startling when Inàste's tear rose up out of nowhere, but we did not make it happen, we were just in the right place at the right time."

"Write that the Creating Spirit showed her grace by allowing the mountain to be formed," Caphalor suggested. "Then you won't have to change many verses of your ode, but keep Imàndaris and myself out of the song please."

Carmondai's frown cleared. "That's fine by me." He put down his beaker and got to his feet. "Then I'll get a move on so that Dsôn can read about the miracle." He nodded to them both and left the room.

Imàndaris watched him through the window as he strode off. Then her eyes wandered to the mountain. "I would never have thought anything like this would happen to us on the Tark Draan campaign," she said quietly. "What luck!"

There was an undertone to her words that concerned Caphalor. "What is worrying you?"

"I'm not worrying. On the contrary: fate has released me from a difficult task, a task my mother imposed on me." Imàndaris lowered her eyes. "I was to do everything in my power to destroy Sinthoras. His reputation, his status, his honor, his services to our land."

Caphalor knew exactly why the powerful älf-woman had instructed her daughter to hound Sinthoras. "Yantarai has never forgiven Sinthoras for abandoning her and going with Timanris."

Imàndaris gave a slight nod. "She was deeply hurt. I am the only one of her children—the one she practically disowned for following a military career—who was able to fulfill her wish. But I had no idea how to go about it: Sinthoras was a hero, a nostàroi! But then he was demoted and had to face a tribunal in Dsôn. I am enormously relieved that I did not have to carry out her wish myself." She walked over to Caphalor and placed her hand on his cheek. "And instead, I found you. My best friend, my beloved, my mentor."

I am so delighted that she is mine. He kissed her gently and enfolded her in his arms. They remained in this embrace for some time.

"It was not very wise to tell me what your mother demanded of you," he said carefully. "Sinthoras is . . . a friend of mine. Admittedly, I sometimes find it difficult to like him when he overdoes the arrogance, but even if he infuriates me, I still respect him. What will you do when he comes back?"

Imàndaris looked deep into his eyes. "I . . . don't know."

Nor do I. Caphalor pulled her into his arms and kissed the top of her head. Suddenly he thought of the demon. *Where can he have gone?* He must find out without further delay.

The door was thrust open again; once more it was Carmondai standing on the threshold, breathing quickly as if he had been running. "Pardon me for disturbing you both, but . . . Sinthoras has been exiled!" He held a new message aloft.

"What?" Imàndaris frowned. "But I thought—"

"You'll have to stop reading letters that are intended for other people, Carmondai." *What intrigues have they used, I wonder, to bring Sinthoras down? It won't have been the truth.* Imàndaris stood at his side to read the text.

"It's not a private letter to you or the nostàroi; it's a public announcement," said Carmondai, defending himself. "Polòtain had him convicted of the murder of an artist: a sculptress that Polòtain had given a commission to. It's unbelievable. A carved stone figure of Robonor has deprived Sinthoras of everything he ever achieved!"

What an idiot! Caphalor could hardly credit how misguided his friend must have been. *His arrogance always made him his own worst enemy.* He turned to Imàndaris. "It does not look as if you will be able to resign any time soon."

Carmondai sank down onto a chair. "What a blow! From our greatest hero to a convicted murderer!" He slapped his thigh. "Samusin is playing one evil trick after another on us."

Caphalor lowered the announcement. It would have to be read out in the conquered territories of Tark Draan, according to instructions from the Inextinguishables. *Perhaps that's really what happened, but it's also possible that Polòtain has arranged the whole thing. Who can say with certainty?* He felt sympathy for Sinthoras, even if he turned out to be guilty of the murder. They had gone through so much together, the two of them.

Caphalor would never have thought that Sinthoras, as a committed member of the Comets, could be brought down by political intrigues in Dsôn. It showed him that there could be no true friendship when politics and power were at stake.

He is alone, ordered to travel west, through Ishím Voróo. I wonder if I shall ever see him again?

Imàndaris touched him lightly on the arm. Carmondai was scribbling like one possessed, trying to incorporate the new turn of events in his epic.

Tark Draan (Girdlegard), many miles south of the Gray Mountains, 4371ˢᵗ division of unendingness (5199ᵗʰ solar cycle), early winter.

Famenia was safely tucked away in her hiding place. There was a smell of damp earth and frost. *Ye gods—Sitalia—let me see out this day!*

Famenia had decided on the soubriquet of the Tried and Tested. No other name could explain what she had been through quite so well. And she was shortly to be tested again. This test, she had decided, would represent the final examination of her apprenticeship. Or maybe it would mean her death, if she failed. *For Jujulo's sake and the sake of my murdered friends!* She clasped her amulet tightly.

She had a new store of energy following her visit to Hiannorum where, having spoken to Hianna, they had arranged for the maga to join the älfar. This would enable her to learn more about the enemy. Famenia prayed that Sitalia might be at the enchantress's side. She had taken on the most dangerous role readily and deserved protection from the gods.

The fresh power Famenia now carried gave her great confidence, but could not displace her fear entirely.

She lay in wait in a hollow in the ground with only brown jute sacking for cover (the elves had heaped leaves and earth on top to camouflage her better) and the darkness. Famenia found the dark hard to cope with, so she carefully rehearsed the spells, formulae and hand gestures she would need. No sound reached her from outside; she could only hear her own breath and that seemed horribly loud. *I wonder how far Narósil has gotten?*

The elf-riders had taken on a great responsibility in capturing Milltown and invading the caves at the same time. If one of these missions were to fail, that would put an end to their entire plan. And the townspeople would suffer an unthinkable loss: that of all their children.

It was very stuffy under the jute sacking; she stretched out one arm to lift the bag in the hope of getting more air.

Bits of soil dribbled down and some snow slipped into the hollow where she lay. The snow would work in her favor: the älfar would never notice her hiding place under its white covering.

Looking out over the layer of fine snow crystals she could see the path leading uphill to the cavern. *All quiet there.* She wriggled her way forward in the hollow to take in a view of the walls around Milltown. *No one to be seen.*

Famenia began to get cold in spite of her thick clothing. She started to shiver; this was not an ideal condition to be in if she were going to issue spells. She kept switching her focus from cavern to town walls.

It had clouded over and snow was falling again. She heard owls screech in the nearby wood, and a fox barking.

Famenia's eyelids grew heavy despite her excitement. *Ye gods of Girdlegard, you—*

Lights flared at the entrance to the cave.

Behind this brightness she could see thick smoke issuing from the cavern mouth. People emerged from the interior bearing torches and flanked by a squadron of mounted älfar who were driving them toward the town.

More älfar on night-mares rode up to the path, directionless and unsure of what to do. Their numbers were growing steadily, from a few hundred to a few thousand. Until they had reached perhaps 8,000.

The elves in the cave won't have been able to deal with many of the black-eyes at all. She tried to quiet her racing heart. *I'm going to be even more vital to the operation! O ye gods!* She had been hoping only a small number of älfar would survive, but Samusin obviously had other ideas.

She twisted to look behind her, where Famenia could see light and hear armor clanking and horses snorting.

This was the second stage of the plan: Narósil and his mounted elf brigade had started out of the forest area and were taking up their positions. They had lamps attached to their shields to help them see and to get the enemy to notice them: the bait in the trap.

Famenia twisted back to face the cavern. It was not long before the älfar took up their stand on the path, ready to confront the foe. The älfar infantry remained at the back while the mounted archers pushed to the front, busying themselves with their weaponry. The unit that had driven the hostages back to the town did not reappear.

I wonder if the elf fighters have managed to take Milltown? Famenia rubbed her hands to get her fingers working again.

The dull noise of many hooves hitting snow came from behind her: the mounted elves had begun their assault against the älfar; their horses' hooves narrowly missed her hiding place.

The plan was that—following the first clash—the elf cavalry would spread out, forcing the älfar to chase them.

Let's hope the älfar fall for the provocation. The snow began to fall heavily, obscuring Famenia's view, but she could hear horses whinnying and the sound of screams and shouts close to where she hid. Some of the älfar arrows must have hit their targets.

Then the elf cavalry turned and galloped in her direction, as if fleeing the battlefield.

Famenia saw at once that something had gone wrong: the elves had been forced to break their attack early due to the hail of älfar arrows and they still had a good 5,000 enemies to contend with.

Then the snow slowed and stopped.

Famenia saw the massed älfar troops on their black mounts riding down the hillside to overtake the elf forces. The night-mares' eyes glowed red in the darkness and sparks flew around their fetlocks. It was a truly terrifying sight.

The enemy swept down like a tidal wave, coming ever closer to her makeshift shelter. The occasional arrow landed nearby; one missed her by inches. There was a brownish liquid on the shaft. *Poison!*

The approaching army thundered ever closer, making the ground shudder and shake. Bits of earth crumbled from the walls of her hideout and tumbled on top of her.

There are simply too many of them! Far too many for one of my firework spells to have any effect. She had expected that only a couple of thousand would survive the elves' attack, but the advancing army numbered many more. Still, Narósil was relying on her, as were Ossandra and all the townspeople, and if she jumped up and tried to run it would be suicide. *Keep calm, girl!*

With the nearest enemy rider not twelve paces distant, Famenia sprang up, slinging the sacking to one side and pronouncing the spell she needed. *Please let this work! It must!* The amulet heated rapidly and her head buzzed with the effort.

Accompanied by an ear-splitting noise, a bright silver wall of magic in the shape of a bell appeared.

The first of the night-mares crashed straight into it, its rider unable to steer the animal from its headlong gallop. The transparent, apparently fragile wall of magic proved to be as resistant as a cliff-face. The head of the black steed burst open on contact. The magic shape gave a happy little sound like a peal of bells. The force of the impact sent the animal's body careering diagonally upward and over the top, its rider flying straight up into the air.

Famenia did not see where he landed. Or how.

The rest of the night-mares came hurtling along to crash into the barrier, setting up a continuous ringing that grew steadily more intense. The magic bell cleaved the sea of death without mercy; a silver rock in a surging black tide.

All these sounds—night-mare death screams, quite unlike any noise a horse would make, the clanging of armor, älfar curses and shouts—wove through the noise of the ringing bells. Famenia was terrified. Blood spattered the magic shield, covering the whole structure with a film of red liquid. Thick gobbets of flesh slithered down the wall.

Famenia could feel the amulet's heat grow more intense. She would soon get burn blisters on her hand.

But the wave of hurtling bodies did not slacken. Inside her magic semi-circular shelter it grew dark as älfar bodies and night-mare carcasses piled up.

The sheer mass of bodies will crush me if I can't sustain the spell! She had not thought of this eventuality when deciding on what magic charm to employ. Her fear increased.

Eventually things grew quieter—a mountain of cadavers surrounded her. She tried not to look at the squashed and deformed faces of her enemies.

Muffled sounds of combat came to her ears and the ground shook.

Could that be the elves riding up? Famenia was dripping with sweat and her hand was burning. *Can't hold on any longer . . .*

She released the spell and leaped backward at the last moment to avoid the collapsing bodies. She did not quite manage to escape them all and a contorted, shattered night-mare with a broken neck plunged to the ground very close to her, trapping her leg under it.

Oh ye gods, no! She tried to pull her leg out from under the beast and was able to release it just before the pile of bodies became a bloodied avalanche.

Famenia crawled over the piles of broken flesh, sobbing. She stayed low, terrified she might be hit by one of the poisoned arrows. After a while she risked standing up and staggered on, casting frightened looks back over her shoulder at the battlefield.

Where her protective bell had been, älfar and night-mares were piled together in twisted heaps; any wounded had been dispatched by showers of arrows from elf archers.

Milltown has been liberated! It is free of the black-eyes! The children are safe!

The remaining älfar were attempting to regroup at the foot of the hill, out of range of the elf archers, but they were now coming under attack from the cavalry under the command of Narósil.

Famenia heard the metallic clang of armor and steel weaponry and witnessed the devastating injury inflicted on the enemy lines. Lances brought death, night-mares were flung to the ground, their riders pierced through; then the elves swung around and rode back to the meadow to gather for a renewed strike: the final onslaught.

Famenia was totally exhausted by the effort of sustaining the bell and her ears were still ringing from the noise. Jujulo had intended that particular charm to be used as a musical instrument for entertainment purposes. She had only been able to hope it could also serve as a protective mechanism. *One more assault and we'll have them.*

She turned to look again and her breath failed her: the älfar were not waiting quietly to be dealt their final blow. They had taken up the pursuit and were careering after the elf-riders.

A female älf led the foray, her long pale hair streaming out behind her like a banner. Nearly all the mounted älfar troops were following in her wake, aiming to prevent the elf-warriors from turning around for a final ruinous onslaught.

The elves realized what was happening and put on a burst of speed to avoid being overtaken. Soon the lamps on the elves' shields disappeared in the distance, the älfar following. This left the last of the älfar infantry standing in front of the smoke-filled cave entrance, wondering what to do.

I wonder how many of the elves are still alive and in the town? How many did Narósil assign to gain access to the cavern? Famenia was afraid that the victory that had seemed so close would turn out to be a rout. She stroked the amulet. It barely made her fingers tingle, demonstrating how little energy it still held.

She sprinted toward the town across the meadow, which was now thoroughly churned up by countless hooves. She stumbled over the clods of earth and over corpses, swerving to avoid hands grabbing at her when she passed injured survivors. Everything smelled of earth and blood, and the sound of älfar moans and of night-mares in pain pursued her until she reached the bridge and crossed into Milltown.

Elves appeared, bows in hand, hurrying silently past her.

Ossandra came running up and threw herself into Famenia's arms. "That was fantastic! You saved us all!"

Famenia lifted the young girl up and hugged her tight. "How wonderful to see you! But thanks must go to the elves." She pointed to the warriors now withdrawing. "Do you know where they are headed?"

"My father said they want to finish it." Ossandra gave her a kiss on the nose. "I am so glad nothing happened to you."

"Come on! Let's see what the elves are doing!" Ossandra nodded and Famenia, still carrying her, ran up the steps to the top of the town walls.

The clouds had vanished and the moon had appeared, as if the sky wanted Milltown to witness the fate of their torturers. The high walkway gradually filled up as more people arrived to watch. Nobody spoke.

They know as well as I do that this has not yet been a victory. Famenia bit her lip until she tasted blood.

Using the mills as cover, the elf contingent had crept up to the enemy and were sending a lethal barrage of arrows at the älfar.

One älfar fell, one after another.

"They deserve everything they get," Ossandra said. "They must never hurt us again!"

When the remaining enemies turned to the mountain in despair and attempted to flee, the elves who had laid the fire in the cavern came over the ridge and threw stones on the foe, forcing them to let go their hand-holds and plunge to their deaths. The population of Milltown cheered.

The town gates were opened one more time and the menfolk streamed out over the bridge armed with scythes, threshing implements, pitchforks and spears, intent on ensuring that not a single älf would survive. Even as the last of the fleeing älfar were killed on the mountainside by boulders chucked down from the ridge, wholesale slaughter commenced on the battlefield.

That decides the outcome. Famenia gently lowered Ossandra to the wall and turned to see what was happening up by the cave mouth. However hard she wished for the elf cavalry to reappear, they did not.

But neither did the älfar.

CHAPTER XX

And so it was that Virssagòn came to Gwandalur on the fringes of the Golden Plain.

And he saw that the mountain where the elves' dragon lived would be nigh on impossible to climb.

For this reason he sent his soldiers out disguised as elves to gather information about the enemy.

What he heard illustrated the way the elves knew no restraint. They saw themselves as the dragon's descendants, called themselves deities and demanded great sums from the barbarians in tribute in return for keeping the dragon quiet.

But Virssagòn saw a chance to get rid of the dragon without having to fight.

He knew the vulnerabilities of dragons.

And the greatest of these—were the elves.

Excerpt from the epic poem *The Heroes of Tark Draan*
composed by Carmondai, master of word and image

Ishím Voróo (Outer Lands), Dsôn Faïmon, Dsôn,
4371ˢᵗ /4372ⁿᵈ divisions of unendingness (5199ᵗʰ / 5200ᵗʰ solar cycles),
winter.

"I can hear you breathing!"

Arviû did not have time to react to this criticism. He heard the stick whizzing through the air and knew the blow was coming from above right, aimed at his shoulder, but could not move out of the way in time. It struck home and he clenched his teeth so as not to utter a sound. If he had groaned he would have earned himself another clout, without question.

"But you are making progress."

Praise from his mentor soothed the pain somewhat, but Arviû was not averse to the discomfort. Only by experiencing fewer aches and stings would he really know when he was improving. "I should not have missed the target," he said ruefully.

"You did not miss. You were spot on and would have hit it," Païcalor answered. "But then I heard you breathe out. We can't have that. It is vital for your safety that you are never seen or heard. Learn to control your body, but don't be too hard on yourself. What you have managed to learn in the few moments of unendingness since your arrival, would have taken most älfar very much longer to master."

"I don't care about what *most* would have done. I want to be the best," retorted Arviû. "I have a goal and I want to reach it as soon as possible— before the nostàroi have finished in Tark Draan and I have nothing to do."

Païcalor stepped aside. "You want to kill elves?"

"Not just kill them." Arviû got to his feet.

He had been lying on the ground between two narrow beams. He had been throwing needle-sharp daggers from that position at the center of the target. He was useless at archery now, but this he could manage. Païcalor, one of the guards from the Bone Tower, had been helping him practice. He had worked with various weapons recently: swords, spears, daggers and iron batons. He only stopped training long enough to sleep, wash, feed or defecate. He was too ambitious to take things easy.

"I shall go to Tark Draan to bring more death and torture to the elves than any of my älfar colleagues," he went on. "They blinded me, but that will become my unique advantage! When the lights are dimmed, their death screams will ring out."

He heard the rustle of Païcalor's robe as he went to the door. "You may become the best ever, Arviû, but you will still need divisions of unendingness before you are ready carry out the task you have set yourself. Tark Draan"—Arviû heard a door open—"will be elf-free by then." The door clicked shut.

Then I'll have to train harder. Arviû went over to the table to collect his outer clothing. When training under the Inextinguishables' bodyguards, he preferred to wear simple breeches and a tight-fitting robustly woven silk shirt. That was all he needed.

He picked up two metal-studded short staves and practiced twirling them in the air, running through the parrying, feinting and thrusting moves Païcalor had taught him. Arviû had had to learn by touch: a new kind of learning. Païcalor would stand behind him, directing his arms and adjusting his stance with movements of his knees.

Arviû had made many mistakes to begin with, but his hearing was much improved and the slightest sound gave him invaluable information about his surroundings. He could hear when weapons were being employed and could accurately judge their speed and trajectory.

That was why it was essential others should not hear him: he must not give away his own position in the dark lest he surrender his advantage over sighted enemies—even those of his own race. The älfar had always been good at seeing in the dark, but even they would have to rely on touch and auditory signals in complete darkness.

Arviû was on the way to becoming a warrior no one would be able to match—unless, of course, he had to fight in the noise of battle.

But I'll have to master that skill, too. Arviû stopped the practice, noticing that he needed to rest his arms and shoulders. *I'll get some food and drink, and have a short break to restore my energy. Then I'll find something else to work at.*

He put on his weapons belt, took hold of the long stick he had been using to steady himself and left the chamber.

His steps were confident as he moved swiftly through the lower floors of the Bone Tower. On this level there were some sighted guards who could help him in an emergency. He used the echo from the tapping of his long stick to help with orientation.

Occasionally he could still get lost, and he had fallen downstairs a few times, but these accidents were few and far between nowadays. Going blind, he had learned, was not the end of life; it only meant a different life. What he desperately missed, however, was beauty; he could not see the elegance of the edifice the Inextinguishables lived in, the decorated walls, the ornaments, the murals, the art . . . all of this was lost to him now.

Soon I'll be able to take on a live adversary! Arviû had been practicing against straw targets and fighting lifeless dolls in an effort to improve his accuracy, but Païcalor had promised he could measure his strength against one of the guards soon. *I don't want to be given any easy options, either.*

Reaching the kitchen area, he collected some food. As he ate, he liked to listen to others talking.

The topic for discussion was the dorón ashont invasion. As far as Arviû could gather, there was a plan to attack the enemy encampment, but he could not catch all the details. They were also speaking of the lethal sickness that was receding, thanks to a loffran root infusion, even though there was a shortage of the plant; and then they spoke of Sinthoras and the recent surprise conviction.

Arviû paid little attention to the content of these overheard conversations, concentrating rather on ascertaining the exact positions of the speakers within the room. He tried to assess the size of the speakers, whether they were seated or standing, how far away they were from him. These would be the details that could facilitate a successful dagger throw. The way their clothing rustled told him they wore simple fabric, little in the way of leather or metal; but some of them must have jewelry of some kind.

Silver maybe? Tionium gives a fuller sound. Arviû enjoyed puzzling while he ate.

As soon as he had cleared his plate, he made his way back to the training area. He wanted to improve his skills with the short staves.

He also enjoyed working with the arm-blades Virssagòn had developed. The contraption consisted of metal tubes, padded on the side, and fastened to your forearm. Stable and erect blades pointing forward and back jutted outward from them. The blades were as long as two hands. Virssagòn had never stopped to explain how best to use them, so Arviû was finding out for himself. His initial tests had proved successful, but he had cut himself a number of times.

With these, I need only make tiny movements to inflict stabs or cuts and I can block sword strokes, but it would not be much help if someone comes at me with an ax. While musing in this way, Arviû had taken a wrong turn. He could smell oiled leather, saddles and bridles and the coats of night-mares.

That's stupid of me! I've ended up in the stables. He knew exactly where he had gone wrong. *Now, where's the door?* He tapped around with his stick to get his bearings.

The stick met wood and clicked against spokes. *Ah, they've got a coach ready.* Arviû went a little farther and was surprised to find a total of eight vehicles apparently made ready for an expedition. *That's quite a wagon train, but Païcalor didn't mention the Inextinguishables were going on a journey.*

In the distance he heard the clink of metal on metal, the creak of leather, the sound of voices.

The sounds were getting closer and he decided on an impulse that he should hide. *Perhaps I can find out what they're planning?* Arviû only had a rough idea of the layout of the stables, but he managed to locate a bale of straw to hide behind.

"... the sighted guards will leave today," said a female älf voice. "It's essential nobody finds out what is happening in the Bone Tower. Load up the extra cart with the Siblings' most valuable belongings and make sure everything is properly covered by the tarpaulins so no one can see what is being transported. Nobody must know the rulers are leaving. The wagon train must look as if it is supplies for Tark Draan, like the earlier transports."

"Of course. We'll take care of that." Arviû thought the other voice sounded like a warrior. "I'm assuming the destination is the crater?"

"Yes. They want to visit the troops and make an appearance at the very spot the Creating Spirit's tear fell to earth."

The warrior gave a short laugh. "Anyone would think the Inextinguishables were not just visiting Tark Draan. It sounds like they want to move there for good."

"What makes you say that?" The female voice sounded suspicious.

"My people have been taking wagon train after wagon train to Tark Draan ever since the campaign started. We were never allowed to tell anyone. I know it was supposed to be a surprise for our troops, but . . . Ergàta, there've been around fifty carts so far. And this train has eight more. What am I supposed to think?"

"It's for a visit. That's all it is," she answered curtly.

The warrior sighed. "Is it to do with the dorón ashont?"

Ergàta laughed. "No, certainly not, Sajùtor! Our army will soon have eliminated them."

The names were new to Arviû, but apparently they were both in the service of the Inextinguishables. *Strange. Very strange.*

"Why are the rulers leaving Dsôn Faïmon?" Sajùtor demanded to know. "Please tell me. If there's trouble on its way I want to warn my family."

"Are you completely insane? They are not abandoning the homeland. They are going to give their blessing to the foundation of a second älfar realm. Nothing further has been decided."

"So, what's with all the secrecy?"

"The population here will think exactly as you obviously do," Ergàta snapped. "Their visit has been planned for ages. It's unfortunate it comes at such a turbulent time." She turned. "Ah, Païcalor."

"I heard you talking and wondered if I could be of any assistance?"

"No," she said. "Sajùtor was about to go and brief his soldiers. He has always given excellent service and is likely to receive praise from the Inextinguishables once he has escorted the last consignment to Tark Draan."

"I was just going, was I?" Sajùtor sounded annoyed at her presumption.

"Yes. And be careful, as always."

Someone left and it went quiet.

Did Païcalor go, too? Arviû could not hear the others anymore and was about to emerge from his hiding place when he heard Païcalor say, "A good thing no one else has been told."

"The excuse about a royal visit is a bit thin." Ergàta sounded concerned. "There'll be rumors."

"They should have fled a long time ago to be sure of avoiding the sickness. These parasites are more dangerous than we originally thought. Even Bolcatòn has died, and he was so convinced he was safe." Païcalor knocked on wood. "I'm as glad as you are to be permitted to leave Dsôn, but the people won't understand."

"It's essential for the future of our race! What use is it if we hang on here in Dsôn Faïmon and all die?" Ergàta was pacing up and down. "I support this move wholeheartedly, even though it brings me pain. The Inextinguishables and the älfar who accompany them will be safe from the parasites and they can found a new city. They'll only make contact with Dsôn Faïmon once the plague is over."

"All the älfar will want to follow them."

"No. Nagsor and Nagsar Inàste will issue an edict to the effect that no one may follow them. It's as simple as that." She fastened a strap. "No one would dare disobey an order from the Inextinguishables. And if anyone did, our archers will pick them off at the Stone Gateway and ensure they meet endingness." It sounded as if she had taken Païcalor by the arm. "You have to understand: they are doing all this for our sake, for our future, for the survival of the race! If things go well there'll be two prosperous and successful älfar realms."

"You're quite right. The Siblings will have considered the options carefully. They have insight and vision." Païcalor sighed. "It is hard to leave so much behind."

"Count yourself fortunate that we're allowed to tag along." The female älf was moving away, Arviû could tell. "We will form the foundation of a new empire, my friend. Who knows what splendid children you and I will have together."

But Païcalor won't be able to see that. Arviû had to think about what he had just learned. The sickness the dorón ashont had brought them was out of control and the Sibling Rulers were leaving the homeland in secret so as not to become its next victims.

Arviû had to agree with what Ergàta had said: Nagsor and Nagsar Inàste *were* demonstrating their far-sightedness. It was a perfectly legitimate way of proceeding. *But there will be panic when it becomes known that they have left.*

He could imagine what would happen: as the numbers of plague deaths rose in the radial arms, the inhabitants would become extremely frightened. And the more frightened they were, the more they would try to find safety. They would want to go to their rulers. But the älfar of Dsôn Faïmon would find their emigration ending abruptly at the Stone Gateway. They would either be forced to turn back or they would be shot.

Arviû let his breath out. *In the name of all infamy!*

"I can hear you breathing!"

Arviû ducked and dodged as a pitchfork pierced the hay bale next to him.

"You'll never learn, will you?" The fabric of Païcalor's robe rustled as he surged forward.

He will want to kill me because I know their secret. Arviû dropped to the floor, holding his cane upright where he expected the attack. The sharp end of the stick went through the guard's foot as he jumped. Païcalor uttered a cry of pain.

Height, location, distance! Arviû retrieved the needle-dagger from his belt and hurled it, his aim deadly accurate.

The scream turned abruptly to a death rattle as Païcalor slumped to the straw-strewn floor. Silence.

Now Arviû was left to decide how to best use his newly acquired forbidden knowledge.

Tark Draan (Girdlegard), south of the Gray Mountains, Enchanted Land of Hiannorum, 4371ˢᵗ division of unendingness (5199ᵗʰ solar cycle), winter.

As soon as he rode into the Valley of Grace, Simin realized that the place name no longer held true.

The trees had withered and their dead foliage lay scattered on a layer of snow. Statues crumbled with every gust of wind. The spell Hianna the Flawless and her pupils had sustained no longer existed. Now, for the first time, the valley had to bend to the laws of nature. The oasis of happiness had gone.

It's that pact she made with the älfar. Simin did not try to hide; he galloped toward the three towers.

The buildings had aged by whole cycles in the past few days. The wood of the bridges was rotten and shingles were missing. Carrion crows and ravens flocked, screeching, above the broken roofs. The birds of death had taken over the dovecotes.

The crows are everywhere. Simin reached the towers and saw the reason the birds had sought out this valley: corpses.

The bodies of the young famuli lay in the snow at the foot of one tower. He glanced up and saw they must have been pushed through the glass windows. Although sharp beaks had already hacked away at the tender flesh, he could see that blades had also been used; in some cases whole limbs were missing, cut off cleanly.

Did Hianna kill her own students? "Hello?" he called, his voice echoing up and down the little valley. Crows hopped out of his path, flapping their wings and squawking at him. "Is anybody there?"

A door banged in the wind, and the snow whirled about him. One of the roof tiles crashed down onto the frozen ground and made his horse startle.

Bringing the animal swiftly under control, he dismounted to inspect one of the bodies more closely.

The young woman could not have been dead long because her body was not frozen. She had died through a stab to the heart and her eyes had been neatly removed with a knife. It looked like a surgeon's work.

The poor girl! He got back up to his feet and began to explore the empty buildings.

Inside the towers there was no sign of disorder, plundering or arson. Occasionally he noted the scorch marks caused by failed spells. *There must have been a chase, a hunt.* He pictured Hianna chasing her charges through the buildings, driving the girls on with magic spells and laughing as she cut them down, one by one.

No. That's not the way she would work. It makes no sense at all. Simin avoided stepping on the rotten bridges between the dilapidated towers. Instead, although it would take much longer, he used the external staircases. *Why would Hianna do such a thing? Wouldn't she try to get her famuli on her side rather than killing them? And she would surely not have condemned her Valley of Grace to decay.*

He continued to look around in the buildings—and found Hianna herself lying in front of an open window. There was snow on her back and a raven perched on her shoulder, pecking away at her earring.

Is it her? Simin could see she was surrounded by tiny triangles of sharp wire. There was a pool of blood around her face. None of his theories about events in Hiannorum fit this picture. He approached the body cautiously, sweeping the barbs aside with the toe of his boot.

The raven squawked, almost as if to stop the magus, then flew out of the window, complaining loudly about being deprived of its booty.

Simin observed the dead woman. "Was that the reward for your treachery? Did the älfar not trust you?" he said, speaking low. "What happened here in the valley?"

He heard a quiet whimpering.

It took him some time to realize that the sound was coming from Hianna. "Ye gods! Still alive?" Simin hesitated, not knowing what to do. *Is it safe to heal her or not?* The whole region was saturated with magic: he was powerful enough to tackle her if need be. *I have to know what happened. And what you have done. When I've learned that, I will let you die as you deserve.*

He lifted her up and carried her to the nearest bedchamber, then lay her down on a velvet couch. He placed two fingers on her brow.

His first spell was to diagnose the extent of her injuries. It told him she had been the victim of a strong poison that was destroying her inner organs. *I don't know this toxin.* She had also been exposed to the cold; she had frostbite on her face and on her fingers. She was severely dehydrated.

Simin brought up a series of spells to neutralize the poison, stop the destruction and repair the damage to her organs. Then he dealt with the frozen extremities. To warm her he lit a fire in the grate.

Finally he sat down opposite her in an armchair to wait. From time to time he made a spell to check her progress and increased the healing power where necessary.

This poison is a tough one, he said to himself. As it was a toxin he had never met before, this strengthened his assumption that it had been älfar who had wreaked this destruction on the Valley of Grace. The question of why they might have done this would have to wait for Hianna to wake.

Simin was reluctant to leave her alone, but hunger drove him down to the kitchens. He returned with bread, cheese and a jug of wine. There was no need to carry water upstairs. He brushed some snow from the windowsill rather than going to the well. *And, of course, the well might be poisoned.*

A whole day passed without the maga opening her eyes, but her breathing was becoming stronger and Simin could tell the healing process was working steadily. Still, many spells would be needed to restore the health of her inner organs. The toxin clearly had terrible effects on humans.

It was not until the third day that Hianna coughed herself awake.

Simin shot up out of his doze. Getting to his feet, he gathered his concentration in order to be able to fend off a potential magic attack. "At last!"

"Where—?" She struggled to sit up, supporting herself on the upholstered armrest. Then she put her hands to her temples. Her face was covered in tiny cuts left by the wire barbs. The poison had left small black spots on her skin: a souvenir of the death she had so narrowly escaped. "I—" She moaned. "It all hurts. Everything hurts."

"Your organs have still got to heal completely. You were poisoned with something that has been destroying you from the inside," he explained, but he was impatient to find out the truth. "Did you kill your students? Or was it the älfar you had a pact with, wanting to have all the magic lands—"

Hianna sobbed and hid her face in her hands. "How could I ever have believed I would be able to deceive those evil beings?" she said, her voice thick with tears. "I brought about the deaths of all of my famuli!

I should have died too, so that they would not have to go to the other side without me!"

"Did you—?"

"No. It was an älf. Before he slaughtered my girls he told each of them that their death came bearing the name Virssagòn." Hianna became hysterical. "And I thought I was such a good actress!"

Simin started to relax somewhat. He was convinced now that Hianna was not pretending. The loss of her students was affecting her deeply. However, he resolved to continue to exercise caution. "I was in the Gray Mountains and I saw you talking to the älfar. Explain yourself."

Raising her head, she looked at him with reddened eyes. "Famenia came here and told me everything. She told me that Ortina had been killed by the älfar. We decided it would be best if I pretended to offer my services as an ally so that I could find out more about them and also about the demon. A female älf, Morana, appeared here in my valley and offered me a pact. I was sure I had been able to fool her. I wanted to write to the others about what I had learned about the älfar, but then this—" Her lip quivered and she wrung her hands as a cascade of tears set in once more.

Simin relinquished all caution and sat down next to her, putting his arms around her shoulder. "You have been braver than I have," he murmured. "And you have paid a high price for your courage."

"He killed them," she whimpered. "O, ye gods! I lay there helpless! I heard their screams and the terrible sounds of his weapons as he cut up their bodies . . . and then . . . it all went so horribly quiet!" Hianna clung to him.

Simin sat by, silent, holding her tight; she could not stop crying. He did not doubt her words. There would come a time when he could ask for a more detailed report of events.

The sun went down behind the hills, turning the sky dark red.

Suddenly Hianna shuddered. "I have lost so much. No one else in Girdlegard must ever suffer what I have gone through," she said, her voice stronger now. "But that's exactly what the älfar and their hideous allies intend. I have learned a great deal about their plans." She lifted her face and wiped away her tears.

"And I have information about the demon," Simin said. "I can cast a banning spell to stop him spreading his undead power over our homeland. If we can stop him we will have made enormous progress. We can do this together!" He embraced her once more. "I am so sorry about what you have gone through . . . and I am sorry that I thought you had abandoned us for the enemy."

"I understand." Hianna freed herself from his embrace. "I know you came here in order to kill me."

"Yes. I could not let the älfar take one of us as an ally alongside the demon."

"I sent messengers to warn the others, Grok-Tmai and Fensa. Virssagòn won't score any more successes." Hianna got up and took a piece of bread from Simin's plate. "I must eat to get my strength up again, then I'll come back with you. Us four and Famenia will confront the demon and the älfar—Girdlegard must never fall into their clutches."

"On my way here I heard one of the monarchs and a few nobles have gone over to the älfar. Our task will be anything but easy. The black-eyes are ingenious and malicious in their planning."

"Believe me, Simin. In me they have an adversary to be reckoned with. They will come to fear me more than the elves or the human warriors." She paused and then whispered, "But first I must bury my girls. My valley is falling apart." She swallowed and put out a hand for support. "But I can't bring myself to look out of the window, let alone go outside."

"Let me do it. Rest now until you are properly recovered."

"No!" She took a deep breath and stared into the flames in the fireplace. "No! I must do it myself, though it will tear my heart to pieces." The warm light made her appear distant, the black spots on her skin recalled the fury lines on an älfar face. In that moment she could have been taken for an älf. The hatred in her eyes added to the resemblance.

"I swear, Simin: I will never teach again. No pupil of mine shall meet her death because she was in my service. I'll put the pupils I sent out to distribute the warnings in your hands, or transfer them to Grok-Tmai or Fensa to look after. And when I die, the enchanted land of Hiannorum shall fall to whoever chooses to take it."

Simin was silent. *That makes two of us who have lost our magic names. I am no longer the Underrated and she is no longer the Flawless.* He looked forward to meeting up again with Grok-Tmai, Fensa and particularly Famenia. Girdlegard already had so much to be grateful to her for. Combining their magic powers they would repel any attack. *We shall hold off the armies! We shall keep the enemy hordes at bay!*

Ishím Voróo (Outer Lands), Dsôn Faïmon, between the radial arms Wèlèron and Avaris, 4372nd division of unendingness (5200th solar cycle), winter.

Téndalor surveyed the scene from his night-mare; it was unusual for him to have such a steed for two reasons: firstly, as a former commander of an island fortress, he had never had the opportunity of riding to battle and secondly, he had assumed that after falling severely injured into the moat, he would be dead by now.

Fadhasi, however, had another mission for him and this was why he had not entered endingness. Instead, he had been washed up on the Dsôn Faïmon side of the bank and had been found and looked after by healers. Fully recovered now, he was eager to fight. Fadhasi had saved the life of his one and only worshipper.

Téndalor stared grimly at the miserable encampment set up by the so-called Army of the Ownerless, and the wall behind it where the dorón ashont had dug themselves in. *I'm going to get my fortress back*, he vowed.

Lamps were burning in the slaves' army camp and a bugle now sounded to alert any sleepers that the älfar had come.

Two camps, one with 6,000 men, and behind that . . . well, it could be 15,000 for all I know. Téndalor assumed the fugitive slaves and crazed óarcos had placed warriors in the first encampment and womenfolk and families behind. *That won't help them one bit.* The Inextinguishables had said no prisoners were to be taken. None of the Ownerless was to survive the night.

Téndalor was in top form. Dsôn Faïmon's army had been sent reinforcements from Tark Draan: a thousand warriors keen to destroy the enemy threatening their homeland and then to continue the battle on the far side of the mountains.

The älfar army was led by Aïsolon: an experienced campaigner and good friend of Caphalor, the Hero of Tark Draan. All the signs were favorable.

Téndalor had not been given details of the strategy they would use to defeat the Ownerless, but word had got around that a small unit had already infiltrated their camp, ready to climb the wall and put the dorón ashont catapults out of action.

As soon as we can get close enough they'll be ours! He was not worried about the numbers of barbarians and óarcos they would be facing. You could give a barbarian a sword, but that did not mean he would know what to do with it.

The ditches that had been excavated around the camp did not present a problem. The älfar army was well prepared and their equipment included portable pontoons. Other vehicles bore mobile catapults that could fire arrows and spears. The attack against the dorón ashont had been planned for some time.

Very soon! Téndalor stroked his night-mare's powerful neck. He was on the army's right flank; Aïsolon had ordered them to push directly into the second of the two enemy camps. *If the Ownerless think their womenfolk are in danger, that will unsettle them and they will split their pathetic forces. They'll do it to protect their young, but they have so many offspring. They breed like rabbits.*

The assault began at a silent signal.

The central unit stormed off, feigning a direct attack on the heart of the camp. The wagons with the mobile catapults rolled forward, their operators sending off the first volleys of missiles.

Téndalor saw the barbarian lanterns moving forward to meet them. They ended up directly under the next arrow bombardment. *Just as planned!*

Then his squadron received the order to attack.

Fadhasi, I slay in your name to bring you honor! Téndalor was riding in the vanguard, keen to be one of the first to draw blood.

His night-mare's sparking hooves trampled the loffran fields flat and the smell of the crushed plants rose in his nostrils. An icy wind struck him in the face as he rode. He glanced at the darkening skies where the first stars were now visible. The dorón ashont catapults, which would normally have deterred the älfar with a hail of stones and arrows and burning pitch, were motionless.

We have tricked them! Téndalor was on the point of letting out a cheer, but restrained himself. He would not celebrate until he had split open his first barbarian head.

Suddenly, fiery missiles shot screaming into the air from behind the dorón ashont barricades.

Those accursed beasts! Téndalor was surprised that only about fifty of these tiny comets headed for the skies and then fell back to earth. Five or six of the howling fiery objects came down on the älfar troops and bounced away. When he realized what the projectiles were, his hatred for the Towers that Walk grew out of all proportion. *Those are our soldiers! The dorón ashont must have discovered them trying to sabotage their catapults.*

The burning warriors screamed as the flames engulfed them: they were being roasted alive. More of these projectiles crashed down onto the mounted troops, knocking several älfar out of their saddles and setting some of the night-mares on fire.

Cheers resounded from the camp of the Ownerless.

Téndalor drove his spurs into the night-mare's sides to speed the animal on. The dorón ashont would be loading the slings and trebuchets again and they had to use the break.

The barbarians were acting as predicted: when they saw that the flank was swerving around the main field of action and heading for the family camp, their sea of lamps spread, thinning out: the enemy was thus weakening its own lines.

Téndalor had no time to watch the rest of the fighting. He kept his eyes to the front. *Thanks be to Fadhasi! We have arrived in too dense a formation for their catapults to contend with.*

Arrows whizzed past him and the ditch surrounding the camp was suddenly visible.

With his archers and spear-throwers giving covering fire, he ordered the mobile bridges brought to the edge of the ditch. Pulleys and counterweights were set in action, moving the segments apart. The first bridge section, with its blade-like edge and iron cladding, crashed through the enemy palisade.

"Tear them down!" Téndalor urged his night-mare across the boards of the bridge, his warriors following suit. He was eager to wreak havoc and revenge and was intoxicated with battle lust. *I don't care if I have to fight hand-to-hand all the way through the barbarian camp.*

The night-mare leaped and landed between the first of the tents. An armed barbarian confronted him with a spear, but Téndalor struck him down with a sword-blow to the throat. He turned his mount and rammed an attacker who had crept up on him from behind. A hoof-kick in the face saw to him, splattering the contents of his head in a shower of sparks.

Téndalor defended the narrow passageway against all comers as more and more älfar crossed the improvised causeway. Now they were so many that it would be impossible to repel the surging throng. The barbarians turned and fled.

"See how they run!" Téndalor laughed and whirled his sword. Women and children in the other camp tried to find shelter and hide. It was a delight to him to hear their cries and moans. *Instead of picking up weapons and fighting, they show us their backs and make themselves as vulnerable as possible.*

The benàmoi of his unit appeared at his side and nodded approval— but an arrow was instantly put through his throat. With a death rattle he slid off his steed, grabbing at the arrow's shaft.

Téndalor had seen the archer: a young man with a bow and a sword at his side. He had hooked his booted feet into the rungs of a ladder leaning against the watchtower, but his hands were shaking too much to notch the arrow for a second shot.

"I'll get you—" Téndalor began, but did not get any further as part of the wall collapsed and dorón ashont streamed through the breach.

Ten, twenty, thirty of them and more leaped through, armed to the teeth, carrying long shields and protected by strong armor. Behind their visors their eyes shone purple, sending bright violet rays of light onto the ranks of the älfar. Above their heads, firebrands soared into the black sky to fall smoking and sparking onto the advancing älfar troops.

The barbarians rejoiced.

It's them! Téndalor remembered how he had felt the first time he had seen one. He had to force himself not to run away.

All the älfar knew full well that the real battle was about to commence.

Chapter XXI

So let them go
if they do not want to stay.

Do not mutter.
Do not complain.
Two cities,
one people,
But which city
will outlast its twin?
Which Dsôn
is genuinely blessed?
Unendingness
will show the truth.
Whoever stays
and survives the plague
will be twice as strong.

Excerpt from the epic poem *The Heroes of Tark Draan*
composed by Carmondai, master of word and image

Tark Draan (Girdlegard), to the southeast of the
Gray Mountains, formerly the Golden Plain,
4372nd division of unendingness (5200th solar cycle),
winter.

I feel like a bird up here. Carmondai was sitting on the mountain that Inàste's power had raised. He was busy sketching his view of the crater despite the frost-laden gusts of wind that assailed him. The evening light was glorious and he could not think of abandoning his task. He did one drawing after another.

Below, the älfar masons had adapted their reclaimed blocks of stone so that no gaps showed at the joins of the buildings. Painters had added runes and symbols as decoration, either drawn free hand, or applied with stencils. With every moment of unendingness the crater camp was being transformed into a collection of beautiful älfar buildings that grew ever taller. The original crude aspect was being replaced with grace, sophistication and artistry. And Carmondai had the perfect view.

There are many scenes to turn into murals when I get home. Carmondai reckoned he must have completed a good hundred detailed sketches so far. When he turned them into finished pieces he would select a range of formats, from huge spreads to miniatures the size of a man's palm. How he loved an artistic challenge.

When his fingers got too cold he packed away his things and began to climb down.

On nearing ground level, Carmondai saw a cloaked figure perched on a rock. He stepped closer and realized it was Morana. She was picking up pebbles and flinging them out; a flute in the form of a death's head lay on her lap.

"It's more fun to send the pebbles spinning across a pond," Carmondai said.

Her pretty face was turned toward the crater edge. She appeared not to hear him.

"Has something happened?" He stretched out a hand to touch her. "Morana?"

She turned her black eyes toward him and her expression held such sadness and soul-wracked depression that Carmondai wished he could capture her image on paper. "You obviously have not heard the news," she answered forlornly.

Carmondai presumed her troubles stemmed from knowing that Caphalor and Imàndaris had become a couple. *Broken hearted. Unrequited love. The old, old story.* "We live for an eternity and we collect a wealth of experiences on our journey. Our feelings—" He stopped.

"No. It's not that." She looked irritated. "We have been forbidden from returning to Dsôn Faïmon," she told him with bitterness. "One of the wagon trains brought the message just now. The Inextinguishables have issued orders to hold the Stone Gateway and to stop any älf from our homeland joining us. And we are not to be allowed to leave Tark Draan."

"*What?*" *Imàndaris will have to tell me that in person before I'll believe it. No, I wouldn't believe it even then! What on earth is behind it?*

He left the site and ran over to the accommodation in which the nostàroi was quartered; Caphalor had the house next door. Morana followed behind him.

Carmondai knocked at the door and opened it to find Imàndaris brooding at the map table. Caphalor was at the window, armed and dressed for a journey that would take place in the heart of winter. He must have seen the poet approach.

Carmondai and Morana entered the room; the latter slammed the door behind her.

They know exactly why I'm here. "Well?"

"What has she told you?" Caphalor's speech was slow as he turned reluctantly to face him. He refused to look at Morana. It was as if they were mortal enemies rather than failed partners.

"Only the rumors." Carmondai did not want to incriminate Morana. "We're none of us allowed to return to Dsôn Faïmon? Is that right?" He stepped over to Caphalor. "How can the Sibling—"

"There is a deadly plague of sickness in the homeland. It has taken over in Dsôn," Imàndaris interrupted. "They thought at first they could contain it, but they were mistaken. I received an order that no älf may leave Tark Draan and none may leave Dsôn Faïmon until the plague is over."

"So the Stone Gateway is to shut once more?" Carmondai rubbed his face with disbelief. "How bad is the situation back home?"

Neither Imàndaris nor Caphalor knew the answer to that one.

Imprisoned and banished. Carmondai had to sit down. He lowered himself on to a chair by the table and laid his folder and pens down. This new occurrence was going to change the way the narrative of his epic developed. Until now it had seemed that Tark Draan signified nothing more than a massive victory for his race, but now it appeared the place was to be the cradle of a new älfar civilization. *I wonder where Sinthoras is now and whether he is carrying the sickness. What if he comes back here after many divisions of unendingness and brings the plague here to us?* "Can anyone tell me about the dorón ashont?"

His question remained unanswered, but it was obvious the two of them knew more than they were letting on. "What do we do now?"

Caphalor ran his hands over his thick winter mantle. "The nostàroi has just instructed me to secure the Stone Gateway while she controls the conquered lands in Tark Draan." He walked over to Imàndaris and kissed her on the forehead.

Carmondai watched Imàndaris close her eyes to accept the caress. She held out her hand as if wanting to make him stay. *But as nostàroi she must let her lover go.*

"I must get going." Caphalor said. "My people are waiting for me. It won't be easy to get to the Gray Mountains quickly in weather like this." Caphalor shook hands with Carmondai. "Until we meet again." Then he swept past Morana, paused and turned to hold a hand out to her.

Morana stared at the proffered hand then looked him in the eyes. She opened the door for him without a word. She had apparently not forgiven him for that unfortunate evening encounter.

Finally she opened her mouth to murmur: "Take care of yourself. The älfar need you."

Caphalor nodded, left the room and closed the door behind him.

Nobody spoke.

Carmondai did not dare to note down his thoughts about the scene he had witnessed. None of what he had seen and heard would ever find a place in his epic. *Maybe I could start a second tale. I could call it* The Legends of the Älfar.

"Morana, go and check the guards at the crater's edge," Imàndaris commanded quietly, with no harshness in her tone. "After that you should prepare for an expedition through the conquered lands to ensure everything is under control. From today you will take over Caphalor's duties. I hereby appoint you to the office of benàmoi. The insignia for your robes and armor should be in your quarters."

Morana needed a breath or two to recover from the shock. Then she gave a bow and left the building.

That did not look like genuine gratitude. Carmondai felt ill at ease alone with the supreme commanding älf. *This is all terrible. Who will ever read my epic? Can I send it—*

"Weren't you going to accompany Virssagòn?" asked Imàndaris, interrupting his train of thought.

"Yes, but he has left without the cavalry and me, and has taken a unit of Ishím Voróo barbarians with him instead. He let me know he would send for me when he has finished his preparations." Carmondai looked at her. "We are completely cut off from home. Cut off from everything." Leaning forward, he tried to look at the maps. *And we are surrounded.* "What is the likelihood of our being able to withstand an attack from the elves?"

"We have a better chance here than the älfar who've remained behind in the capital, faced with the plague and the dorón ashont." Imàndaris had not moved since Caphalor's departure. "I can understand why the Inextinguishables have issued these orders."

Carmondai tried to catch her eye. "You haven't answered my question about the dorón ashont. I swear I'll keep it out of the epic."

She nodded. "Caphalor trusts you and so I will trust you, too. Our race is battling the dorón ashont and a whole army of runaway slaves. We badly underestimated the threat." Imàndaris looked thoughtful as she took a seat opposite him. "I sent a messenger south to Horgàta, but neither she nor her squadron have survived an attack by the elves."

"No!" Carmondai had heard more than enough bad news.

"5,000 warriors, wiped out; attacked by the heavy cavalry that escaped Sinthoras and Caphalor in the battle of the Golden Plain. A sorceress assisted them, I understand. We have lost an important advantage."

"I . . . am still optimistic. I'm sure Virssagòn will prevail against the dragon-riders."

Imàndaris gave a tired laugh. "We'll be lucky if we can even manage to keep *this* Dsôn. Our plan to kill Girdlegard's sorcerers has failed. Virssagòn was only able to slay two of them and a third was removed by a troop of guards in the Gray Mountains. The rest of them have been alerted and warned. I expect they will join forces with each other. And *what*," she leaned forward for emphasis, "*what* shall we do then?"

Carmondai was about to suggest that she refer the problem to the academy staff as they had their own, albeit limited, power. But of course, they would not be allowed in to Tark Draan. *And anyway, they would not be able to withstand the concerted efforts of the local wizards.* "And our demon?"

"Exactly! What about our confounded demon?" she exclaimed, slamming the table with her fist. "There has been no sign of it. Perhaps it has followed Sinthoras into exile. I don't know. I'm becoming convinced our gods have abandoned us." She turned to the maps and pointed. "Make sure you remember where these lines fall. They show our greatest victories against Tark Draan. Soon they might all be gone."

Carmondai saw she had lost any confidence she might have had at the outset of the campaign. "An enormous challenge faces you, Nostàroi. It is your task to create a new homeland for our people. Here." He pointed up to the mountain. "It was you and Caphalor who raised the tear of Inàste. Look on it as your sacred task to build a second Dsôn!"

"A second Dsôn?" she repeated, throwing herself back in her chair. For a long time she was lost in thought. "You speak the truth, Carmondai. I must not give up and wallow in my own sorrows. I have a mission, a task that Inàste herself has given me." She smiled. "My thanks, Carmondai, I may call on you often in the future to dispel my doubts and renew my courage."

"I shall be there for you, Nostàroi." He returned her smile. "Now, please excuse me. I need to find Virssagòn—I won't wait for him to summon me; I always like to form my own opinion of a situation." He packed his things together, got to his feet and left.

It had grown dark in the crater. On the southern side of the hollow the captured humans from the conquered town of Sonnenhag were working by lamplight to straighten the sheer crater sides.

A new cradle for älfar civilization. Carmondai saw Morana with the laborers, observing them closely. He had noticed her doing that quite often. *How can anyone be so interested in barbarians?*

To the north, Caphalor climbed the steep winding path out of the crater with his troops. He saw Carmondai and waved.

Carmondai returned the greeting and then looked around to find Imàndaris standing directly behind him. Her hand was raised in a farewell salute. *Ah, so it wasn't me he was waving at.* Smiling, he took himself off to his quarters to organize things for his trip to Gwandalur. *Easy mistake to make.*

*Ishím Voróo (Outer Lands), Dsôn Faïmon, between
the radial arms Wëlëron and Avaris,
4372nd division of unendingness (5200th solar cycle),
winter.*

"Yes!" Jiggon had managed to shoot the älf standing at the mobile bridge through the throat. He was surprised at his own luck, because he had actually been aiming at the black-eyes to the left of the one he hit.

His original target swirled around, saw Jiggon on his precarious perch on the ladder and turned his red-eyed steed.

He's coming straight for me! Jiggon's boot slipped on the ladder and he nearly fell. "Attention there! Form a circle!" he called to his men. He couldn't notch his next arrow.

The fighting men ringed the lookout tower and took up what Ataronz, their trainer, had termed a hedgehog formation, which meant they had their spears pointing at all comers. Any enemy approaching at speed was bound to skewer himself. Jiggon leaped down and saw four armed älfar heading their way. He chucked away his bow and shouted: "Shields high! Or they'll shoot us like rabbits at harvest time!"

Behind him he heard a grinding sound and a series of thumps. Looking around he saw that the acronta had torn down their own ramparts in order to join their allies.

The godlike ones aren't going to desert us! That had been Jiggon's greatest concern. If the gigantic acronta had simply remained behind their wall, the Army of the Ownerless would have had little or no chance of standing up to the älfar attack.

He took the fact that they had torn down the stones of their own fortifications to mean that the decisive onslaught was about to take place. *They don't need their stronghold anymore.*

The projectiles from the trebuchets hissed into the air. Gobbets of burning pitch fell on the advancing älfar ranks, throwing up a wall of flame as they hit the ground.

We will defeat our oppressors! "Come on, there! Keep your courage up!" Jiggon yelled to his troops, then picked up the shield that Ataronz had given him. He did not know where the óarco was, but he wished him luck—and good hunting.

The älfar who had just now been considering a frontal attack on the hedgehog formation turned their night-mares and made straight for the acronta.

This allowed Jiggon a little more flexibility. "Hedgehog! Close ranks! Get closer together. Shields high and move to the right," he commanded. "Small steps, like Ataronz said—make sure no one trips!"

Slowly but surely, his spiked formation approached the bridge the älfar had come over. He was eager to ensure that no more of the enemy could use it. Women and children were running frantically, trying to get past them and onto the safety of the bridge; they completely ignored his shouted warnings.

Jiggon knew that anyone making it to the far side of the bridge was as good as dead: the älfar reserves were waiting out there in the dark, listening out for the signal. *I'm pretty sure we haven't seen all of them yet.* Now and then he risked a glance over the top of his shield to see how the main battle was progressing.

The älfar had concentrated their entire effort on repulsing the eighty acronta who had come through the hole in the wall. Ten of that number were guarding the gap and the others were heading for the black-eyes in small groups. The badly reduced numbers of Ownerless did not bother them; the acronta were following their own stratagem.

Jiggon had to admit the acronta were dealing out their punishment effectively. Each of them was carrying several weapons, either at their side or on their backs. As they were taller than anyone else on the field of battle, they presented a terrifying sight. They worked their way in a line through the throng of älfar like barbarians wielding scythes through a field of hay. They slammed into their smaller foes with shields and cudgels, or spiked mace-heads the size of a young calf. Any älf in the way would fly a good half dozen paces through the air, smashed to smithereens or cut to pieces.

However, Jiggon also noted that some of the acronta were wounded. A few were limping and others had fallen to their knees, brought down by the constant rain of älfar arrow-fire. Turning to the left, Jiggon saw an acronta felled after receiving ten or so spear thrusts to his upper body. With a supreme effort, the mighty figure dealt death blows to thirty of his adversaries, even while injured and nearing the end. His bright yellow blood coursed from gaping wounds.

"To the bridge!" Jiggon urged his men on. "And then into the middle!"

The soldiers followed his command and marched straight on to the wooden planking, which did not even sway under their weight. When Jiggon signaled to the hedgehog formation to jump, the bridge did not even shake.

He started to doubt their chances of damaging the solid construction. "Curses!" He got one of his people to go down on all fours so he could climb up on his back for a better overview.

There were several fires burning in the Ownerless camp and the flames were spreading fast; the straw used for the soldiers' bedding providing a ready source of fuel.

Forget the tents! After the battle we'll all be able to sleep in our oppressors' palaces. Jiggon was trying to jolly himself along, but deep inside he was pessimistic. There were twenty acronta still standing on the battlefield and four of them were attempting to hold the wall breach against an älfar onslaught.

In the flickering light of the flames, Jiggon could see all the dead bodies. Most of them were Ownerless. Dead black-eyes were only to be found in any appreciable numbers where acronta had fallen.

The fighting spirit of the älfar was undimmed. Jiggon observed how they let their sword blades whirl through the air, how they loosed arrow after arrow at the foe, aiming at the visors of the Towers that Walk in order to bring them down with a shot to the eyes. The Army of the Ownerless had been broken up into isolated groups that were being chased through the camp.

We're going to lose! Oh ye gods! Jiggon felt stupid. *As if it makes any difference whether I can destroy the bridge or not!* He jumped down from his comrade's back. "Run to the defense canal!" he called to his troop, his voice faltering.

"Why? What's happening there?" Pirtrosal, not much older than Jiggon, regarded him with a horrified expression. The others all exchanged incredulous glances.

"We can jump in and swim over to Ishím Voróo and save our skins!" Jiggon pointed to the acronta defending the breach. Two more Walking Towers had been slain. "We have lost the battle. The black-eyes won't spare any of us!" He thought back to what his father had said back then in the hut when Jiggon had tried to persuade his family to rebel. *We should have been more cowardly and remained in slavery . . .*

"But how can we be losing?" Pirtrosal screamed, scared out of his wits. "We've got the Towers that Walk on our side . . . and . . . and there are so many of us!"

Jiggon noticed that the acronta catapults had ceased their fire. That must mean the älfar had reached the fortress and had captured these siege engines. "Get to the canal!" he repeated, his voice grim with disappointment. "The älfar are occupied with the Towers that Walk. This is our chance. Chuck all your equipment away. It'll only slow you down."

They came out of formation, throwing down spears and shields. Even their armor. Running full tilt through the dark, they followed the sound of the water.

"Over there!" Pirtrosal shouted. "On the right!"

Too late, Jiggon saw a hundred red points of light glowing in the gloom and heard heavy snorting. A hoof stamped and tiny lightning sparks shot out around the fetlocks, throwing light on the legs, belly, neck and head of a black charger.

Night-mares! Less than two paces away!

A latecomer firebrand soared up from the fortress, a bright tail that illuminated humans and black-armored riders in its wake. White steam rose from the nostrils of the mounts standing in a densely packed row.

Jiggon's stomach lurched and the hair on his head stood on end. Without knowing it they had run past a unit of reserve älfar. He stopped and stared.

One of the älfar broke into malicious laughter. The rest joined in.

They only allowed us to run away for a joke! Jiggon reacted to the evil mirth with a shudder of fear. *We will never reach the canal!*

A command in an obscure tongue resulted in one of the line advancing and drawing his sword.

"Game on!" the älf shouted, this time in the human language. "If you get to the water you live."

Is it possible? Jiggon staggered back and stared up at the mounted adversary.

"Start running if you want to live. Your barbarian chums are almost at the bank by now."

The night-mare revealed its snapping, vicious teeth. The solo rider advanced.

Jiggon whirled around and ran like the wind to escape death. His troops were ahead, running for all they were worth, pushing and shoving each other in their haste to get away. Some had tripped, dragging others down as they fell. Some managed to scramble back to their feet. There was no *esprit de corps*, no common cause; it was every man for himself.

"Faster!" Jiggon shouted. "You have to run faster! The moat isn't far off!" He overtook them, leaping over fallen bodies. His legs were young, strong and rested. He no longer had his heavy shield or spear to weigh him down. Another twenty paces and he was racing over the flat ground at the head of his men.

There was the canal moat, its bank so close now. *Any moment!* "Quickly! Nearly there."

Behind him he heard the first scream. Jiggon did not dare to look around. Naked fear drove him on while his comrades were slain.

Jiggon launched himself in a mighty leap to get as far as possible into the stretch of water.

But there was no water.

He fell into empty air.

Tark Draan (Girdlegard) southeast of the Gray Mountains, to the east of the former Golden Plain, 4372nd division of unendingness (5200th solar cycle), winter.

Carmondai was not worried about crossing Gwandalur. Virssagòn and his barbarians had gone ahead and Carmondai was sure they would not have left anyone alive that could pose any threat to him. *Sinthoras will be having a harder journey.*

He had followed the road leading east from the Golden Plain, riding a night-mare someone had lent him. The black steeds were faster and had far more stamina than horses and there was no longer any need to pretend he was an elf. *The masquerade is over.*

Carmondai was surprised to find that there was no frontier post, no barrier and no fortress at the border between the Golden Plain and Gwandalur, only a little sign in an indecipherable script hanging on an intricately carved post. He assumed this marked the border and he was now in Gwandalur.

Snow lay on the ground and he saw neither village nor lone homestead as he crossed the empty landscape. *At least it wouldn't take me long to draw . . .*

A mountain appeared on the horizon, its summit piercing the clouds: the lair of the dragon. *I wonder if the elves live in the mountain, too? It would make things easier for them. And it would explain why there aren't any houses.*

It was difficult to judge the distances, but he thought it would be a couple of moments of unendingness before he reached the foot of the mountain.

Another night in the open air, or maybe two or three. He cursed under his breath. He was not fussy and certainly not spoiled, but having to sleep outside under a tree or in a hole in the ground was no joke in winter.

I wonder if there are any barbarians in Gwandalur? I could stay in one of their houses. I wouldn't have to talk to them, like Morana does. She's spent far too much time with humans; she's nearly one of them herself now.

Late in the afternoon the wind stopped and the sky cleared and, shortly, Carmondai rode past a shallow valley. A stubby tower with smoke coming out of the top squatted in the middle of the valley. On the side of the building there was an extension, propped on poles against the main wall. Around the base of the tower there were a few crude huts; it was clearly not an elf settlement.

Barbarians. They're like rats. They get everywhere. He turned his night-mare, heading down from the little hill they were on toward the bottom of the valley; they rode through a newly planted area of pine and birch. From the saddle he could see over the tops of the young trees and saplings.

Earth, hidden under last year's snow,
still given over to the elves.
Soon to be converted and exalted.
Step by step, blow by blow.
One älf will suffice . . .

Out of the corner of his eye he noticed saplings swaying. Someone was moving through the plantation, coming straight for him. His night-mare snorted a warning, having got wind of the danger.

Carmondai had just enough time to draw his sword before an elf in a dull gold breastplate shot out of the wood and thrust him out of the saddle. Carmondai landed on his back in the snow.

Rolling over, he jumped to his feet and looked to see where his enemy was, but the elf had ducked back into the cover of the small trees. *Virssagòn hasn't been as thorough as I would have expected.* He noticed drops of blood on the snow. *Is that mine?* He did not feel any pain. *It must be the elf who's injured!*

Carmondai threw his bag containing his notebook and pens to one side in order to be freer in his movements.

The armored elf appeared from the undergrowth again, wielding a broken sword. He struck four swift blows that Carmondai was able to parry before diving back into the thicket. This time Carmondai saw that his opponent was bleeding badly from a wound on the thigh.

I bet you could tell me a story or two! Carmondai set off after him, following the trail of snapping branches. He noted where the twigs had lost their layer of snow.

He went deeper into the dense plantation until he reached a small clearing, two paces wide.

The elf was standing there, sword in hand, breathing heavily. He called out some kind of a challenge to Carmondai. He had no idea what it was, but it did not sound friendly.

Suddenly there was a rustling from all sides and the sound of branches breaking. A score of barbarians clad in furs and animal-skin jackets emerged from the trees, swords and clubs at the ready.

"Got him at last!" shouted a man with a long blond beard.

Carmondai realized they must be mistaking him for Virssagòn. *He certainly used to be more thorough. In the old days he would never have left an enemy alive.* "Yes, you've got me—even though I'm the wrong älf. I advise you all to hide again or you'll never see another daybreak!" He pointed his sword at the elf. "I only want him. The rest of you can get lost."

The elf shouted something again, incomprehensible for Carmondai. The barbarians attacked, rushing him in a wild, unruly throng, reliant on the fact he was grossly outnumbered.

Two he brought down with fast, sure, stabbing movements to the chest. He darted through the gap he had created and dived into the undergrowth. "Come and get me!" he called. "Your deaths bear the name Carmondai!"

They followed.

Carmondai had tricked them into surrendering their greatest advantage: instead of staying together they took him on one by one. The branches got in the barbarians' way, hampering their sword arms, and there was no room to wield clubs with sufficient force to do any damage.

You've the elf to thank for this. He sent you after me. Carmondai showed them what an älfar blade could do—severing branches, clearing space, before striking the body of his adversaries. "Your death is called Carmondai!" he yelled. Seven, now eight, barbarians fell bloodied to the snow to breathe their last.

The rest turned and fled, but their heavy winter clothing snagged on the trees, slowing them down. Carmondai comfortably dispatched them one by one, slicing off their heads, stabbing them, or hacking off their limbs so they collapsed screaming.

After a few moments he had seen to all of them and had cleared a red-stained path through the undergrowth.

And where is the one who started all this? He returned to the clearing to find the elf still there. Brandishing his dripping sword, Carmondai announced: "Your barbarian underlings are all dead. The stupid deserve to die, my friend." His breath was coming somewhat more quickly than normal, but he had not exhausted himself. *How is the elf going to react?*

The elf's face showed no distress. "I wanted to see the way you älfar fight," he retorted. "I wanted to see where your weakness lies."

"And did you find it?"

The elf nodded. "And that is why I shall defeat you."

"You? With your broken sword? I don't think so."

"I need nothing more in order to kill you."

"You know I'm not the one your barbarians thought I was." Carmondai approached his adversary with caution.

"I know. The other one had better armor. And he didn't even look like you." He lifted his weapon. "He was the one that destroyed the sword of my forebears. After I have killed you I shall pursue him and make him pay."

"Those are fine plans for a corpse." Carmondai considered how best to overpower the elf and take him prisoner. Then he would force information out of him about the mountain and its dragon. "Why do you allow humans to settle on your land?"

"We own no land."

"So this isn't Gwandalur?"

The elf gave a laugh. "Of course it is, but your way of thinking is petty, outdated and backward, like the elves of Âlandur. We don't have an empire or divide our land: Gwandalur is everywhere our dragons can fly and humans pay us tribute. We are not constrained by arbitrary lines on some map. Our only exception is made for the elves of the Golden Plain." He took his sword in both hands. "Is there anything else you would like to know before I put a stop to your questions?"

"Yes. When did my comrade come through here?"

"A day ago. He was on his own and looking for something."

Trophies. Carmondai knew how Virssagòn liked to collect particularly attractive limbs so as to make souvenirs out of them. He would show visitors around his collection on winter evenings and had an anecdote to go with each item. His latest acquisitions were selected from among Hianna's female students. "You've been hunting him down?"

"I found myself by chance in the humans' village, taking their tribute levy." The elf was becoming impatient. "I have been considerate enough to answer your questions. Now you tell me: Why are you here in Girdlegard? What do you want here? Your army will soon be routed. Is that what you want—to die so far from home?"

"What we want is to wipe out all the elves. We've dealt with the Golden Plain. Gwandalur is next."

His opponent laughed at him. It sounded more arrogant than any älfar laugh. "You intend to storm the mountain? Good luck with that! Our dragon-riders will turn your army to ashes!"

"I've heard the dragons can't fly in wintertime," Carmondai reacted to the taunt. "Their blood is cold and slow."

The elf frowned. "Is that what they say?"

"Our scouts are good." Carmondai swirled his sword through the air and the last drops of barbarian blood flew off the blade, making a red line in the snow in front of the elf. "Whenever you're ready, just step over the line."

"And did your spies find out what the dragon-riders look like?"

Carmondai could not remember. He looked at his enemy's dull gold armor. *Those figures on the metal, are they dragons?* "I suppose you are one of them?"

The elf gave a malicious grin. "You have guessed correctly. Now, have a little think, black-eyes, however did I manage to reach that village?"

"On a—" Carmondai had been about to say *horse,* but he hesitated in the face of this haughty expression. *What if the dragons* can *actually take off in the cold season? If so, why haven't I seen any?*

A broad shadow covered the clearing and snow was swept from the branches. Then he heard an almighty roar.

Looking overhead, Carmondai saw a green dragon with a huge body and a tail of the same length. Its wings were spread wide and its muzzle was open as it got ready to roar again. *So that . . . By infamy! The frost doesn't affect them at all! The nostàroi must be told, immediately.*

The dragon folded its wings and dived down to earth. Carmondai, still staring at the beast, heard the elf's armor scrape as he moved and lifted his sword at the last moment. Their blades clashed in midair.

The elf attempted to strike him in the head, but Carmondai evaded the blow, drew his sword back in and glanced upward to seek out the dragon. *Best if I try and stay really close to the elf so this creature can't get me.*

"And suddenly you don't seem so confident," mocked his opponent. "Fengîl obeys the slightest signal. I only have to waggle my finger and—" The elf broke off in the middle of his sentence and his eyes rolled up in his head. Gouts of black blood emerged from his mouth, ran down his armor and splashed onto the snow; then he released his hold on the broken sword, fell sideways to the ground and did not stir again.

Virssagòn must have used poison on his blade. Close above his head Carmondai could hear the dragon snorting and its wings flapping.

He flung himself down, praying the beast's claws would miss him.

Chapter XXII

The coming death.
It had three faces.

Nobody had ever seen them
so they could not be recognized.
The coming death.
With faces of steel,
of flesh
and of alchemancy.

The cruelest effect
was brought about
when all three faces united.

Epocrypha of the Creating Spirit
Book of the Coming Death
101–115

Ishím Voróo (Outer Lands), Dsôn Faïmon, Dsôn,
4371ˢᵗ / 4372ⁿᵈ divisions of unendingness (5199ᵗʰ / 5200ᵗʰ solar cycles),
winter.

Polòtain stood in his courtyard early one morning looking at the sculptures that had just been delivered. After Sinthoras had been exiled, the mood in Dsôn had lightened. The name of the nostàroi—once so admired, but at the same time feared—had no power over the älfar any longer. Polòtain had had no difficulty finding another sculptor to take over the commission.

He strode around the figures. *One for my beloved Robonor and one for the unfortunate Itáni, who paid for her courage with her life and secured my revenge.* He kissed the marble figures symbolically on their cold, lifeless mouths.

Then he signaled to his serfs that they should take the figures and place them in the marketplace, so that the citizens of Dsôn could see a double version of his victory over Sinthoras.

Polòtain strode back into the house and climbed to his glass-roofed extension. There he would take his daily dose of Ioffran infusion to protect himself against the purple phaiu su. There had been rumors that some älfar had become ill despite taking the brew, but he preferred not to give credence to these reports. And anyway, he had become accustomed to the taste. *I have eliminated the plague called Sinthoras; these relatively harmless parasites won't hurt me.*

Seated, he had his servants bring the hot drink and some biscuits. Unlike many of his neighbors, he had never had any problems with unruly slaves and none of his had joined the Army of the Ownerless.

"Out with you," he commanded, and the veiled barbarian women hurried back down the stairs.

Then he put his feet up on the upholstered stool, took the cup in his hands and sipped the tea, while enjoying the view over the Black Heart.

Polòtain adjusted his capacious black and silver silk robe. It was soft to the touch and pleasant on the skin. For the first time he was acutely aware of his age. He wondered how Carmondai managed to cope with the harsh campaign life he had volunteered for.

The burdens of the last few divisions of unendingness were starting to recede from his shoulders. He had achieved his sworn objective, albeit in a roundabout fashion: to bring about the fall of his enemy Sinthoras.

I should have preferred it if he had been banished to Phondrasôn, but this way he is condemned to permanent solitude. The shame is too great for him ever to return to Dsôn Faïmon, even after the forty divisions of unendingness have passed.

His gaze lingered on the roofs and strangely empty streets of Dsôn. *They've all crawled off to hide. There's no reason to fear. No älf should ever be afraid of anything.* He saw the sickness as a test of endurance that the älfar had been visited with. It would eliminate the weak and leave the best specimens alive.

Since the site of the outbreak had become public knowledge, Polòtain had found out everything he could about this sickness. His mother had once told him about a threadworm pestilence that had once hit their race. Though it had been a milder version, the parasites had died off eventually, starved of nutrition.

That's exactly what will happen this time, too. Polòtain sipped the infusion. *We just need to take protective measures.*

He did not believe that the dorón ashont had infected the town deliberately. He thought it more likely that the unfortunate älf had become infected with the parasites in Ishím Voróo: it was sheer chance. According to reports, he had crawled through any amount of filth in his efforts to escape. *He could have picked it up then. The dorón ashont are not bright enough to think up a scheme of these proportions.* Putting the goblet back down on the table, he picked up a biscuit. He could imagine the battle at the island fortress. *Then the horrors will be over, once and for all. The Army of the Ownerless! What a joke. We ought to change their name to the Army of the Lifeless.*

Plans were already afoot in Dsôn to use the rebels' cadavers: a pile of bodies was to be placed in each vassal town as a warning never to rise against the älfar again.

Polòtain had suggested rehousing the vassal peoples in settlements on the other side of the defense moat, thus increasing älfar territory.

He expected the Sibling Rulers would agree, given the events of recent moments of unendingness.

Security through expansion. The Comet campaign motto had been adopted by the residents of those radial arms most affected by slave rebellion.

Polòtain picked up a pen and started to record his thoughts on political strategy and how best to deal with the serf question. *We gave the barbarians too much freedom. We should keep them in their own towns, like animals in pounds. That's the only way to control them properly.* He liked this idea. He would present it at the next meeting with the Inextinguishables.

One thing was certain, he thought: the Constellations have lost influence. He took a mental note that his next speeches should blame the exiled Sinthoras for all the failures of the Tark Draan campaign. A second wave of attack could be started in the spring. A glorious victory awaited and the destruction of the elves would be assured.

He looked out of the window and considered his choice of wording for the discourse of his next address. *If we had had more land on the other side of the moat, the dorón ashont would never have gotten so near. Thus it follows that Dsôn Faïmon must extend its borders as soon as the sickness has been overcome, by at least 200 miles in all directions.*

He smiled as he scanned the notes he had written. *And I thought I had retired from all that. This feud with Sinthoras has given me a taste for politics again.*

Polòtain got up from his armchair and walked out through the large balcony door onto the viewing platform that ringed the building. With a warm southerly wind playing in his hair, he did not find the cold too bracing.

He took deep breaths and filled his lungs with fresh air. *Ye infamous gods, I have you to thank for this outcome. After all the pain I suffered, now Robonor is avenged.*

He saw his neighbor Nèlosor in the process of having a new work of art installed in the courtyard and raised his arm in greeting. The work looked to be from Tark Draan and had the style of the bonesmith Durùston. *I wonder if I should plunge back into the intrigues of the empire?*

The daystar was sinking toward the crater edge and ceding power to its rising cousin. As the moment of unendingness drew to a close, a cloudless sky promised a biting frost.

A faraway rumble sounded like distant thunder.

Polòtain looked around, but could not see storm clouds anywhere on the horizon. *It can't have been the catapults. The battle is much farther away and the wind is blowing in the opposite direction.*

There was another rumble.

The windowpanes of the tower shook in their frames and two of the pieces of glass cracked from top to bottom.

An earthquake? We've never had an earthquake here in Dsôn! Polòtain left the balcony and was about to go down the stairs to a safer part of the building, but something to the northwest caught his eye. In the light of the dying sun a powerful foaming jet shot out of the crater wall. From this distance, the gushing fountain seemed small, but at its origin, it would probably be around twenty or thirty paces broad; the water steamed in the cold air, sending up a yellow fog.

Wherever is the water coming from? He tried to think what to do. *Should I go and inform the watch?*

It was many miles to the far side of the crater. Dsôn was not in any danger from a flood: the water would dissipate and drain away before it ever reached the outskirts.

But the sight of that gushing water brought back distant memories.

The memory of a story his grandmother had once told him, about the origins of Dsôn Faïmon.

She had told him that. A violent shudder hit Polòtain's property and he was thrown off balance. Cups jumped off the table and smashed on the floor tiles; part of the balcony fell away and plunged down into the courtyard. All the windows in the little tower shattered. He put up his arms to protect his face from the flying glass.

Then it grew quiet again.

Impossible! He struggled to his feet and looked at the surging water. *I remember. She told me it had dried up long before the moat was dug.*

A huge boulder hurtled down from the crater wall and the fountain became a cascade, boiling and foaming its way into the hollow in which

Dsôn had been built. The yellow clouds of gas formed an impenetrable fog over the water, but Polòtain could see the vast hole above the waterfall grow broader and broader. The surge continued. *The old river has come to life again!* The constant stream pouring into the crater would be enough to flood Dsôn. *Unless it stops soon we shall all drown! I must get out and onto higher ground.*

He ran down the steps, shouting for his servants, and yelled to Godànor to pack a few vital things and to get the carriage ready.

When the courtyard gate was eventually opened, he was confronted by the sight of crowded streets: älfar, slaves, night-mares, and wagons forced their way between rows of houses, all trying to make their escape in different directions. Voices. Neighing. Rattling wheels . . .

Ye gods of infamy! What do you have in store for us? Polòtain thought he could even hear the sound of the cascade above the hubbub. Dsôn formed the Black Heart of the empire and lay at its very center, but it was also the deepest point in the depression. Unless the water could be stopped, the crater would fill up together with all the radial arms in a matter of moments of unendingness.

"We must get out of here!" he shouted, swinging himself up into the smallest carriage.

"Master," countered a terrified slave, "We'll never even reach the exit!"

"Godànor!" he yelled. He got the servants to attach four night-mares to the wagon instead of horses.

The young älf, still doing up the last strap on his armor, came running up. "I'm sorry! I was out the back and—"

Polòtain pointed to the driver's seat. "Get me out of here! Out of Dsôn! I don't care how you do it!"

Godànor nodded, shoved the barbarian off the seat and grabbed the whip.

"And the rest of you! Watch the building! Look after it!" he ordered his distraught household. "I'll be counting every single coin when I get back."

Godànor drove the night-mares with furious blows of the whip in his hand. They dashed out through the open gate. Biting and snapping, they pushed their way through, ramming other vehicles and thrusting them aside. Any foot traffic was trampled under their flying hooves.

Polòtain hung on for dear life as the coach juddered and jolted over holes in the road or rolled over fallen bodies. Chaos reigned and screams filled the air. The wooden vehicle survived impacts with other carts and crashes into stone walls. "Make for the south. Take the Cajoo road and then head for Nagsar Square!" Godànor was pulling on the reins for all he was worth in an effort to control the animals. "Get to the edge of the crater! There's a narrow path that leads up."

"Not to Riphâlgis?"

"No. That's where everyone will be heading. The roads will be jammed. Not many know about the little path." Polòtain looked around. The crush was growing thinner. The coach wheels were red-stained and blood had even sprayed into the interior. The night-mares and Godànor's armor were also spattered with red. Their escape had been at the expense of others' lives. Guilt was very far from his mind.

He saw the yellow cloud of steam behind them rising and spreading in the air. *This is not normal. What sort of a river is this? You would think it's not water at all. It's more like liquid sulfur. Boiling liquid sulfur.*

They did not slow down.

Godànor urged the night-mares on; they protested noisily at the vicious blows of the whip, but kept running, their sparking hooves drumming on the ground and scattering the bone pellets of the road surface.

They left the densely populated city and reached the outskirts to find waves of refugees on the move.

Polòtain commanded his grandson not to let up and not to spare the animals. "Take the right fork!" he shouted, seeing the first groups of älfar on the narrow path that led to the top of the crater. *Not too many of them as yet. That will soon change.*

After a few miles Godànor halted the carriage where the path started to climb. His way was barred with a jostling horde of people. "We're here!" announced Godànor.

Polòtain wondered whether he should try the ascent on one of the night-mares, but decided on another tack. He got out of the vehicle and joined the ranks of the fleeing multitude together with Godànor.

He felt hot despite the winter temperature. He was being pushed and shoved and no one seemed to respect his name or his rank. It was each to his own.

Progress was so slow. It was an age before they had reached the first of the steps. He had no idea how much time had passed. *One, two splinters of unendingness?* He forced himself up the narrow stairs, reckoning he and Godànor were now perhaps a dozen paces above the ground.

Looking back, he could see the wave flooding through Dsôn accompanied by the yellow cloud of gas; the hissing sound was audible even at this distance. Where the flood hit, whole buildings were dissolving. *That is not ordinary river water!*

Before the river, walls, wood, whatever the material, disintegrated. Edifice after edifice was affected, as were the älfar in the streets. Every object. Every living creature. All was caught up in the flow, surrounded and liquefying. This was the process that was causing the clouds of gas.

The first fumes reached the escaping crowds. Polòtain coughed. The smell was like sulfur: it made your eyes smart and your mouth burn . . . *It's acid! How can a river turn into acid?*

The älfar screamed in horror as they realized what fate had in store for them.

Those at the base of the slope started to push and shove their way onto the path that meant safety. Pressure from below brought the first casualties, as those on the steps lost their balance and tumbled. Where they fell on the waiting throng below there were injuries and deaths.

Polòtain grasped hold of Godànor and pushed his way up, his back pressed into the wall of rock. They were hardly making any progress. *Ye gods of infamy! The whole city is dissolving!*

The yellowish liquid flowed on a wide path, as if savoring the destruction. The outermost fingers of the river reached the feet of the crowd. Älfar screamed out and fell. No one falling into the flood emerged again. Some tried to survive by clambering up on top of abandoned vehicles or up into the branches of trees, but there was no protection.

Polòtain's supposition proved true; it was indeed acid. He could see that quite clearly. Wagons disintegrated, night-mares struggled through the lethal mass as half skeletons, the flesh burned off their bones.

The yellow clouds thickened, obscuring his view. He could not stop coughing. Every breath he took seemed to steal more air from his lungs. All around him the fleeing hordes were choking.

Polòtain felt his senses leave him. His legs turned to jelly. "Help me, Godànor!" he groaned. He was near suffocation in the poisonous fumes; he slipped down despite Godànor's grip. "Please! Please don't let go of me!"

He slipped out of his grandson's hold, fell, and was kicked and trampled by strangers and forced aside. Some climbed over him, shoes struck him in the head and in his ribs. Someone stood on his wrist, fracturing it.

Finally he rolled over the crumbling edge of the path and plunged down through the toxic mist until he crashed on to something solid. Through watering eyes he saw it was the roof of a coach that was floating in the yellow lake, foaming and fizzing as it dissolved.

A large, glass barrel-like object drifted past; there were fflecx symbols on the side, but he could not work out what they meant. *Is it them? Have the alchemancers diverted the river and poisoned it? I thought they were all dead?*

With a crunch and a crack the carriage split and the wreck tilted precariously.

Next to him bodies fell into the acid; älfar who had fallen from the slope shrieked as they died in torture. The harsh biting fumes would ensure no one reached the safety of the top of the crater. Not a single inhabitant of Dsôn would survive this splinter of unendingness.

Dsôn Faïmon's Black Heart is lost! What has happened to the Inextinguishables? Polòtain's hands had been in contact with the burning substance and his fingertips were hissing as they melted away, revealing the white bones. He screamed and coughed, spitting blood.

The worst thing was the realization that his single-minded pursuit of Sinthoras through the courts had probably saved his sworn enemy's life. *If only Sinthoras had stayed, if only the hearing had taken longer, then at least he would have ended up in this lethal brew!*

Choking again, he fought for air. *When I think of everything I have done! Is this my reward? I only wanted justice for Robonor! This is how I am repaid!* His surroundings turned into a single yellow surface with no recognizable contours.

Our gods have all abandoned us. Polòtain rolled over and dived headfirst and open-mouthed into the deadly acid lake so as to shorten his suffering.

Tark Draan (Girdlegard), southeast of the Gray Mountains, Gwandalur, 4372nd division of unendingness (5200th solar cycle), winter.

That night, Virssagòn drew close to the mountain where elves and dragons lived; since the confrontation with the lone elf-warrior he had no more contact with the enemy. *He must be dead by now, even if the poison takes a little time. The fact he ran away from me will only have postponed his death.*

He was close to the foot of the mountain. The walls of rock rose sheer and sharp into the sky and pointed crags reared out of the stone. Sturdy trees had wound their roots around the rocks. It reminded him of the new tear of Inàste that had grown in the crater.

I wonder where the cavern entrance is? Virssagòn began to work his way around the base of the mountain. He kept to the shadows so as not to be seen by any nearby sentries. His night-mare had been left in a nearby wood so that the creature's red eyes would not betray his presence.

This time he really wanted to succeed.

He was dismayed at not having rid Girdlegard of all of its mages. *Maybe I was just too slow in carrying out the plan? But I don't see how I could have managed it any quicker; the distances were simply too great.*

Grok-Tmai had been the next name on his death list, but the magus had been forewarned by the deceitful Hianna, and Virssagòn had assumed there would be a trap, so he avoided that confrontation. Disposing of sorcerers was more or less impossible if the intended victims had prior knowledge of the attempt.

If Morana had kept out of it and let me kill Hianna in the first place, I'd have been filling my trophy collection with bits of the other wizards, but I'll make up for it by wiping out the elves.

The Ishím Voróo barbarians he had recruited would be arriving from the southeast within the next splinter of unendingness, Virssagòn reckoned, and he would need them for the assault on the mountain; he had told them he was going to open up an entrance for them.

Of course, that was a lie.

His real intention was to find out whether the cold weather actually did prevent dragons from functioning. It did not matter that the barbarians would die, of course, and the test would give him valuable information about these scaled creatures.

Dragons. Tark Draan is truly a cauldron of surprises. He tried to remember when he had heard of these airborne lizards last appearing in Ishím Voróo. In his own lifetime there certainly had not been any dragon issues—no serious altercations. His people avoided them wherever possible, knowing them to be devious and untrustworthy; their powerful wings made them unpredictable adversaries.

I seem to recall one of our armies slew a dragon in the west of Ishím Voróo when the beast had tried to demand tribute. That must have been a dozen or more divisions of unendingness ago. Virssagòn spat. *The elves do the same thing with the barbarians around here.*

He had verified the scouts' reports on this matter: the peasants he had come across so far had spoken of the elves as a pestilence; they longed to be free of them, but did not have the courage to take up arms against them. Understandable.

Having got a third of the way around the base of the mountain using the bushes and shrubs as cover, he saw the entrance: a gate big enough for a dragon to pass through. It was locked and had a yellow metal cladding to reinforce it. *I'll take a closer look.*

He went nearer and soon he could detect the relief pattern on the metal by starlight. On it, some kind of deity was creating the dragon and an elf simultaneously. This presumably indicated that the elves were just as divine as the dragons they flew around on.

It must be pure gold! There were precious gems set into the metal, testimony to the wealth of the elves. Diamonds sparkled in the moonlight, giving off rainbow shimmers. Virssagòn knew of races in Ishím Voróo who would happily go to war for the value of this gate.

Above the gate there were broad arrow slits with firelight flickering through. The elves had fashioned the cliff by the entrance to look like a dragon: the gate formed a huge muzzle.

A dragon cult: formed to worship the scaly creatures of light and the children of Sitalia. Virssagòn crouched low in the shadow of the mountain. *Quite some elves!*

He looked up, scanning the rock face, searching for an opportunity to get inside. He could see light shining higher up on a platform. *Those will be lamps for the sentries. Or . . . could that be where the dragons come in to land? Can they take off at night, I wonder?*

Those lamps could be a navigational aid; if so, the dragons were indeed capable of flight in the winter months.

The next opening, again with a stone platform in front of it, was much farther up, above the gate, but he wouldn't be able to climb that: his armor was heavy and hardly suitable for rock-climbing.

Well, then, maybe I'll get in through the apertures their archers fire from. That would only mean climbing a short way. He could not decide.

If he were spotted inside the elf stronghold, there would be no chance of escape. He knew his own capabilities and weaknesses. He was no fool. He was not about to underestimate an enemy whose numbers he could not even guess at. *Fools are always the first to die.*

He made his decision and began to make his way forward, darting from shadow to shadow. He did not wish to overuse his älfar powers at this stage. The bright snowfields surrounding the mountain were the worst possible surroundings for an undercover älf. Creating areas of shadow and spreading clouds of darkness would immediately attract unwelcome attention.

As he reached the gate he listened carefully, taking only shallow breaths.

There was no sound. The sentries above the gate were apparently still unworried, even though the Golden Plain had been invaded. *A further example of the confidence the elves place in their dragons.*

Let's get on. Virssagòn examined the immediate vicinity, looking for jutting sections and any cracks that would afford toeholds. He found a possible route up the cliff and made a start on the ascent.

He was only a short way up when a piece of rock came away under his gauntlet.

He twisted around as he fell and landed on his feet, absorbing the impact with a somersault. He had not made any noise as he fell and there was only a small *crunch* of snow as he landed.

But the little landslide of stones that followed him alerted the sentries.

Lamps approached the arrow slits and voices were heard. Searchlights shone down from the battlements.

I am no mountaineer. Virssagòn had no option but to use his powers to avoid being spotted. He dimmed the elf lights, and enveloped himself in shadow as he pressed his body flat against the cliff.

He heard a deep clattering sound and then the noise of eighteen bolts being drawn back. One half of the gate creaked open a little way. The elves had become wary and wanted to check to see what was happening outside.

Virssagòn launched himself into the air and clung to the golden dragon claws on the decorative relief. He climbed two or three paces higher while the elf sentries below him stepped out through the gate. *They will find my tracks and sound the alarm.*

He knew he had to get inside—the sentries had relieved him of the choice.

He clambered sideways to reach the edge of the open gate in order to slip around to the inside. When the gate was closed he would be hanging above the sentries' heads. He would only have to wait until they went away.

The elves found his footprints and shouted to the bowmen in the alcoves above.

Samusin, don't let them see me! He maintained the aura of darkness he had surrounded himself with, but if they looked directly at him, or used strong torchlight, his presence would be revealed.

Roving cones of light as wide as a tree canopy lit up the whole area, stamping dazzling circles on the snow. The searchlight beams wandered over the snow as the elves attempted to locate the intruder.

Looking up, Virssagòn realized that rotating machines composed of many lamps and huge mirrors were producing these beams. *Good job I didn't decide to run away. I would not have got far.*

A second armed troop of elves passed below him, leaving the shelter of the mountain and following his prints. An älf in leather protective clothing would leave no tracks, but Virssagòn's penchant for heavy armor meant his feet would sink into a soft surface such as snow.

He continued on his way around the edge of the gate.

The sentries withdrew into the mountain while the search party followed his tracks. The gate creaked slowly shut. Virssagòn had to make haste now if he was not to be squashed; it was no easy thing to get around the edge of the gate and he could feel no ornamentation on the other side to give him a handhold.

The opening was getting very narrow.

I'll have to risk it, but if there's nothing to grip on the inside, I'll fall at their feet. He swung around to the back of the gate just as it clanged shut.

A broad retaining timber that strengthened the gate structure provided the handhold he needed. He hung there swaying to and fro like a flag until he could pull himself up on to the horizontal wooden strut.

The guards were not looking for him inside the complex. They moved off through a vast hall and disappeared through a side door. Virssagòn could hear them walking up some stairs.

He breathed a sigh of relief. However, the incident would mean all the elves were alert and on their guard. He might have to wait several moments of unendingness before things calmed down again.

But tomorrow the barbarians will be attacking. The elves will assume their intruder was a scout sent by the humans and they'll forget about me. It'll be fine. I'll just have to be patient. He looked around. *I'd prefer somewhere else to wait, though. I'm too easy to spot up here.*

He slid down, jumped lightly to the ground and ran to the side of the hall. There was a passage leading straight on; Virssagòn took it.

This brought him to the bottom of a vertical shaft incorporating a spiral ramp hewn out of the rock.

Virssagòn assumed the ramp would permit an injured dragon to get safely back into the interior of the mountain if no longer able to fly. And horsemen and vehicles could use it without any need for a lift. *Clever idea.*

Nothing about the inside of the mountain looked hastily conceived and every inch of the walls was decorated with symbols or murals. Elf art was not to his taste, but he had to admit that the elves were a whole lot better at handicrafts than the groundlings. They could almost compete with the skills and aesthetics of the älfar. The mountain must have served the elves as a home for many, many divisions of unendingness.

Something else struck him: how quiet it was.

The alarm must have only alerted those elves on sentry duty; the rest of them were likely to still be asleep.

I'm not complaining. Virssagòn went up the ramp and farther into the mountain's interior.

The upper stories were arranged in circles with frequent openings off the central shaft. He took one of the corridors, listening out. He could hear the sounds of sleepers moving, low conversations, a little music. Sometimes there would be a smell of food, or else fragrant oils. The walls, as in the main hall, were smooth and polished in places. The floor was either made of flagstones or covered in carpets. The higher he got, the more opulent it became—the residents of the top floors had taken much more care with the ornamentation and comfort.

Virssagòn assumed the lower regions were reserved for soldier elves who would not care so much about luxury.

The ramp ascended through many hundreds of paces; small lamps on the walls spread a pleasant red glow.

At last he reached an area where there were no living quarters. The passageways were wider and he could hear chains clanking. There was a loud, deep snorting very close by, as if a huge bellows was being worked. The air had an acrid smell and a wave of heat swept toward him.

Ah! I have located the dragon. He started to feel nervous.

His knowledge of dragons was restricted to what he had learned from legend. He did not know how refined their sense of smell might be and he had no idea what the creatures were capable of, or in what ways they might be vulnerable. He did not even know where their hearts were located. For a warrior such as himself, who always made sure he was well informed about any adversary, this was an unsatisfactory state of affairs.

Virssagòn crept along the first corridor he came to, always following the sound of the creature's breathing.

He saw a small door, which he opened carefully.

Two elves lay in their beds. The room smelled of leather and metal. He could see leatherware such as belts, bridles, harnesses and reins. There were also iron rings and hooks; presumably all the equipment needed for controlling a dragon in flight. It was like a tack room.

Those will be the dragon-riders. He left their chamber, silently closing the door, and moved on.

The temperature and the smell increased. He started to sweat.

On his right he saw iron bars. In front of the metal grating there was a series of pulleys, and levers and chains went up to the roof and through the rock: it was a cage.

The dragon slept in its enclosure, anchored by metal bands, its wings kept clamped to its sides. It lay on a bed of hot ash and glowing coals, its head resting on its short front legs. Its eyes were closed.

Virssagòn calculated the creature's torso must be a good eight paces long and its coiled tail was probably the same length when extended, though its head and neck were relatively short. The scales shimmered grayish white in the light of the glowing coals. There was a two-seater saddle suspended above the dragon's back.

Of course they can fly in winter! Virssagòn scowled. His mission here was suddenly gaining in significance.

Chapter XXIII

Snow
falls silently.
Covering the bodies
of those who died
in battle.

Blood
flows silently
Seeping from the bodies
of those
who took no care.

Death
comes silently.
It slips past the fires
of those who are afraid
of the night.

Excerpt from the epic poem *The Heroes of Tark Draan*
composed by Carmondai, master of word and image

Ishím Voróo (Outer Lands), Dsôn Faïmon, between
the radial arms Wèlèron and Avaris,
4371ˢᵗ/ 4372ⁿᵈ divisions of unendingness (5199ᵗʰ/ 5200ᵗʰ solar cycles),
winter.

Téndalor took up his bow and notched a long, dark arrow, pulling back
the string until his recently healed wounds smarted. *Die!*

His fingers released their hold and the missile shot off, striking the
dorón ashont directly through the slits of his helmet. The target, the last
of the dorón ashont still standing in the breach of the walls, already had
several arrows sticking out of his torso, but it was Téndalor's steel-tipped
arrow that finished him off. He swayed and eventually landed on top of
his dead comrades.

Téndalor gave a whoop of joy at his success and clambered, together
with several of his colleagues, over the enormous corpse. *I'll soon have
control of the island fortress once more. I've won it back from you.*

Still balancing on the remains of the collapsed wall, he stopped in
surprise: a whole section of land was missing. The water that had been
in the defense moat was pouring down into a yawning abyss and clouds
of steam rose up, soaking his face and shimmering in the moonlight.
He had assumed the sound of the river was the noise of catapults firing. *They have excavated a huge hole and are emptying the defense moat!
Do they still have an army in Ishím Voróo?*

Aïsolon appeared at his side. Noting the cavity, he immediately commanded his troops to withdraw. There were no dents on his armor, but
plenty of yellow and red splashes of blood. "There are no enemies left to
defeat. Off to Dsôn! Fast!"

"Why have the dorón ashont done that to the defense moat? What
did they hope to gain by it?" Téndalor asked. "Where's the water going?"

Aïsolon's expression showed deep concern. "It is flowing into the bed of
an ancient waterway. The river was there at the time our ancestors founded
the city, but they diverted it and used the water to feed the defense canal."
He turned and ran off. "We must get to Dsôn and warn the inhabitants!"

The underground river leads to the Black Heart? Téndalor had a metallic taste in his mouth. He tried to swallow, but could not.

The defense moat had lost a good half of its water, but three rivers fed it, so it had not gone dry.

Téndalor considered the geography of the star-shaped realm. *Dsôn will fill up first, like a bathtub, and then the radial arms will flood!* "Aïsolon! We have to block the hole they have dug!"

The commander of the army looked back at him. "Can you explain exactly how you would do that? Soil would be washed away at once. The water pressure is too strong. Dsôn needs to be warned and then we'll have to leave it up to the experts to find a solution. We can't stop the flood." He raced off.

Téndalor's entire body felt numb and he could hardly walk. He grabbed the next riderless night-mare and rode as quickly as he could in the direction of the capital, hard on Aïsolon's heels.

The animal he had taken moved quickly. Before he knew it Téndalor found himself at the head of the column racing to Dsôn.

He caught up with Aïsolon. "How did the dorón ashont know about the old river bed?" he called. "How come we didn't know about it? Why did we wait so long before attacking?" Even as the commander of an island fortress he had not known about the diverted river.

"Perhaps their forefathers made charts of the region? I expect they have already taken the rest of their army along the dry river bed." Aïsolon looked extremely worried. "This will not end well, Téndalor! Water is more powerful than any catapult when it comes to inflicting damage!"

He knows my name! The elation, however, was short-lived. In his imagination he could see the dorón ashont lined up in a circle around the crater, smiting any of the älfar who managed to escape the rising waters.

Side by side they galloped over the plain. Their night-mares sensed the urgency and did not falter in their headlong race, though the sweat foamed at their sides.

The sun rose and showed the älfar a sulfurous yellow cloud hovering over the site of the city.

Téndalor and Aïsolon approached from the northwest. The entirety of the dorón ashont's army waited on the crater's edge. The front ranks were looking down into the crater, while at their feet a broad waterfall poured into the basin.

Téndalor reined in his night-mare and looked down on his homeland. The sight that greeted him left him horrified: Dsôn no longer existed.

Yellowish vapor drifted over a bubbling cauldron of dark liquid. Even if the level of the water was not especially high, it had been enough to swallow up every tower and spire. Not a single building or roof was to be seen. Not even the Inextinguishables' famous Tower of Bones. There was nothing to suggest the Black Heart of Dsôn Faïmon had ever stood in this place. There was only a seething expanse of hissing, foaming liquid.

"It's acid," said Aïsolon, completely at a loss. "Oh ye gods of infamy! They transformed the river into acid." He stared at the dorón ashont. There were hundreds of them now: the enemy's banners fluttered in the breeze high above the center of the älfar realm. "Ye gods! They have done away with the entire city and its people. It's all dissolved!"

Téndalor shuddered at the thought of the intense fear the fleeing älfar must have experienced. *If I had been able to hold my island fortress, none of this would have happened. They would all still be alive. I bear the death of thousands of älfar on my soul.* The faces of friends he had lost paraded past his inner eye, staring accusingly at him. He did not know how to react to this immeasurable disaster. "Aïsolon . . . kill me," he whispered.

"What?"

"I . . . They were only able to put their plan into action because I failed to hold the island fortress."

Aïsolon shook his head. "No. I shall need you. You will ride against the dorón ashont at the head of our army. If you survive the battle, the gods will have forgiven you." He pointed to the yellow waters. "The acid will have reached the radial arms. The life of every remaining älf is vitally important now. Who knows how many of us there are left?" He pulled his mount's head around. "Get back to the army. We must defeat the dorón ashont—they shall all die!"

Fadhasi, you are an unforgiving deity. Téndalor drew his dagger and scratched out the tiny symbol on his armor. *You saved me from the waters once, only to heap shame and guilt on my shoulders.* He followed his leader.

They had covered a quarter of a mile when cracks started appearing in the snow and clouds of yellow gas began venting from them. Riding through these fumes gave him a coughing fit and he felt as if he were about to suffocate. Even his mount was suffering badly from the toxic steam and slowed its pace. The acid air stung his eyes.

"The ground is breaking up under our feet!" croaked Aïsolon. "Ride quickly!"

They urged their night-mares on as parts of the ground fell away under their hooves. The animals stumbled frequently, but somehow managed to keep upright; miraculously, neither of the älfar was thrown.

At last they reached terrain where the cracks were less defined and they were able to regain solid ground.

The night-mares had reached the limits of their endurance and their legs were shaking. Téndalor's mount collapsed first, followed by Aïsolon's, but the riders were lucky enough to jump clear, landing on soft earth as their animals fell.

Téndalor looked south toward the dorón ashont.

Their army was running for its life. The huge creatures were leaping over the cracks opening in the ground, disappearing by the dozen in the gaping chasms, swallowed up in the steam.

Samusin punish them! Slay them all!

"Let us give death a helping hand," said Aïsolon grimly.

The älfar took their bows and sent their arrows winging toward the Towers that Walk. The injuries they were able to inflict on their targets were sufficient to slow them down, and those that slowed fell victim to the chasms in the rock.

Of all of the dorón ashont, only the nimblest were able to escape the horrors of the turbulent earth—but then the whole region sank with a tremendous rumbling noise, taking the last enemies of the älfar with it.

"Samusin be praised!" Aïsolon lowered his bow.

I give no praise to Samusin. The deaths of the dorón ashont could never make up for the loss of all the älfar who had died.

Aïsolon inspected his exhausted animal. "We can't wait until our mounts recover." He pointed north. "We must make our way on foot to rejoin the army and report what has happened." He strode away, followed by Téndalor.

"And what happens now?"

"You have survived the battle," replied Aïsolon. "The gods of infamy have decided you are not to lose your life."

Perhaps I do owe my survival to the gods of infamy, but what value do I put on this life of mine? "No. I meant: what of our people? Our whole race?"

"That will be our next task, Téndalor. We must locate the Inextinguishables and ask them."

"But . . . if they were in the Tower—"

"They are called the *Inextinguishables*. Do you understand? They bear that name with good reason." Aïsolon's words were confident and convincing. "Our army will keep their eyes open for any survivors and set up a camp for them. After that we'll have to think about ways to stop that river so that we may rebuild the city of Dsôn."

Téndalor hoped that the Inextinguishables still existed, so that the surviving älfar might be shown a way out of this disastrous situation. Without their rulers, he felt, their race was doomed.

Tark Draan (Girdlegard), southeast of the Gray Mountains, to the east of the former Golden Plain, 4372nd division of unendingness (5200th solar cycle), winter.

The dragon flew in overhead and snatched the dead elf. Carmondai looked up from his prone position. The creature rose back up to the skies with powerful strokes of its wings, making snow swirl through the air.

That was a close shave. Why did the dragon not go for me? Carmondai stood up and brushed the snow from his clothing. *Will it be coming back?* He scanned the horizon.

The dragon, flying east and as small as a bird now, soon disappeared entirely.

It looks like I'm safe. Carmondai surveyed his surroundings. *I ought to explore the village. There won't be many barbarians left if Virssagòn passed this way.*

He returned to the plantation and crossed it to reach his night-mare. Two barbarian corpses lay on the ground at the feet of the creature. They had bite marks in their throats and their torsos were half-consumed. Steaming guts hung out of the night-mare's muzzle.

Lack of caution is death to a stupid man. Carmondai led the night-mare over to a group of huts, sword in hand, ready to fight, but there was no one there to attack him. Not even a dog barking, which was just as well: he did not like dogs; they stank and dribbled and hardly ever obeyed—and they would betray their master for a piece of meat.

A strange tower stood in the middle of the huts. The snow just at its base had melted and Carmondai could feel warmth issuing from the walls. He moved around it and discovered a wheel-operated iron trap that a handcart could pass through. There was a ramp constructed of bricks leading up to the trap.

What is this? Curious, Carmondai began to work the mechanism.

The trap opened and a room appeared. Sparks as big as his hand flew out of the door—the heat was intense. Carmondai took a few steps up the ramp to look inside.

A thin layer of coals had been spread on the ground and dragon manure was burning, polluting the atmosphere with an acrid smell.

It's a warming tower. Perhaps this is how the dragons are able to function even in winter: these towers prevent their blood from thickening.

If there were more buildings like this, the elves would be able to use their dragons all winter long. This meant they could attack the älfar army whenever they felt like it.

He sketched the tower with its upper extension; did a drawing of the dragon from memory and another of the kind of armor the elves wore. He drew every small detail that could prove useful.

He was surprised that Virssagòn had left the little tower standing. *What is his game? Has he found out more than I have?*

Even though the thought made him uneasy, Carmondai decided to spend the night in the hamlet—he could explore further and report back to the nostàroi.

He looked in the houses and discovered footprints indicating that any barbarians who might have been there, had left. *Were they afraid of Virssagòn? But he would have left a trail of blood and there is none to be seen. Or have they run away for fear of the dragon?*

He chose the largest of the huts, one with two rooms, and having put his night-mare in the shelter out front, made himself a bed in the loft. He felt safer from attack up there should anyone approach the village, and his night-mare would warn him if there were any nocturnal visitors—and with any luck eat them on sight.

Tark Draan (Girdlegard), Gray Mountains,
4372ⁿᵈ division of unendingness (5200ᵗʰ solar cycle),
winter.

"Keep an eye on furnaces number six and seven; the pressure's quite high and we don't want the substance overcooking." *Too many duties are the enemy of perfection.* Durùston strode like a commander between rows of groundling smelting ovens. Since the älfar victory these furnaces had been serving a very different function.

The boilers were ranged in rows to the right and to the left, and each one had coals glowing white-hot under them, fanned by the huge bellows. Durùston's apprentices and serfs busied themselves throughout the hall by checking the contents simmering in the containers.

"Crew to boiler number four: the elf bones should be ready now. Prepare to drain the vessel." He looked up at the air vent; the stinking steam was collecting in front of it. "Send a couple of mechanics up to check what's happening with the vent. *We're* practically being broiled alive, let alone the remains of our enemies."

Everyone in the vicinity broke into laughter.

Durùston wiped his face; drops of sweat splashed onto his thick brown leather apron. *I could do with double the number of boilers and twice as many assistants.*

He knew that, back in Dsôn, the population were keen on owning souvenirs collected from the victory over the elves, whether they be bone ornaments, strings of beads or rings. In fact, with the extra raw material the nostàroi kept sending him—barbarians and elves rounded up from the furthest corners of the Golden Plain—he could barely keep up with demand.

Some of the delays were his own fault: he had extremely high standards and was fully aware that each finished piece would impact on his reputation, so he would not sign off a work until satisfied that it could not be improved.

Time to check on the smithy. Pulling off the leather cap that protected his hair from the sparks, he left the fume-filled hall and went into the smithy next door, where an agitated blond älf awaited him. This newcomer had arrived only a few moments of unendingness before. Durùston knew he was one of Khlotòn's nephews, but could not remember the young älf's name. *It was his uncle's influence that made me accept him, rather than any natural talent.*

"I have made a discovery!" the blond älf called excitedly, running off.

Durùston stood still and watched him go. "Can I see it from where I am, or do you expect me to come after you?" He was not in the best of moods. He was intensely dissatisfied with something he was working on. He had everything he needed to create a work of art no one in Dsôn could match—in particular the beautiful captives from the Golden Plain, but today he had no inspiration. Someone brought him a beaker of water and he downed it in one. *What's the fellow's name, for pity's sake?*

"Forgive me," called the blond älf, still beside himself with excitement. He had returned with a small pot in his right hand and a carved bone in the other. The small container held a viscous fluid that looked rather like quicksilver. "Here!"

"I can't see anything worth getting excited about," Durùston grumbled.

The älf placed the pot down, knelt on the flagstones and spread a layer of the paint on the bone. He blew on it gently and passed it to Durùston, eyes gleaming with enthusiasm. "It's dry! And it is—"

"Silvery." Durùston accepted the piece. "So what? I've seen quick-drying paint before . . ." He fell silent. His fingers skimmed the section that had been treated. *Metal?* He flicked it with his fingernail, producing a slight ringing tone. He stared at the elf disbelievingly. "Give me the pot." When it was handed over he noticed immediately that it was lukewarm to the touch. *It's not molten metal.*

"It hardens at blood heat," the other explained.

"Tell me your name."

"Khlotònior. I've done a few experiments with it."

"You developed this yourself?" Duruston applied some of the substance to another part of the bone he was holding. He watched as it instantly hardened, then he dropped the bone and stamped on it with the heel of his boot. The bone crumbled and turned to powder, but the new layer, thin as a leaf, only changed its shape slightly, flexing and becoming longer and thinner. *That's it! It's just what I've been looking for.*

"It was pure chance, I must admit, master." Khlotònior stepped back respectfully. "I was cleaning out the last of the molds the dwarves had in their stores, to see if we could use them. I heated the contents and poured it all into a collecting vessel. And *that's* what happened." He indicated the little pot. "I didn't do anything special. I just noticed the luster and the texture. That's why I tried—"

"Yes. All right." Duruston had gathered that it was not going to be possible to recreate the special qualities of this substance. He took the hardened metal from the floor and placed it in a clean mold, which he put on the glowing coals of the nearest forge. Before long the substance had vaporized. *It cannot be used again. Excellent.* "How much of it is there?"

"A large bucketful, master." Khlotònior had been watching Duruston's experiment. "I hung it up over the fire so that it would not solidify." He pointed over to the right.

Duruston nodded. "Well done. From now on you will have the vital task of checking out all the smithies and forges in the Gray Mountains and bringing me any more of this that you find. Find the molds they used, and, if need be, find yourself some groundlings to help you work out what has formed this compound."

Khlotònior was bold enough to attempt to voice an objection. "But . . . Master Duruston, I wanted to be apprenticed to you so that I could learn how to metallize bone."

Duruston laughed cruelly. "We do not die. There is plenty of time. Find me more of this marvelous stuff first and then I can still get around to making a sculptor out of you."

"That won't make my uncle very happy."

"It is up to an apprentice to carry out all the unpleasant tasks." *And if you annoy me, I could send your blessed uncle a special sculpture entirely composed of your body parts.* Durùston dismissed him with a gesture.

Khlotònior bowed and withdrew.

I hope I never see him again. The groundlings might capture him. Or kill him and there'd be one less idiot cluttering the place up. Sculptor, indeed! Durùston went over to where the bucket hung and looked at the fluid silver compound. *It needs a name. I'll call it durùsilver.*

And he knew exactly what he was going to use it for.

Hurrying out, he ordered two of his trusted workers to mind the bucket, and set off again to the part of the mountain where he stored his creations.

He crossed one hall after another that were full of finished ornaments made from bone, coats of arms, candlesticks, ceiling pendants and wall panels, all waiting to be transported back to the homeland. Some of them had inlays in gold or some other less precious metal; some were set with gems. The groundlings had certainly hoarded enough of these things and Durùston was putting them to better use—they no longer sat in boxes and chests where no one could see them.

He was proud of what he and his apprentices had already produced, but he was eager to take on the challenge of using a newly discovered material. *It will serve my creative urges well. It shall be a splendid gift for the Inextinguishables.*

Durùston reached a door where four heavily armed älfar stood guard. "Bring her to me!" he ordered impatiently.

As the door opened, a thick wall of stale air escaped from the room behind. The commander of the watch disappeared through the door and came back with a female elf. Her curly blond hair framed her face like an aura and her wrists were bound with chains. She looked exhausted. Her only garment was a thin linen vest.

"Shall I come with you?" the guard asked as he handed the Durùston the end of the chain.

"No. I'll manage." Durùston set off. He could hardly wait to try out his idea. He made the elf walk slightly ahead of him so that he could keep an eye on her. She could not escape, but he wanted to ensure there were no surprises.

They had hardly crossed the first hall containing the *objets d'art* when her pace slackened. She moaned when she saw the skulls and bones. She seemed to be saying a prayer.

The elves' language is obnoxious. "I think your friends have done quite well, all things considered. Being made into art is better than dying on the battlefield and then turning into food for the vultures." He laughed. "They will have pride of place on an älfar cupboard, or the wall of a nice warm kitchen. It's another form of immortality, really, my pretty one."

The elf turned her head and spat at him. The gobbet landed on his leather apron.

"Aprons are always useful." Durùston gave her a shove and she stumbled back against a pillar made of bone. He pointed at it. "I needed the bones of one hundred of your kind for that. Do you want the details of how I made it?" He laughed again when he saw the disgusted expression on her face. "You simply don't know how to appreciate art, obviously."

He pushed her into his chamber and had her washed and scrubbed. Inspecting her flawless body he tried to choose. *Clothed or naked?* He decided on a nude version and led her back to the workshop, where he handed the chain to one of his apprentices.

"Take her to the center of the room," he instructed, kicking over a low wooden platform for her to stand on.

The two älfar put her in position. Durùston took down the bucket from where it had been hanging over the fire and collected a metal ladle and a paintbrush, which he hooked through the strings on his apron. The special compound was lukewarm. *This will be my first piece of art working on living material. First and last.*

He turned around and walked up to the elf. He noted no trace of fear on her face. Her expression was one of revulsion. "I am Durùston, one of the most celebrated artists Dsôn has to offer. With your help, I am now going to be the best," he told her. He poured some of the compound over her feet and the raised stand; it tinkled as it solidified. Now the elf-girl was securely anchored to the floor. "You can let go of her now, and remove her chains."

His workers did as they were bid and then stepped aside.

She seemed not to feel any pain and the process continued without incident, but her face changed as she realized what he was intending to do.

"My first idea was to get you to drink it and after that I was going to remove your flesh, but that would be a waste." With the ladle in hand he walked behind her and poured a generous portion down her back.

He watched, fascinated, as the liquid flowed over her shoulder blades and down her spine, adapting to every slight contour. The fluid even entered her pores.

She tried to squirm free, but the hardening metal prevented any movement. Pinioned, she groaned, and redoubled her efforts, but the armor casing was too strong. She screamed.

Perfect! Durùston applied a second ladleful, a third, a fourth, over shoulders, thighs, and rump.

With each application the elf became less of a living being and more of a statue fighting to resist immobility. The viscous substance flowed over her body before quickly hardening. Her struggles gradually ceased.

Durùston brought out his brush and guided the paint to any areas not yet covered, transforming the elf into a silver mannequin. He left her head untreated.

It makes every muscle stand out so clearly. And the tendons! Beside himself with artistic fervor, he stroked the fine bristles meticulously over the last few blank places on her upper and lower body. *This way I can preserve every intricate detail.*

He would not be distracted as he worked on the metamorphosis.

The silver paint in the bucket was running dangerously low.

Durùston stood up and looked her in the eyes. "Are you ready to die?" *This has to work!* He took a deep breath. "You will be my masterpiece," he whispered. Before she could answer, he poured a ladleful of silver into her mouth, stopping up her throat instantaneously. She gradually suffocated.

I must not miss the opportunity! Durùston held the brush poised; he watched her eyes intently, waiting for the arrival of death.

There was an alteration in the pupils.

Now! Durùston brushed the paint over her face at that very instant. "Yes!" he cried excitedly, covering the rest of her countenance with the metal. "I have captured death!" He was about to cover her hair, but the container was practically empty. There was just enough left to anoint the hairline, while her locks stayed blond.

Durùston was pleased with this effect. He was suddenly aware that all his apprentices had entered the studio. He hurled his ladle, brush and the bucket into the furnace, where the remaining durùsilver smoked and vaporized.

"Look at what I've done!" he enthused. "Look at this masterpiece! I shall be sending it to the Inextinguishables as a gift: Veïnsa, the princess of the Golden Plain, at the exact time of her death!" He gave a contented sigh. *No one can ever emulate this effort.* "Watch her carefully for me," he instructed his most trusted pupils. "Don't let anyone come near."

He left the workshop utterly exhausted and made his way to his rooms. After a short rest, a bath and some food he would compose an explanatory letter to accompany the gift. That way, when it was sent to the Sibling Rulers, they would be able fully to appreciate the work that had gone into the creation of this statue, which was not, of course, a statue at all.

Tark Draan (Girdlegard), to the southeast of
the Gray Mountains, Gwandalur,
4372nd division of unendingness (5200th solar cycle),
winter.

Virssagòn did not sleep that night. He went back to the room with the sleeping elves and haunted their chamber like a living ghost, torturing them with cruel dreams and ruining their sleep. He smiled as he watched them writhe to and fro in their beds, giving out frightened moans.

After a swift search of the rest of the level, he had discovered that this was the only occupied room. The other rooms were empty, but the dragon cells all had scaly occupants.

The two elves are probably on guard duty. If Virssagòn had read the situation correctly, they would be the first to fly out against the barbarian army when it appeared and he did not want to miss seeing that.

As the first rays of sunlight came through the small windows, there came the sound of a gong, followed by an alarm call.

Aha. My barbarians are on their way. Virssagòn quickly left the room and concealed himself near the dragon enclosure to observe the riders saddling their mount.

It was not long before the two elves came running in wrapped in furs with their armor fastened over the top. They wore thick leather headgear topped with helmets secured by chinstraps.

They handled levers and pulleys swiftly in an automatic routine: the saddle was lowered and it clicked into place on the iron framework on the dragon's back, the clamps holding the wings were removed and an elf entering the creature's cage fed leather straps through bolts fastened through the dragon's scales. These were on the head and throat, and around the muzzle; all of them showed scarring and crusts of dried blood. They had been screwed directly into the animal's flesh.

I see! That's how the dragons are steered. It's pain that does it. Virssagòn had to admire the elves' ingenuity.

The second elf swung up into the saddle and checked the arrow quivers and spear holders to see if they had their full complement. While one of the riders piloted the dragon, the other one would operate the weaponry.

The elf who had attached the leather straps spoke to the animal, stroking its head. Then he took his seat. Fishing a lance from the wall he poked it between the bars of the cave and activated a lever on one of the pulleys.

This set the chains in motion and the entrance was revealed. Wind swept in through the opening and Virssagòn caught sight of one of the landing platforms.

The elves each put on belts that would ensure they did not fall out during any violent maneuvers, then hooked something else on to their armor.

What could that be? Virssagòn saw a wire leading from the armor to the dragon's neck, where it was fastened to a bolt, but it didn't look like it had anything to do with the steering. Virssagòn thought for a moment. If the dragon were to lose his rider, the wire would rip out the bolt and probably slit the creature's throat. It looked like an insurance feature. *The elves and the dragons don't trust each other completely.*

The creature's powerful back legs were still chained up. It strained impatiently at its fetters.

The pilot called something out and tugged hard at the reins, causing blood to drip from where the bolts protruded. The dragon immediately became docile—on the surface, at least.

But Virssagòn had read the expression in the creature's eyes: an urgent desire to kill its tormentors. A wild nature, solely constrained by fear of pain. *That's good!*

The lance tip swept around and touched a second lever that would free the chains anchoring the dragon. As soon as the creature was freed, the flight would begin.

Virssagòn came out of the niche, pulled two pointed weapons from the holsters behind his shoulders, and hurled them both at the elves. The custom harness the holsters were attached to was especially helpful: one only had to reach behind one's head, grab and throw; no time was wasted.

The hardened points of the weapons pierced the elves' helmets and penetrated their necks, killing them before they'd had a chance to notice him. They both hung dead in the saddle.

Those safety belts did not help you much. The dragon eyed him suspiciously, apparently able to recognize that Virssagòn was no elf.

"Take a good look, my friend." Virssagòn unfastened the wires from the elves' reinforced jackets and yanked the two corpses out of the saddle. They thumped down on the ground. "Remember, you owe me your liberty," he told the dragon. He did not allow his own nervousness to show while he was close to the dragon's mouth. He pulled the leather reins out, throwing them away. He then lifted the safety wire and removed the loop from its catch.

The slitted eyes of the white-gray dragon followed every move he made.

"Are you interested in avenging yourself on your tormentors, perhaps?" Virssagòn reached through the bars and moved the lever back. Finally, the dragon's back legs were freed. Virssagòn moved to the side to give the dragon room to maneuver. "Shall I go and release your friends?"

The dragon rushed past him and onto the platform. It unfolded its wings and they flapped and cracked as they caught the wind. With a screech the creature launched into the air and out of Virssagòn's field of vision. He heard another loud cry and a whooshing sound, then silence returned.

He was disappointed. *It would have been too good to be true. It would have saved me a lot of work.*

The gong sounded again.

The elves will send out replacements. I should get going. He ran back through the corridor and up the ramp toward the other dragon cells.

It was lucky for Virssagòn that the other guardrooms were not occupied. He freed half a dozen of the scaled creatures at his leisure. Like the gray-white one they all took to the skies and never looked back at their mountain prison.

They had obviously been mistreated, so Virssagòn had secretly hoped at least one of the dragons would respond to his kind words and become an ally, but this did not happen. He slit the throat of two of the dragons while they were still chained—it would not do to give them too many troops to fight with, for who knew which army they would turn on?

He left the dragon quarters and looked out into the corridor, inching his way forward. *Ah, here they come,* he thought, looking down.

The elves had realized what was happening and were swarming, armed, into the corridors. It would be almost impossible for him to avoid them. Ten were heading straight for where he stood.

The sun was climbing in the sky and sent its rays, reflected off upright mirrors, deep into the interior of the mountain. He would not be able to hug the shadows any longer.

I shall wait until the barbarians attack before deciding on my next course of action. I should be able to avoid capture until then. Virssagòn concealed himself in one of the empty dragon cells. He stepped out onto the platform to watch events on the battlefield unfold.

The barbarians advanced on three fronts in double rows: a strategy designed to conserve energy. The humans at the front beat the snow down to help those bringing up the rear. They had brought ladders with them, but it had not been possible to construct heavy siege equipment in the short time available. Of course, the barbarians were working on the assumption that Virssagòn was going to open up the entrance for them. *Try praying to your gods; you'll need their support.*

Below him and above, riders piloted the rest of their dragons into the skies; loose chains hung down from their claws. Elves in the dragon-rider uniform sat firmly on their saddles, prepared for conflict.

Virssagòn saw no chance for his allies. *But watching the battle should be exciting.*

Even at the first assault the dragon-riders made huge inroads as they flew in low over the barbarians' heads. The long chains the dragons held dragged through the snow and crashed into their victims, flinging men aside and knocking gaps in the lines. The lucky ones were able to struggle back onto their feet with only slight injuries.

The barbarians sped up. The attack had only renewed their resolve to get to the mountain.

Virssagòn saw the six dragons he had released dive in formation out of the heavens and plunge down to attack the humans. They plowed through the lines, snapping wildly and flew off with their prey, devouring their flesh while still in flight. Bloody gobbets and bits of metal fell onto the soldiers.

Cursed brood! Is that all the thanks I get? Should have slit your throats like I did with that last pair.

A called question came from behind.

Virssagòn turned around slowly and found himself threatened by five elves wielding spears. Behind them came three others with bows at the ready. "I presume you are asking who I am?" he whispered in response. "Then hear this: I am your death."

One of the archers said something in the elf language. The one in front pointed to Virssagòn's eyes in horror. "Älf!" he hissed.

Virssagòn spread his arms out from his body to the sides and then back, as if about to dive into a lake. "Who wants to embrace death?" he said quietly, a cold smile playing on his lips.

With this unnatural arm movement he had activated a mechanism in his armor, releasing tiny concealed steel springs that propelled rivets toward the enemy.

The sharpened points hit home, knocking the elves bleeding to the ground. The silvery poison the tips contained killed within two heartbeats. Virssagòn was passionate about his sophisticated armor and enormously proud of the secret refinements.

Two further elves appeared at the cell door, raising their weapons.

You won't get me. He stepped to the side and plunged down off the platform to land on the one immediately below.

Somersaulting, he rolled back in through the open cage doors of the dragon cell below, drawing his sword and the short metal stave as he did so.

He came to a stop and looked up to find he was face to face with a dragon.

Virssagòn hit the creature on the nose with the iron stave so that the creature's teeth missed him by inches, snapping on air. He ran behind the dragon to be confronted by the two elves from the room above. He plunged his sword into the first of the two riders and broke off the lance that had been thrust at him. Then he hurled the stave at the second elf, hitting it between the eyes. The enemy dropped unconscious to the floor. Virssagòn pulled his sword out of the first elf's torso, avoiding the jet of blood that spurted in its wake. The elf would inevitably bleed to death. The carnage had taken but a moment.

"I give you your freedom!" he yelled at the dragon. Then, before it could turn, Virssagòn snatched up the broken lance end and rammed it into the creature's skull from behind. The scaled monster perished with a loud screech.

Virssagòn heard the rattle of armor. More of the enemy confronted him. *They have come after me, but the cowards are using that ramp instead of leaping out like I did.*

He slit the unconscious elf's throat with his sword and, taking his iron stave, launched himself off of the edge of the cave to land on the stone jetty below.

As he fell he caught sight of the battlefield.

The barbarians had not advanced more than a few hundred paces toward the mountain entrance and the snow at their feet was red. The army was in disarray and many were running to save themselves. This only made them easier targets for the diving dragons and the elf bowmen's arrows.

A textbook massacre. Virssagòn was unmoved by the fate of the slaughtered barbarians, but he was annoyed at the waste it represented: he had wanted the barbarians to at least get to the gate in order to provide a distraction.

When he landed he found himself in front of a large iron grid in the rock.

Now what? There were no further platforms right or left he could jump to and on the one above him he could already see elf faces peering over the edge. They could see, looking down, that he was cornered.

Can I hide inside a crack in the rock? Virssagòn looked at the rough surface of the mountain. The rock crumbled away as he put his hand out to it. He recalled his initial fall by the gate and was in no hurry to repeat the experience from the height he was currently at.

A first spear landed close, splintering on the stone, and two arrows hit his armor, ricocheting harmlessly off the metal: a tribute to its robust construction.

One of them will hit me on the head soon, no matter how ineffective their training. He slipped back to the entrance, hoping the crew would open the gate to grab at him. Otherwise he was going to get shot; that much was clear. He deflected another arrow with his raised sword.

A dark shadow surged down from the sky with a furious screech and skimmed the platform the elves were standing on. Screaming, they plunged over the edge and bounced down the rough rock of the mountainside. The flesh was ripped from their bones.

The liberated dragon that had saved him then returned in an elegant swoop and landed on the newly empty stone jetty, folding its wings.

Does it want to get inside again? Virssagòn could hardly believe his eyes. All the released dragons had gathered on the stone platforms facing the direction of their cells—but then, as if in response to a silent command, they simultaneously spewed their fiery breath through the grating into the mountain's interior.

Flames shot out of the guardroom windows and propelled burning elves to the exterior.

Virssagòn hoped the cells he was currently standing in front of would stay shut. *What unpredictable, changeable beasts these dragons are.* He glanced down at the battlefield again. The barbarian army lay routed and the elf-riders were completing their final circuits.

Virssagòn was suddenly aware of his misunderstanding. *Of course! That's it! Hunger motivated the creatures I released. They were in need of sustenance and now they have returned to wreak vengeance on their tormentors!*

The dragons disappeared into their cells. The low rushing sound that accompanied the flames gushing from their nostrils was slightly muffled now. Fire and smoke were disgorged at various places through apertures in the mountainside as the conflagration inside the mountain spread.

Virssagòn laughed out loud. *So the barbarians did serve a purpose in the end! Without them, the dragons would have been too weak to take their revenge.* He sat down on the jetty to watch events as they happened.

The dragons the elves were piloting also rebelled abruptly and executed hair-raising aerial stunts to throw off their saddles. Some purposefully crashed landed, together with their crew. Virssagòn saw some larger specimens carrying four elf-warriors hurtling intentionally toward the cliff-face. The dragons had begun to revolt.

He heard loud hissing coming from the gate behind him. A wave of heat hit him. It felt as if the stone was blazing with invisible fire.

Virssagòn sprang to his feet as the gate slowly opened. Bars broke away from the grating and there was a fearful noise: the dragon that the elves had imprisoned behind the bars had broken free and activated the opening mechanism.

The dragon is unlikely to make an exception for me. He took the spear he was still holding and snapped off the shaft so that he could use the blade like a knife, then he drew out his dagger and climbed out sideways from the narrow platform, hoping to evade the dragon's sightline. He rammed the metal blades into the slim gaps in the rock to give himself a hold.

Virssagòn gradually worked his way down until he was hanging diagonally underneath the jetty. He was very keen that the beast should not spot him.

A roar sounded above his head. The platform shook.

There was a clatter when the clawed feet landed and then a mighty white dragon leaped off the jetty, unfolding its wings and floating with a howl of hunger toward the last humans, who were desperately trying to escape across the snow.

That was a good move, getting out of the beast's way. Virssagòn watched the scaly creature land in the middle of the band of humans and attack them with its claws, striking them dead with its tail before devouring them. *The elves have been arrogant enough to keep the dragons as if they were normal animals, thinking to control them by means of keeping them hungry and inflicting pain.*

The white dragon's body measured fifteen paces, plus a long tail and a long neck. Once the wings were unfurled it would never have fit through the vast gates. Virssagòn was fascinated by the animal's grace in flight and in killing, despite its gigantic proportions.

By now there were no more elves in the air. The dragons they had been riding were either dead on the valley floor or smashed to smithereens on the side of the mountain, surrounded by the mangled bodies of their riders. The only dragons still in flight were the ones recently liberated by Virssagòn.

Virssagòn had found a good spot where he could use his feet to help keep his balance, thus relieving the strain on his arms. He was waiting to see what the white dragon would do next.

The beast had finished its meal and flapped its broad wings, whirling up clouds of snow. Suddenly it shot out of the white cloud of flakes, giving a baleful cry that the other dragons joined in with. Its muzzle and the pale chitin plates on the underside, throat, tail and feet were all covered in barbarian blood.

An impressive sight! Virssagòn felt reluctant respect for these enormous creatures. He would never be able to defend himself against them, he realized. To stay safe, he swirled darkness around himself in his niche under the narrow platform.

The white monster landed on the ground at the gateway and spat bright fire against the golden patterns carved on the gateway. At the first round of flames the relief started to melt and at the second, the metal cladding liquefied completely. The dragon pushed through the ruins of the gate and poked his head into the mountain's interior.

Virssagòn could only guess what was happening, but when another muffled rushing noise was heard, and blazing jets of fire shot out of the lower part of the mountain, hurling ash into the open, he was certain he knew. The white animal, supposedly created by Sitalia as brother to the elves, was employing his lethal fire-breath time and again.

A number of elves opted to jump out of the windows in panic or they plunged out in flames, dying when they hit the ground. The smaller dragons spat fire through the upper levels, creating such heat that normal breathing was impossible without scalding the lungs. Virssagòn could see from the flickering light that flames were shooting out of the opening in the rock above him.

Exactly how long the dragons gave vent to their hatred it was impossible to say, but eventually the white dragon withdrew. It licked its snout, let out an ear-splitting roar and flapped its wings powerfully, rising from the midst of a glittering cloud. It made off toward the south and the smaller of the species followed it into the distance.

That was my masterpiece. Virssagòn climbed back up onto the stone ledge, only to be soaked by a veritable cascade of meltwater.

The whole mountain was steaming and its covering of snow was melting.

It'll be some time before it's safe for me to go inside the mountain. He looked down. *I have no alternative but to climb down the cliff face.*

It was a tough decision for Virssagòn to have to make, but in the end he took off his precious armor, leaving it in relative safety by the entrance, which was still emitting an incredible temperature and the odd cloud of ash. *I'll come back for it as soon as I can.*

He clambered down nimbly and without the encumbrance of the heavy armor.

Ishím Voróo (Outer Lands), Dsôn Faïmon, between the radial arms Welèron and Avaris, 4371st and 4372nd divisions of unendingness (5199th/5200th solar cycles), winter.

Jiggon fell down the slope, rubbing his skin raw. *Where the blazes is the water?*

He grabbed at a thick root and halted his fall. Clods of earth and some gravel rolled past him to splash into water far below. So the river was still there, but for some strange reason there was a lot less of it than there should have been.

As his eyes got used to the darkness, Jiggon assessed his whereabouts.

He was hanging a couple of paces above swift-flowing waters, which looked more like a mountain torrent than the placid defense moat he was used to. A waterfall he could just see roared into the darkness. *What have the dorón ashont done? Have they drained the moat? But what on earth for? All that effort instead of using rafts to cross it?*

Jiggon knew how to swim, but he did not let go of the root he was clinging to. A vague feeling of unease warned him it might be better not to dive into the flood. He did not know where the racing waters might take him.

I wonder if the black-eyes are still watching? He pushed against the bank of the river with his toes, looking for some solid support. Slowly but surely he made his way back up and found a jutting ledge he could grab hold of.

When he arrived under the shelf he listened carefully before heaving himself up over the edge, his arm muscles protesting at every movement. He would not have been able to hang on much longer.

The quiet immediately struck him.

He could hear nothing but the wind, and could see snowflakes and ash falling, uninterrupted to the ground; some got in his eyes. He rubbed them. The ash stung and made his eyes water.

Dead dorón ashont lay strewn across the battlefield, as did älfar warriors, night-mares and humans. The last remaining tents in the Ownerless Army's camp were still burning. The battle had been fought and lost.

With streaming eyes he looked again.

Where are they all? Jiggon was alone.

There were no älfar stalking the field, and there were no live dorón ashont as far as he could see. No humans seemed to have survived: the Army of the Ownerless had been wiped out—with the exception of himself.

The wind turned and he was enveloped in smoke from the burning camp. The smell of singed corpses made him sick to his stomach and he vomited.

He had not the remotest idea what would become of him, nor what he ought to do. He did not even pray; the sight of all of those dead bodies had removed his faith in the gods. They had not intervened. No deity had stood with them.

All in vain. He pictured the faces of his family and of his comrades in arms. He recalled what Khalomein had said shortly before the battle and had a sudden insight.

Jiggon turned his head and looked toward Ishím Voróo. *That's where my future lies, not here. I'll never be a slave again.*

He dragged the armor off a dead älf, took his weapons and went off in search of a safe path.

Chapter XXIV

Hear what victories they won, the Heroes of Tark Draan!

For most, the time of endingness was still far off, and many would go on to achieve true fame.

But Dsôn Faïmon was never to recover from the damage inflicted by the dorón ashont.

And so the Inextinguishables had to come to a decision that was to ensure the survival of the älfar but that brought pain to all.

Excerpt from the epic poem *The Heroes of Tark Draan*
composed by Carmondai, master of word and image

*Tark Draan (Girdlegard), to the southeast of
the Gray Mountains, Gwandalur,
4372nd division of unendingness (5200th solar cycle),
winter.*

Carmondai had left before first light, heading in the direction of the mountain where the elves lived with the dragon. He torched the village he had stayed in overnight, hoping that the warming-tower would also be destroyed.

After a few miles he came across a dragon lying dead in the snow; in its claws it held the remains of a half-consumed elf—the same elf he had fought in the woods. The poison that had done for its master had eventually caused the dragon's own demise. *It probably hated the elves, then. That's a relief. I was afraid that it would come back and get me.*

As the daystar rose in the sky, he saw the mountain not far away— and an army advancing toward it.

Must be Virssagòn's barbarians. Damn! I'll be too late. Carmondai was about to spur his night-mare on when he saw dragons flying out from the mountain and swooping down on the warriors.

He brought his steed to a halt. *Too dangerous.* He rode over to the shelter of a tree to observe what was happening. So many impressions were crying out to be recorded. So much needed sketching!

He was obviously witnessing a rebellion. Some of the dragons, led by a particularly impressive dragon with white scales, had turned on their masters and were attacking the elves' mountain. Carmondai was transfixed by the image of the steaming rock, the inside alive with red and orange tongues of dragon-breath. He was inspired by everything he beheld.

Finally the dragons took off one by one and flew south, completing a circuit overhead, as if to show off to the artist.

Carmondai sighed with relief as they flew on. *Not an enemy I'd have wanted to take on.* He stowed away his drawing equipment, mounted his night-mare and galloped toward the mountain, where the fires still burned.

As he rode, the flames began to recede and the smoke got thinner, giving way to the steam vapor rising off the slopes.

Even if Carmondai preferred to write about events he had actually witnessed, he was enormously glad that he had not accompanied Virssagòn on this particular outing.

I hope he has not met endingness. His death would make for good reading in my epic, of course, but it would sadden me and it's not what he deserves.

Carmondai passed through the area where the Ishím Voróo barbarians had been mown down by the dragons. Snow stained red from human lifeblood spurted up as he galloped through, kicked into the air by the night-mare's hooves. He was forced to reduce his speed as he rode through the despoiled corpses.

At last he reached the entrance.

A gateway stood empty and unguarded, the walls within black with soot.

Carmondai could hardly believe his eyes when he saw the golden lake that had solidified in front of the entrance. The white dragon's claw prints were clearly visible in the hardened gold.

None of the elves will have survived that inferno. Nothing can live through heat that melts gold.

"Late!" He heard Virssagòn's voice to the right. "What kept you, Carmondai?"

"I was here in time for my purposes. I doubt I'd have survived if I'd come any earlier," he replied with a laugh. "What an inferno! How come you've not got your armor on?"

"It was easier for the descent. I was there." He pointed to the fourth platform up. "The only thing for it was to climb down the cliff. It was a little too hot for me to come through the inside." He gave an answering laugh. "Did the battle look good from where you were?"

"My paintings will celebrate your glorious deed," Carmondai promised. But then he wanted more information: "Tell me, was everything part of your grand plan, or did it just happen?"

Virssagòn grinned. "I'd call it a plan that just happened, but it's the final result that matters." He came over. "Can you give me a lift? My nightmare ought to be somewhere over there if the elves haven't killed it. We can't get inside the mountain anyway. It'll probably need about forty divisions of unendingness before the rock has cooled sufficiently for me to go back and retrieve my armor. But I want to tell the nostàroi what I have achieved. Then I'll come back with a unit of mounted spear-carriers and make sure there are no elves skulking in a crevice somewhere."

"Of course." Carmondai hauled him up on to the saddle and they rode back the way he had come. "How many dragons are dead?"

"I don't know, but it must be at least half a dozen. And I have no idea how many elves I've killed. It's a shame. It would make an impressive story for your epic."

"Why should you get the credit? It was the dragons," Carmondai teased him. *Well, well. He's very keen to have me honor his deeds in my masterpiece.*

"But I was the one that motivated them," Virssagòn protested.

"What about the white dragon and his . . . entourage? I saw them fly off south; do you think they'll come back?" Carmondai was distinctly uneasy at the thought the dragons could reappear. He had seen with his own eyes what they were capable of.

"I could not have done anything about them: dragons can wipe out whole armies with their breath. Let's pray to the gods of infamy that they fly right over the mountains and never come back. I'm pretty sure they'll want to avoid the whole region after what the elves did to them."

"Let's hope so." Carmondai did not know how assess the battle, or what conclusions he could draw: was it a victory or had it merely given his people an advantage for the war in Tark Draan?

They reached the place where Virssagòn had tethered his night-mare. The steed had disappeared. So they rode back together on Carmondai's mount through the snowy landscape that had once been Gwandalur, back toward the new älfar realm.

Now there's only Lesinteïl and Álandur to sort out. "Tell me what it was like inside the mountain, Virssagòn," said Carmondai, taking out his notebook. "What was it like inside, before the fire?"

And Virssagòn described the mountain fortress before its destruction in the dragon-breath inferno.

Tark Draan (Girdlegard), to the southeast of the Gray Mountains, formerly known as the Golden Plain, 4372nd division of unendingness (5200th solar cycle), late winter.

I need an alternative word for "killing." A word that sounds grander, more epic. Carmondai sat at his desk in the generously proportioned stone building allocated to him by Imàndaris. Recently, all his time had been spent writing up his notes or consulting his sketches. He almost never left his quarters, or bothered to find out about events elsewhere in Tark Draan. *Slaughter. That's a good one.* He scribbled away, amending the passage.

This was his way of coming to terms with the shock of Dsôn's annihilation.

Carmondai uttered a sigh. *Isn't this all a complete waste of time?* When he finished his poem, how would he get it duplicated? There were no chancelleries back home anymore, of course, where he could get scribes to do the copying. And who would read it, anyway? *Any survivors have more than enough to contend with.*

Carmondai leaned back and surveyed the scene outside.

There was a buzz of activity in the crater. Slaves toiled ceaselessly to put up buildings and straighten the crater edges. A second Dsôn was being born.

Carmondai felt torn in two. He longed to return to the radial arms to support what was left of his own people, but he was frightened that he would catch the parasite-borne disease that had somehow survived Dsôn's annihilation. That was not how he wanted to end his days.

He drank some water flavored with preserved berry juice. As there were no supplies to be had from Dsôn Faïmon, there was no option but to make use of Tark Draan's local resources. In the spring they would start working the fields of the Golden Plain; they had managed to procure a few seed samples from the homeland.

I wonder when the blockade will be lifted? He got up and went over to the window. Imàndaris was striding toward his house through the melting snow wearing her full nostàroi armor. He opened the door to her before she knocked. "Greetings." He held out his hand and she grasped it.

"I hope I'm not disturbing you?"

"Not at all. I'm giving my mind a little rest." He admitted her.

Her gaze took in the piles of paper that lay on the table, chairs, window ledges and stairs. Random thoughts, finished pages from the epic poem, sketches and finished illustrations had been written or drawn upon them, and there were easels in the corner of the room at which he had been working at two pictures simultaneously. Pots of paint stood nearby and there was a smell of solvent that Carmondai only became aware of after he had taken a breath of fresh air at the door. And now he noticed the splashes of color on his robe: green, brown and red. The nostàroi's visit pulled him out of his creative haze.

"You had all that in your folder?" she asked him, impressed.

"Wait—let me make room for you to sit down." He smiled and removed a heap of papers from one of the chairs. "Some of it, but most of it is recent." *I wonder what she wants?*

Imàndaris settled on the chair and studied him. "We hadn't seen you for some time and had been getting worried."

"Who is *we?*"

"The älfar of Dsôn Balsur, that's who."

He raised his eyebrows. "So that's what we're calling the new realm?" *The new child has arrived and has been given a name. This is the end for Dsôn Faïmon.*

"That is the name the Inextinguishables have chosen."

Carmondai thought he must have misheard. "The Siblings are here in the crater?"

Imàndaris's joy at this development wasn't as enthusiastic as he expected. "They happened to be on their way here to inspect the new mountain when the dorón ashont wiped Dsôn out. Caphalor thinks the Towers that Walk used the stores of acid the alchemancers had accumulated. Survivors claim to have seen glass barrels with fflecx symbols on them."

The Inextinguishables. Carmondai could not believe his ears. It meant that Dsôn Faïmon had been totally abandoned, once and for all. "Is the blockade over?"

"No. Caphalor still has troops stationed at the Stone Gateway. He writes that there are still new cases of the parasite-sickness causing death in the camps outside the gate. A single victim can infect a further hundred with the purple phaiu su." Imàndaris gave a deep sigh. "There's a reason for my visit: I've been asked to oversee the construction of Dsôn Balsur according to the wishes of the Inextinguishables. I need your help, Carmondai."

"Me? Surely we have experts—"

"The experts are dead or in Ishím Voróo," she interrupted, seizing hold of his hand. "Please! You have a fertile mind and wide-ranging gifts."

This was flattering, but a very challenging task to take on: he would have to finish his epic, do all the illustrations and build a city at the same time. "What has happened to Dsôn Faïmon? Have the Sibling Rulers said anything?"

"They told me that the new empire is to be based here. Anyone who wants to remain in Dsôn Faïmon may do so when the effects of the acid have lessened, but the elves' former Golden Plain is to be the new älfar home. They said the crater and the Creating Spirit's tear are signs that the old is to be cast aside and the new embraced. Dsôn Balsur is to emerge with its center here. We will subjugate the other elf lands from this base. The elves of Lesinteïl and Âlandur will be eliminated. The whole of Tark Draan will belong to us. They will be making an official announcement very soon."

He could tell how dejected she was from her tone of voice. The news depressed him, too. It was hard to give up Dsôn Faïmon after all those divisions of unendingness, after all the wars that had been fought in its defense, after all the hardships the älfar had endured for its sake. *Does the homeland mean nothing to our rulers?* "Right. It's to be Dsôn Balsur. I see." He repeated the name quietly a few times. "How many inhabitants are there in the new realm?"

She gave a forced laugh. "A few thousand."

The wildest thoughts raced around his head: the älfar rate of reproduction was slow; this would make the conquest of Tark Draan in the coming divisions of unendingness difficult, to say the least. *Toboribar's óarcos will outnumber us ten to one. And the barbarians breed like rabbits.* "We shall have to pray to the gods of infamy that the plague will be over soon so that the survivors can join us here."

He had an intimation of the tragic fate awaiting those left in Dsôn. The outcome of the battle at its walls would soon be known. Without the island fortresses and the älfar to defend them, it would not be long before the scum of the earth would plunder what was left of it. The survivors were in dire peril.

His people were certainly resilient, but they were weakened now to a greater degree than ever before. Carmondai knew of no ancient saga, no epic poetry, no heroic ballads that told of any similar fate. *And I am here in Tark Draan.*

"We won't be praying to the gods of infamy."

"What do you mean?"

"The Inextinguishables have decided that our people will no longer worship the gods of infamy. They let us down and do not deserve our respect. There are to be no further prayers, offerings or hymns." The nostàroi was upset about this. She pushed back her bright red hair. "It won't be long, Carmondai, before we shall have two new deities for whom we'll have to make a new throne of bones."

Now Carmondai had to sit down. He plunked himself down on a pile of drawings. Dsôn Faïmon was in its death throes and the Infamous Ones were no longer to be called upon. The new Dsôn Balsur had feet of clay. Carmondai stared at Imàndaris without seeing her. *Here was material enough for a further five epics.*

"Will you help me?" he heard her ask.

He was confused. Having actively helped to bring about the conquest of Tark Draan, he had refrained from giving himself any of the credit in the heroic record of events that he was composing, because no one was allowed to know that he had impersonated Sinthoras. *And what if I were granted fame as the founder of the new Dsôn? Why should I decline an opportunity to go down in history and legend? Is this perhaps my overdue reward for my brave deeds? But the responsibility is huge.* He wasn't happy about the extra work, but the possibilities of it intrigued him.

"As soon as the plague is over and the blockade is lifted, the remaining älfar will make their way here, full of hope," he said pensively, getting to his feet. "Nostàroi, I swear that you and I shall build a Dsôn that outshines the old city in glory and splendor. It will be a symbol of our new beginning as a people—a sign of the new era and of our resurrection after the hardest of fate's blows!"

Imàndaris stood up and embraced him. "I thank you with all my heart! We shall construct a town with majestic squares and imposing streets, winding lanes and magnificent buildings. I shall appoint you to the highest rank at my disposal so that you shall have every authority to issue commands—"

"—to everyone apart from yourself and Caphalor. Oh, and to the Inextinguishables, of course," he broke in. "I shall leave my epic for now. There will be time enough for that in the future, when we have our completed city at our feet. I shall get Durùston to advise me. I'll commission the finest works of art from him to elevate the status of Dsôn Balsur even more." He held out his hand, palm upward. "Show me the plans, Imàndaris. I'll get straight to work."

"I don't have them with me. I wasn't sure you would accept." She went to the door. "Oh, have you heard?"

"About what?" He saw from her expression that it was good news that she was about to give.

"Arviû is back. He arrived with the last supply wagons sent from Dsôn Faïmon."

"He must have had protection from the gods of—" He broke off, not knowing what deities he was supposed to thank for Arviû's safe passage. He scratched his head. *Damn. Another rewrite.*

"He had the protection of fate," she supplied. "Our one-time master archer is training to be a warrior."

"He is blind!"

"He's been learning skills from the guards in the Tower of Bones. He told me that he won't appear in public until he has managed to overcome ten opponents in combat. That's ten älfar opponents." Imàndaris let herself out. "If you see how he moves now, you won't believe that he can't see. Another division of unendingness and he'll meet his own challenge. He is determined to do whatever he can to bring about the end of the elves."

From sharp-sighted bowman to instrument of lethal revenge. Imàndaris grinned as she saw Carmondai make a couple of notes. "Arviû. He'll have a tale to tell, I warrant. No, I'll tell it for him. He's an älf bold enough to stand up to fate." He waved her off. "Go and get the plans, Nostàroi. We've got a city to build!"

Imàndaris looked as if she had something else she wanted to say. "Can you keep a secret?"

"Anyone who can write a story can keep a secret," he answered with a wink.

Her face glowed, revealing her relief and her delight. "The Inextinguishables have decided to reinstate Caphalor to high office. He has been appointed my deputy!" On that note, she left.

But is it what he wants? Carmondai tidied his room and sorted the papers roughly before putting them aside to make space for studying the Sibling Rulers' plans. It was no routine task he had been given. He was looking forward to it.

Taking what he had produced so far for his poem, together with all the notes and sketches he had made, he wrapped the written pages carefully in waxed paper to protect them from damp. *At least things have more or less come right for Caphalor. The Inextinguishables appreciate his talents and they know that the troops respect him. Dsôn Balsur will need an experienced general like him.* His notes totaled eight parcels, and he placed them in a wooden chest for safety. *I wish Sinthoras well. May he make a new future.*

Imàndaris brought him the plans and they spent the whole of the evening examining them. They were both sure they could turn this vague list of specifications into an overall design for an impressive, robust and deadly älfar realm in Tark Draan.

Tark Draan (Girdlegard), Stone Gate Path in the Gray Mountains, 4372ⁿᵈ division of unendingness (5200ᵗʰ solar cycle), late winter.

"You down there!" Caphalor shouted down from his tower to a group of älfar trying to approach the gate. They carried their possessions on their backs, their mantels were torn and shabby and their breeches torn. *It's hard, but it's important not to take pity on them.* "Stay away from here! In the name of Nagsor and Nagsar Inàste, I command you to retreat and wait in the camp for new arrivals with all the others. If you come a step nearer I shall be forced to have you shot."

They looked up and then deliberated among themselves.

"Take aim," Caphalor ordered his archers to either side on the battlements. They raised their long-distance weapons and made ready.

Seeing this, the älfar turned tail and ran.

Caphalor hated driving off the refugees, but it he had to protect the others at Dsôn Balsur: those that were healthy had to stay that way. He thought aloud. "The sentries on the Ishím Voróo road must have been asleep. They should have stopped them."

"Perhaps the sentries are already dead?" suggested one of the archers, lowering his bow. "The parasites do not respect rank or position."

"That would be a problem. We need people to keep discipline down there." Caphalor looked over at the barricades his soldiers had put up. There were catapults loaded with arrows and spears lined up along the whole path; he was standing to the right of the tower.

You could not do anything without the necessary discipline.

He had arranged for the refugees to be sorted into a hierarchy of camps. The new arrivals had to wait at the far end. Only after fifty moments of unendingness, when it was clear that they were not infected with parasites, would they be allowed into the next compound. The second interim camp was carefully observed; if the älfar here showed no signs of sickness after a further ten moments of unendingness, they could move on to the third encampment. That was where the healthy älfar would wait for Caphalor to let them pass through.

Soldiers in the camps—the same troops who had been sent back to fight the dorón ashont—controlled the system and enforced discipline. Caphalor knew a few of them from the Tark Draan campaign. They would ride up to the barricade every morning to report to him and to hear his orders. They carried out his commands at arm's length.

Aïsolon, my good friend. Protect those who, like yourself, have chosen to remain loyal to Dsôn Faïmon. He often thought of his comrade who was carrying out that essential task.

His mind would travel constantly to his own family, not knowing what had become of his children: they could still be alive, or they might have succumbed to the acid . . . The cruel uncertainty was anguish to his soul.

And he thought about Sinthoras, traveling through Ishím Voróo. *He could give people courage, hope and a vision of a new life. That's if he's still among the living.*

Caphalor looked at the tents pitched close to the gateway path. Walls had been hastily erected to separate the three camps; ditches one pace wide filled with acid from Dsôn acted as a barrier against crawling parasites.

The plague was not easy to control. They were still losing many victims and there were frequent new infections. All in all there were around 4,000 älfar refugees housed in shameful conditions just outside the Stone Gateway.

What utter misery. Caphalor clenched his fist in anger—but there was no one he could call to account for the fate that had struck his people. The dorón ashont had died in the acid just as thousands of älfar had done. Samusin had intervened. But he still had these dark thoughts . . .

He did not know how he would react if a friend of his or one of his children came pleading at the gate to be admitted. He could only hope the situation would never occur.

An älf marked by a long, hard ride appeared at his side and handed him a leather wallet bearing the seal of the Inextinguishables. "A message for you, Caphalor. For your eyes only."

Despite the presence of the archers, he opened the seal and took out the missive.

Scanning its content, he did, however, move several paces to the side for privacy. These were lines that should never be seen by a third party.

Highly valued and imperially blessed Caphalor,

You have proved yourself an honest and upright älf over the course of many divisions of unendingness. You have carried out your appointed tasks without complaint and you have not argued with us over your removal from the office of nostàroi. Regard this period as a time of trial and testing.

Those älfar who felt entitled to interfere in the concerns of our state have been proven wrong. They deceived themselves, all the älfar in Dsôn Faïmon and us.

A new age has begun: an age of challenges; an age for a new generation of älfar and a new empire carrying the name Dsôn Balsur.

And just as we need you—a far-sighted warrior with an excellent mind, a cool head and an unrelenting fist—we also require älfar with the gifts and temperament of Sinthoras.

Exile seemed the only option, but we have come to realize that his banishment was based on false statements from corrupt witnesses. Polòtain died in the flood and has thus escaped the punishment that would have been due.

We hereby command you as follows: you are to make your way in all secrecy to Ishím Voróo and to seek out Sinthoras. Find him and bring him back so that he may, together with yourself, lead assaults on the elves in Lesinteïl and Âlandur. Not as nostàroi, but in the capacity of a highly respected benàmoi.

Our people are severely weakened and are in great need of heroes to look up to. You and Sinthoras are just such heroes. The battle of the Golden Plain is still spoken of with awe.

On your way, Caphalor! On your way!

And bring the Hero back to us.

This letter is your permit to travel in Tark Draan.

The imperial seal had been stamped in the wax beneath the text.

Anyone would think they wanted to reappoint me as nostàroi. I would not accept. Caphalor looked over the battlements and past the camps toward Ishím Voróo. Memories of his previous journey flashed through his mind: he and Sinthoras had been sent away to win the mist-demon as an ally.

The memories were not pleasant ones.

There was no hint now of where the demon might be. *He has abandoned our cause.*

Caphalor had an inkling that this was why the Sibling Rulers were recalling Sinthoras; they would be desperate to call on the demon's powers given the starkly reduced numbers of surviving älfar. Only with his help would the Tark Draan campaign be successful.

They aren't even considering the plague, or that I might pick up the infection. Caphalor looked at the camp. *I'll go this very night.*

He quickly left the tower to find and brief his deputy. Then he would write a note for Imàndaris. She had to be told what his mission was and why he was leaving for the wilderness once more.

In the middle of the night, certain that most of the älfar in the camps would be asleep, Caphalor rode through a gap in the barrier. Thick snow was falling.

His night-mare, Sardaî, was loaded up only with the most indispensable items for the journey. Comfort was not a concern, but speed was. He made sure he was not showing any kind of insignia and took care to cover his armor with a wide mantle. Nobody would know who was heading quickly north that night—and nobody would suspect that an älf would ride from the safety of Tark Draan through a tent village that still harbored the plague.

Sardaî easily jumped the acid-filled ditches and raced past the guards' braziers. No one stopped him, no one called out. Those waiting in the camps were not interested in the solitary rider—not, that is, until he was confronted by a veiled figure at the far end of the new arrivals' compound.

Parasite land. "Out of my way!" barked Caphalor, swerving aside.

The älf mirrored his movement almost as if begging to be ridden down.

Caphalor had no mercy and set his night-mare to charge straight on. At the last moment the figure darted aside.

What the blazes was that in aid of? He looked back over his shoulder and saw that the cloaked älf had snatched one of his saddlebags. *A thief!* Caphalor reined Sardaî in and turned. *I'm not letting you get away with that.*

He raced back. It was in that saddlebag that he had stored the vital imperial letter: the letter describing his mission and allowing him to pass—and the masked älf was holding it. He seemed to have recognized its significance and was rushing through the camp toward the gate, waving the paper in the air and shouting.

The commotion woke the other occupants and they came streaming out of their tents: living obstacles to Caphalor's passage.

"Faster, Sardaî, but mind who you kick!" Caphalor urged his mount.

A desperate race ensued between the thief and the black steed. Caphalor helped where he could with skillful use of the reins, and encouraged the night-mare to leap over the ditches, but all of the dodging and swerving meant lost time, and the daring thief had already gained a head start.

It is vital he doesn't get through to Tark Draan, or he'll take the parasite infection with him. Caphalor drew his sword. The masked älf was destined for a swift death anyway: he had seen the content of the letter.

The archers on the battlements had followed what was happening. They took up their positions and raised their bows.

The thief had already left the last of the three camps behind him and was racing up to the barricade when he stumbled, quickly regaining his footing, flourished the letter and shouted: "Let me through! I've got a pass from the Inextinguishables! Here! Read it for yourselves!"

I've nearly got you! Caphalor saw no further hindrances and urged Sardaî to fly like the wind. The night-mare stretched out with sparks flashing around his hooves, more like a lightning storm than a horse.

"Stop where you are, thief! Hand me back the letter you stole and I'll let you live."

But the masked figure, already near the barrier, did not hear him. He was illuminated by search lights and torches. The sentries operated their catapults, adjusting the trajectory.

I warned you. Caphalor hurled his sword.

The weapon whizzed through the night and struck the thief on the nape of his neck. He fell to the ground without a cry, without any sound at all. He rolled over and over, the paper flying up into the air as his grasp loosened. The letter was carried off by the north wind and landed behind the barrier.

"Oi, you there on the night-mare," the sentry yelled down at him. "Stop right where you are or I'll fill you full of arrows."

"I am Caphalor!" he called out, but in the simple attire he had selected for the journey and with his face hidden by his hood, no one would recognize the benàmoi of the Gateway.

"Oh, sure. Stay exactly where you are. Or die!" came the scornful rejoinder.

I have to get that letter back! "Jump, Sardaî!" He forced his heels into the night-mare's flanks and the beast launched itself into the air.

The catapults snapped into action.

Arrows hissed just under them as the creature leaped over the barrier. On the other side they were quickly surrounded by lance-bearers. Caphalor saw the letter lying next to Sardaî's left fore hoof.

"Slow down," he called to his soldiers, throwing back his hood to reveal his face. They lowered their spears, but seemed unsure as to what they should do. Their orders said clearly that no one who had been in Ishím Voróo was to come through to Tark Draan. "I dropped this." Caphalor slid down from the saddle to retrieve the letter, showing it to Ofardanór, his deputy, who had come running over.

He could hear shouting from the compounds. That wild chase had caused great upheaval and the thief's dead body lay only a few paces short of the barrier. His fate had upset the others and they were incensed.

Ofardanór read the lines and, with a meaningful hard look, ordered his soldiers to stand down their weapons. "He is allowed back in," he announced, holding up the permit. "This is special permission from the Inextinguishables." He handed the letter back to Caphalor.

Caphalor could see that the handwriting had become smudged in the relevant part of the letter. Ofardanór had not been able to read the permission. *I certainly appointed the right älf for my deputy.* He thanked him quietly and climbed up onto the barrier to see what was happening in the camps. *Mayhem over there. I can't risk it again tonight.*

He jumped down to stand next to his second-in-command. "Shoot fire-arrows at the corpse and make sure nothing escapes from him, in case he is a worm-carrier."

Caphalor went back to Sardaî and took the bridle to lead the night-mare back to the stables. *The Sibling Rulers will have to issue a new pass. I can't depend on others being as loyal as Ofardanór.*

Back in the stable he checked over Sardaî and found a long shallow cut on one flank, still bleeding. The thief had slit the saddlebag strap with a blade. *Serves him right that he died like that.*

He took the saddle off carefully and attended to the wound. Sardaî snorted with discomfort, but allowed him to do it. Stitches would not be necessary; the injury would heal by itself with the help of the salve that Caphalor was applying.

As he inspected the saddlebag, he remembered losing one on his last ride to Ishím Voróo. But this time it had been stolen, not lost. *Maybe I should forget about taking luggage.*

His thoughts wandered and returned to the state of the camps he and Sardaî had charged through to catch the thief. He was tormented by the images of misery and suffering his people were subject to. *I am responsible. Sinthoras and I, we're both responsible for following the Sibling Rulers' orders.*

If they had never found the mist-demon and won him over as an ally, the demon would not have attacked the kingdom of the fflecx and eradicated that race. And then the dorón ashont would not have come across the gnomes' unguarded stores of chemicals and Dsôn would not have been destroyed.

If Sinthoras and I had failed in our mission, many, many lives would have been spared. The Heroes of Tark Draan are answerable for all of the glory and all of the destruction. Caphalor shut his eyes and made a solemn vow to do everything in his power to protect his people better in their new homeland. *Samusin, give me the strength I shall need to make amends.*

Sardaî gave a whinny of warning.

"How kind you are in caring for him," said a familiar, but totally unexpected voice.

Caphalor's eyes widened in surprise and he whirled around. "You? Here?"

He stared at Sinthoras a good four heartbeats long. The long blond hair shone like gold and he was wearing a guard's simple armor.

"How did you get in here?" Caphalor asked, astonished. He added with a smile, "And tell me who I've got to execute for not noticing you."

"Your people are good. I would not have got past them." Sinthoras came up to Caphalor and embraced him. "It's so good to see you!"

"You very nearly missed me." Caphalor returned the hug warmly, not thinking about the parasites Sinthoras might have brought with him. "I was on my way to Ishím Voróo."

"I know. That was quite a commotion you caused, going out and coming back!" Sinthoras clapped him on the shoulders. "Ye gods! Ye gods! To think I would ever see you again! What were you going to do out in the wilds? Or were you being sent to Dsôn Faïmon?"

Caphalor had gotten over the shock. "Tell me how you got in to the fortress and I'll tell you about my mission to Ishím Voróo."

"I kept to the terms of the Inextinguishables' sentence."

"And those would be?"

Sinthoras pointed east. "I was to keep going west until I could go no farther. So, of course I did just that. I went west and came around again in the east," he said with a grin. "I wanted to get to Dsôn Balsur, but when I heard the Inextinguishables were there I thought it would be better to ask you to speak to them on my behalf, because I don't think they would accept my version of events."

"That's . . . unbelievable!" Caphalor laughed out loud. *This is the type of thing I have missed so much.* "You should hear yourself! You tell lies bold as brass!"

"Me? Telling lies? You think people might assume I'd got to Tark Draan before you built the barriers and that I'd been hiding here ever since?" Sinthoras was amused. "Well, they could say that, but they can't really prove it, can they? I promise you—if you ride west for long enough you'll arrive back in the east. Of course, I have no idea how long it might take to do that. And anyway I was only exiled from Dsôn Faïmon. And—" He laughed again. "Count the graves of those I've slain in the name of the Sibling Rulers. Must be far more than the 10,000 they demanded of me, so I've already met two conditions toward ending my banishment."

"You are quite incorrigible. Heroically so." Caphalor had calmed down now and held out his partly indecipherable letter. "You can save your transparent excuses. Read this. The Inextinguishables want us both back."

His friend's eyes sparkled. "Do you mean that?"

"Yes. Your name is to be cleared. You won't be a nostàroi, and nor will I, but we're both back with the army as benàmoi." *And we can work off our guilt.*

Sinthoras sat down on a bale of straw and read the letter with tears of joy streaming down his cheeks. "That is—" He cleared his throat and wiped his face. "I really have been out in the wilderness," he said emptily. "The thoughts that went through my head . . . I can't describe what it was like, Caphalor. I contemplated founding my own empire, raising my own army and setting off to save Dsôn. I was in despair and tortured myself with recriminations . . . and never more so than when I put the blade of my knife to my own throat. The worst thing . . . But, Caphalor! Both of us?" He jumped up and hugged his friend once more, overwhelmed with joy. "I shall have a reputation to be proud of; I'll be respected and admired. And I'll rip out the tongues of all those who gave false witness and blackened my name."

That sounds a bit more like our old Sinthoras. Caphalor clapped him on the back. "Then off we go. I don't have to bother going to Ishím Voróo now. Though I rather doubt whether any of your enemies are still around."

"They can't all have died of the sickness, though I would have wished it for them."

Caphalor was surprised at his friend's continued high spirits. "You don't know what happened to Dsôn?" Sinthoras looked blank. "The city has been completely destroyed. The dorón ashont obliterated it in a river of acid."

All jauntiness drained away from the blond älf's face. He mouthed the name Timanris, and clung to a wooden pole to stop himself falling.

"I can see we'll have to drown our troubles in wine before we set out to join our rulers."

Sinthoras put his hand to his throat, shaking his head in disbelief. Words would not come.

"I'll tell you everything that has happened." Caphalor stroked Sardaî's nostrils affectionately and left the stable in the company of Sinthoras.

His own situation had improved due to his banished companion's return and he had regained something he had thought lost forever: hope.

Now he saw his first task would be to try and restore some of the same thing to Sinthoras.

It was not going to be easy.

Tark Draan (Girdlegard) to the southwest of the Gray Mountains, enchanted land of Siminia, 4372ⁿᵈ division of unendingness (5200ᵗʰ solar cycle), spring.

Simin the Underrated was proud of his assembled friends: Grok-Tmai the Worrier in his gray and black robe; Hianna the Flawless, her opulent attire swapped for a simple lavender-colored dress; Fensa the Inventive in a flowered outfit; and Famenia the Tested, wearing a costume best suited to a court jester on holiday.

They were all seated around the table and it was *his* proposal they were all studying. His own suggested draft for a banning spell.

They each read through the text in silence and made notes, consulting learned tomes.

Famenia gave up first with an apologetic gesture. She was very young to take on the task of succeeding Jujulo the Jolly and did not feel up to handling this kind of magic. Simin nodded indulgently.

The afternoon hours drifted past.

Hianna was the next one to put down her quill; Grok-Tmai followed suit. A little later Fensa completed her suggested amendments.

"Well?" asked Simin impatiently, unable to wait any longer. "Famenia, you don't have to say anything."

She nodded gratefully, relieved that she would not be forced to make a fool of herself.

"I'd like to start," said Grok-Tmai. "The basic approach for this spell is sound, but in my opinion there's a fatal mistake in the first line."

This grudging objection gave rise to a heated discussion between the various magi. Many new proposals were put on the table and many of them were quickly rejected.

Simin had to admit that he had made a couple of assumptions that had not been thoroughly thought through, but he considered some of the other objections quite laughable. However, with the exception of Famenia, they had all contributed valuable ideas. Famenia had hardly understood what the others were talking about.

Evening drew in, but it found them still arguing and splitting hairs. They did not break off their discussion until late in the night when tiredness overcame them all.

Simin had picked up a few useful hints as to how he could revise and improve the formula and he thanked the others for their assistance. "There are so many aspects to consider. I'm glad to have the benefit of your views. With our united efforts we will find a way to keep this mist-demon out of Girdlegard for good. Let's get to bed now and meet again at dawn to carry on our discussion. We have made an excellent start."

They applauded. One by one they stood up to go to their rest, disappearing into the chambers he had set aside for them.

Famenia stayed where she was, looking sad and fiddling with a quill.

Simin read her expression. *She's feeling superfluous, I expect.* "Don't be upset. Jujulo could not have known what challenges his apprentice would one day have to face." He came over to where she sat and stroked her hair as a father might.

"So what use am I at all?" she said, downcast. "I can produce a few gusts of wind, a fireworks display and an illusion or two."

"And without those skills Milltown would never have been saved," he reminded her. "Talent and imagination were needed to adapt the music spell to serve as a barrier in that way."

"It was stupid, really. My ears were still ringing four circuits later." Famenia smiled in spite of herself.

Simin put his arm around her. "Famenia, what you did was amazing. Between ourselves," he said, giving a conspiratorial wink, "none of my pupils would have dared to do what you did. Jujulo's gift of humor is a weapon we'll often need to keep our spirits up. And anyway, it's always a question of *how* a spell is employed. You have shown you understand that." He gave her an encouraging hug. "You are well on the way to becoming an excellent maga. And things in Girdlegard will settle down, you'll see. It'll all come right in the end. The pacts the monarchs entered into with the älfar have already fallen apart. We all applied pressure to make that happen. You, too: you are the liberator of Milltown. Who's going to confront a sorceress with a reputation like that? We'll defeat the elf-slayers and their dark hordes!"

"If you say so, master."

I don't seem to have completely succeeded in cheering her up, but she's looking a little more confident. "Don't call me master. You are a pupil no longer." Just as he was about to leave the room something else occurred to him. "Can you tell me what Jujulo was researching most recently? We always wondered if he really was only working on the entertainment side of his art."

Famenia gave it some thought before answering. "It was not a secret. He had never wanted to turn lead into gold or to explore the depths of Tion's nether worlds, or to gain enormous power. He wanted to make the humans in his magic land happy; he loved to hear them laugh. He'd have wanted to make all of Girdlegard happy. That's what he trained me to do."

That's just what I thought. A big kid at heart. I miss him. Simin knew that Jujulo had sent out his best apprentices to learn from the world and give delight to those they encountered on the way. Their audiences had appreciated their little tricks and clever illusions. "As I said: we all need a bit of fun. It's a wonderful gift!" He tossed an apple over to her, but she did not catch it very adroitly. "Oh, I'm sorry. I thought, as one of Jujulo's best pupils you'd be a bit of a star at juggling."

"No, I can't juggle."

"But what did you do when you were traveling?"

"We did magic tricks. Not juggling." Famenia grinned.

"I meant when you were out on your trials being tested, far away from the enchanted ground. Somewhere you wouldn't have had any magic source." Simin was really keen to find out. "I expect you told amusing stories to entertain the humans you met."

"I used this." Famenia brought out her amulet.

"I don't understand."

"It allows you to store the magic power you need. It may not be much but—"

Is that possible? Simin strode back to where she was sitting. He ran his fingers over her talisman. It made his fingertips tingle and he felt the magic the amulet held. "Jujulo found a way . . ." he whispered. "He played the fool but he was cleverer than any of us!" he whooped. "Famenia! How many of these things did he produce?"

"One like this."

"Only one? Oh." *Got excited a bit too soon, didn't I?* He had been hoping that they could use the stored magic to confront and defeat the demon directly at the gateway. "That's a shame. Perhaps you know how he did it, though?"

"No."

Simin's optimism faded as quickly as it had come.

"But there are lots of smaller ones. They just don't hold as much magic," Famenia explained. She had kept him in suspense deliberately. "He made forty altogether. One for every one of us going out on tour. The amulets and rings don't last forever and they start to crumble eventually, but they can be used quite a few times. At least I think so."

"Well done that magus! The fool was the wisest of us all." Simin took her face in his hands and gave her a big fat kiss on her forehead. "He's given us the possibility of stopping the demon in his tracks. Him and you. I'll see you later on."

With that he ran off into his study. Sleep could wait. First of all he had to redesign his spell.

. . . *And so you have read all about the Heroes of Tark Draan.*

Not everything was included, for they lived through too much.
Some events were not covered because I was not informed.

One splinter of unendingness I may sit down and find the time to write the final story and complete the epic poem or to continue the legends of the älfar.
When Dsôn Balsur is built and a new Tower of Bones rises above the Black Heart of the älfar empire—but not until then!

But I can tell you:

that Virssagòn invented weapons of such ingenuity that all the peoples of Tark Draan felt envy and shame. Many elf fortresses fell because of his skill, and Arviû, for whom he designed the deadliest lethal throwing blades, became his closest friend.

that Arviû attained manifold revenge for the loss of his eyesight. His raids on the elves were the bloodiest ever experienced, and a moment of unendingness on which he did not kill more than forty by his own hand would not have been worthy of the name.

that Morana, attracted by the ways of the barbarian, took it upon herself to roam through Tark Draan to learn more about them and even went so far as to form ties of love to some—or what she thought was love. She never returned to Dsôn. I do not know what became of her.

that Horgàta and her warriors were never heard of again, though the Inextinguishables sent Virssagòn south to seek them out. All trace of them was lost at the gates of the realm of the Secondling dwarves. Barbarians who trade with the dwarves of the Secondling tribe reported that an elf horde had sought shelter there, but that both Horgàta and the elves were chased out through the southern gate and away from Tark Draan. What happened to them is not known.

And that Sinthoras and Caphalor are the greatest heroes of all, despite not being nostàroi!

They were responsible for planning the assault on Lesinteïl, the northern elf kingdom, and inflicted immense damage on the enemy.

The struggle is arduous and mile for mile is still fought over, up to the present moment of unendingness.

It was these two heroes who enclosed Âlandur in many places with a wall to bring the elves to their knees.

And it will be these same two älfar who will ensure our victory over the elves and the whole of Tark Draan.

I have no shadow of a doubt about this.

It is as true as the fact that Dsôn Balsur will never fade!

Concluding stanzas from the epic poem *The Heroes of Tark Draan*, composed by Carmondai, master of word and image

EPILOGUE

Tark Draan (Girdlegard), Gray Mountains,
4372ⁿᵈ division of unendingness (5200ᵗʰ solar cycle),
spring.

"What's wrong with this idiot shrontz?" Shoggrok confronted the óarco currently held with chains fastened around some stalagmites. Its body was covered in deep cuts and it did not look as if it had any blood left. It was squatting on the ground, its eyes dull and lifeless. "Is it still alive?"

The horde of óarcos with Shoggrok looked up sheepishly at the imposing leader of the last of the Kraggash.

"Toboribar has ordered all his troops to go south." Shoggrok had been given the task of gathering up stragglers and driving them out of the Gray Mountains. He took his work very seriously. Following the defeat at Sonnenhag and the treacherous betrayal by the black-eyes, every arm capable of wielding a sword was urgently needed. He pointed at the chained prisoner. "He belongs to the troops. Take the chains off; we'll take him, too."

"But . . . he isn't one of us anymore," one of them objected. "The demon has transformed him. He should have been dead ages ago, but he keeps hitting out and biting if we go near."

"We really can't use him," agreed another óarco. "He's completely insane. We ought to leave him here for the black-eyes to play with. Or the other way around."

The captive made a wild lunge, screaming horribly. The chains went taut and forced him back. One of the stalagmites snapped in half. Even Shoggrok flinched, taken aback at the sudden show of aggression.

"There! Did you see that?" squeaked the first óarco. "He'll tear us to pieces!"

The mostly dead óarco hopped about in fury and tried to grab the Kraggash leader with its claws. Baring its teeth, it displayed black bile dripping from its muzzle. It was not about to quiet down.

Shoggrok drew his sword. "You are right. It'll cause more trouble than it's worth," he grunted, striking out. "He stays here."

Sparks flew as the blade clanged against the steel collar, then cut through the animal's neck so the head came away from the shoulders. One of the óarcos caught it, laughing. The captive's body collapsed to the floor.

But instead of blood, a silvery fog shot out of the stump.

Shoggrok jerked backward. "What's that?" He hit out with his sword at the shimmering mist, but to no effect.

<My hearty thanks, you brainless creatures!> they heard inside their heads. <You have released me from my prison.> The óarcos all cowered away from the cloud. <It's high time I got a look at Tark Draan. I waited for Sinthoras to keep his promises for far too long. I'm going to take what's due to me!>

Shoggrok had heard tell of the demon that the black-eyes had won over as their ally. *However did he get inside the óarco?* He stared at the corpse.

When he turned around again the demon had disappeared. And so had Shoggrok's horde of óarcos.

"Hey!" he yelled, furiously. "Where are you, you band of cowards? We've got to go south!" He found his warriors hiding in the nearest tunnel.

They started out on their march south.

When Shoggrok left the Gray Mountains that evening to join their prince, Toboribar, they came across the demon again. He was hovering up and down in midair just ahead of them, and whizzing from right to left.

"Whatever he's up to, he looks like he's having fun," laughed one of the óarcos.

"He's waving at the clouds," chuckled another of them. They competed with each other to make the stupidest suggestions about what the demon was doing.

Shoggrok thought it looked more like the demon was not able to cross some invisible barrier, like a fly constantly buzzing into a windowpane. "Well, let's leave him to it." He gave the order to break into a jog. "We need to get away from here before the demon gets inside one of us. That flashing cloud thing belongs to the black-eyes."

The group moved away fast, leaving the mountains and the demon behind.

A NOTE FROM THE AUTHOR

When I finished writing *Devastating Hate* and looked at the publication date of the previous volume, I realized that more than two years had gone by.

More than two years!

That's a very long abstinence from these rascals, but they've been given plenty to do.

It was important to base the action in several different parts of Girdlegard and to include other characters, humans and älfar alike. That is why the focus is not solely on Sinthoras and Caphalor this time.

If you are wondering why you don't learn much about the dorón ashont, I have to tell you that's exactly how I wanted it. It would have led to an imbalance if I had gone into more detail. And no, I don't intend to give them their own novel. It's obvious that they will play a role in the future stories as they have already with the dwarves.

You might assume I'd be taking the story directly on from here.

But I am sticking to my original plan and am going to jump ahead time wise: the next part of *The Legends of the Älfar* will fall in the lost period of 250 cycles between volumes three and four of the dwarf saga.

The action will take us deep into the caves of Phondrasôn, part of which will be familiar to my readers as the Black Abyss in the dwarf series. This is where Tungdil once disappeared and from whence a gâlran zhadar emerged.

Many of the mysteries and secrets waiting in the dark caves and chasms will be revealed—Tungdil's own secrets among them.

If you want to know what happens next to Sinthoras and Caphalor and to find out more about Morana, try looking in the books about the dwarves.

What Carmondai, Virssagòn and Arviû get up to next might one day see the light of day in some shorter älfar legends—perhaps an anthology?

Do not worry: Carmondai has kept all his notes carefully and put them by for later.

Acknowledgments

Quite a few people have made major contributions to help bring this volume to print and I should like to thank them all.

Tanja Karmann, Petra Ney and Sonja Rüther have done another fantastic job as my test readers.

My thanks, then, to them and to my new editor Peter Thannisch and to Carsten Polzin from Piper Verlag. I would like to thank everyone at Piper for their support.

Further thanks to HellScreen, who are planning to bring the älfar to life in the virtual world at www.albae-online.de.

I can't wait!

Glossary

acronta, term used by humans to refer to the dorón ashont

benàmoi, high älfar military officer grade

botoicans, a race with latent magic skills that live in the west of Ishím Voróo

cnutar, symbiotic creatures composed of three units which can meld and disperse at will

cûithones humanoid race in Ishím Voróo

dorón ashont, also called the Towers that Walk or acronta; colossal creatures whose race the älfar had thought all but exterminated

durùsilver or **bone silver,** a metal that hardens instantly

fflecx, *also known as alchemancers and poison-mixers,* a black-skinned gnome-like race

gàlran zhadar, dwarf-like people skilled in magic

gardant, leader of a guard unit

intigrass, a medicinal herb prescribed as a distillation

loffran, a medicinal root

nightfern, greenish-black foliage grows to the height of an älf

nostàroi, supreme älfar commander

óarco, orc

obboona, humanoid race also known as Flesh-stealers,

pace, a measurement that equates to around a yard

phaiu su, blood-sucking arachnoid creatures, many types found

Phondrasón, underground place of banishment

ryma blossom, reddish-black briar that gives off an intense rose and carnation perfume at night

shrontz, term of abuse: idiot

sotgrin, wolf-like predator

Tark Draan, refuge of the scum (Girdlegard)

tharc, älfar board game of strategy using miniature figures

thujona berries, slightly hallucinogenic, consumed fresh or as an infusion

utron viper, extremely deadly species of poisonous snake

quwiksilver, toxic metal in liquid form

A Unique Interview with Superstars Sinthoras and Caphalor

Sinthoras and Caphalor, one-time nostàroi of the älfar armies, are back and some might say, bigger—and wiser—than ever. Over wine served in intricately carved bone chalices and loffran root (the purple phaiu su curse that decimated their population is still a worry), the two gorgeous stars are here to discuss glory, bust-ups, banishment, the hated elves and, of course, each other.

I: I think it's safe to say you two have had a bit of a rollercoaster ride on your journey to Tark Draan. But let's go back to the beginning. You two were once enemies—how did it feel to be told you would have to work together to find the demon—and what did you think when you succeeded?

S (trying the wine): What, by the infamous gods, is this? It looks like wine, but it tastes appalling!

C (raising his eyebrows): I'd say they haven't found the best of vintages. We should make the butler drink it until his guts burst.

S (moves the wine away): To start with, being bound together with Caphalor like this was a shock. We have different ways of thinking.

C: Very different. And I'd be lying if I said we understand each other now.

S: Well, we understand each other, we just don't agree. Still, we got the job done.

C: That's certainly true.

I: So you could say you're frenemies?

S:—

C:—

I: *Let's move on then. Sinthoras, it is widely known that you offered the metaphorical olive branch to Caphalor. What made you change your mind about working with him?*

S (taking a paint brush from his pocket, dipping it in the wine and beginning to draw on a napkin): Well, sometimes you need some support to achieve really big goals.

C: We both know opposites attract, and they're at their best when they overlap—in certain, limited ways. (Looks at the picture and addresses Sinthoras.) You're not as good as you were.

S: I'm a little out of practice and, anyway, this isn't blood, just bad wine.

I: *You have both lived through enormous tragedy: Caphalor, you lost your life-partner and your daughter, and Sinthoras, you were betrayed by Timanris, then both of you lost Dsôn to a river of acid. Do you think this has informed your actions since and shaped the älfar you are today? Has it brought you closer?*

S: It has showed how hard you have to work to achieve your goals. Hard, and fast, because you never know what the future will bring.

C: It's made me tougher. Or, let's put it this way: I rarely show mercy now. Firstly because I do not want to be seen as weak, and secondly because if you offer mercy to your enemy, you often find yourself facing them again.

S: At first I thought he'd [Caphalor] lost the will to live [after these events], which would have been a real problem for *me*.

C: I like his sympathetic ways (he says sarcastically). He's always thinking about other people.

S: Of course! Other people only turn into problems.

I: If you had to live with humans, elves or dwarves, which would you pick?

S: I'd choose . . . suicide. Nothing else would be bearable.

C: I'd take humans, because they're so easy to influence. I'd get those silly souls to start a war with the elves and the dwarves, and then I'd live in peace.

I: If you were the Inextinguishables for a moment of unendingness, what would you do?

S: Build myself a nicer palace. I find the design dated, personally.

C: I'd bring in order and unite Comets and Constellations. We can't get lost in political games again—that was our undoing. Whoever looks too closely at the inside of his fortress, isn't watching the outside world.

I: Do you think you have made each other better people?

S: Even better?

C: What my friend is trying to say in his inelegant way is that we learned from each other what we each lacked. That's probably the best way of putting it.

I: Sinthoras, you were accused of murder and banished to the west. Do you have any comments on the matter? And Caphalor, what was it like not having Sinthoras to watch your back?

S: I did and do certain things to reach my goals. I don't see anything wrong with that, as long as the goal is a worthy one. And I'd never try for a goal that wasn't worth my time.

C: I missed him a bit. And then just as I was getting to enjoy life without him, he came back. Tragic.

I: Caphalor, you have been accused of being a closet Comet—and since you invaded Tark Draan, the Constellations have been slowly declining in popularity. Do you have anything to say to those who think you betrayed them?

C: Sometimes you start out as a star, but only following a comet can show you new goals and new ways. After my short time on the ground, I now know the way to become a star once again.

I: You're both seen as leaders, not just in war, but in matters of beauty too—art, music, and especially, these days, fashion: so what are your fashion hates?

S: I hate all that fake jewelry the barbarians wear. It makes them look rich, when they aren't at all. It's just painted sheet metal! What's the message: "Look at me, I'm a faker and can't afford anything nice, but I pretend to be someone of standing"? It's embarrassing. For everyone. When I meet someone like that on the field of battle, they're the first one I kill.

C: Most people have completely forgotten everything they learned about color pairings. Green and blue, for example, is a terrible combination—and yet you see clothes in these colors all the time. And *barbarians*! They try to wear as many colors as possible. It's an assault on the eyes.

I: If you could choose to make art or wage war, what would you pick?

S: War is the best way to find opportunities for new art. Think of what you can do with blood, with bones, with all these things you can make into new artworks—including the organs of the dead.

C: And waging war is an art in itself, to my mind. Barbarians charge blindly into battle, without any kind of foresight. That's why our people remain undefeated—because no one else has our skill.

S: (Sinthoras nods) Mostly, yes. But I do like staying by my easel, peacefully. That way I paint very calm, controlled pictures. After a battle, my blood is still up and my hands are wilder.

I: *And, finally, a bonus question for our readers: what's next for the two benàmoi?*

S: Oh, we have a few little jaunts left.

C: There are things to discover and examine, before we commit to new battles. Let's not kid ourselves: the Hidden Land will be ours before long.

S (laughing): Who can stop us? A dwarf? (signals for more wine)

I: (Sinthoras hands me the napkin)

S: Please. A gift. A brilliant portrait in bad wine. That was the best I could do with it.

So that's all from the two benàmoi, but don't forget to check back in for the next installment of The Legends of the Älfar: *The Dark Paths*, to follow the stars of the Tark Draan campaign!

About the Type

Typeset in Garamond Premier Pro.

Garamond Premier Pro is a product of type designer
Robert Slimbach's study of Claude Garamond's type designs.
Th is interpretation of the Garamond extensive typeface is refined,
versatile, and yet contemporary with current typography.

Typeset by Scribe Inc., Philadelphia, Pennsylvania.